T0043384

PEARL
IN THE
SAND

TESSA AFSHAR

MOODY PUBLISHERS

CHICAGO

Scripture quotations are taken from the Holy Bible, New International Version®, NIV®. Copyright © 1973, 1978, 1984, 2011 by Biblica, Inc.™ Used by permission of Zondervan. All rights reserved worldwide. www.zondervan.com The "NIV" and "New International Version" are trademarks registered in the United States Patent and Trademark Office by Biblica, Inc.™

Published in association with the literary agent Wendy Lawton of Books & Such Literary Management, 52 Mission Circle, Suite 122, PMB 170, Santa Rosa, CA 95409-5370.

Edited by Paul Santhouse, 2010; 2020 by Pamela J. Pugh
Interior design: Erik M. Peterson
Cover design: Faceout Studio
Model - Brandon Hill Photography
Red Cord - Brandon Hill Photography
Cover photo of background copyright © 2019 by Clari Massimiliano/ Shutterstock (475443451).
Cover illustration of border copyright © 2019 by Dream_master/ Shutterstock (522271156).
All rights reserved for the above.
Author Photo: Matthew Murphy, MurphyMade LLC

Library of Congress Cataloging-in-Publication Data

Names: Afshar, Tessa, author.
Title: Pearl in the sand : a novel - 10th anniversary edition / Tessa
   Afshar.
Description: Chicago : Moody Publishers, [2020] | Summary: "Can a Canaanite
   harlot who made her living enticing men be a fitting wife for a leader
   of Israel? Shockingly, the Bible's answer is yes. This 10th anniversary
   edition of Pearl in the Sand includes new features that will invite you
   into the untold story of Rahab's journey from lowly outcast to redeemed
   child of God. Rahab's home is built into a wall, a wall that fortifies
   and protects the City of Jericho. However, other walls surround her too,
   walls of fear, rejection, and unworthiness... Years of pain and betrayal
   have wounded Rahab's heart-she doubts whether her dreams of experiencing
   true love will ever come true... A woman with a wrecked past-a man of
   success, of faith... of pride. A marriage only God would conceive!
   Through the heartaches of a stormy relationship, Rahab and Salmone learn
   the true source of one another's worth and find healing in God"--
   Provided by publisher.Identifiers: LCCN 2020017843 (print) | LCCN 2020017844 (ebook) | ISBN
   9780802419866 (paperback) | ISBN 9780802498786 (ebook)
Subjects: LCSH: Rahab (Biblical figure)--Fiction. | Women in the
   Bible--Fiction. | Jericho--Fiction. | GSAFD: Bible fiction. | Love
   stories. | Christian fiction.
Classification: LCC PS3601.F47 P43 2020 (print) | LCC PS3601.F47 (ebook)
   | DDC 813/.6--dc23
LC record available at https://lccn.loc.gov/2020017843
LC ebook record available at https://lccn.loc.gov/2020017844

Originally delivered by fleets of horse-drawn wagons, the affordable paperbacks from D. L. Moody's publishing house resourced the church and served everyday people. Now, after more than 125 years of publishing and ministry, Moody Publishers' mission remains the same—even if our delivery systems have changed a bit. For more information on other books (and resources) created from a biblical perspective, go to www.moodypublishers.com or write to:

Moody Publishers
820 N. LaSalle Boulevard
Chicago, IL 60610

3 5 7 9 10 8 6 4

Printed in the United States of America

For Emi,
My sister, my friend, my great joy

A NOTE FROM THE AUTHOR

Dear Reader,

During a visit to Florence over twelve years ago, I noticed that Ponte Vecchio—the famed bridge that has straddled the Arno River for almost seven hundred years—had tiny shops built right into its walls. They bulged out of the sides of the bridge like odd-shaped barnacles sticking out of the hull of a ship. Walking over this bridge, I was reminded of the story of Rahab. The Bible tells us that Rahab lived in the bowels of a wall too. Her house was built right into the defensive walls of Jericho.

As I crossed Ponte Vecchio, I wondered what it was like to live in a wall. Then I realized that we all know a little something about that. Most of us have to contend with walls in the interior places of our souls. Walls built on foundations of fear, rejection, loss, pride; walls that keep others at bay and shield us from drawing close enough to get hurt again. Now I was hooked. I wanted to write about walls, about living in them, about pulling them down. I wanted to write about Rahab.

At the time, I had a terrible habit of writing stories and leaving them unfinished. Partway through the story, I would convince myself that it was boring or plain bad, and no one in their right mind would want to read it. Mostly, my trouble stemmed from fear. I was so afraid of failing that I preferred to leave my stories incomplete rather than have them be pronounced unsatisfactory. Even though I had wanted to be a writer since childhood, I found it preferable never to write a book than to write one and see it fail.

Jesus had to bring a lot of healing to my heart before I could write a novel. I had to learn to trust Him more than the whispers of fear. To entrust my calling to Him rather than to my own limited strength.

One New Year's Eve, as I was praying about my future, I felt very strongly that I was to write a book that year, and to finish it. That night, I made a commitment to the Lord that, regardless of how I felt, I would finish this novel. I would write out of obedience when I ran out of confidence.

That year, I wrote *Pearl in the Sand*. What I didn't know as I penned Rahab's story was that few publishing houses at the time were accepting biblical fiction. If I had known that, I would have given up on this story and worked on a different idea. God, in His grace, preserved my heart from discouragement by keeping me in the dark. Just as Noah built a boat before a single cloud marred the sky, I worked on my own personal ark—a novel based on a biblical story when few in the industry had any interest in the genre. Of course, God's timing was impeccable. By the time the story was finished, the industry was awakening to a burgeoning interest in the genre again.

Pearl in the Sand is a book that examines our worth in God's sight. It focuses on forgiveness and redemption. But it is also a story about the healing of a broken marriage. For me, the story of Rahab became truly interesting *after* her marriage to Salmone. Only God would think of putting together a former Canaanite harlot with one of the leaders of Judah, a man who belonged to one of the foremost families in Israel. How would such an unequal relationship survive? How could it thrive?

The more I considered these questions, the more I realized

that Rahab's story is the story of God's outrageous grace. And in that sense, it is my story and yours. That was the novel I wanted to write.

Through Rahab's and Salmone's various struggles in *Pearl in the Sand*, I wanted to capture the wild nature of grace, of divine love, of the insane new beginnings that God allows. There is a lot of romance in this novel. But perhaps the greatest one is between God and Rahab. And often, God and the reader.

Having written a novel that, at the time, did not really fit the genre, I had no idea what to expect from readers. Would they be able to relate to it? Or would they walk away?

I was flabbergasted upon hearing the news that three days after the release of the book, we had to go into our second printing. I knew, then, that God was using this story in a special way that had nothing to do with me.

I started receiving the most astonishing emails and Facebook posts from readers. A man told me that he had been a church-going Christian for years, but it wasn't until he read the earring scene that he experienced his worth to God for the first time. Women poured out their stories of abuse, of violation, of rejection. I have cried a lot of tears over the years, reading my precious readers' letters. One woman told me that she could never find words to explain how she felt. But this book finally gave her a way to express *her* story. A therapist told me that several clients came to see her after reading *Pearl in the Sand*, recognizing in themselves patterns of brokenness we see in Rahab. Perhaps my favorite letter was from a man who told me he was a construction worker, 250 pounds, covered in tattoos, and he cried like a baby when he read the scene with the pearl earring.

The letters have kept coming over the years. *Pearl in the Sand* has been translated into eight languages, so I hear from people around the world. I find this astonishing. This was my first novel, and I wrote it with the mistakes of a novice. In fact, there were certain aspects of *Pearl in the Sand* I always wanted to improve. There was a particular verse I had missed in the plotline, which I needed to address. And I wanted to make the flow of the writing better. I find the readers' connection to this book remarkably humbling, because it is clearly not because of any special talent on my part.

That is why Moody Publishers' willingness to release this revised edition means so much to me. Their grace in opening this new door is no less a blessing than the fact that they took a chance on this story in the first place. Few writers are given a second chance. I am utterly grateful for this one. I can only hope that the fans will enjoy our revised, anniversary edition.

I pray, whether you are coming to this story for the first time or for the tenth, that this new edition will minister to your heart. May you fall in love with God in fresh ways and discover you are more beloved than you ever imagined.

With profound gratitude,

Tessa

2020

CHAPTER ONE

Rahab tumbled into consciousness courtesy of an impatient nudge. "Stop your laziness, girl. Your brothers and father are almost ready to leave." Her mother gave her one more unnecessary shove.

Rahab groaned and gave up on rest, forcing herself to rise from her pallet. Every muscle protested the simple movement, and she winced in pain. For two months she had been doing the work of men, waking before daybreak and wrestling the land all day with little food, water, or rest to renew her strength. It was useless—even at fifteen and only a girl she could see that. Their land had produced nothing but dust. Like the rest of Canaan, Jericho was in the grip of a brutal drought.

Though she knew their efforts to be wasted, every day she pushed herself almost past endurance because as long as they stayed busy, her Abba had hope. She couldn't bear the thought of his despair.

"Child, hurry," her mother snapped.

Rahab, who had already folded her bedroll and was almost finished dressing, continued her silent preparations at the same pace. She could move no faster if the king's armies were at the door.

Her father entered the room, chewing halfheartedly on a piece of stale bread. His face, pale and drawn, glistened with sweat. Rahab finished tying her sash with a quick motion and snatched a piece of hard barley cake that would serve as breakfast and noonday meal. Giving her father a tight hug she said, "Good morning, Abba."

He stepped out of her embrace. "Let me breathe, Rahab." Turning to his wife he said, "The north and west fields are barren. The only thing growing there is wind. The east field where I planted flax fared even worse. All that remains is the southern field. If I find nothing growing there today, I am giving up."

Rahab sucked in her breath just as her mother let out an agitated wail. "Imri, no! What will become of us?"

Her father's lips flattened into a tight line. Without bothering with an answer, he walked outside. In a haze, Rahab followed him, her gaze glued to his stooping back.

Her brothers Joa and Karem were waiting by the door. Karem stood munching on a raisin cake, a luxury their mother saved for her eldest son. His wife of one year, Zoarah, stood close, speaking in tones too soft for Rahab to hear. In spite of her worry, Rahab smiled at the way they held hands. Theirs had been a love match, a rare occurrence in Canaan. Although she teased her elder brother at every opportunity, Rahab's heart melted at the thought of such a marriage. Sometimes, under the cover of darkness when the rest of the family was long asleep, she lay awake, dreaming of having a husband who would cherish her as her brother did his Zoarah.

Joa, the youngest at fourteen, slumped against the cracked garden wall, his shoulders hunched up to his ears. Rahab had not heard him string three words together in as many days. It was as if the drought had dried up his speech as thoroughly as it had scorched the earth. His tall frame had grown gaunt, and dark circles haunted his eyes. He had probably left the house with no food in his belly. She reached for the bread wrapped in her belt, tore it in two, and took half to her brother. Insufficient even for her, it would have to do for both of them.

"You eat that, young man."

Joa ignored her. She sighed. "You don't want me nagging at you all the way to the farm, do you?"

He glared at her with irritation, then held out his hand. She lingered to make sure he ate, then traipsed after their father.

As they hastened toward the city gates, Rahab noticed that even Karem, who was rarely given to broodiness, had turned ashen in spite of the hot sun. He broke the silence that hung over them. "Father, I went to Ebrum in the market as you told me. He refused to sell me oil or barley for the price you said. Either he has doubled his rates since you last purchased from him or you are mistaken about the price."

"Send Rahab, then. She negotiated last time."

"Rahab. You might have said." A good-natured glint lit up his eyes. "One glance at her pretty face and every thought of sums and profits leaves Ebrum's flat head."

"Not so!" Rahab objected, her voice rising higher with annoyance. "My face has nothing to do with the price. I am better at bargaining than you, that's all."

"Bargaining you call it? Batting your eyelashes more like."

"I'll bat my broom at you if you don't watch your tongue."

"Hush," their father commanded. "You two make my head hurt."

"Pardon, Abba," Rahab said, instantly chastened. As if her father needed more trouble. She must learn to subdue her tongue. Father carried the weight of their survival on his shoulders. She longed to comfort him, not become an additional burden.

Hard as she tried, she could think of no words that would console him. Instead, following instinct, Rahab reached for her father's hand and held it. For a moment he seemed unaware of her presence. Then, turning to gaze at her with an unfocused expression, he registered her proximity. She gave him a reassuring smile. He pulled his hand out of hers.

"You're too old for hand-holding."

She flushed and hid her hand in the folds of her robe. Her steps slowed and she fell behind, walking alone in the wake of the men.

At the southern parcel of their land, they began examining rows of planting, looking for healthy seedlings. Other than a few hard-shelled beetles, they found nothing. Although Jericho's natural springs had not dried up over the past months, the water they had carried from the city wells by the bucketful dried up almost as soon as it touched the heated soil. They needed a river to save their harvest; the handfuls of water they managed to feed the ground simply evaporated in the unrelenting sun before the young seedlings could drink enough to survive.

By noon, they had finished their careful inspection. The

southern field lay as ruined as the rest of their land, swallowing their seeds and spitting up death.

"What's to be done? *What's to be done?*" Father muttered under his breath.

Rahab looked away. "Let's go home, Abba."

Before she could step over the threshold of their house, her mother shooed her out with a wave. "Leave your father and me to ourselves."

Rahab nodded and walked back out. She sank down against the crumbling mud wall, alone in the lengthening shadows. She longed to find a way to help her family, but even Karem and Joa had been unable to find work in the city. Jericho, already bursting with desperate farmers in need of work, gave them no welcome. How could she, a mere girl, be of any use? The sound of her own name wafting through the window brought her distracted mind back into focus.

"We should have given her to Yam in marriage last year instead of waiting for a better offer," her mother was saying.

"How were we supposed to know we'd be facing a drought that would ruin us? In any case, the bride price he offered wouldn't have seen us through two months."

"It's better than nothing. Talk to him, Imri."

"Woman, he doesn't want her anymore. I already asked. He's starving right alongside us."

Rahab held her breath, not willing to miss a single syllable of this conversation. Under normal circumstances the thought of eavesdropping wouldn't have entered her mind, but something in her father's tone overcame her compunction. She flattened herself like a lizard against the wall and listened.

"Imri, there will be no going back if we do this."

"What else can we do? You tell me." A heavy silence met her father's outburst. When he spoke again, his voice was softer, tired sounding. "There's no choice. She's our only hope."

Rahab felt her stomach drop. What was her father scheming? Their voices grew too soft to overhear. Frustrated, she strode to the end of the garden. In a dilapidated pen, two skinny goats gnawed on the tips of a withered shrub, already stripped to bare wood. With the men and Rahab working the fields every day, no one had found time or strength to clean the pen. A putrid stench made her eyes water, and Rahab covered her nose with her fingers.

She frowned as she considered her parents' conversation. They had been referring to her as the means of the family's salvation. But it wasn't through marriage. What other way could a fifteen-year-old girl earn money? Taking a sudden breath, Rahab put her hands to her face. *Abba would never make me do that. Never. He would rather die.* This was nothing more than a misunderstanding. But the knot in her stomach tightened with each passing second.

With a sigh, Rahab shoved the blanket aside and rose from her pallet. The world lay shrouded in darkness, the dawn still a long way off. But she could not sleep. In the dim light of the single burning lamp, she began to fold her meager bedding.

"Leave it."

Startled by her father's unexpected voice, Rahab dropped the blanket. "Abba! You are up early."

"Your mother and I have been discussing your future, Rahab," her father said. "You can help your whole family, daughter. Help us survive this drought. It will be hard on you. I am sorry—" he broke off as if at a loss.

The silence stretched, full of monsters. Nausea clawed inside Rahab's belly. She shook her head. Her father cleared his throat.

"You have to . . . you have to earn some silver, Rahab."

"How?" she said, her throat dryer than their land.

"The way of women. The way of our gods. You understand my meaning?"

She understood too well. Horror seized her so tightly it nearly choked off her breath. She shook her head again. "You can't mean it," she said, her voice a broken croak.

Her father exhaled a long breath. "There is no other choice."

Rahab staggered and sank down, her knees hitting the hard floor with a loud bang. She felt as if she had been pierced with one of Jericho's iron-tipped spears. Her chest burned. Her worst fears had come to pass. The nightmare she had dismissed as a misunderstanding the night before *was* real. Her father meant to sell her. Sell her as a harlot. He meant to sacrifice her future, her well-being, *her life.*

"Many a woman has had to do it—younger even than you," he said, his face turning red.

Rahab threw him an appalled look. She wanted to scream. She wanted to cling to him and beg. *Find another way, Abba. Please, please! Don't make me do this. I thought I was your precious girl!*

"I thought you loved me!" The words emerged a broken whimper, accusation and plea and desperation entwined in a mangled jumble.

"Love won't fill your belly, girl," her father growled.

"I would rather go hungry!"

"It's not your choice." Her father's eyes narrowed. "This family needs you."

Rahab felt chilled as she stared into those eyes. Stone-hard implacability stared back at her, unblinking. Unyielding. And Rahab knew in that moment. Every hope, every dream, every childish expectation for happiness was about to be wrecked at the hand of the man she loved most in the world.

Her face turned marble-cold as something deep within cracked. She swallowed her pleas and her hopes. She swallowed every word.

You'll never be my Abba anymore, she vowed.

From the time she had learned to speak, she had called her father *Abba,* the childish endearment that captured her adoring affection for this man. But her Abba was gone. In his place stood a stranger. A betrayer. The sorrow of this realization was almost more overwhelming than the reality of having to sell her body for gain.

As though hearing her unspoken words, he snapped, "What choice do I have?" Rahab turned away so she wouldn't have to look at him. The man she had cherished above every other, the one she had trusted and treasured was willing to sacrifice her for the sake of the rest of the family.

This was not an unusual occurrence in Canaan. Many a father sold his daughter into prostitution for the sake of survival. Yet it made her father's choice no less of a betrayal. She tasted ashes and ground her teeth until her jaw ached.

Her father rubbed a trembling hand over his scalp. "In the temple, you will receive honor. You'll be treated well."

Rahab gasped as if he had struck her. "No. I won't go to the temple."

"You will obey me!" he yelled, his voice echoing in the small chamber. Shaking his head, he gentled his tone. "We need the money, child. Or else we'll all starve, including you."

Rahab strangled a rising scream, forcing herself to sound calm. "I am not refusing to obey you. Only, I won't go to the temples. If I have to do this, let's not bring the gods into it."

"Be reasonable, Rahab. You'll have protection there. Respect."

"You call what they do there 'protection'? I don't want the respect that comes with the temple." She turned and looked him squarely in the eye. He dropped his gaze.

He knew what she was talking about. The year before, Rahab's older sister Izzie had given her firstborn child to the god Molech. That baby had been the joy of Rahab's heart. From the instant her sister announced she was pregnant, Rahab had felt a bond of kinship with him. She'd held him minutes after his birth, wrapped tightly in swaddling, his tiny, perfect mouth opening and closing like baby kisses intended just for her. Love for him had consumed her from that moment.

But her sister wanted financial security. She was tired of poverty. So she and her husband Gerazim agreed to sacrifice their son to Molech for the sake of his blessing.

They paid no heed when Rahab begged them to change their minds. They were determined. "We'll have another baby," they told her. "He'll be just as sweet. And he'll have everything he wants rather than be brought up poor and in need."

Rahab went to the temple with them on the day of the sacrifice. She went hoping to sway her sister, hoping to make her see reason. She pleaded, begged, prayed. Nothing she said moved Izzie and Gerazim.

Her nephew wasn't the only baby sacrificed that day. There were at least a dozen children. The grounds were packed with people watching the proceedings. Some shouted encouragement to the priests who stood before enormous fires, covered from neck to ankle in white, offering supplications. Rahab recoiled at the sight, wondering about the nature of a god who promised a good life at the cost of a priceless baby's death. What kind of happiness could anyone purchase at such a price?

She held her precious nephew in her arms for as long as she could, cooing to his wriggling form. He smelled like sweet milk and honey cakes. Rahab nestled him against her one last time as she kissed him goodbye. The baby screamed when rough hands wrenched him from Rahab's arms. She stumbled back into Gerazim and found Izzie already slumped down. The sound of the baby's final shriek as the priest reached the raging fire still haunted Rahab, a nightmare that never quite faded.

That was the day Rahab promised herself she would never bow her head to Canaan's gods. She hated them. For all their glittering attraction, she had seen them for what they were. They were heartless murderers. Thieves of joy.

Now Izzie and Gerazim's land lay as wasted as her father's. So much for Molech's blessing. She would never seek it. No, the temple wasn't for her.

"Rahab," her father pleaded, biting an already ragged fingernail. "Think of the life you'll have outside the temple. You're young. You don't understand."

It wasn't that she felt no fear. Life for prostitutes outside the temples was hard, risky, and shameful. But she feared that life less than she feared serving Canaan's gods.

"Please, Father. I will not survive temple life." Daughters were expected to obey their parents without question. Her objections and pleas could be construed as disobedience. Her father could take her to any temple by force and sell her, and she would have no recourse. She told herself her father would never stoop to such means, but then remembered assuring herself only the night before that he would never ask her to prostitute herself either. The very ground under her feet had been shaken. Nothing seemed secure anymore.

Karem, who had walked in halfway through this exchange, burst out, "Father, you can't do this to the girl! Her life will be ruined."

Imri slashed the air with an impatient wave. "And you have discovered a way to support the family through the winter, perchance? You have arranged for a job? An inheritance from a rich uncle no one knew about?"

"No, but I haven't tried everything yet. There are other jobs, other possibilities." Rahab's heart leapt with hope at her brother's support. But the hope died quickly with her father's response.

"By the time you realize your confidence amounts to nothing, your pretty bride will be dead of starvation. Rahab is our only sure means of survival. Our only means," he repeated with brutal assurance.

Karem dropped his head and did not speak again.

Rahab pulled her knees to her chest, unable to swallow her tears. Her father moved to the opposite side of the room and sat in a corner, staring into space. Unspoken words rose between them like a wall. A wall as high and impregnable as the walls of their city.

Loneliness, vast and cavernous, slithered inside Rahab and settled into her bones.

In the end, Imri could not refuse his daughter's one request. Rahab's unwillingness to enter the temples placed her parents in a quandary, however. How were they supposed to find customers for Rahab? At the temple the rules were straightforward. But doing things Rahab's way meant none of them knew how to procure a well-paying clientele.

"There's a woman who lives round the corner from us; she used to train the temple girls," her mother said. "Now she helps girls who are on their own."

"I know the one you mean," Imri whispered. "She seems hard."

"I know her too." Rahab had seen the woman slap one of her girls until blood spurted out of the girl's nostrils. "Perhaps that is not the best plan."

"You are always contrary to my suggestions," her mother said, her voice trembling with reproach. "Do you know how much this hurts *me*? Do you know what it does to a mother's heart to have to bear her child's pain?"

"No, I probably do not," Rahab said, her words stiff as wood. She thought it politic to swallow any obvious references to her own pain. That would only set her mother off on another attack of guilt and suffering, and Rahab did not feel up to comforting her while grieving her own shattered dreams.

"Look, why should I give half my profits to a woman who will mistreat and cheat me? If the intention behind this enterprise is to earn enough money to see us through the year, we can't afford a greedy partner."

"Rahab, we don't know how to . . . how to manage this affair," her father said, banging his fist on the wobbly table.

The taste of bile rose in her throat. Ignoring it, she rasped, "Take me to Zedek the goldsmith. He'll know what's to be done." Her father ran errands for Zedek now and again. He was a rich man, goldsmith to the king, and well connected among the aristocracy of Jericho. For the last six months, every time Zedek saw Rahab on the street, he stared at her with an intensity of desire that even she couldn't mistake. She knew he didn't want her for a wife. He would have asked her father already if that had been his intention. But she was willing to bet he would pay well for the other.

And she intended to make him pay very well. If she had to go through this horror, she would gain a little something besides her family's bread for the drought year. She would free herself from her father. She loved him still, loved her family. But she determined never to be dependent on their protection again.

"What has Zedek got to do with it?" her mother asked.

Imri didn't answer her. He mopped his head and said, "As you wish."

Rahab snuck into the garden to weep in private.

23

"How much will it take to feed us for a year?" Rahab asked her father as they walked toward Zedek's shop. Her legs shook with each step, but she refused to give in to the fear that strangled her from the inside out.

"Why?"

"Ask for that much. Plus a gold necklace, earrings, and bracelets for me."

"Girl, you're pretty, but not that pretty. No man in his right mind would pay that much for one night, not even for you."

Was she attractive enough to tempt Zedek to part with his fat purse? She knew she'd been drawing men's eyes for the past two years, since her body had blossomed and her hair had lost the wild wiriness of adolescence and settled into soft curling masses of deepest red and brown. Would she do for Zedek? "Not one night," she replied absently. "Three months. He gets to have me while I'm still young and fresh . . . before anyone else . . ." Her voice trailed off. She couldn't bear the thought of facing this thing one night at a time, with different men spinning in and out of her life. A steady lover might become tolerable with time.

"I'll ask, but don't expect him to accept."

"It's a good bargain. He'll accept. Mind you, three months and not one day more." Her father looked at her like he'd never seen her before. Perhaps he hadn't. She hardly knew herself.

Zedek was a well-fed man with protruding front teeth. He dressed richly, ornamented with gold from his beard rings to the dainty bells on his woven shoes. When he saw Rahab and her father walk into his shop he came straight over, shoving the hireling aside. "Good day, Imri," he said, staring at Rahab.

In his dark irises she could see tiny reflections of her own face—thin nose, full lips, large hazel eyes puffy from tears. She had washed her hair for this visit, and now it peeked from under its veil, an unruly mass of bright chestnut coils surrounding her face and cascading down her back. Recalling the reason behind that washing she blushed with shame and desperation—and held Zedek's gaze.

Her father cleared his throat. "May we speak with you, my lord? Privately?"

Zedek haggled hard, but Imri, to his credit, did not budge. Zedek stared at Rahab, fingers rubbing his lips, and threw out one last sum. When Imri shook his head, the goldsmith walked away. Rahab took her father's hand and rose to go. He shot her an agonized look, but Rahab pulled hard and he stood. Zedek, perceiving their determination, came back and accepted their offer. Rahab noticed that her father looked astonished. She schooled her features into a bland mask, covering her own surprise. Like her father, she could hardly believe that Zedek was willing to pay so much for her.

For three months, Zedek was her master. He liked that she knew nothing. He liked that for the first week she cried every time. He liked comforting her afterward too. He wasn't cruel to Rahab. He never beat or abused her. And if a disgust of herself and of him settled into her stomach, she never let him see it.

When the three months were over, Zedek gave Rahab a bag full of gold. He threw in a pair of anklets in addition to her original demand, and when she tallied the coins, she found he had overpaid her as well. She assumed a mistake. "My lord," she said, "you gave me too much."

"My little Rahab refusing money?"

"I don't cheat my customers."

"Customers?" He rolled his eyes. "You've had but one. And you aren't cheating me, girl. I'm giving it to you."

Rahab bowed her thanks and clutched the money, half hoping that Zedek would ask her to stay longer. He was right. She hadn't known any man other than him. She didn't care for his touch, but she would prefer being the consort of one man than the plaything of many. Zedek showed no interest in continuing their association. Clearly he had had his fill of her.

She returned home and handed the bag of gold to her father. "From Zedek. Payment for three months."

Her father peered inside the bag and gasped. "So much! I never thought he would give so much!"

"That's the last of it. He's finished with me. He doesn't want me anymore." Rahab blinked back the tears.

"What did you expect?" Imri threw her a quick glance before returning his attention to the bag. "It's a wonder he stayed with you as long as he did, Rahab. He's a man of the world. He's accustomed to the best."

Meaning she was not the best. Rahab slumped on a cushion. Her father's words hammered home a truth she hadn't dared admit to herself. Once a man really came to know her, he would not want her anymore. She must be undesirable or insufficient in some way. Her father knew it. Zedek knew it. Now she knew it.

She felt cold. Laying her head on her knees, she wrapped her arms around her legs, and began to rock. Her father went into the next room to show her mother and brothers the gold. If not for the occasional gifts of wheat and oil from Zedek, their family would have starved by now. This gold would see them through the rest of the year and buy seed for the following year's harvest.

She heard her parents' muffled voices as they spoke in the next room. "Imri, what's to become of her now?" her mother asked, her voice thin and reedy. "Can't you persuade Zedek to keep her?"

"How am I supposed to manage that? He's bored with her and that's that."

"What are we to do with her, then? No one will marry her now."

"You knew the answer to that from the first day, woman. She'll have to make the best of it. We all will. Her looks will serve her well. There must still be men who want her. For a season anyway."

Rahab curled deeper into herself and swallowed a moan. Without thinking, she took a fistful of the lavish silk of her dress in each hand, bunching the fabric the way a scared infant might cling to a blanket. She choked as she thought about her future—about all the Zedeks who would spin in and out of her life. Her bed.

She mourned the dreams that would never be, the destiny she would never have. She mourned the choices lost to her. A loving husband. Children. Her own family. Finally, exhausted from crying and the strain of loss, she shut her eyes and lay on the cool floor. A shaft of sudden clarity pierced through the haze of misery.

She did have one choice. Though she was reduced to selling her body for money, she could choose her own lovers. She could begin and end every liaison according to her own desire.

She had tasted rejection from Zedek and it was too bitter to swallow. This bitterness, at least, she would avoid. She would be master of her own heart. She would let no one in, and she would cast each one out before they realized, as Zedek had, that she was unlovable.

During the months Rahab had been under Zedek's protection, she had met other influential men of his acquaintance. Several of them had hinted that they would be happy to replace Zedek if given the opportunity.

Rahab chose carefully, and only one lover at a time. She was stinting in her acceptance of men. Her clients were few, but generous. Her unusual selectiveness enhanced her popularity among men of the higher classes. Each wanted to be chosen over the others. Rahab became the competition they sought to win.

"Rahab, you are the most beautiful woman in Jericho," more than one man told her. "Even the king doesn't have a woman in his household who compares with you," they whispered in her ear.

Some days such words put a smile on her face, a shallow joy that never lasted. In her heart she believed that these men who claimed her to be incomparable would tire of her inside of three months and discard her like bones after a feast.

Sometimes after being with a man, she would curl on her mattress and shake, unable to stop. There were days when she would kiss her lover goodbye, smile at him as though he were the center of her world, close the door, and vomit. She hated what she did. But she did not stop. She believed she had no alternative. What else could she become after what she had been? Her life was locked into this destiny.

By the time Rahab was seventeen, she had enough silver to purchase an inn on the city wall. Leaving home came easier than she imagined. Two years of absent nights and shamed days had taught her to distance herself from her family. Her body followed where her heart had long been. She did not love her family any less than before. Often in her little inn, she was lonely for them. Yet, she found that being with them only made her lonelier. Increasingly, she gave her time to the demands of her inn.

Most innkeepers in Canaan were also harlots, so much so that the terms had become interchangeable. Rahab, however, separated her professions. Not everyone who stayed at her inn was welcomed to her bed. She made certain that her inn gained a reputation for simple elegance and comfort. Decorating it with woven tapestries and rich carpets, she avoided the gaudy ornamentation common among other inns.

The location helped. Jericho was nestled behind the protection of a double enclosure of walls. The outer wall with its stone base and impossible thickness contained a number of businesses as well as military towers. Those merchants fortunate enough to live in the outer wall enjoyed the benefits of a constant parade of patrons. As a result, the outer wall had turned into a fashionable address, and in spite of the inevitable diminutiveness of the establishments built into it, represented some of Jericho's most desirable properties. By the time Rahab turned twenty-six, her inn was as popular as she herself, though like her body, it often remained empty. It was that very exclusivity which made it a sought-after destination.

CHAPTER TWO

The first time Rahab heard about Israel, she was sprawled under a carelessly flung linen sheet, watching through half-closed eyes as her lover, Jobab, paced restlessly. His brow was so knotted it reminded her of a walnut shell. She could see he was agitated, but waited with patience until he was ready to speak. Men admired women who kept quiet at the right times.

When he finally tired of striding about like a trapped lion, he asked, "Tell me, Rahab, have you heard of the Hebrews?"

Rahab shrugged. "No. Friends of yours?"

Jobab's lip curled. "Hardly. The Hebrews crushed King Sihon and his sons last night. The great king of the Amorites was routed by a band of nomads."

"What are you talking about?" she asked, pulling the sheet around her and sitting up. "That's impossible." Sihon, one of the great kings east of the Jordan River, ruled over his land like an eagle in an eyrie. Men called him undefeatable. His kingdom was one of the most secure in Canaan.

"He *was* conquered, I tell you. By the Hebrews. Their leader, an old man named Moses, sent a message to Sihon requesting permission to travel the King's Highway in peace. Sihon denied them passage. He then mustered his army and attacked them at Jahaz. He must have thought it would be an easy victory. Would you believe, it didn't take long for the Hebrews to turn the battle." Jobab stopped speaking and stared at the scarlet carpet as if words failed him. "They're fierce. They don't even have proper armor. So when Sihon's army started to run—"

Rahab's chin snapped up. "Sihon's army *ran?*"

"What am I telling you? They were pulverized. And those not killed, ran. But the armorless Hebrews ran faster and caught up with them. They even killed some with slings. Sihon's glorious capital, Heshbon, brought down by slings."

Rahab's mouth dropped open at his words. To her, as to all who first heard of these events, they seemed outlandish. Impossible.

"That can't be!"

Jobab ignored her outburst. "All Canaan is in danger now."

Rahab rubbed at the pounding pulse in her temple. "Who are these Hebrews? I've never heard of them. How do they wield such power?"

"That's the wonder. They are nobody. A bunch of runaway slaves." Jobab sank down to the floor and slumped against the wall. "Forty years ago they ran away from Egypt, and they've been wandering in the wilderness ever since. They have no cities, no walls, no fields to plant or plow, no vineyards to harvest. Everyone has ignored them."

"What you say makes no sense. How could an army of slaves run away from Egypt? As if a pharaoh would ever allow it. This is an empty rumor." She looked at him, her fears reined in. Crossing her arms, she leaned back against a pillow.

Jobab raised his arms in exasperation. "Rahab, you're simply too young to know about it. Forty years ago, there was a great revolt in Egypt among the Hebrew slaves, led by this same man, Moses. He claimed his god wanted Pharaoh to free the Hebrews. Pharaoh refused at first, but so many plagues befell the Egyptians at the hands of the Hebrew god that Pharaoh *had* to let them go. Egypt was in ruins. Then, at the last minute, he changed his mind. As the Hebrews were leaving, Pharaoh mobilized his army and pursued them."

"Don't tell me the slaves brought Pharaoh's chariots down with their slingshots." Rahab smirked.

Jobab sighed. "Nothing so ordinary. Their escape route brought them to a dead end against the sea. Behind them came Pharaoh's invincible army. Before them lay a body of water impossible to cross. They were doomed. And then their god parted the sea."

Rahab raised an eyebrow. "Come now."

"He parted the sea, I tell you! Divided it right up the middle. They walked straight through to the other side on dry ground with the water piled up all around them. Then, when Egypt's chariots and men of war tried to follow, the waves came crashing down on top of them. Every single one of them perished. Egypt has not yet recovered its great strength after that loss."

"You believe this?"

"I know this," Jobab said without hesitation. And he was not a man to swallow tall tales.

But if Jobab was right, who could ever sleep safe in their beds again? What kind of god wielded so much power? If this was all true, who could stand against him? She began to understand the scent of fear that clung to Jobab.

Bending, she picked up her shift from the woven rug on

the floor and pulled it over her head. "Do you wish to stay the night? I can cook you supper if you want." Better she focus on her own menial tasks than the workings of kings and gods. What had she, a mere innkeeper, to do with such great events?

But she couldn't get Jobab's stories out of her mind. In the morning the soldiers at the gate confirmed news of the destruction of Sihon. Heshbon had fallen to the Hebrews. Surely that was frightening enough without bringing magical powers into it.

Along with everyone else in Canaan, Rahab soon heard more distressing news about the Hebrews. In the months following the defeat of Sihon they triumphed in other astonishing battles. They besieged and captured the walled cities of Nophah, Medeba, and Dibon, killing all their inhabitants. With every defeat Canaan grew more petrified. Rumors abounded. The Hebrews were giants. They were numberless. Their weapons were forged of a metal no one could break. They had winged horses. They grew larger than life with every victory.

Rahab disbelieved these exaggerated accounts of the Hebrew people. She recalled Jobab's words about the destruction of Sihon. The Hebrews were nobodies. People who wielded no sophisticated weaponry, and had no armor, no land, no riches. This was the true picture of Canaan's new enemy. And yet they were vanquishing nation after nation, army after army. What was it about these people?

Jericho, sophisticated Jericho with her ancient double row of walls and well-trained army, grew pensive. Canaan boasted many walled cities, but none to compare with Rahab's home. The walls of Jericho were a marvel. They were so thick that people built houses and places of business into them. In the land of Canaan, when they wanted to make a point about someone's strength, they compared them to the walls of Jericho. But even the people of Jericho were unnerved by the astonishing victories of the Hebrews east of the Jordan River.

Sacrifices increased in those months as people sought protection against the threat of this terrifying foe. Rahab could smell the burning flesh from the temple fires a league away. The priests grew slack-jawed and grey from lack of sleep. People poured into the temples and high places at such a rate that the king finally had to appoint soldiers to keep order. Rumor had it the temple prostitutes were kept busy day and night. Rahab pitied them. She hoped they were too exhausted to think or feel anymore.

The desperate idolatry of her people did not attract Rahab. The more she saw their faith in practice, the more she reviled it. Not even fear and desperation would drive her into the arms of Asherah, Baal, or Molech.

Her life went on despite the upheavals outside her walls. She left Jobab, and for a long season her inn and her bed were empty. Fewer people traveled those days for fear of marauding foreigners. She had enough gold saved up that the temporary lack of income didn't worry her. Her father's land could always use an extra pair of hands, and she spent her days in the fields, doing the hard work of farmers. Her skin grew brown and her nails ragged. *Not good for my trade,* she thought, examining their rough edges one afternoon under the hot sun. The realization made her smile.

At fifteen, all she had wanted was this life. But then, she had had hopes of marriage, of love, of true companionship. That life and all its promises were a faded dream, now. She could not afford a farmer's back-breaking labor as an unmarried woman. Nor would she return under her parents' roof to become the object of their neighbors' scorn and her family's shame.

That evening, when she received an invitation from the king's cousin to attend a glittering feast at his home, she decided to accept. She must not remain absent from the sophisticated crowd who put bread on her table and filled her purse with gold.

Rahab chose a dress in flowing cream linen edged with delicate silver embroidery. Her clothing never marked her as a harlot. She dressed as any fashionable lady in Canaan might, leaning toward simplicity rather than high style. She found that the curves of a woman's body, when displayed with clever modesty, proved far more attractive than any dramatic garment. Ignoring current fashion, which demanded tiny elaborate curls sculpted on top of her head, Rahab left her hair loose down her back. She wore long dangling earrings and matching armbands on her bare arms. She did not intend to stay long, but merely to make an impression.

"Rahab!" her host exclaimed as he spotted her walking in, his long face wreathed in a smile.

She removed his hand from her hip and made a graceful curtsy. "Your servant."

"I wish you were."

She smiled into his eyes. "Your villa sparkles this evening, my lord."

"Now that you are here, it certainly does."

She laughed. "The dangerous royal charm." Her host was only a distant cousin of the king, and liked being referred to as *royal*. His hand was snaking too close to Rahab's lower back again, and she hastily stepped away, bumping into a hard body. Turning around, she exclaimed, "Your pardon."

She knew the man by sight. He served as a high general in the army—one of Jericho's leading men of war. What was his name? Debir, she remembered.

"Evasive maneuvers," he said straight-faced. "I understand." Small laugh lines crinkled around his eyes. Rahab flushed and turned her head for a quick look. Her host had moved to another conversation.

"A friendly skirmish," she replied.

He grinned. "I am Debir."

"I know. Your reputation precedes you, my lord. I am Rahab."

"I know. Your reputation also precedes you."

She inclined her head. "It is rare to see you attending a feast, lord."

"Alas, I find I do not enjoy empty chatter."

"Nor do I. I prefer intelligent conversation, but there is not much of it in my profession."

He laughed. "Nor in mine."

They spent the next hours in each other's company, speaking with a natural ease that was rare for Rahab. She found Debir's sharp humor and acerbic commentary on Jericho's society refreshing. He was not a charming man. He never even tried, a relief to Rahab who had grown accustomed to men offering empty courtly manners and little substance.

They discovered a mutual understanding bordering on respect

for each other that night. Within the first hours of his acquaintance, Rahab decided to accept Debir as her lover.

Rahab knew that Debir came to her not out of lust or sentimental affection, but out of a simple desire to be relieved of responsibility for a few hours. Even a steady man like Debir needed a place where he wasn't continuously pestered for decisions and judgments and wisdom. Everywhere Debir walked, he shouldered the weight of endless expectations. His three wives and numerous children relied on his guidance as heavily as his troops in the king's army. So Debir came to Rahab simply to be.

Unlike her other lovers, he appreciated Rahab's wit and enjoyed conversing with her. As a result he would often speak to her about matters of state, something the average man of Jericho considered above a woman's comprehension. He never shared state secrets. There was too much soldier in him for that. But he would talk to her about the wars that raged around them, and of the change that was settling over Canaan.

"It seems the Hebrews have besieged Og," he told her one night, the planes of his face smooth and curiously expressionless as if he hadn't just proclaimed the most devastating news to reach Canaan in a hundred years.

Rahab gasped. Og, the king of Bashan, was reputed to be a giant both in stature and in ability. His iron bed was considered one of the wonders of the world, thanks to its remarkable size. No Canaanite could imagine anyone having the temerity to march against Bashan. "Now they'll *certainly* be destroyed," she said.

Debir raised an eyebrow, but said nothing.

"You don't agree?"

"Let's say I don't think it's a foregone conclusion."

"You don't think Og can beat them? You think they can overrun the city of Edrei?"

"Edrei is a different matter. It's protected by a gorge on the one side and a mountain on the other. Nestled right into the side of it. Militarily speaking, Edrei is impenetrable. I can't see how even Moses and his magician warriors could get in."

"So? Isn't that where Og is?"

"For now, yes. He's settled in, and all he has to do is sit tight and wait the Hebrews out. It will be a long and grueling siege, and the Hebrews can't afford to sit idly and do nothing for that long. They'll need food, water, and fresh grazing land for their cattle. Eventually, they'll have to give up and leave."

Rahab frowned. "I thought you feared Og might lose. Now you're telling me he doesn't even have to fight to win."

Debir walked over to the window and gazed out at the plains and hills leading to the Jordan. His smile didn't reach his eyes as he turned back to face her. "A conceited king will find it hard to hide rather than fight. He may not lose, but he also doesn't win. Og is a warrior, and his pride matches the size of his shanks. It will take a great deal of sense to keep him sheltered in Edrei."

"And you think he has more pride than sense."

"Let's just wait and see."

Og chose to march. Like the proud fool he was, he took his whole army out to meet the Hebrews in battle. One soldier survived long enough to tell the story, and a passing merchant brought it to Jericho. Edrei had been attacked by swarms of hornets. The city was thick with them. They drove the horses wild, and there was no escape. Their stings were so bad they killed the very young and old. Their strong men howled with pain and cursed with vexation. Og could not bear it. To be imprisoned in your own kingdom by an inferior enemy was bad enough, but the added indignation of being stung by hornets was too much for him. Was he a slave that he should cower in his own domain, hiding from mere vagabonds? So he marched out together with his sons and his army to engage the Hebrews.

And the Hebrews killed every single one of them and took possession of their land.

"It won't be long now before Moses sets his sights on Jericho," Debir said after telling Rahab the story of Bashan's defeat. He was lying on his back, staring at the ceiling. "We are the first great city west of the Jordan, and if he understands anything about warfare, he'll make us his next target."

Her mouth turned dry at this pronouncement. "Well, for pity's sake, don't open the gates and rush out to meet them if they come. We'll be safe inside our walls."

With his thumb and middle finger, he flicked a fly that had settled close to him. He had faultless aim. The fly pitched over in death. Turning toward Rahab, he said, "They crossed the Red Sea, you know. When they ran away from Pharaoh. The sea parted for them and collapsed over the Egyptian army."

Rahab flopped down on a feather-filled cushion and leaned back against a tapestry. "Don't tell me you believe in that nonsense."

Debir looked at her from beneath bushy brows. "I do believe

it. I have believed it for almost forty years since I first heard about it. Their god is mighty beyond our experience."

Her smile was tinged with sarcasm. "Another bloodthirsty god. Excellent. Just what Canaan needs."

He shook his head, his eyes sparkling with amusement. "You have the strangest notions, Rahab. It's a wonder the gods don't strike you down."

"I leave them alone and they return the favor. Why do you believe this nonsense about the sea parting and Pharaoh's army drowning, Debir? It's not like you to credit rumors."

"It's no rumor."

"You saw this with your own eyes?"

Debir ran a hand through his hair. "No. But I saw it through the eyes of someone who *did* see it firsthand. One of the Hebrews."

Rahab bolted upright. "You know one of them?"

"Forty years ago, I did." Debir rose from the mattress and came to sit near her. "I met him just before my military training. If I hadn't been so young, I would have recognized him for the spy he was. At the time though, I believed him to be a merchant like he told me. He saw me at the gate and gave me a week's wages to give him a tour of the city."

Her eyes widened. "Why didn't they attack us back then? Why wait forty years before starting their campaign?"

"I don't know. This Moses must be getting on in years. He was their leader back then too."

"Maybe he'll die before they come against Jericho."

"I have a feeling even that wouldn't stop them. The man I told you about, he said their real leader is their god. It was this god who sent Moses into Egypt to free the Hebrews from slavery.

He told Moses he had seen the affliction and misery of his people, and was concerned about their suffering. He wanted them released from Pharaoh's yoke."

Rahab frowned, her mind racing. In her experience, words like *concern* were not in the gods' vocabulary. Yet if Debir was correct, here was a god who had compassion on human suffering. The thought of a god of compassion did something odd to her heart.

Without warning, she felt the squeezing hand of longing. Longing to be *seen* as the Hebrews had been seen by their god. Longing for someone to look upon her suffering and care enough to rescue her.

With ruthless precision, she squelched the traitorous desire. "Well, he wasn't very compassionate to the Egyptians if he drowned the lot of them. Is it only the Hebrews he cares about? Didn't he consider the weeping wives and mothers back in Egypt?"

Debir lifted a fat curl lying on her shoulder and pulled it softly. "*I* wouldn't have shown the Egyptians any compassion if they had treated *my* people as they did the Hebrews. Incredibly, the Hebrew god gave the Egyptians plenty of opportunities to release his people without bloodshed. He gave them warning upon warning. But their pride was too great. They wouldn't bend to his will. If they hadn't chased after the Hebrews, they wouldn't have drowned."

Rahab pulled her hair free from his hold. "What else did this man tell you about their god?"

Debir shrugged. "He sounds very odd. He allows no statues to be built of him so you can't see or touch him. He claims to be the one true God, present everywhere, ruling over everything. It would be laughable if it weren't for the power he seems to display."

"A god you can't see? What would be the point? How are you supposed to believe in what your senses tell you isn't even there?"

"I don't know, but the Hebrew spy told me he did not find this an impediment. He claimed there were other ways to experience god apart from statues and man-carved images."

Rahab leaned on her elbows and pinned Debir with a steady gaze. "Such as?"

"I didn't become a follower, Rahab. I'm no expert at their religion. I can tell you he is ridiculously strict. For example— and you'll find this interesting—he forbids prostitution even as part of worship. One of the places I took the Hebrew was a temple. He covered his eyes when he saw the prostitutes mating with the worshipers and told me that according to Hebrew Law, they would have been stoned."

"Stoned?"

"You would make a very bad Hebrew, eh, Rahab? Or a very dead one."

She swallowed. There was a flagon of wine sitting next to her and she poured some into an ornate silver cup for herself, forgetting to offer any to Debir. It tasted like dust. She barely said a word after that, and Debir, unaccustomed to a brooding Rahab, took his leave.

CHAPTER THREE

Nobody knew better than Rahab the destructiveness of her trade. Nobody knew better what it did to your soul when you gave your body without emotional attachment, without commitment, without hope of a future. No pleasure could fill the gulf of loneliness that widened with each day. There were days when she wanted to strangle the men who pawed at her without a thought for her heart. And there were days when she thought her own death might not be a bad fate. She felt part dead already. It seemed that the Hebrew god agreed with her. So he was a god of compassion. But for Rahab, he had only stones.

She could hardly blame him, for she hurled stones at herself every time she gazed in a mirror. But that night, Rahab lay awake, tortured by thoughts of a compassionate god who chose to rescue his people from their afflictions.

The next afternoon Debir came again, and to make up for her silence the previous day, Rahab prepared his favorite meal, roasted fowl stuffed with figs, served with sweet cinnamon bread. She poured him rich, red wine, cleaned his hands and feet with perfumed oil, and then settled herself on the cushions at his feet.

"Tell me more about the Hebrew god." The request burst from her lips before she had a chance to silence it. Dread warred with an inexplicable hunger as she waited for Debir.

He swallowed a large mouthful of bread. Debir might be a nobleman, but he ate like a soldier, always in a hurry as if pursued by iron chariots. "I thought you found him offensive."

"I find him . . . curious."

Debir picked up his cup. "The Hebrew god is as tenderhearted as a woman."

"What do you mean?" For Debir, a woman's tenderness was no compliment. But Rahab found the description intriguing.

"The day I took the spy to the temple, the priests were sacrificing three young boys. The spy wept when he saw it. I will never forget his tears. He was a large man, well-built and heavily muscled—not effete in any sense, except for these tears running the length of his face. As a young man I thought him weak, crying like an untried boy at a sacrifice.

"He asked me if I felt no revulsion. 'Of course not,' I said. He told me his god would never bear such a thing. Then he said, 'Your hearts are stone. Your people have grown hard beyond redemption. Even the Lord cannot reach you. And He is God in all heaven and earth.'"

Rahab turned toward Debir, holding her breath. A god who cherished life? A god who cared for unnamed babies? A god who could see Canaan's iniquity and declare them *beyond redemption*? Again she felt that longing, stronger than before. The irony of it didn't escape her, the pitiful irony of a prostitute from Jericho longing for the god of the Hebrews.

"So you think their god is wiping us out as judgment?" she asked.

Debir shrugged. "I'm not a priest. As a soldier, I can tell you they are winning victories they shouldn't be winning. Their god baffles me. He appears to have more power than any of our gods. Power *and* compassion. I've never seen anything like it, and I don't care to face it now, if you want to know the truth. I hope the Hebrew god is satisfied with the land on that side of the Jordan. Let them settle over there. Then maybe we can do business with them."

"But you don't think that's what will happen."

He leaned over and refilled the silver cup. "If I were their general, that's not what I'd do. Trapped between Midianites and Edomites and Amorites and Egypt, how would they ever be safe? If this god desires to give his people rest, leaving us untouched would not make a good plan."

"Are you afraid of him—of this god?" she blurted out.

The fact that she had asked him this question would have been an insult to any other man. But Debir took no notice of the impropriety of her words. He stood suddenly and began to pace in the narrow room. "The *Lord*. That's what they call him," he said, dropping to one knee very close to Rahab. She could feel the warmth of his wine-soaked breath as he spoke. "Everyone's afraid. Even the barracks are filled with dread. If Og and Sihon couldn't withstand the *Lord*, how can we? He isn't interested in terms. He isn't interested in compromise. He is like a consuming fire. You ask me if I'm afraid. Rahab, I have never known fear . . . until now."

"You think we're going to die." It wasn't a question. She could see the conviction stamped on every line of his face. The Lord. Finally, she had encountered a god of power *and* compassion. And he was her enemy.

"Yes. I do. I imagine it's not going to happen for many weeks yet. The river is on our side because it's at flood stage. You can't cross a whole army through it at this time of year, but as the waters dry up, they will come."

"How will they get through our walls? No one has been able to do that, not for centuries, not since they have been extended."

"You're right. No *army* can get through these walls. But we're not talking about an army; we're talking about a god. No wall can withstand his will." Debir bowed his head as he said this, and she caught a glimpse of something she never thought to see on his face. Despair. He had no hope. In that moment she became convinced of Jericho's doom.

When Debir left, Rahab was filled with a sudden desire to be outside, away from the constraints of her small home. Her sandals clattered down the stairs inside the dark bowels of the wall and then, relieved, she emerged into the bright day. Taking a deep breath, she began to walk, her feet moving of their own accord.

She plodded blindly down the main avenue that led to the king's palace, passing the thick palms that lined and shaded the road. Her steps wavered before the temple of Molech. It had been long years since she had walked through Molech's threshold. Impulsively, she entered the ornate double gates. It was not the hour for sacrifice yet, and the pit of fire burned low, like a sleepy demon with one eye open.

Rahab stood over that pit, which had once greedily devoured her greatest treasure, turning him into a handful of ash. "Well, you have finally met your match," she whispered. "For years, you have roamed among us like a hungry lion, seeking whom you will devour. Now there is one who can devour *you*." She smirked. "Good riddance."

The next morning, on her way to the market Rahab turned down a narrow lane and came upon a group of noisy children. She gazed at them with an indulgent smile. Her smile faded quickly as she realized the nature of their game. They had surrounded a beggar and were pelting him with stones and obscenities. The old man crouched in a corner, his trembling hands covering his face.

A sharp rock hit the man's forehead. Blood welled up on the wrinkled skin and began dripping into his eye.

One of the girls pointed a finger at the beggar and shouted, "Look how his white beard is shaking—he's starting to cry! Hit him again!"

"Cry nothing," laughed a boy. "I think he might wet his pants!"

"Eeuw!" Several spectators gasped, and cheered with laughter.

"Leave him alone!" Rahab bellowed.

The boy, about to hurl another rock, stopped short and stared at Rahab. Her fine clothes must have made an impression. "My lady?"

She gestured for him to drop the stone.

He frowned. "Lady, he's just a beggar, can't you see?"

"Leave him alone, I said."

They were all gaping at her now. "We aren't doing anything wrong," one of them said defensively. "Didn't you notice his stench?"

"That's right. He's only an old beggar!" the boy added.

Rahab grew very still. It was true that her people treated vagrants worse than stray dogs. She herself would have walked right by him without a glance on most days. She might not have tormented him, but she certainly wouldn't have given his plight a second thought.

She examined the young faces before her. They displayed no remorse. No conviction. No regret. These were mere children, yet already they had learned to step on the weak and hate the helpless.

"Get out of here," she insisted. They obeyed her, partly because she was an adult, but also because her clothes were finer than theirs. The people of Jericho did know how to respect money.

She knelt by the old man. "Are you hurt badly?"

He shrank back and said nothing. She saw that his cut was superficial, another injury to add to the scores he had received in the course of his life. Reaching inside her linen pouch, she found a few silver coins, probably more than the old man had ever seen in one place. Placing the coins in his palm she said, "Go and find a safe place to wash and sleep. And put some warm food in your belly." His jaw dropped open, and she saw that his teeth had rotted away. The pathetic sight of that mouth, toothless, filled with decay, stinking of putrefaction, made her heart melt with pity instead of disgust.

He wrapped shaking fingers around the coins. Raising that

wobbly fist he cried, "A curse on them! A thousand curses on those children!"

"Shhh," Rahab whispered. Without understanding her own actions, she reached out and held the man as a mother might hold a dear child. To her astonishment, he began to sob, heaving convulsions that seemed to have no end.

With painful insight she realized they were not much different. She too had putrefying wounds, though they were deep within. She too was forsaken. She too was rejected. Her life too had been wasted. No, she felt no disgust for him. Only sorrow and pity.

When he had quieted, she rose up. "Lady," he rasped. "No one has held me like that since I was a boy."

Rahab smiled and nodded. Drained by the encounter, she began to walk away, then broke into a heedless run toward home.

She recounted the story to Debir when next he came to visit her. He shrugged, dismissing it with ease. "He's a beggar, Rahab. I don't know why you bothered."

Rahab studied him silently. Debir was closer to a friend than anyone she had known since childhood. She liked his forthrightness, his intelligence. She basked in his unusual acceptance of her. And yet she had to admit he was hard. Impenetrable. "Do you think the god of the Hebrews would care about beggars?" she asked, trying to goad him into some feeling.

"How should I know? Am I a Hebrew? He cares for babies and slaves. Maybe he cares about beggars too."

Rahab turned away bleakly. "And yet he plans to destroy us."

"Yes."

She felt torn between fear and longing. Terror toward a god who despised her people and longing for a god who championed the forgotten. Terror won. Without thinking, she reached for Debir's hand and held on to its rough, broad surface until her fingers turned white. "Debir, let's escape. Let's run from Jericho."

"There is no escape. Don't you see? The *Lord* has marked out this whole land for his people."

"We'll go somewhere else. We'll—"

"Rahab, stop. I'll not run. Why should I bend my knee to this wandering rabble and their tenderhearted god? I am a man of Jericho, a lord of Canaan. I will not betray my position or my people." He pulled his hand out of hers and moved away.

Rahab opened her mouth to argue and then closed it again. Debir felt none of the pull or longing for this new god that she felt. He was only afraid of his power. And that fear did not compare to the measure of his pride. How could Rahab pit herself against Debir's pride when his own fear of the Hebrew god could not dent it?

A great sadness settled over her as she studied his tense back. Their time together was at an end, she knew. He was a man who believed he had no future. A man preparing to die. Dying men returned to their families. Suddenly the very things they avoided as annoying or cumbersome seemed precious and worthwhile. Their harlots no longer answered their needs.

She approached him and waited until he acknowledged her with a glance. She caressed his face with a tender hand. "May you live long, my lord."

"Are we saying goodbye?"

"It is best."

He nodded with a soldier's disciplined movement. "May the god of the Hebrews deal kindly with you. Our own gods seem to have abandoned us."

"I abandoned them first, so their loss is no great sorrow to me."

He gave the ghost of a smile. "I will send you a token. Don't bother saving any of it. Spend it as soon as you can."

In the ensuing days Rahab spent long hours brooding over her future. She thought about the destructive ways of Jericho and the pointless passions of her countrymen that led only to unhappiness. She thought about the Hebrews and their strange customs. Most of all, she thought about their god. She could not pluck him out of her thoughts. Could there really be a god who ruled over everything? Could he be real, this phantom of the Hebrews who saved some and condemned others with incomprehensible rationale? Did he really champion slaves?

After three days of being haunted by her thoughts she knew she was in need of a diversion, and decided to call on her family.

"Do my eyes play tricks on me or is my younger daughter actually honoring me with a visit?"

Rahab's smile was dry. Her mother reached on tiptoes and gave her a quick kiss on the cheek. "Izzie and Gerazim are here too. The whole family's together."

For a moment Rahab felt a wrenching pang. If she had not happened by, would they have invited her? And why should they? She had spurned so many of their invitations in the past. Though she often sent gifts, her visits were few.

"I'll be glad to see everyone," she said honestly.

"Is that my little sister?" Izzie cried and ran over to envelop Rahab in a hug. "Looking ravishing as always. Come and soil your exquisite robe. I'm preparing the meal and I could use your help." She leaned closer so that only Rahab could hear her. "Mother is causing me to lose my mind."

Rahab laughed, feeling the tension drain from her body. Cooking with Izzie sounded delightful.

"Mother, now that I have Rahab, you can rest from cooking," Izzie announced. "Why don't you go enjoy your grandchildren?"

"What, and leave you girls to ruin our supper? I don't think so."

Izzie growled under her breath. "Pardon, but I have been running my own household long enough to manage a family dinner. As for Rahab, she owns a famous inn."

"Thank you for the reminder, as if I could forget," Rahab's mother said, her lips turning white.

Now Rahab remembered why she rarely visited. Izzie dug a sharp elbow into her side. "Ignore her. You come with me." To Rahab's relief, their mother did not follow, and she spent two hours helping prepare several dishes for the family's supper. Her sisters-in-law, Zoarah and Joa's wife, Hurriya, joined in after a while and Rahab found herself laughing over stupid stories. She had missed her family. They were far from perfect. But they were the only family she had.

As the days unfolded, she found herself spending more and more time with them. With the women she weeded the garden, fetched water, made cheese and yogurt from goat milk, bartered in the bazaar, and spun wool. In time, the season for harvesting the flax and barley arrived, so Rahab joined her family in the fields more out of a desire for companionship than for financial gain. Debir's "token" turned out to be a substantial bag of gold large enough to see her through a year. If she had a year, which she doubted.

She didn't believe she had a future anymore. Still, she scraped her hands raw, pulling flax from the root to protect the fragile stems that would yield linen. Who would live to use these stalks? Who would put the yarn on a loom and weave them into linen? Who would dye them? Sew them? Wear them? And yet she pulled and pulled, until the field about her was cleared and her bundles piled high.

Her family wasn't immune to the dread spreading over Jericho as continuous reports of Hebrew victories reached their gates. By its very nature, harvesting forced them to think about the future. And their future boded ill. The enemy was close.

The night they completed the harvest there was little of the usual joviality that accompanied the last day of reaping. Rahab took her share of the flax stalks home in an old cart and laid them out on the roof to dry. She was exhausted from her labors. Too weary even to wash the sweat from her skin, she slid down against the wall and rested her head on her knees.

She hurt, flesh and heart. An overwhelming sense of isolation swept through her. For all the time she spent with her family these days, and despite their kindness toward her, she felt as if she belonged to no one. She longed for sleep to release her from the pain of thinking. Of *feeling*. But sleep would not come.

She was trapped. Trapped in the solitude of her heart, which no amount of companionship seemed able to pierce. Trapped in her body, the body of a harlot besmirched by a dozen men. Trapped in Jericho, which stood trembling before an enemy whose advances could not be turned away by walls of stone and mortar. Trapped in Canaan, which was marked for destruction by a god who claimed to have dominion over the whole world.

Was there anyone who could set her free from so much bondage?

Her thoughts turned again to the god of the Hebrews. If he were truly the one god over everything as the Hebrews claimed, did it not follow that everyone who lived on earth belonged to him in some way? If he were the one real god—a stretch to believe such an outlandish claim—but if he were, could not even Rahab the harlot, Rahab the Canaanite, Rahab the nobody make a request of him?

Rahab sat up straighter. What would she have to lose by it?

"God of the Hebrews," she began, before lapsing into silence. She had no idea how to speak to a god after so many years of enmity with them. "God of the Hebrews," she began again with determination. "I have heard of your power. Your people say you are the one true god. They say you hear their cries.

"If these are not the wild tales of desperate men, if you are truly what they proclaim you to be, then I wish you would reveal yourself to me."

The pale rays of dawn woke her from a deep sleep. She still sat where she had collapsed the previous night, against the wall, in a heap. Rahab was amazed that she had slept soundly through the night. Not for months had she known slumber so uninterrupted. The words of her prayer to the god of the Hebrews suddenly rose to the forefront of her mind. An unseen god. A god with no form or image. A god no one could touch. The god of her enemies. And yet on this early morning she sensed a peace beyond anything she had known these many years. Was this the doing of the unseen god? Or was she losing her mind? Would her mother be saddened or cheered to know about her madness? What was worse—having a mad woman, or a harlot for a daughter?

She rose with a grunt. Her day servant would not arrive for several hours yet, and Rahab could not wait to wash. She stank of dried sweat and farm soil. *She stank of honest work.* Filling a large basin with tepid water, she added a few drops of rose water and oil and began to cleanse her skin of its dirt. The peace lingered. If this was madness, she accepted it gladly. If this was the doing of the Hebrew god, then he was everything his people claimed him to be. If this god was the enemy, she belonged to the wrong side.

A glance out the window showed a cloudless blue sky, and Rahab decided to go for a walk. She chose a winding path lined with young date palm trees, a beautiful road that led toward the marketplace. Without warning, the stench of charred flesh and the pounding of drums assailed her senses. Looking up, she examined her surroundings and found herself near the temple of Baal. Not ten paces away stood a prostitute, waiting, and half tumbling out of a dress that no longer looked fresh. Their eyes met. This was someone's daughter, Rahab thought. Someone's sister. But her life had been sacrificed, exchanged for the promise of prosperity.

Abundance, fertility, health—Canaanites sacrificed their children in hopes of greater gain and satisfaction of every kind. Next to money, they worshiped lust. In satisfying one desire, they hoped the gods would satisfy all their other desires as well. Financial security and sensual pleasure mattered more than life in Jericho.

It had been years since Rahab parted company with the gods of her people. Now she saw that the trouble wasn't merely with their gods. The root of Jericho's problem was her people. They chose these standards. They chose this order and abided by it. They lived in sin and called it good. Even Debir had chosen death over the humility of a new start. And Debir was the best of them! Canaan had turned into the very pit of the world, and Jericho was the pit of Canaan.

Was this why the god of the Hebrews sought to annihilate them? Did he see no hope for them? No redemption? The answer welled up within her. They had gone too far. And they were arrogant about it. Defiant. The weak, the helpless: nameless babies, sickly beggars, and young girls forced to serve in the temples—like this girl, staring at her through vacant eyes—had no recourse. No justice and no hope of salvation. They either perished, or died a slow death by growing bitter and refusing to forgive. While the powerful pawed and pillaged and used and violated as they pleased. This was her home. This was her heritage.

Unsettled, Rahab made her way to her parents' home. In the small garden, she found Joa, tending vegetables.

"Rahab!" he called out and straightened.

"I was planning to buy some food in the market, but lost heart before I arrived."

"All of Jericho has lost heart. Come and pick vegetables with me."

Rahab knelt in the dirt, careless of her fine tunic. "Joa, do you think the god of the Hebrews is real?"

"Perhaps you should ask Og or Sihon that question. Oh, wait. They are dead."

She nodded slowly. "He is powerful."

"And bloodthirsty."

Rahab frowned. "He forbids the sacrifice of children, you know. He does not allow human sacrifice at all."

Joa straightened. His eyes were shadowed as he looked at her. "You have no fondness for our gods."

"I do not. I am not certain I have any fondness for our people, either."

"Rahab!"

"Think on it, Joa. Where is the goodness of Jericho? Where is its mercy?"

Joa lowered dark brows. "We're no different from anyone else. Everyone is the same."

"Everyone is *not* the same. The Hebrews don't live by our standards."

"*The Hebrews!*" Joa spat the word with venom.

"You can hate them all you wish. But *they* don't put their daughters to work as harlots in their temples."

Joa flushed. He pulled on his ear, leaving a trail of dirt. "They are our enemy, Rahab. They mean us harm."

She waved a hand as if that stark reality was irrelevant. "Their god, Joa, isn't merely powerful. He cares for the welfare of his people."

"And you think that helps us, somehow?"

"It helps us to know that there is one god in this forsaken world who has a heart of compassion."

"Helps *you*, maybe."

"Yes. It helps me."

"Wonderful. He will put you to death with great compassion, I am sure."

Rahab's smile was bitter. "I am full of regrets, brother. Death does not seem so frightening just now."

At home, Rahab found she could neither sit nor eat. Pacing from room to room, she eventually climbed the narrow ladder to the roof where the flax was drying. Sinking down on the bundles, she stared into the distance, over the boundaries of Jericho's farmlands. Somewhere beyond the horizon the Hebrews were preparing for war.

"Am I seeing what you see when you look at Canaan?" she asked her invisible foe. "Have I seen us through your eyes?"

The day had turned hot, and Rahab yanked off the diaphanous veil on her head with an impatient hand. A soft breeze lifted the heavy weight of her hair from her neck. She raised her face to its caress.

Through the rafters in the roof, she heard a soft knocking on her door. It had been many days since she had received a visitor. She meant to ignore whoever was seeking her company. But the knocking continued, quietly persistent. With a sigh, she pulled up her veil again and carefully made her way down the ladder.

"Who is it?" she asked through the barred door.

"I am Malakbel, lady. My lord Debir sent me."

Rahab pulled open the door in surprise. After receiving his gift, she had not expected to hear from the general again. A stooped, white-haired man stood at her threshold. With a small bow he offered her a roll of papyrus. Accepting the letter, she broke Debir's familiar seal and read.

Rahab,

This is my slave Malakbel. Forty years ago, he too met the Hebrew I told you about. I have sent him to you with my compliments. The army found nothing of use in his knowledge. But I thought you might find him more helpful than we did.

Debir

Rahab rolled up the papyrus and gazed at the stooping man who stood patiently at her door.

"Malakbel, is it?"

"Yes, lady."

"Do you know why your master has sent you to me?"

"Yes, lady."

Rahab beckoned her visitor inside. "Tell me what you know," she invited simply.

"You want to know about the god of the Hebrews? May I inquire why?"

Rahab shrugged. "He seems . . . interesting."

"You are curious, then." His eyes sparkled with bright intelligence as he studied her.

"More than merely curious," Rahab said, plucking at her sleeve.

He nodded. "He has captivated you."

Her face warmed. "It sounds ridiculous, I suppose. I only know what Debir told me, and that is little."

The old man smiled. "It is not ridiculous. I have felt the same tug on my heart for forty years." He turned toward the window, looking at the darkening sky. "Unlike us, they have only one god, these Hebrews."

"You can't serve him and another god at the same time?"

"Not at all. He is like a bridegroom who will not welcome his bride into his house if another husband is tagging along. Besides, he considers all other gods false."

Rahab sneered. "Can't blame him."

Malakbel's beard shook as he laughed. "I have reached the same conclusion myself."

"But the Lord is different?"

"Oh yes. He wants a world without murder, adultery, and thieving. Without lying and jealousy. Without bribes and oppression. He even forbids the murder of slaves and the abuse of foreigners who live among his people. Imagine that! Imagine living in such a world!"

"It would be nothing like Jericho."

"True."

"Malakbel, are you going to run away from Jericho? From Debir? Are you going to try to join the Hebrews?"

"No, lady."

"But you believe in their god! You can try to save yourself from the coming destruction."

The stooped back turned away from her. "I am a dying man. Too many beatings. Too many years of hard service. I could barely climb the stairs to your house. I shall never make it out of Jericho. I will be in my grave before the Hebrews come. Pity. I should have liked to see the Lord conquer this city."

The life of a slave was harder even than that of a harlot. Rahab could not imagine the indignities Malakbel must have endured through the years. No wonder he was eager to witness the destruction of Jericho.

After her unexpected guest left, Rahab returned to the roof and settled once more among the flax. She mused over Malakbel's revelations.

"God of the Hebrews," she said, her whisper mingling with the quiet wind. "Surely my people displease you." A dozen memories flashed through her mind: the children's cruelty; the beggar's curses; Debir's unbending pride; murderous priests; the lust of faceless men; greed that placed gain above the well-being of the heart. Her gaze turned inward. Was she so much better?

She felt the blood drain from her face and gulped a mouthful of night air. "I am no different," she admitted. "I am no different." Her fist clenched. "God of the Hebrews, if you are able, take the weight of this sin from me."

In her mind's eye she saw her bed and remembered what it represented. Every fiber held the memory of her iniquities. Her insincerities. Her lies. Her lust. She had always blamed others for her life. Her father's betrayal. Her mother's self-absorption. Her family's needs. The perfidy of men. The faithlessness of the gods.

She had been wronged many times, there could be no doubt of that. But she had also made her own choices. Would not God hold her accountable for them? "I am sorry," she whispered. "I am sorry for it."

She slumped on the scratchy flax, tears burning her eyes, choking, suffocating as guilt twisted inside her like a wild creature. "If you are god of heaven and earth as you claim, help me, for pity's sake!"

Without warning, the peace that had rested on her in the morning, returned, settling over her like an embrace. It was a force, that peace. A power more awesome than the chariots of Jericho, more mighty than lightning. Rahab's breath hitched.

For a moment she could not think. Words eluded her. She lay under the weight of that peace and felt it wash over her like a living river, cleansing what it touched.

"God of the Hebrews, is that You?" She croaked as the mighty weight of otherworldly peace finally lifted off. An unreasonable conviction filled her mind—the conviction that this god was true. This god was God, and present to her at this moment.

"You are real! You are the God of heaven and earth. Perhaps I'm mad, but I believe it."

For the first time in years she felt anchored to something secure. Something good. "Whatever You choose to do. Whatever happens to Jericho or to me, I promise I will set that life aside. For as long as I live, I will set that life aside."

CHAPTER FOUR

S almone!" shouted a familiar voice with annoying insistence. Salmone hunkered lower behind the rock. He loathed giving up a rare moment of privacy, an elusive luxury when you traveled with multitudes of people. His friend Hanani called out again. "Time to come out of hiding, O Great Commander. Joshua has business with the leaders of the tribes."

That drew Salmone's attention. With a sigh he untangled his long legs and straightened. "Stop straining the sheep's ears. You found me. What does Joshua want?"

"Do I look like one of his advisors?" Hanani asked, scratching his beard and yawning. "He just said to find you. He wants to meet with all the leaders."

Salmone nodded. The closer Israel drew to the Promised Land, the greater his list of responsibilities grew. He acted as advisor, mediator, warrior, decision maker, coordinator, organizer, commander, and cattle herder. His father, Nahshon, had held even greater responsibility as the leader of the entire tribe of Judah, and under his tutelage, Salmone had grown accustomed to the burdens of duty early in life.

"Thanks for fetching me, Hanani," he told his friend and began to stride back toward the camp, his curiosity piqued. Joshua didn't call pointless gatherings. A man of action, he used his time with careful frugality.

Salmone found the men already assembled around Joshua, and sat where he could best hear. Joshua's stocky figure stood ramrod straight on a sloping hill. His salt-and-pepper hair waved in the warm breeze. Nothing else about him seemed to move. "I have news of Moses," he started, but his voice wavered and he paused.

Two days ago, Moses had called the people of Israel together. "I'm getting on in years and am no longer able to lead you," he had announced. The crowd had objected in dismay, for Moses still showed the vigor of a man in his prime in spite of his advanced age. His eyes had the vision of a young man, his muscles rippled as he moved with the crisp economy of a born athlete.

To the murmuring of Israel, Moses had merely raised a silencing hand. He was used to objections from them, and their insistence no longer swayed him. "The Lord has informed me that I shall not cross the Jordan with you." A collective gasp had met this shocking pronouncement. Moses ignored the rising alarm and continued. "God has chosen Joshua to be your leader, and so I name him, and so I bless him.

"It's time to leave fear behind or you'll be robbed of your destiny. You don't need confidence in yourselves or in your own power. Be strong in the Lord. When disaster seems close, don't be discouraged. God will never leave you." When Moses had finished his address, he had set out for Mount Nebo. That was two days ago, and now Joshua had fresh news of him. The gathered leaders held their silence, barely breathing.

"Before he left, Moses again laid hands on me and blessed me," Joshua disclosed. Salmone could see the bobbing of his Adam's apple as he swallowed several times. "Moses told me he would not be coming back from Mount Nebo. He was right, as usual. The Lord has informed me that His servant Moses is dead."

Some of the men gasped; others sat stunned. Could it be true? Had Moses died? They understood that none of Moses's generation save Joshua and Caleb would live to enter the Promised Land; Moses himself had said as much.

Salmone stared at Joshua in disbelief. He noticed the glint of unshed tears in Joshua's brown eyes and knew with sudden certainty that he would never see Moses again. Throughout Salmone's life Moses had been there like a beacon guiding his people. Surely there would never be another man with his faith. Surely Israel had lost her greatest leader. Salmone put his hand on the front of his tunic and tore it. The men around him looked at Salmone wide-eyed. It was as if his action made Moses's death a reality.

Joshua nodded and tore his own tunic. "Tomorrow," he said, "Israel will begin grieving for Moses formally. We will have thirty days to shed tears and mourn. Then we must move. The Lord is about to give us this land. Tell the tribes. Prepare them for grief. Prepare them for obedience." He raised his arms. "Prepare them for victory!" he shouted.

Salmone rose with the rest of the leaders and walked back toward his tent, dragging with every step. He was an old hand at mourning. He had lost mother and father. He had lost a young wife. Tears would come, he knew. Yet rejoicing was not far behind. Finally, *finally*, after a lifetime of wandering from wadi to wadi, from valley to plateau, from gravel paths to limestone fields he was in sight of home. He gazed around him and took in the mobile camp that formed the only life he had ever known. Tents, large and small, dotted every cubit of the landscape. Makeshift pens held livestock—sheep in some, goats in others, with a few cows and oxen spread throughout the camp. Their smell and dust filled the air. What would it feel like to live in a house, to have a barn, to own land? He was about to find out. Home meant more battles and trials, but it also meant a fresh hope for the future.

As he strode toward his tent, Michael, Sethur, and Jedaiah cut across his path. Good. These were men of influence who would help him spread the news.

"Is it true, my lord? Is Moses really dead?" Michael asked. He was a stocky man several years Salmone's senior. There was a steadiness about him that Salmone liked and trusted.

Salmone nodded. "Yes. I'm afraid it is. The greatest loss we have ever known, and yet Joshua assures us that we will be marching into the lands west of the Jordan in a month."

"Lord have mercy!" Sethur cried. "We're undone! How can we win any battles without Moses?"

Salmone looked at Sethur through eyes narrowed with calculation. "Undone, are we? I suppose God can't manage to fulfill His promises without Moses."

Sethur made a slashing gesture in the air. "God used Moses to free us from slavery in Egypt. He used Moses to keep us alive in this forsaken wilderness. He used Moses to lead us to victory in every battle we have ever fought."

Salmone crossed his arms. "And now He will use Joshua. Or do you have a better plan, perhaps? Would you recommend going back to being Pharaoh's slave?"

"I'm just saying—"

"Then *stop saying*. You are spewing panic. Our faith was never in Moses or in any other man. Our faith is in the Lord God. Every one of us is replaceable. Even Moses."

"Does Joshua have a plan?" Michael asked.

"It's still early. You know Joshua. He talks to God more than he talks to us. He'll have a plan in time. We have a whole month to grieve for Moses first." As Salmone turned, his eye caught Jedaiah and he flinched. The man was trying hard not to weep. Salmone berated himself for a fool. How could he have forgotten the deep affection that Jedaiah held for Moses? A special bond had existed between the older man and the younger. To Jedaiah, Moses wasn't merely a remote hero. He was a beloved advisor.

Salmone clasped Jedaiah's shoulder. "I am so sorry. I know how much Moses meant to you. And I know what you meant to him."

Jedaiah's lip quivered like a little boy's, and large tears slid down his cheek, disappearing into his beard. "I didn't even have a chance to say goodbye."

"I'm sorry, Jedaiah," Salmone repeated, grieved for his friend. He had learned enough from his own anguish not to offer platitudes. Loss had to be borne. There were no short ways around it. "We'll begin formal mourning for him tomorrow. If you wish to play a special part, you should go and see his family."

Jedaiah nodded. Salmone guessed that having something practical to do would provide an outlet for his grief. Jedaiah departed at a half run toward Moses's tent.

"So we'll be going into battle soon," Michael said into the ensuing silence.

"Indeed. God is giving us the land."

Sethur said, "You seem very confident of victory."

"I am, Sethur. My confidence is in God. You know how our parents' faith deserted them. You know even though they had Moses, they refused to fight for fear of losing. I don't intend to make that mistake. God is giving our generation another chance. I don't propose to lose my opportunity as my father lost his."

Sethur licked his cracked lips with a nervous tongue. "I don't want to lose my opportunity either."

Salmone clapped him on the back. "Good man. Trust God. And when you run out of trust, just obey Him."

For the next twenty-four hours Salmone applied his substantial energy to calling out the most influential men and women under his command, passing on the news of Moses's death, and instructing them on the coming preparations. Life without Moses seemed unimaginable. Perhaps the Lord meant them to realize that flesh and blood could not bring about their ultimate destiny. Only the Spirit of the Lord could. Israel's warriors had nothing to recommend them against the battle-hardened soldiers and walled cities of Canaan. All they had was God. And wrapped up in faith, this seemed more than enough.

When the thirty days of mourning were over, Joshua called the tribal leaders together. It was evening, and the leaders crowded into Joshua's large tent. Salmone's long, hard-muscled limbs were wedged between Caleb and Elidad, one of the leaders from the tribe of Benjamin. He could feel their scratchy homespun robes rubbing against his skin, their elbows digging into his ribs. A curious contentment washed over him—contentment at being surrounded by his brothers in the faith. Their companionship comforted him. A sense of safety seeped inside his bones.

In the tight space, Joshua's voice rang out like the whoosh of a loosed arrow. "We must get the people ready to cross the Jordan River."

Elidad cleared his throat. "But Joshua, the Jordan is at flood stage. It's impassable. Wouldn't it make more sense to wait a couple of months? It's been nearly forty years. What's another two or three months?" Salmone swiveled around to stare at Elidad in astonishment. To his shock, he saw a number of heads nodding in agreement.

Joshua's eyes narrowed. "Is this the counsel of the Lord, Elidad?"

Elidad shifted on his mat. "Well, no. Speaking sense, that's all, Joshua."

"Let me tell you something, every one of you. Human wisdom won't win us these battles. It will be God alone, as it has been since the day Moses led us out of the bondage of Egypt. We aren't called to be men of war as other nations understand warfare. We are called to be a people of faith. Our shield is God's Law. Our sword is His Word. He is our strong tower, and

He alone will give us victory. Otherwise we might as well dig our graves now."

A silence fell upon the men. How easy to forget they could not live as other nations. How easy to slide into pride and human reasoning, leaving no room for the ways of God. Finally Elidad broke the silence again. "If the Lord leads us into the churning waters of the Jordan, we will follow, Joshua. We will follow Him anywhere." Salmone felt his tightened muscles relax.

"Good." Joshua's grin flashed the white of a perfect set of teeth. "Now listen. Go through the camp, each one of you. Tell the people to get their supplies ready. Tell them we'll be crossing the Jordan before the week is over.

"One more matter. I'm planning to send two men west of the river to spy for us. We need to collect information on Jericho. I am not looking for heroics. Just go in, assess the situation, and return. I'd like to know what sort of welcome awaits us."

Salmone jumped up. "Send me, my lord."

"No, Salmone, I need you here. But fetch your friend Hanani. I will send him and Ezra."

Swallowing his disappointment, Salmone bowed his head in obedience. He had long since learned to rein in his impulses. The thought of Ezra and Hanani's excitement at being chosen by Joshua for such an important mission made him smile.

Flooding had made the fords nearly impassable. Hanani and Ezra had to cross the hard way—striving against the force of the water in tandem by creating bodily blocks for each other, one

72

standing still, bearing the force of the river on his back, while the other stepped ahead. With sheer determination they flung themselves against the relentless currents, battling concealed eddies and violent torrents as their feet fought to gain purchase on the slippery bed. Exhausted, they finally managed to pull themselves out onto the west bank by holding on to branches dragging in the water. They had come too near to drowning.

After catching his breath, Hanani threw an agonized glance at Ezra. There was no way the people of Israel could pass through that river.

"Let's go directly to Jericho," Hanani suggested. "It's what Joshua is most interested in, and our time is short."

"It's also the most dangerous part of our mission, Hanani. Passing through the city gates without getting caught won't be as easy as gathering manna."

Hanani pulled on his dark beard. "That's unavoidable. Just keep your chin down and try not to stare like an Egyptian calf when we get there. We'll enter during the afternoon bustle and hopefully no one will notice us."

"I won't stare if you don't babble like a girl. Your accent will give us away before you finish your first sentence."

Hanani cast his friend a mock glare. "At least I know how to talk. What about you? 'Hello, Mi-Mi-Miriam.' So profound. So charming. I'm sure Miriam ran home and begged her brother to give her to you in marriage after *that* conversation."

"Oh, eat your beard."

Hanani was too distracted to continue bantering; his half-hearted barbs were only an attempt to mask the heft of anxiety preying on his mind. He suspected Ezra struggled with similar worries.

The day became uncomfortably hot, and their drenched clothes dried quickly. Soon, the two men stripped off their outer robes and traveled in their simple homespun linens. The road to Jericho was covered by delicate gravel, which was easy on the feet. Hanani, whose feet had grown resilient from years of marching, barely felt the strain of the walk.

Though still leagues away, Jericho's walls came into view. As the men grew closer, they saw that the thick stones at the lower level of the wall gave way to mud brick so thick, soldiers marching two abreast on the parapet passed oncoming guards without even rubbing elbows.

"Nice stonework," Hanani muttered.

Ezra grunted. They had already discussed their plan. They would walk in brazenly, blend with the crowds, keep their ears open, and walk out toward nightfall without speaking to anyone. Hanani knew their real job was to listen. How were the inhabitants of Jericho reacting to Israel's victories east of their land? Were they even aware of the events of the past few months? Were they preparing for battle?

Their plan went awry from the first step. The guards at the gate were checking everyone. Each interview seemed lengthy and detailed, undermining the spies' intention of entering without being noticed. As the two men approached, one of the guards blocked Hanani's path and another thumped a beefy finger against Ezra's chest. "What are you doing here?" he demanded.

"Merchants," Ezra said.

"Where are you from?" the guard persisted.

"Midian, mostly. But we travel around."

The guard frowned. "You talk funny."

Hanani glanced around in desperation. There would be no fighting and no running. The gate area was thick with guards. Audacity would be their only hope. "We talk funny because of the dust of the road, brother. I am dying of thirst. And this one," he nodded toward Ezra, "is so hungry he could swallow a camel and its mother. Let us by, friend. We have money to spend in Jericho."

"Yes, let them by, friend," came an unexpected female voice. "They have money to spend at my inn. It's been an age since I've entertained travelers, and you aren't helping, Hamish."

Hanani turned to look . . . and drew in his breath. A woman wrapped in light blue linen lounged against the wall of the watchtower. Her chestnut hair fell below her waist in shiny ringlets, barely covered by the translucent veil fluttering in the wind. Large eyes were fringed by thick curling lashes, and her slender nose was like an arrow pointing at full lips, too red for nature's bounty. The blue silk of her dress clung seductively to her curvaceous figure leaving little to the imagination. Hanani gulped. An innkeeper, she had said. Everything about her was forbidden to him. Nervously, he dropped his gaze.

Fortunately, the guard seemed as distracted as Hanani. Losing interest in the interrogation, he faced the woman. "Rahab! Business can't be so dismal that *you* would entertain men wearing homespun."

"Of course business is dismal. Thanks to you and your soldier friends who scare away my customers. Now let these nice young merchants come into my inn so they can spend lots of their silver on good Jericho wine."

The guard considered this. "What do I get out of it?"

"I'll give you a cool jug of my barley water tonight. But only if you stop harassing my customers."

"Get me the barley water first," Hamish demanded. Hanani threw a quick glance at the woman. She stared at them with narrowed eyes, then turned on her heels and disappeared up a staircase carved into the wall. He was certain she had just saved their lives.

"You two, stand aside over there. If she returns you can go with her. *If* she returns. She's wasting her effort if you ask me. I don't see much silver coming out of those worn bags."

Even standing to the side, their presence drew too many curious stares. Saved by an innkeeper—a *zonah*! Perhaps death by torture would not be so terrible a fate after all. He could not imagine explaining to Joshua this particular turn of events.

Finally the woman named Rahab returned. She sauntered over to Hamish the guard, taking her time, swinging her hips with every step. Hanani appreciated that undulating walk, for as she approached, every man turned from scrutinizing him and Ezra and focused instead on Rahab.

"Here is your drink, young soldier. Now hand me my customers and make a nuisance of yourself with someone else."

Hamish took the jug from her and laughed. "Hey, fellows, look what I've got." He showed off the jug to the other soldiers at the gate. "Barley water made by Rahab's own lily hands. And none of you is getting a drop."

Hanani and Ezra didn't linger another second, but followed Rahab as she led them into her inn within the very walls of Jericho.

CHAPTER FIVE

No one could have been more surprised than Rahab to find two Hebrew spies ten cubits from her door. She knew them for Hebrews the minute she set eyes on them. Besides their unfamiliar accent, it was the way they carried themselves. They looked trim and well-muscled like soldiers, not soft like merchants. Certainly they had raised the guards' suspicion, and if she had not interfered, they would have been arrested. Jericho had been shaken by fear of the Hebrews since the fall of Og. Every stranger approaching their gates was examined with more zeal than finesse.

Any other citizen of Jericho would have insisted these two be interrogated. But Rahab found that she could not bear the thought of God's people being tortured.

As she stepped forward, she had no plan or clever ploy. She only knew that she had to remove the spies before the guards' curiosity turned violent.

Now there were two Hebrews traipsing behind her like lion cubs following their mother. Who would kill her first? The

Hebrews or Jericho's soldiers? She had definitely lost her mind. But even as she censured herself for foolishness, she wondered if the Hebrew God approved of her brazen rescue.

When they crossed the threshold of her inn, Rahab faced her guests with a smile. "Please sit down, my lords. You must be tired after your journey. Would you like some refreshments?"

The men stood just inside the door, their movements stiff, as if they preferred not to touch anything. The shorter one, his beard twitching with a nervous jerk, shook his head. "No, thank you. We brought our own."

Rahab motioned them to the table and set goblets of wine before them. The nervous one pulled something wrapped in cheesecloth from his worn bag. He was so jittery he knocked over the goblet of wine and Rahab had to fetch a rag to clean up the mess. As she moved about, their eyes never rested on her face or body, but seemed to run to and fro, seeking any place to look besides her.

She remembered Debir telling her that harlots were condemned to death by these people. Was she repugnant to them? Her brows knotted at the thought. She determined to try and win them over. Earn their good opinion. How hard could it be? She had half the men of Jericho eating out of her hand. Surely Hebrews could not be that different. "What are your names?" she asked.

"I'm Ezra, and this is Hanani," the taller man said. He had surprisingly light skin in contrast to his dark hair, and a crooked nose saved him from being too pretty for a man. The one called Hanani glared at him, obviously considering this surrendering of information inappropriate.

"We're not here for . . . for . . . anything other than a place to stay. We don't want . . . any . . . er, that is, we just want a place to rest and we'll be on our way," Hanani said.

Rahab rose and took a step back. Her voice sounded cold to her own ears. "You're merely guests at my inn." And then to her amazement she found herself admitting what she had told no one else. "I have repented of that other life."

For a moment, they all stared at one another at a loss for words. Finally Rahab said, "Rest easy. You're with a friend. But I must warn you that you're not safe."

"What do you mean?" Hanani demanded, shooting to his feet in a sudden motion that overturned the wine goblet again, though this time at least it was empty.

She bent and picked it up. "I mean that I know you are Hebrews. And every guard out there is going to arrive at the same conclusion once they consider the evidence."

"Where did you get such an idea?" Hanani asked, eyeing the door.

"Peace! I mean you no harm. You are safer in my house than out there. Didn't you see how suspicious the guards were when you tried to enter the gate? Your accents are strange to us. You have the bearing of soldiers. And Jericho is on heightened alert because of the many battles you have won east of the Jordan. If I had not distracted them, you would be under their whips and knives by now."

Ezra cleared his throat, as though that final word picture had stuck in his gullet. "Why should we trust you?" he asked.

Rahab glanced out the window toward the gate. "Because, if I'm not mistaken, that runner is carrying a message even now to the king's men. They're bound to come looking for you soon."

Hanani moved to stand next to her, flattening himself against the wall so he wouldn't be seen. By his expression Rahab knew that he had picked out the messenger. He didn't miss a group of the guards looking up in the direction of her inn either. One of them said something and spat on the ground. "We need to get out of here," he said to Ezra.

"How?" she asked, her brows arching. "Go down those stairs and you'll be captured." She covered her face with her hands for a moment. *I can't believe I'm doing this.* "Listen, I have a better idea. I will hide you."

"Why would you do that?" Ezra asked, his voice dripping with suspicion.

"Well, it's not because of your charming manners." Rahab pursed her lips in an attempt to calm the ire that Hanani and Ezra's wariness provoked in her. She supposed she couldn't fault them for their skepticism. She didn't half understand her own motives.

Why was she risking her neck to help two unpleasant Hebrews? Because of their God. She wanted to be on His side. Bone deep, she believed more in their God than she had ever believed in the gods of Canaan. *I want to help you because I'd rather follow the Lord than the ways of Jericho.*

But she couldn't say any of those things to the two men who studied her with wary eyes, their bodies tight with tension. They would never believe her. Instead, she smoothed her skirt and settled for half of the truth.

"I don't want to stand against your God. Now do you want to live or not? Because your time is running out."

The mention of God seemed to deflate their agitation. "All right," Ezra muttered.

Rahab gestured toward the trapdoor that led to the roof. "I'm drying stalks of flax up there. Go fetch the ladder from the room behind you and hide yourselves up under the flax. Dusk has come, and no one will see you in the darkness if you're careful."

Her inn was built high up; its roof jutted slightly past the edges of the wall, hanging over into the city side. Three times a day, guards marched past the roof of her house. Rahab knew that the next watch was not due until early morning, which made this a safe hiding place for a few hours.

Something of the urgency in her voice finally moved the men into action, and they fetched the heavy ladder, their feet silent on the thick carpet. Rahab climbed the ladder behind them and settled them under layers of flax until their bodies were hidden from view.

"It's a long way down," Hanani whispered as he glanced around.

Rahab recalled her own butterflies the first time she had climbed onto the roof. "There's room enough," she assured him. Other dangers loomed much bigger than the height. "Understand this," she warned. "My life is in danger as much as yours. If you're careless, I will die a worse death than you, for I am now a traitor to my own people."

As she climbed back down into the room, she heard the sound of a stifled sneeze. Even the closed trapdoor merely muffled the noise. Rahab squeezed her eyes shut and cringed. She had seen people have that reaction around drying flax. But a simple sneeze on this night could mean her head.

The next sound she heard was the clatter of feet on the stairway. She froze. *The ladder!* Grabbing it, she began lugging it into the back room. It weighed more than she expected. Usually, either her servant fetched it, or she dragged it on the ground. But she dared not make any noise that might alert the approaching soldiers to the movement of heavy furniture. Beads of sweat collected on her forehead as she took one tiny step after another, the ladder hoisted high in her aching arms. Her foot caught the edge of the bottom rung and she stumbled. The ladder nearly went flying out of her hand. The footsteps were getting closer. Gasping, she took a few dancing strides, and regained her balance.

The footsteps reached her door just as she shoved the ladder against the wall, where blue linen curtains hid it from sight. Rahab barely had time to heave a sigh before the knocking began. She turned and saw to her horror that one of the Hebrews had left his outer garment on the cushions. A small squeak escaped her lips. Next to the cloak, the remains of their repast were plain to see. She shoved everything under the covers of her bed and pulled the embroidered coverlet back over them, hoping the soldiers would not notice the odd lump. Just in case, she threw a couple of extra pillows from the floor onto the bed. Another series of knocks, impatient and louder, made her jump.

"Hold on to your chariots. I'm coming," she called and pulled open the door. Two men in the king's uniform stood outside. "The king's guard! Don't tell me the king is longing for my company."

Their lips twitched before a curtain of seriousness fell over their faces again. One of them had eyes that bulged frog-like under bushy eyebrows. Those eyes were alert beneath their lowered lids as he exclaimed, "No. His majesty is well cared for, thank you, Rahab. We are here for your guests." He stretched his neck and looked beyond Rahab into the room. Hardening his voice, he barked, "Bring out the men who came to your inn. They're spies, here on a mission against our nation."

Rahab gasped. "Spies! I could have been murdered in my bed!"

Frog Eyes shifted impatiently. "Yes, yes. Bring them out, woman."

"I'm not a magician. How am I to bring them out if they're not here?" she croaked.

"Are you denying that they came in to stay with you?"

"Of course not. They came in, all right. But how was I to know they were spies? I thought they were like any other travelers. It's not my fault they left."

"They *left*? When? Where did they go?"

"At dusk, just when it was time for closing the city gate. They hardly spent any time here and even less money. I don't know which way they went, but if you go after them you might still catch up with them. It wasn't that long ago."

The two men shoved her aside and came in, scrutinizing the chamber. Without warning, one of them moved over to the bed and kicked it. Rahab took a sharp breath. If he found the Hebrew's garment, her arrest would be certain. His boot missed the jiggling pile in the center by a thread before he turned away. Sweat broke out on her brow as Rahab finally exhaled. The guards moved into the next room, carelessly shoving furniture around, inspected the wall outside the window to ensure no one was dangling from a rope, and finding nothing, left without apology.

A platoon of the king's armed guards awaited the two soldiers below stairs. She watched them open the gates and set out in pursuit of the spies on the road that led to the fords of the Jordan. As soon as the pursuers had gone out, the gate was shut once more.

Rahab leaned against the wall, her breath coming in jerky gasps. Putting a trembling hand to her head, she began to laugh. She had managed it. She had saved the Hebrews and her own skin in the bargain. She had turned traitor against her country, her people, and her way of life. The enormity of her decision hit her like a millstone. She had betrayed her countrymen to the Hebrews. No. Not to the Hebrews. *To the Lord.*

Gingerly, for she found her knees were shaking, she went to fetch her guests from under the flax. Back in her rooms, they washed and drank a little water, eating thin wafers from their bundle. Rahab knew she should lead them back up to the roof in case the king's men decided to return. But impulsively she blurted, "Will you tell me about the Lord?"

Ezra who was sitting closest to her threw her a surprised look. "What do you mean?"

"I want to know about the Lord, your God. Will you tell me about Him?"

"What would you like to know?"

"Everything."

Hanani snorted, then laughed aloud before Ezra's elbow in his side stole his breath. To Rahab's delight, the men did not refuse her. For a whole hour they regaled her with stories of the

Lord. How He had taken care of Israel by His might and compassion through their long exile in the wilderness. And how He was the one true God. With every word Rahab grew hungrier for this God—*the* God—whose face she had never seen.

Finally, with regret she said, "I have kept you up too long. You must hide on the roof once more. The king's men may return."

Hanani and Ezra crawled back up the ladder, their feet dragging this time, and once more lay beneath the flax. She went up with them and lingered for a few minutes to see them settled. The smell of drying flax filled her nostrils, rich and clean.

"You must leave very early, before sunrise," she said in hushed tones lest someone overhear. "The guards walk the perimeter of the wall at first light, and they might discover you if you haven't left."

Hanani nodded. "We heard you speak to the king's men. Why did you, a . . . woman from Jericho, protect men of Israel?"

She was kneeling on the parapet, while they lay hidden by the stalks of flax. If anyone had bothered to look up, they would have seen only Rahab. The night had grown dark, and she felt the heaviness of it upon her like a smothering blanket. Stars shimmered in the midst of that blackness like pinpricks of hope. She thought about Hanani's question. Why *had* she helped the enemy? Why had she made her name the object of every Canaanite curse for generations to come? Because, against all reason, it was the right thing.

"I'm helping you because I know the Lord has given this land to you. Fear stifles my people. We have heard how the Lord dried up the waters of the sea for you when you came out of Egypt. We have seen what you did to the two Amorite kings,

Sihon and Og. When we heard of these victories, our courage failed. But *I* know the Lord your God is God in heaven and on the earth. I know it is He who fights your battles and wins them for you. This is why I saved you."

She did not say how desperately she wanted to belong to Him for fear of their ridicule. She was convinced that they would revile her. That the Lord Himself would reject her. So instead she set about to make a bargain with Him through His men. "Hanani and Ezra, I've shown kindness to you. I've saved your lives. So now will you return my kindness? Will you swear that you will spare me and my family when you come against this city?"

Hanani pushed aside the flax until his face became visible. In the darkness, Rahab could see the white of his eyes. "You have no doubt that God will give Israel the victory, do you?"

Rahab shook her head.

"You have great faith. I never thought to find the like outside Israel."

His words brought tears to her eyes, and she turned away so he wouldn't see their sheen in the starlight. They were words of approval from a man who not long ago had found her worthy only of contempt. And she had won his approbation not by feminine manipulation, but by her faith. Yet what good would his approval be to a dead woman?

"Will you save our lives, then? Will you spare the lives of my parents and my brothers and sisters and their children?"

Hanani reached out and touched the hem of her garment. "Our lives in exchange for yours," he promised, the fierceness behind his words convincing her. "Rahab, if you don't tell anyone what we're doing, we'll treat you with mercy when the Lord gives us the victory."

Rahab gulped around a large lump in her throat. Was this real? Had she, in fact, managed to purchase life for herself and her family? "May the Lord bless you," she whispered.

"And you," Hanani said with a grin. "If not for you, we'd be lying in our shrouds instead of in flax right now."

"Try to snatch a bit of sleep. I must fetch you down soon. You still have some adventures ahead of you."

Rahab remained wakeful through the night. She kept thinking that she had made a bargain with the Lord through His men, and He had accepted it. She had done something for Him, and now He was doing something for her.

Not taking any chances, she rose and climbed onto her roof long before dawn to fetch the men. They slept like peaceful babes. It occurred to her that they had more courage than spy craft. Surely one of them should have kept watch. They owed their safety to their God, not their skill. Perhaps God had chosen her to play a part in that plan of safety. Back inside the house, she showed them the window. "You need to climb down the wall. The guards are thick about here, and if you go down the stairs they will spot you.

"Last night I saw the king's soldiers take the road toward the fords of the Jordan. You will need to avoid that road. Go instead toward those hills in the north. Hide yourselves there three days, because these searches never last longer than that. Then you can go on your way."

"I've been thinking," Hanani said. "You can't expect an army to ask for directions in the middle of battle. You'll need to mark your house somehow so that our forces will recognize and spare it." He looked around for a moment until his eyes fell on a thick scarlet cord that framed a tapestry. "You must tie this scarlet cord outside the window. Also, you must bring your entire family into your house. We can't guarantee anyone's life outside this inn. Their blood will be on their own heads. But we'll take full responsibility for the safety of anyone who remains in this house. Only Rahab, if you betray us, our oath won't be binding anymore."

"I promise I shan't prove disloyal to you or to God."

"You're an extraordinary woman," Hanani exclaimed, and Ezra nodded.

"And you two begin to grow on me," she replied with a pleased grin.

"We must move quickly before it grows light," Ezra interjected. "It's too far down for your ladder. Do you have any strong rope, Rahab, or were you expecting us to fly?"

"The Lord parted the sea for you. He can provide you with a pair of wings, surely?"

"Yes, but while we wait for them to sprout, perhaps you would be good enough to fetch some rope." Hanani tightened his belt, preparing for the rough descent ahead.

"Rope you shall have, my Hebrew friend." Rahab rummaged in a chest until she found a sturdy length of date-palm rope, and Hanani, wasting no time, tied it about his middle with a secure knot. Ezra lowered him outside the wall, his chest heaving with strain as he carried the weight of his friend's body. Hanani's feet touched the ground just outside Jericho.

Ezra tied one end of the rope around his waist and looped

the other through a hook in the wall where Rahab normally hung a lamp. His brow became more knotted than the rope as he handed her the free end. "Do you think you can bear my weight? The hook might break my fall if you lose your grip, but at that speed, I suspect my back would snap anyway."

Rahab's mouth went dry. "I won't let go. Only . . . don't dawdle to see the sights or anything. Get down as fast as you can."

Ezra sputtered. "Don't worry. I've seen enough of Jericho. But I'll be back to fetch you and your family on the day of war. Now, hold tight to this rope; my life rests in your hands." He gave Rahab one final encouraging smile and climbed over the window ledge. He hung there by the tip of his fingers for an infinitesimal moment as Rahab wedged her feet against a corner and wrapped the rope several times about her arm. Then he let go. Rahab gave a muffled screech as she was pulled forward with a wrenching force. Her feet slid across the floor, yanked by Ezra's dangling weight, and she pictured him falling toward the ground. Holding on with her whole might, she jammed her feet against the wall and held on.

"Oh God oh God oh God help me" she choked. Then she found her balance, caught her breath, and started to loosen the tension bit by slow bit. Ezra tried to help when possible by wedging a hand or foot in the cracks between the rocks, but these were few and far between, so Rahab ended up bearing his whole weight most of the way down. Never had she borne such a burden. That man weighed two of Rahab on a well-fed day.

Planting her feet more firmly, she hefted the rope until her palms bled and her arms were bruised with the friction she tried so hard to control. She ignored the blood and ignored the sting and kept at it, allowing the hook in the wall to carry some of the weight. Ezra had made it halfway down the wall when the rope slipped from Rahab's arm, peeling a good portion of her skin with it. He shot down with alarming speed. Rahab had no breath left with which to exclaim. Using her whole might, she grabbed the rope and held on, leaning her body back. Ezra was half a man's height from crashing to the ground when she finally managed to slow his descent. Slowly, his feet touched down in a gentle landing.

The men began to run toward the hills as soon as Ezra freed himself from the rope's tangled knot. In the predawn darkness, Rahab lost sight of them before she had a chance to blink twice.

With an alacrity inspired by danger, she pulled up the rope and stored it away as fast as she could in case the soldiers returned to examine her house again. Then the ladder, and finally she tended to her burned and bloody arm and hands. At least the men had remembered to take all their belongings this time, God be thanked.

What remained now was to convince a family from Jericho that they were safer in the Lord's hands than in the hands of their own gods. To convince them to place their lives in the promises of their most dreaded enemy.

CHAPTER SIX

A re you mad?" Joa exploded.

"Have you lost your mind?" Karem bellowed.

Rahab opened her mouth, but Joa had more to say. She appreciated the interruption. She did not feel qualified to defend herself with any great gusto.

"If they find out you harbored Hebrew spies, they'll kill you. And they'll kill us for having had the misfortune of being your family."

A stretch of shocked silence followed Joa's words. Rahab swallowed hard. "Why should they find out?" she asked, straining to keep her voice steady. "Look, what do you have to lose, any of you? If you say nothing, no one in Jericho will be any the wiser. But if the Hebrews do come and overrun our walls as they have done to all the other cities, our lives will be spared.

"Next week you and your families come and stay with me for a while. You can go to work as usual, but not too far. An alarm will be raised if their army is sighted, and you will have time to run back here to safety. And if they don't come, you can go home without loss. Only think what would happen if they attack Jericho and defeat our army and you are not here; think of what you would forfeit then. For weeks you have spoken of little but your anxiety about our future. Now you have no need to worry. Your lives shall be spared no matter what happens."

"How can you trust them? You're taking the word of lawless pagans! What good is that?" Joa spat.

"Their God treats oaths with gravity, and they obey Him strictly. Again, I put it before you: What will you lose by following my suggestions?"

In the end, everyone decided to stay with Rahab for a few weeks. They spent the next seven days buying necessities, which the rest of Jericho was also doing for fear of an impending siege. It made for long lines, astronomical prices, and frustrating and sometimes fruitless waits. At least they were one of the few places in Canaan that need not be concerned about running out of water. Jericho possessed several prolific natural springs within its city walls.

Everyone worried about a lengthy besiegement. Rahab prepared for a short and conclusive one. She bought little, for she suspected that when the Hebrews won, she would only be able to take away what she could carry on her back.

How Israel would accomplish this feat, she could not imagine. She only knew that they would bring down the walls of her native city. The Hebrews would conquer Jericho.

Hanani and Ezra lingered in the hills for three days as Rahab had advised. Hanani rationed their small store of food to ensure it would last until they returned home, and a delicate brook provided plenty to drink. The skies opened up and poured on the second day, soaking them until they sat shivering and miserable in their wet cloaks. But the rain also washed away any tracks they may have left behind, and although they took turns keeping watch at night, Rahab showed herself reliable once again, and no one from Jericho came for them.

Early the fourth day they came down from the hills and set out for Israel's camp at a jog. It took most of the day to reach the Jordan. Hanani stared at the river's turbulent waters and winced. The waters frothed and danced in murky violence. The hard rains had eroded the banks on either side, making the crossing even more treacherous than before.

Ezra jumped in without hesitation, and Hanani, not about to remain behind, took a deep breath and followed suit. He found it tough going from the first step, but realized he had to keep moving or the current would devour him. He pushed on, barely able to see through lashes matted with water. As he squinted toward the opposite shore he spotted Ezra, slightly downstream. He was in serious trouble. Though closer to shore, Ezra was clearly caught in the grip of a fierce eddy.

Hanani groaned. He had to find a way to reach Ezra. Up ahead, he noticed a long, vine-like branch dragging in the water. Sending up an incoherent prayer, he moved toward it. He could only hope that it would prove sturdy. Keeping one eye on the branch and one on Ezra, he pushed himself harder. There! Just as he reached for the vine he saw Ezra go under. Clinging to the branch he allowed the current to pull him toward where he had last seen Ezra. *Where are you, my friend? Come back where I can see you!* Suddenly, a dark head popped up.

"Ezra!" he shouted, and reached out with his free hand, his other anchored to the vine. Disoriented, Ezra ignored Hanani's call. Hanani grabbed a fistful of his hair and pulled with all his might.

"Aghh!" Ezra managed to turn and cling to Hanani's arm. Hanani swung around and began to fight his way to the shore. They had to crawl the last few steps, finally collapsing on dry land, panting and spluttering, grateful for the air that filled their lungs. Hanani stood on shaky feet and pulled Ezra up beside him.

"Thank you," Ezra managed, then doubled over to empty the contents of his belly. Volumes seemed to spew out of him. Half the river, at least. Hanani grimaced.

"All right, now?" he asked when Ezra's heaves had subsided.

"Yes. Thank you for saving my skin."

Hanani held up a hand. "The river Jordan has nothing on the wrath of your sister should I have carried your dead body home."

Ezra's bluish lips split into a weary grin. "Home sounds good—let's go. I've had enough of spying."

Hanani was elated when he caught sight of the familiar tents dotting the arid landscape. As he suspected, word of their return quickly spread, and Joshua came to meet them in person.

He rushed through his greetings before getting to the point. "Come, come. Time runs short. I rejoice at your safe return, men. Now you must tell me what you found. We will meet in my tent." With that he walked away.

Hanani, sore from nearly drowning and the long walk that came before, tried to keep up with the older man without betraying his fatigue. Out of the corner of his eye he spied a familiar form.

"Hanani and Ezra!" Salmone called out, running toward them. "*Shalom!* What a sight you are," he said with a grin, pointing his chin at Hanani's stained clothes and tangled hair, four days without the attention of a comb. "How good to have you both back."

"Yes, yes. It is good," Joshua interrupted. "But we can celebrate later. This son of Judah has a report to make. Salmone, you can join us, since Hanani is under your leadership and a personal friend besides."

Salmone fell into step beside them. Hanani, who had known Salmone all his life, noticed his friend's taut muscles and pursed mouth, a sure sign of the knot inside his belly. Salmone was burning with curiosity. Hanani spared him a glance and a grin, trying through his tiredness to convey his elation. *The report is good, my friend,* he expressed without words. *This is not a repeat of the disaster from a generation back.* Salmone's mouth relaxed. Among friends of old, friends who had waged war and cobbled peace alongside one another, words weren't always necessary.

Joshua walked into his tent and flapped it shut. Evening was falling, but the air inside remained stifling. Hanani took no notice. Like other Israelites, he was accustomed to harsh weather and nomadic inconveniences. Joshua spun around as soon as he sealed the tent. "Well, speak up. What did you find out?"

Hanani's gaze lingered for a long moment on the fluffy cushions the covered the floor, and he wondered if he could sit down before making his report. Sighing, he decided Joshua would disapprove, and shifted his stance to take the pressure off his aching muscles.

"The Lord has given the land into our hands," he said. "The people of Jericho and the rest of Canaan speak of us in fear."

"They expect defeat," Ezra continued. "They're petrified of our people."

Joshua smiled. "This news will reassure our men. Now start from the beginning. You've been gone for days. Where did you stay?"

No cushions seemed to feature in Hanani's immediate future. He rubbed his burning thigh with a knuckle. "We hid in the hills these last three days, because the king of Jericho sent a search party after us." Thinking of the rest of his report, Hanani chewed on his mustache. "We spent the first night in Jericho."

"Really? Where in Jericho did you stay?"

"At an inn," Ezra provided.

"An inn?" Joshua's head snapped up, and Salmone's neck jerked around so fast Hanani thought it a wonder it remained attached to his body. "You mean the house of a *zonah*?"

"It wasn't like that, Joshua. Rahab helped us. She saved our lives," Hanani assured him.

Salmone rolled his eyes. "Just what we need. Canaanite prostitutes rushing to our aid."

"It wasn't like that," Hanani repeated.

"So you keep saying. Yet, you call her by name as if well acquainted." The mild manner in which Salmone spoke did not fool Hanani.

Taking an uncomfortable gulp, he rushed to explain, his words tumbling one over the other. "The guards spotted us the moment we tried to enter the gates. They have grown suspicious of strangers because of our victories. Anyone remotely resembling an Israelite attracts instant attention, and our accents gave us away. Then, just as things began to grow ugly, Rahab stepped in. She told the guard we were her guests and cajoled him into letting us go. She hid us under the flax drying on her roof when the king's soldiers came looking for us. I'm telling you, she saved our lives at the risk of her own."

"Why would a woman of Jericho do such a thing? Why would she betray her people for the sake of two unimpressive strangers?" Salmone asked.

Hanani examined his friend with surprise. The handsome face, square jawed, with a nose too straight for a soldier, had hardened with suspicion. His eyes appeared tense and accusing. Hanani jutted out his chin. "Pardon?"

"No offense, but you had little money and even less sophistication to recommend you to a city woman like that."

"Quiet down, everyone," Joshua interrupted. "You say this woman saved your life. Did she tell you why?"

"Joshua, she did it because of the Lord. She had more faith in God than our fathers and mothers. She spoke more like one of us than one of them. Ask Ezra."

Ezra nodded, his head bobbing like an apple at the end of a thin branch. "She said the Lord is God in heaven and on the earth."

"That seems . . . extraordinary."

"Exactly what we thought, Joshua. Neither of us wanted anything to do with her, but after the way she spoke of the Lord and saved our lives, we had to, uh, I mean it only seemed right, don't you agree, Ezra?"

"*What* only seemed right?" Joshua prompted, an eyebrow arched.

"Well, uh, we made her a promise," Hanani stammered. "She endangered her life to save us. First she took us into her inn. Then she lied to the soldiers after she had hidden us. She even lowered Ezra from her window. On a rope. Delicate thing she was too." Seeing the look in Salmone's eyes, he rushed on, "This lumberjack Ezra must have broken her back." Ezra nodded again, not offended. "And on the way out, she told us to hide in the hills for three days so the search party wouldn't find us. So actually she saved our lives four times."

"I see. You spoke of a promise. May we be privy to it?"

Hanani pulled on his ear. "We promised to spare her life and the lives of her family members if she helped us. She knows we're going to conquer Jericho, you see. She believes God has given us the victory. So she has asked for mercy before the battle even begins. That kind of faith should be rewarded, don't you think? Wouldn't God Himself reward it?"

Salmone, who had remained silent through most of this soliloquy, bellowed, "Are you trying to be amusing?"

"This is no prank," Joshua stated, his voice a mere whisper. Salmone stared at Joshua in disbelief. The older man merely nodded his head, as if privy to some information available to him alone. "I believe they have done well."

"Joshua, they have promised a harlot and her entire family that we won't touch them, even though God told us to destroy Jericho *in its entirety.*"

"But don't you see that it could only be the hand of the Lord that has led them to this woman's house? If she hadn't noticed them, they would have died. In all of Jericho, was there another who would have helped our men? Another who acknowledges the Lord? Others might fear Him now that His fame grows, but would they serve Him? And how was it that at precisely that moment this woman noticed Hanani and Ezra? It is the hand of God and no other, Salmone. Who knows but that it was His plan from the beginning?" Joshua thought for a moment. "I will keep this promise."

Salmone was stunned. His emotions had soared and dipped like the outline of a camel's back as he had listened to Hanani. First, he had been filled with elation at his friends' safe return, then he had plunged into dismay when he heard that they had spent the night with a *zonah*. That was a serious infraction of the Law. Then with relief he had found that the men had not touched her. Now they were making her out to be some heroic figure of faith and granting her redemption.

He supposed he understood Joshua's reasoning. Yet to spare the life of a Canaanite *zonah* seemed to take the mercy of God to a ridiculous extreme. Would God allow a whole nation to be put to death while sparing the life of one so unworthy? Salmone would never disobey Joshua. But that did not mean he agreed with him, either.

By morning the sprawling camp had heard the news that they were to prepare for departure. That same day they took the first step of their journey toward Jericho, and come evening, they camped by the bulging banks of the river Jordan. For two days, Joshua and the leaders of the tribes fasted and prayed, seeking the will of God. On the third day they knew with certainty that God had a miracle in store for them.

The people weren't told what to expect, only that they should follow the Ark of the Covenant, the sacred container that housed the original stone tablets of the Ten Commandments. Joshua didn't want doubt to shake the people as they waited through these final hours, so he chose to withhold the more astounding details of the coming day until the last possible moment. He would only say, "Tomorrow, the Lord will do wonders among you."

The next morning excitement rippled through the camp like bolts of silent lightning. Joshua called the tribes together and told them to expect a most wondrous thing: "The Ark of the Covenant of the Lord will go into the Jordan ahead of you. As soon as the priests who carry the ark of the Lord set foot in the Jordan, its waters flowing downstream will be cut off in one heap."

A collective gasp rose up from the people. Salmone, who was standing next to Hanani and Ezra, saw their faces pale. He had heard the story of their river crossing and knew them to be less than enthusiastic about setting foot in those furious waters again. He placed a reassuring hand on each back.

"God has a different treat in store for you this time, my

friends. Your garments shall not even grow damp. Forget the idea of a swim. This time, you will stroll."

The two men stared at him, a mixture of wonder and doubt coloring their faces. Salmone laughed. "Be strong, my courageous friends. You are about to witness a miracle like our fathers and mothers experienced during their escape from Egypt. God appears to have a particular purpose for choosing such an unlikely season for our crossing. He wants to teach us about His power and glory."

Salmone didn't say that he believed God wanted this younger generation to have a firsthand experience that would prepare them for the hardships of conquest. He wanted to part the waters in order that He might part their hearts and make sufficient room for Himself.

Hanani scrunched his nose. "It would be easier if God's lessons about His greatness didn't include so much risk to our necks. I mean, walking into the middle of a raging river isn't exactly normal behavior, is it?"

Salmone chewed on his lower lip in an effort not to smile. "I suppose we are incapable of truly learning to trust God without paying a cost. To see these waters part, we must be willing to step into them."

He squeezed Hanani's shoulder, trying to impart wordless reassurance to his younger friend before moving to take up his position at the head of his people while they waited their turn. His eyes grew damp as he realized how deeply he needed to depend on God. On ordinary days as he took on the busy work of shepherding thousands, it was easy to fall into a mindset of self-reliance. Subtly, his will took over, and he started depending on himself to a greater measure than he did on God. His gifting, his human strength, his solid, reliable fortitude carried him through many a demanding task. But on this day, the impossibility of such an attitude struck him hard. Stripped of every illusion of control, Salmone experienced a new sense of freedom, for comprehending that God alone must be the source of his strength liberated him from the burden of false responsibility.

As if waiting for Salmone to arrive at this precise moment of utter surrender, the priests stepped on the water's edge, carrying the ark. Upstream, the waters instantly stopped flowing. They piled up in a heap a great distance away, at a town called Adam, while the water flowing down to the Salt Sea was completely cut off. The riverbed before them turned into a wide highway. So immense was the pathway that the people crossed the miraculous breach in great clusters, while the priests stood on muddy ground in the midst of them. The whole nation of Israel walked to the west of the Jordan into the Promised Land, stepping on the back of God's miracle. They lingered long enough to collect twelve mighty stones from the middle of the Jordan riverbed and built a monument as a sign for generations to come.

To Salmone, the sight of the Jordan returning to flood stage the moment the priests stepped up onto the west bank was perhaps even more glorious. No one could call the events of this day a coincidence after this. No one could doubt the Lord's intention and might.

That evening, Israel camped in the land that would become her new home. It became a season of firsts. The first time the sons of Israel were circumcised after generations of neglect.

The first Passover they celebrated on the western banks, remembering their deliverance from Egypt, from slavery, from death. Their first harvest of grain from farmlands they had not planted.

And it became a season of lasts as well. The last time they tasted manna, the miraculous food that had sustained them for almost forty years. The last time they wandered like the homeless. Salmone realized that before long they would be learning to farm and plant like the rest of the world. The only thing standing between them and an ordinary settled life was war.

His stomach knotted at the thought. He had weeks to reflect on such things as he, along with the rest of the young men who had been born in the wilderness, recuperated their strength after being circumcised with flint knives. There could be no assault on Jericho until they regained their vigor. God, who had been in such a hurry to get them across the overflowing river, was content to let them wait for the most important battle of their lives.

Joshua could not sleep. The men of Israel had almost recovered their strength and were ready for war. He knew that Israel's fate rested in the balance of the coming battle. And the knowledge weighed on him. How often the Lord had to rise up and encourage him. How often he needed God to strengthen his resolve.

With supple movements for a man of his age, Joshua silently rose from his bedroll and grabbed a coarse robe. Leaving his tent, he walked until his steps carried him outside the camp of

Israel. The sun drenched the sky with light by the time Joshua neared Jericho. He was close enough to see the walls, which meant he was close enough to see that not even scaling ladders and battering rams, which Israel did not possess, would make a difference. The city was not conquerable. He dropped his eyes to the ground and tried to win an internal battle with discouragement.

As he raised his eyes, he gasped with shock. A few paces in front of him stood a man holding a drawn sword. The man was tall and muscle-bound, a warrior born and bred by his look. And his sword was nothing ordinary; it shone like moonlight, jewel-encrusted at its base and sharpened to an impossibly fine edge. Part of Joshua wanted to run in the opposite direction, but he too was a courageous soldier. Who was this man and what was he doing here? Joshua clenched his jaw and stepped forward.

"Are you for us or for our enemies?" Joshua asked, his narrowed eyes searching the man's expression.

Close up, Joshua could see that the warrior's face was stamped with an unearthly peace. It was impossible to guess his age. There were no lines, no sagging skin, no scars. And yet the eyes held an ancient wisdom. Joshua could not look away from his unblinking gaze.

"Neither," he replied.

Joshua raised an eyebrow. Neither friend nor foe? *Who was he then?* The man's next words wiped every thought from Joshua's mind.

"I am the commander of the army of the Lord, and as such I have now come."

Joshua fell facedown on the ground. He found that he could

hardly move. Like Abraham, he was being honored by a heavenly visitation. A sense of awe filled him, overflowing into worship so that for long moments he could not speak. Finally, he managed to gulp in a lungful of air. With shaking voice he asked, "What message does my Lord have for His servant?"

He forced his knees to bend, his back to straighten. With effort, he managed to stand, facing the heavenly warrior like a soldier ought. The impassive face glowed for a moment, the perfect skin haloed like the moon.

"Take off your sandals, for the place where you are standing is holy."

Hurriedly, Joshua obeyed. Around him a heavy silence settled. After a time, Joshua dared to look up only to find that the commander of the host of the Lord had vanished with as little flourish as he had appeared. Slowly, Joshua fell to his knees. What did it mean? Why had God sent him this visitation? If God had sent him the commander of His own army, why had He not taken Israel's side?

Then it dawned on Joshua that God was not on Israel's side; rather, He beckoned Israel to be on *His* side. Joshua couldn't claim God for himself or for his own interests the way the people of Canaan used their idols. The Lord had claimed Israel as His own possession. It was up to Israel to align itself with God's will.

As Joshua dusted the dirt from his tunic, he was struck by another realization. He wasn't Israel's military commander. He did not have the ultimate responsibility for this impossible task. God had assigned the commander of His own armies to fight the battle. Suddenly, Jericho's walls did not seem so impossible. Not with the army of God rising up against them.

CHAPTER SEVEN

Jericho waited in alarm like a pig sensing its impending slaughter. Spies brought back terrifying reports of the Jordan parting and the Hebrews walking across the riverbed as if strolling through a field. They reported that their enemies were more numerous than ants. The king ordered the gates of the city sealed. No one went out and no one came in. Rahab wondered what he hoped to accomplish. If the burgeoning river could not hold them back, how would dressed stone and mud brick do so?

But the Hebrews did not attack immediately. After crossing the river at flood stage rather than waiting for its waters to subside as any normal nation might have done, they now seemed in no rush to attack. They rested. They feasted. They lounged about. Rahab puzzled over their behavior with the rest of Jericho. The waiting grated on them.

When the Hebrews deigned to come, as if finally they had roused themselves to bother with Jericho, something of an anticlimax accompanied their approach. First came their armed guard, and then what looked to be priests carrying trumpets made of rams' horns and an ornate box, which they carried with exquisite care. Bringing up the rear came the main force of their fighting men. Their trumpets made an eerie sound hour after hour as they walked around Jericho's walls in endless procession. At the first sight of them, the watchmen of the wall began raining down arrows. Rahab, keeping vigil at her window, held her breath. The arrows fell just short of the Hebrews, as though they had calculated to the cubit the measure of Jericho's bows. Yet they did not fight back. They merely marched, step after step, cubit after cubit, furlong after furlong. The people of Jericho had never seen anything like this. What were they doing? Showing off their strength? What good would it do them against their mighty double rows of walls?

The first day, the Hebrews marched around the city once and left. The second day they came again, early, so that babies were roused from sleep by the blowing horns and added their own crying to the din. Rahab's family came to her house and did not leave after that day. They spoke little. With the rest of Jericho they watched and waited, feeling helpless and on edge.

Rahab learned to talk to the Lord in the silence of her heart, for her minuscule inn was crowded with people and afforded no privacy. She had no idea if He could discern her thoughts. She hoped if He did, that He did not consider her words disrespectful or inadequate. Yet she found that speaking to Him soothed her fears. And there was much to fear. For the army of the Hebrews was never far from Jericho.

By the third day, the wall guards began to heckle the marching army. The Hebrews didn't react. None of them spoke. Staring straight ahead, they just marched on and ignored the soldiers. They couldn't hear much anyway, Rahab guessed, given the clamor they were making with their horns.

The fourth day they came and the fifth. Tensions mounted and tempers flared in the city. As if having an encroaching war at their gates wasn't violent enough, men broke into fistfights over insignificant things and women screamed at old friends with little provocation. From her post at the window Rahab overheard the gossip of the soldiers as they discussed the state of affairs in Jericho. She heard that temple sacrifices had multiplied. No one was wasting the blood of rams or bulls, now. Animals were precious commodity during a siege. They were sacrificing humans. They made the Hebrews' work easier for them, Rahab reflected.

Many people hid inside their huts with their hands over their ears, weeping. Others kept heckling from the wall, competing to generate the most admired insults. They were a creative people and amused themselves. None of it seemed to confound the host of the enemy.

On the seventh day the Hebrews changed tactics. Showing up earlier than before, they didn't stop with one march. They kept on walking, twice, three times, four times, five times, their horrifying horns blowing and blowing. Even the hecklers fell silent and grew grey with fear.

Rahab stood at her window throughout the day and tried to spot Hanani or Ezra, but they were too far away. She kept fingering the scarlet rope to make certain it had not moved. It draped outside her portion of the wall like a thread of hope. On this scarlet cord hung her future and her life, and the lives of those she loved. Her future hung in the balance of a rope. *No,* she reminded herself. *My future hangs in the balance of God.*

After the seventh interminable march around the city, the trumpets grew louder, unbearable almost. Then as one, the multitude raised their voices in a shout that made Rahab's hair stand on end. The force of their voices made the ground shake, and she put her hands over her ears, trying to drown out the noise.

Even through her clutching hands, however, she could hear the noise increasing. The ground shook. Rahab leaned out of the window and saw to her left and right that Jericho's impregnable walls *were falling down!* They were crumbling and collapsing all around them. Without ever an arrow being shot, without fire or battering rams, with nothing more than a shout, the Lord had ripped down Jericho's fortress. Jericho had been defeated.

Rahab's eyes dampened. She felt numb with the shock of what she was seeing. As the dense powder of stone and mud and mortar began to settle, Rahab grasped the extent of the damage. Apart from her own section of the wall, which miraculously stood unharmed, as far as her eyes could see the entire defensive structure had crumbled to the ground. In some areas a small hedge, no taller than Rahab's knees still clung to its foundation; in others, not even that remained. The inner wall encircling the city had fared no better.

To her horror, Rahab noticed limbs protruding from under large pieces of masonry. The carnage of war had begun. She realized she needed to alert her family, who were clinging to each other in the back of the room away from the window.

"Gather your things together," Rahab cried coming out of her daze. "Get ready. The walls have collapsed and they'll be coming for us soon."

"The walls have *collapsed*? Was that the noise we heard? But it cannot be possible!" Joa's voice was hoarse beyond recognition. "Let me see."

Rahab moved aside and let him look. His chest shook and a small sound escaped his lips. "No . . . *no*! How did this happen? They never even came within shooting distance. Was it magic —a powerful incantation of some sort?"

"No." Rahab recalled Ezra's brief warning that the Lord disapproved of magic, mediums, and fortune telling. "It's the power of God."

Karem came to stand next to Joa. "Look!" He pointed with a finger. "The rest of the wall has fallen, but this part where we're hiding is still standing. If this section of wall had failed we would have been crushed like those poor people. This God, it seems, has preserved our lives."

In the middle of the worst day in the history of her people, Rahab found herself smiling. Not Hanani, not Ezra, not the armies of Israel, not a forced promise, but God Himself had chosen to spare her life. His own hand had sheltered them.

With more confidence, she said, "Come everyone. You have to be ready. There won't be time for dallying once they come for us. Grab what you can carry as I have told you. Leave behind whatever isn't essential."

The children were crying. Rahab's sister and sisters-in-law were crying. Her mother and father were crying. Her brothers wiped silent tears from their faces and began picking up their bundles. Their whole way of life was over. God had rescued them, but they were too numb and brokenhearted to be grateful yet.

They could hear the Hebrew army moving into Jericho. The sounds of fighting rang out. Running feet. Screams. Weeping. Scuffling. Clashing metal. Then Rahab heard someone running up her stairs. For a moment she froze. What if they didn't keep their promise? What if they betrayed her? Then she remembered Hanani's words and knew that he would keep faith.

The door burst open and there was Hanani himself with Ezra behind him. They were covered in dirt and grinning from ear to ear. Seeing them gave her a rush of strength, and she ran toward them laughing and crying at the same time. "You came. You came for us!"

"Didn't we promise? Joshua, our leader, has sent us to take you out of Jericho. We'll lead you to a place not far from Israel's camp. Make sure you bring everything you'll need. The city will be burned to the ground. We have been commanded to leave nothing standing." Politely both men ignored the gasps and fresh tears of Rahab's family members. Bewilderment silenced the occupants of the room as enemy struggled to become friend.

It was easier for Rahab who had had time to consider the coming destruction. She already had faith in the might of the Lord, in the truth of who He was. "Thank you," she whispered, but could think of nothing more to say. On impulse, she grabbed the scarlet cord and shoved it in her sack. She would always treasure it in memory of the Lord's goodness to her. It would serve her as a reminder that He had chosen to save her.

The stairs to her inn remained as solid as ever, impervious

to the wreckage that reigned everywhere about them. Hanani went first, then Rahab and her family with Ezra bringing up the rear. An unexpected stench brought tears to Rahab's eyes. The odor of burning wood and flesh, of blood, of mud dust and ashes made her throat burn. Rahab's hands were full and she couldn't cover her nose. She began breathing through her mouth, trying hard not to gag. Just as they were about to emerge from the stairway, Hanani came to a sudden halt, and Rahab, bowed under the weight of two bulging sacks, plowed into him.

"Oh! Pardon."

Hanani shook his head. "Don't look down," he said to her. Then raising his chin he addressed everyone. "Don't look down. And cover the eyes of the children."

Rahab felt the blood draining from her face. Hanani began to move again, and she followed him, her mouth dry. A body lay lifeless and bloody across the threshold. To move forward, Rahab had to take a wide step over its torso. She tried not to look. Still she saw that its neck came to an abrupt and messy end where a head should have been. A dismayed croak escaped her lips. She turned her face away only to see the head, rolled away near a pink rosebush, eyes staring wide, mouth open more in surprise than agony. She recognized that face. It was Hamish the guard. A fat horsefly flew out of his lifeless mouth, and Rahab bit her lip to keep from retching.

She forced herself forward, pasting her gaze on Hanani's back, ignoring everything but that small patch of fabric, the muscles underneath it bunching and relaxing with each step. Because she lived in the wall, the carnage they passed was limited. It was still more than enough horror to last a lifetime. Whenever she heard the words *war* or *battle* after that day, these were the images that her mind would conjure up.

Rahab set down her bundles and covered her nose and mouth with a shaking hand. The sounds that surrounded her were horrifying and unmistakable—the sounds of violent annihilation. Near where the great gate to the city used to stand, Hanani came to a sudden halt and turned. "I must tell Joshua we found you. Don't move from here. Ezra, I will return shortly!" He yelled in order to make sure he was heard over the din. Ezra waved a hand to signal he understood.

A tall warrior moved quickly toward their waiting group. He pivoted with a lightning movement toward her, brandishing a broad sword stained red. Rahab gasped and raised her hands in unconscious entreaty. Ezra jumped from behind Joa and cried, "Salmone, stop! They're with us!"

The man bent his face toward her, and for a fleeting moment, Rahab found her gaze locked with his. His eyes narrowed as they studied her. A dark sternness marked the well-formed features, making him look far from inviting. He was beautiful, but cold.

"You had better get them out of here before someone else cuts them down," he bit off.

Hanani was now running toward them. Hearing the man's words, he cried, "We will, Salmone. Straightaway. I was reporting to Joshua."

Rahab had an impression of impatient ire before the man turned and shouted to a group of soldiers who ran to obey his command. Only after his back turned did she breathe again.

With relief, she resumed her interrupted march behind Hanani, step-by-step, as he led them out of the ruins of her city.

They had walked for an hour in unbroken silence before Rahab could find her voice. "You'll fight other cities?"

"Yes," Hanani said.

She nodded. Of course the Lord wasn't satisfied only with Jericho. Hadn't Debir told her as much months before? The thought of him brought tears to her eyes. All too well she now knew his fate—the fate he had chosen. She mourned for his loss—the loss of the only friend she had had in Jericho since girlhood.

Their trek proved long, and although Hanani and Ezra helped them with their bundles, her family stumbled along, bowed beneath their sorrow and loss even more than beneath the weight of their worldly possessions. The younger children had to be carried most of the way. Rahab tried to ignore the stitch in her side and kept up as best she could. Sweat made uneven tracks on her flesh where she was covered in the thick dust of Jericho's fallen masonry.

Just after noon, they arrived at a small hilltop surrounded by palms and a few acacia trees. "We must leave you here for now," Hanani told them. "Joshua asked us to bring preliminary reports of the war to Israel's camp. On our way back to the city we'll stop here again to bring you water. You have no well nearby."

Rahab curtsied to them. "You have saved our lives."

"As you saved ours," Ezra said with a nod.

They were grateful to have shade. No one was hungry, and the children, exhausted from their grueling walk, fell into sleep without fuss. Izzie helped Rahab spread some blankets to create a more comfortable atmosphere. They also strung her scarlet rope between two date trees and hung a blanket over it to create a space that afforded a measure of privacy. From Jericho's walls to a blanket. They had been reduced indeed.

The nine adults sat huddled together, trying to derive some sense of assurance from one another's proximity. Rahab kept thinking of Hanani's claim that Israel would continue its war on Canaan.

And where would that leave Rahab and her family? At the mercy of other Canaanite gods and people? At the mercy of another indefensible attack from Israel?

She realized she wanted so much more than this temporary respite. She wanted a security that lasted. She wanted a nation that she honored. She wanted the Lord.

On impulse she blurted, "I want to ask Ezra and Hanani to intercede on our behalf with their leader, Joshua. Perhaps they'll let us live with them."

A shocked silence met her announcement. Then Joa pivoted toward her. "Has your brain baked in the sun, woman? The Hebrews are murdering our people as we speak. You want to live with them? How do you think they'll treat us?"

"It's out of the question," her older brother concurred. "We'll stay here out of respect until they come back. Then we'll move west. Canaan has other cities. We'll settle far from here."

"And what will you eat?" she challenged. "Your farm belongs to the Hebrews now. How will you support yourselves?"

"Same way we would if we stayed with those foreigners, Rahab. We would work," Karem responded.

"As laborers, you mean? And how long before you starve? Surviving was hard enough when you were masters of your own fields."

"You think these people are going to gift us with land?" Joa asked, his tone bitter with sarcasm. Turning, he punched the nearest tree trunk with a balled-up fist. There was a sickening cracking sound and Rahab winced, hoping he hadn't broken his fingers. He put his knuckles in his mouth and turned away. She saw that they were raw and skinned. Her shoulders sagged.

"They live differently from us," she said after a few moments. "No one in their midst starves. The Lord provides for them."

"The Lord! The Lord! I'm sick of hearing that name," Joa shouted. "I want to get away from Him—as far away as I can."

She moved to his side. "Joa." But she couldn't think of anything to say that would be a comfort to him, so she hugged him tightly instead. He began to weep. "This is a nightmare," he kept saying over and over.

Rahab's father and mother came and sat near him, looking helpless and close to tears themselves. Her sister and sisters-in-law had been busy trying to start a fire and prepare some warm food, and missed most of the exchange. Drawn by Joa's misery, his wife, Hurriya, came to huddle next to him, followed by Izzie and Zoarah.

"What's going on?" asked Izzie.

"Rahab wants us to move in with the Hebrews," her mother replied.

"Would they let us?"

"Izzie! You can't mean you'd want to," Gerazim admonished.

"Well, where else are we going to go?"

"Exactly," Rahab cut in. "You cannot go far enough west in Canaan to get away from the Hebrews. They'll come sooner or later—in our lifetime, or in your children's. Haven't you comprehended that yet? They want this whole land. The only safety is with them. As one of them."

"Would they make us slaves?" Izzie asked.

"Of course not . . . I don't think." *Blight! They wouldn't, would they?* If they wanted slaves they would have taken them prisoner. "I think if we are willing to worship the Lord alone, and give up our gods, they might let us live with them—as free people."

Izzie's brow crinkled. "Give up our gods? I'm willing any minute of the day."

Her husband stared at her like she had just announced she had taken up Rahab's former profession. "Izzie, what are you saying?"

She turned on him with a vehemence that silenced everyone before she even spoke. "I gave Molech my child. My child! And what did it gain me? Besides misery and regret, what have I reaped from that sacrifice? So many years, and I've been barren. No blessing. No wealth. I have seen more power in the Hebrews' god in the last seven days than I have in our own deities my whole life. I say good riddance to them. Bring on the Lord. Rahab, I'm with you." She bit her lip with small even teeth, and then in a smaller voice asked, "Do you think they'll take someone who has sacrificed her child to Molech?"

"They will if they take a former harlot."

Karem pushed a hand through his hair. "Rahab, are you sure they're going to attack other lands in Canaan too?"

"Positive."

"You haven't been wrong yet. If it weren't for you, sister, we'd be dead, every last one of us. None of us has had enough sense to thank you. We owe you our lives. And I for one don't want to live through another battle like that. I'm willing to join the Hebrews if they'll have us as equals, and not as slaves. My family and I will stand by you."

Izzie looked at Gerazim. He jerked his head in a faint nod, looking green and sick. Rahab couldn't blame him. What did they know about the Hebrew life? It spread before them like a starless night.

Rahab's parents were quiet, looking from Joa to the rest. Joa sat mute, staring toward where Jericho used to be, his lips trembling. His wife huddled next to him, and his children, still somnolent from sleep, came over. But even their clinging nearness didn't draw him out. The whole night he shivered against that tree. When Rahab woke up in the morning, he was in the same place, his mood as black as before.

"Joa," she whispered and hunched down in front of him. "What is it? What eats you so?"

"They're the enemy. I feel like you've gone over to the enemy."

"Do you want to take your family somewhere else in Canaan? You may if you choose, brother. They have given us our lives free of conditions."

"If I go I'll lose the rest of you. Haven't we had enough losing already?"

She nodded. *More than enough.* "That Hebrew camp is the

only chance at life in the long run. You can learn to live with your enemy, turn him into your friend, or you can go where you and your children will have no future. Those are the only choices you have."

"Rahab, why do you want to serve their god?"

How could she put into words something she barely understood herself? "Because He is true." As answers went, it was sorely deficient. But Joa seemed to grasp it. He gulped hard. Then nodded.

"I will go where you go," he said, but he said it with defeat, not with hope.

Rahab's parents added their agreement after that, as she knew they would. The whole family stood in unity, yet for vastly different reasons. To Rahab, the Hebrews were hope. They were an answer to a longing she scarcely comprehended. Her sister came because she had nothing to lose, and her husband followed as he always did. Rahab's older brother Karem came because he saw the practicality of it, and he made the pragmatic compromise necessary for his family's survival. Joa came out of despair.

Whatever their motives, Rahab had managed to convince her family to cast their lot with the Hebrews. But could she convince the Hebrews to want them?

When Hanani and Ezra returned, she drew them aside and wasted no time on pleasantries. "Can we join Israel? I've heard there are some foreigners in your midst. Would you take us in as well? Would you let us live with your people?" Her unrehearsed words tumbled over one another.

From under dark curving eyebrows Hanani looked at her and quickly away. "That wouldn't be up to us. But we'll ask Joshua when everything concerning Jericho is settled and he has time to deal with other matters."

"Remind Joshua . . . remind him that I have set aside the life of a *zonah* for the sake of the Lord. I will never go back to it."

Hanani considered for a moment. "You really have stopped because of the Lord?"

Rahab nodded. "Months ago."

"Our people stone a woman for such a sin. She becomes unclean in the sight of God. It is good that you have stopped. We'll tell Joshua, Rahab, but we can't promise anything."

"I understand. Thank you."

"Joshua believes that the Lord Himself sent you to Ezra and me. Perhaps that will move him."

She smiled. "Well, the Lord didn't save me and my family just to lose us in another Canaanite town. What would be the point? He must have spared us for a purpose."

Hanani shook his head. "Do you never doubt our victory?"

"Of course not. How could the Lord fail?"

"I think Israel will always remember you for your faith, Rahab," Ezra said.

Pleasure pierced her heart. Was it possible she could be remembered for something other than her former profession?

CHAPTER EIGHT

Salmone dropped to his knees on a heap of charred masonry. The short sword he had wielded for long hours clattered to his side. He swallowed, his throat convulsing. The smell of death surrounded him, and he fought hard against a sudden urge to empty the meager contents of his stomach. A swarm of flies buzzed around him, drawn to the scent of blood drying on his clothes. He let them, too tired to swat them away.

Peripherally, he became aware of a man striding toward him. Joshua. Salmone wished he would go away and leave him alone to make some kind of peace with his internal torment. But Joshua kept on coming, his steps unwavering. He climbed Salmone's heap and stood over him for a moment. A strong arm, brown from the sun, wrapped itself around Salmone's rigid shoulders like a familiar blanket.

For a moment Salmone avoided that comfort, drawing deeper into himself. Then dropping his head, he allowed the tension to drain out of him. "I'll never get used to the killing," he whispered, his voice raw. With a trembling hand he rubbed the side of his face, leaving ash streaks on his cheek.

"God takes no pleasure in this either, my son," Joshua said.

"Then, why?"

"You know He hates iniquity the way a mother hates whatever pestilence harms her children. Like the days of Noah, the children of Adam can pile so much corruption upon corruption that their very being grows dangerous to all that breathes. So God's holiness rises up. If these people were willing to repent, to change, God would have spared them."

Salmone squeezed his eyes closed. "How long will we be at war, do you think, Joshua?"

"Like Noah's flood, this part of our history is constrained to a season. This is only a short part of our story. It is meant to reach an end. God has other plans for our people. He promised Abraham that all the nations of the world would be blessed through him. Through us. That is our ultimate destiny."

Salmone rubbed the back of his neck. "May the blessing not tarry. This is one job I can't wait to be released from. I suppose I sound ungrateful, given everything the Lord has done for us."

"You sound weary." Joshua straightened and surveyed the devastation around him. "We'll be returning to the camp soon. The very ground of this city is cursed. We will not spend a single night on this soil."

Salmone became aware that someone was running toward them. Hanani.

"My lord!" He panted as he reached them. Unaware of the storm of emotion Salmone had only just sheathed, he smiled lightly. "Glad you're safe," he said to his friend before turning his attention back to Joshua. "Now that you are done with the arrangements for the city, can you spare a few moments?"

"Yes, O renowned spy. How did events proceed with Rahab and her family? Did you see them to safety?"

"We did. In fact that is what I wished to speak about, my lord. She asks for permission to live with Israel. She and her family."

Salmone snorted, but Joshua ignored him. "Does she now? Singular woman, this *zonah* of yours."

Hanani flushed. "She definitely isn't mine, and I don't think she's even a *zonah* anymore. She said to tell you that she has given up that life. Months ago. For the Lord."

Joshua tugged on his beard with a callused hand. "I am convinced she has been sent to us by God. Though she can't know much about the Lord, she follows hard after Him. Since our wanderings began, we have taken less worthy outsiders into our midst. If she and her family give up their idols and agree to live according to our laws, then I believe I shall allow her to join us."

Salmone, who had kept his comments to himself, exploded. "You can't mean that!"

"Can't I? And why would that be?"

Too roused to heed the dangerous light in Joshua's eyes, Salmone said, "We have just put their whole people to death, in case you forgot. You think they're going to live with us peacefully after that? We'll have to sleep with one eye open for fear of being stabbed in the night by Jericho's survivors seeking revenge."

Joshua nodded. "A reasonable concern. Except that this woman herself helped with the destruction of her home by aiding our men. And her family helped right along by keeping quiet. If they were so concerned for Jericho, they would have tried to save it while they had the power. They will be harmless enough in our midst. Sorrowing, I dare say, but not vengeful."

"And what about Rahab?"

Joshua bent his head to the side. "What about her?"

"She's a *zonah*, whatever she claims. She's unclean."

Joshua raised up a hand, palm up. "I think you and I had better have a walk together." That was Joshua's *commander* voice, brooking no disagreement. Salmone obeyed, his steps wooden.

Joshua said nothing until they entered a secluded grove just beyond where Jericho's walls once stood. Salmone chafed under the heavy silence, knowing he had displeased the older man. Joshua came to an abrupt halt and turned to face him. "Such a heart of pride you have been harboring, my young friend."

Shocked, Salmone's eyes bulged. "My lord?" The formal words of address almost choked him as they came out.

"It's unpleasant, this business, I know. But I must speak with you forthrightly. Salmone, your judgment on this woman is erroneous.

"Not that I blame you, mind. I understand the root of your opinions; I know how you formed them. It's part and parcel of the way you young ones grew up. Your generation has had a hard lesson to learn. Your parents' and grandparents' lack of faith and disobedience changed your lives. Instead of being born and raised in homes of your own, you've endured the hardships of a meandering existence. You have never known the routine of a stable home life. The one security you young

126

ones have known has been the Lord. It has made you cling to God in a way your parents weren't able to do. Perhaps your children's generation won't inherit your resolve either. Maybe that's why God allowed you to become wanderers in the first place.

"But there is an underside to every strength, and yours is showing right now, Salmone. You have grown judgmental in your attempt at righteousness."

"I'm merely stating the facts."

"Ah yes. She's *unclean*. Vile with sin. What an unfamiliar concept to the nation of Israel. Because our greatest leader Moses never killed a man in rage. And our high priest Aaron never fashioned an idol of gold. Your own spotless ancestor, Judah, certainly didn't ignore the rights of the widow of his sons. And God forbid he should walk by a pretty girl he mistook for a prostitute and turn aside into her tent. What a sore torment Rahab would be to pure, unblemished Israel."

Salmone ground his teeth. "Are you comparing an adulterous woman to Moses?"

"In a way. I think you have forgotten, my young friend, that the blood of the spotless lambs on Passover covers your own sins too." Salmone turned red, and Joshua nodded. "Do you remember my telling you about meeting with the commander of the army of the Lord? He told me that day that he was neither on our side nor the side of our enemy. It gave me a glimpse of the Lord's heart. He is on the side of all who are on His side. And Rahab is on His side. Only your pride blinds you to that fact.

"Pride is the bane of the righteous," Joshua continued. "On the outside you may seem more upright than a woman with such a past, but God sees us from the inside. You've been so busy trying to keep the commandments, trying to do everything right, that you forgot your inner world can never bear the scrutiny of a holy God. And you have missed the self-righteousness that's crept through your front door. You are mistaking condemnation for good judgment."

Salmone gaped, speechless.

"Now I'm going to give you a new assignment to help you with your problem. I am putting Rahab and her family under the banner of the tribe of Judah. Specifically, I'm putting them under your charge."

"But—"

"Stop. Don't say another word unless it's, 'Yes, my lord.' I expect you to treat these people with respect. Help them settle in. Teach them our ways. Have I made myself understood?"

"Yes, my lord." Salmone's lips hardly moved as he spoke. He felt frozen. Never had Joshua reprimanded him so completely. The man he admired most thought him self-righteous. Proud. Judgmental. *Over a Canaanite zonah.* He had fought hard to gain Joshua's trust. The opinion of his mentor meant the world to him. And his criticism cut like a flint knife. His words snaked into his heart with bitter bile.

His original objections to Rahab had been a matter of principle; he had had no personal feelings against the woman. But after this encounter with Joshua, a distinct dislike of her settled like a stone in his gut. She had yet to step into Israel's camp, and she was already causing division. Looking for Hanani, Salmone strode back toward the heap that was once the city of Jericho. Joshua had given him an assignment and he meant to discharge it well. He also had every intention of forcing the Canaanite to show her true colors.

He found Hanani sitting down to a meal of date cakes and roasted grain. In his mind, Hanani was tainted by association. He had pushed Rahab forward, after all. "Where did you take that woman?" Salmone barked. "Joshua has placed her and her family under my leadership."

Hanani swallowed his mouthful of date cake. "You mean Rahab? They're about an hour outside our camp. We can stop by on the way home, if you want."

"No. It will be past midnight by the time we get there. We'll deal with them in the morning."

"Uh, you don't sound too happy about it."

"Me? I'm leaping with joy. I always wanted a Canaanite adulteress and her morally destitute brood in my tribe. That ought to bring peace and tranquility to my people."

"Salmone, I don't think—"

"That's right; you don't," he snapped, and walked away.

Salmone spent the next hours receiving reports, taking note of the wounded, hearing accounts of battle, and making sure those who needed direction received it. Shoving his churning feelings into a side pocket of his mind, he allowed his usual warmth to flow over his men, praising acts of valor and commending initiative. After a final meeting with the commanders who reported to him, he allowed himself to head for home.

Just outside Israel's camp, he stripped off his clothes, washing off the blood and sweat of battle until he was ceremonially clean. Then he trudged into the camp, drained and weary to his bones. Knowing that messengers had already brought news for wives and mothers and sisters waiting at the camp, he made a straight line for his tent.

His younger sister Miriam, named for Moses's famed sibling, almost threw him on the ground with the force of her body as she slammed against him in a fierce hug.

"*Umph!*" he mumbled, trying to catch his breath. "If the soldiers of Jericho fought the way you hug, we might not have won."

She smacked him on the arm. "I'm so glad you're safe."

Salmone patted her head, forgetting that she was now a woman grown not a child. "Safe and sound and bleary with exhaustion."

"To bed with you, then. Tomorrow, you can tell me about the battle and the wall falling. Ezra described it, but he had to be brief. I bet your version is more exciting."

"Bloodthirsty girl. Away before you give me nightmares."

Salmone crawled into his pallet, stretching aching muscles, trying to unwind. He didn't pray, not even to praise God for His miraculous intervention or his own safe return. He told himself he was too weary, but in a deeper recess of his mind he was aware that what kept him from God was not exhaustion, but anger. He felt angry about the argument with Joshua. He felt angry about the burden of Rahab. And most of all, he felt angry about the possibility that Joshua might just be right about him.

Morning dawned bright, and for Salmone, not cheerful. Miriam came in with breakfast and an elated smile. Everyone in Israel grinned this day. Their cheer irritated him. They didn't have any unpleasant chores to mar the taste of victory on their lips. They didn't have to deal with a Canaanite *zonah*.

What was he to do with these foreigners anyway? He couldn't breeze into camp with them in tow. There were a hundred rules and laws that they could unknowingly break within the first hour. He decided to leave them where they were until they had received some basic tutelage.

"What's wrong with you, brother? Were you injured yesterday?" Miriam asked, frowning at Salmone.

He sat up and punched the pillows behind him, ostensibly to fluff them. "No, I wasn't injured."

"Then why are you acting like a camel with a sore tooth?"

He raked his hand through his hair, making it stand up in dark spikes. "It's complicated." It didn't help that he was still groggy.

Miriam snorted. "Well hurry up and dress. I'm going with you to help."

"To help what? What are you talking about?"

"Your complication. I believe its name is Rahab."

Salmone sputtered. "How do you know about Rahab?"

"Calm yourself. You'll give yourself desert fever. Joshua asked me to give you a hand."

"You! What for? He's put a slip of a girl to spy on me— my own sister, no less!" He threw her a look that practically screamed *traitor*.

Frowning, Miriam waved a dismissive hand. "Of course not. He asked me to help with the women. You'll have an awkward time trying to explain the laws pertaining to them. I'm to help them fit in."

"Oh."

"Apology accepted. Such a churl is my only brother, and on the day of Israel's great victory. Why, may one inquire?"

Salmone shrugged. "I don't see eye to eye with Joshua on this. I think it's a mistake to transplant these people into our camp. If God led us to spare them, so be it. I'd rather not shed any more blood than I have to. But should they join us?"

"She sounds like a brave woman of faith. What do you have against her?"

"She is a *zonah*, Miriam. Come to think of it, I'm not sure that it's wise for you to spend much time with her. Let Joshua send his own sister if he feels compelled to help them."

"Hanani and Ezra spent a whole night with her. Alone. And they haven't been corrupted. I dare say I shall be able to withstand any nefarious influence she might have. Besides, Joshua asked me personally, and I'm not going to disappoint him."

"Well, Joshua should have asked my permission first."

"Take it up with him if you want. Now, when are we going to visit them?"

Salmone groaned. He couldn't fight both Joshua and his sister. They were the two people in the world who wielded the greatest influence on his heart. And in truth, he wasn't worried about Miriam. She could manage ten Canaanite harlots without coming to harm. He was merely looking for excuses to thwart Joshua's plan.

"Right now. We are going to visit them right now. Let's go find Hanani so that he can show us the way. Ezra knows it too, come to think of it. We'll take the first one that crosses our path."

They found Ezra not far from their tent, humming a sunny tune as he carried water.

"Ezra!" Salmone called.

"Good morning, Salmone." His smile widened as he noticed Salmone's companion. "Morning, Miriam."

"Hello, Ezra. My brother and I need your help."

"Anything. Anything you—"

"Yes, yes," Salmone interrupted. "I need to get to Rahab's campsite. Can you take us?"

"Of course. We settled them at an oasis not far from here." He looked about for a place to put his water jug, then changed his mind and placed it back on his shoulder. "I'll bring this. They need fresh water."

Salmone made a gagging noise under his breath.

Ezra and Miriam chatted most of the way, or at least Miriam spoke and Ezra listened with enthusiasm. Salmone ignored both and spent his time wondering how long he would have to be saddled with these last remaining residents of Jericho before they could be forced to reveal their wickedness.

A small camp came into view. Under the shade of tall palms, children played a game while a woman watched. Four women were preparing some kind of meal over the fire. One man gathered firewood, another slept, and two were engaged in quiet conversation. The scene appeared familiar and domestic. Innocent. Distinctly unsinister. This family had lost everything and everyone they knew, Salmone realized. They must be devastated. He swallowed a sudden lump of guilt. In his mind, they had become abstract, two-dimensional beings, without humanity. The scene he walked toward stripped that blindfold from his eyes.

Rahab's family noticed them approach and stopped their activities. Even the sleeping man was roused, and the children quieted down. When they drew close, a woman stepped forward. She was dressed in a modest gown of rich linen, her hair covered by the folds of a dark veil. Large eyes looked at him through thick lashes. They widened with recognition before she hastily lowered them. He hadn't forgotten her face either, not even after their brief encounter in a burning city. She had skin so translucent the sun seemed to go right through it. Her unusual coloring—golden eyes and chestnut hair peeking through her scarf—heightened the exotic femininity that stamped her every feature. Salmone gave himself a mental kick. Was he truly standing there, admiring a Canaanite woman? Never mind Miriam, he was the one in need of protection.

She turned to Ezra, and gave him a quick dip of respect in the manner common to Canaanites. "Welcome, Ezra."

"Good morning, Rahab. I have brought you a little water."

Rahab! This was Rahab? Had a woman ever looked less like a harlot? Where were her dangles and bobbles? Where were her sheer veils and clinging skirts and face paint? Where was her brazen expression and her forthright sexuality?

Ezra interrupted Salmone's dazed thoughts with an introduction. "Salmone, this is Rahab, who saved Hanani and me from certain death. Rahab, this is Salmone, son of Nahshon, one of the leaders of the tribe of Judah. And this is Miriam, his sister."

Rahab dipped another curtsy, deeper this time in respect to Salmone's position. "You honor us with your presence, my lord." After introducing the members of her family, she asked, "Would you share a meal with us? We have some fresh pan bread and raisin cakes."

Salmone, annoyed at having to spend half his day dealing with people he little trusted, and even more annoyed at finding himself impressed by Rahab's looks and manners, curled his lip. "No. We have come to tell you that Joshua has decided your family can move into Israel's camp. Conditionally."

Before he could open his mouth and spell out his conditions, Rahab shocked him by prostrating herself on the ground. "Thank you, my lord. Thank you. May God bless you." Her wide eyes were drowned in unshed tears.

"Rise up, woman," he snapped. "I cannot talk to you with your face in the sand." Miriam gasped. Salmone ignored her. In truth, he hadn't intended to sound so harsh, but the sight of Rahab's tears and importunate humility moved him too deeply for comfort. Annoyed with his own unbidden response, he ground his teeth until his jaw ached. The woman would wreak havoc in Judah if allowed. Knowingly or unknowingly, she would unleash corruption.

As if reading his thoughts, Rahab's face turned the color of chalk, and she scrambled to her feet. "Pardon."

Salmone pinched the bridge of his nose, wishing someone would wipe that wounded look from the woman's face. "Listen, I said conditionally and I meant it. You must give up all your idols and false gods. Do you understand? All. The Lord is a jealous God. He will not put up with idolatry. If you wish to live with Israel, you must dedicate yourself to the Lord. And you must keep our laws. Joshua has put you under my care, in the tribe of Judah. I am now responsible to teach you what you must know. When you have been prepared, then you may move into our camp. Until then you must stay here."

Rahab's older brother stepped forward, bowing with diffidence. "My lord, how are we to learn these laws? And how are we to learn about the Lord?"

"My sister Miriam will help your women. I will send any man I can spare every day to teach you. Now you must tell me, are you willing to give up your idols and worship the Lord only? For understand this: the punishment for idolatry will most probably be death."

The same brother answered. "Rahab has already explained to us that we must give up the gods we grew up with. We have, every one of us, chosen to do this, for the Lord is mighty. He has proven Himself great above all other gods. But we are very ignorant, I fear."

At least they acknowledged their lack of wisdom. Humility could pave the way for a successful assimilation, Salmone conceded. Before he could respond, the younger brother stepped forward. There was something tight-lipped and sullen about his attitude. This one was struggling with his decision, Salmone guessed. He sharpened his focus on the younger man, gauging his attitude, trying to read his expression. Was there hatred? Revenge? Violence? He tensed, unconsciously taking a battle-ready stance.

"Shall we be slaves to the Hebrews if we come and live with you?" His voice wavered, despite his obvious effort to sound calm. Salmone thought he detected fear, even mistrust, but not violence. He willed his straining muscles to relax. The question was a reasonable one.

"No. You're not our captives. Your sister purchased your lives and your freedom by saving our men before the war began. You would join us as free people. But there is no compulsion for you to join us. You may leave if you wish. You aren't in our debt. Your lives were purchased fairly."

"And how would we live? We owned a small plot of land before . . . in Jericho, I mean. We made our living as farmers. How shall we feed our families if we join you?"

Salmone shrugged. "Your young men will go to battle with the rest of the men. You shall have a share of the land and plunder same as the others. Your women and children will stay at our camp and help with daily upkeep."

Several of the family gasped at once. "Battle?" one of them choked.

Well what did they expect—that their Canaanite origin would exempt them from unpleasant chores? What did they think joining another nation meant?

"If you join us, we will expect you to live as one of us."

Rahab who had moved to stand behind her brothers stepped forward again. Her voice was so soft Salmone had to strain to hear it. He noticed that she avoided his gaze. "My lord, my brothers and father have never been trained for war. They are skilled farmers. I have been told that some of you will be settling in the land that was once Og's and Sihon's. Will you not need to till the land and work it soon? Having traveled most of your lives, you may perhaps find farming a challenge. If your men are gone a good deal of the time, the heavy work of the farms will fall on women with no experience. You could lose much in the process of learning. My brothers and father can help. They could teach your people the skills they need. They are familiar with the land in this area—the crops that grow well and those that perish. They understand what feeds the ground and what drains it. Would it not be an advantage to Israel to use their farming knowledge rather than waste their lives in battle for which they haven't been trained?"

Salmone threw her a sharp glance. In a few moments, she had managed to establish her family as an indispensable commodity to Israel, while also giving a notable reason for them to avoid fighting. And not once had she resorted to using anything like feminine wiles, which he would have renounced with some pleasure. He was astonished to find her blush under his scrutiny. She lowered her eyelids; it made him stare at her even harder. Never had a woman so utterly puzzled him. Or drawn him. The thought almost made him groan. He wanted to run as far away in the opposite direction as his legs would carry him, and then borrow another set of legs and run those ragged too.

CHAPTER NINE

Rahab studied Salmone surreptitiously. He stood rigid, hands balled into fists at his sides, surveying Rahab and her family the way a shepherd might survey a pack of flea-riddled wolves. That he had no love for them he did not bother to hide. The only thing colder than his manners were his words. With one breath he delivered the best news she had ever heard in her life while at the same time robbing the joy right out of it.

When Salmone announced that he would be their leader, her heart dropped to her feet. There was an implacable strength about Salmone that she found intimidating. Years of wandering the desert had made his tall frame lean with muscle, and recent battles had honed him like a knife's edge. But it wasn't his physical power or even the stony good looks that she found so imposing. He had a penetrating quality in the way he gazed at you as if dissecting your soul. Judging by the rigid line of his mouth, whatever he found in Rahab gave him no pleasure. Though she tried to hide inside her brand-new respectable clothes, Salmone made her feel like a misbehaving child.

After being so publicly upbraided, Rahab locked her mouth tight and spoke as little as she could. Until he casually released his final thunderbolt: her brothers were expected to go to war alongside the rest of Israel.

She had thought of this possibility during the long waiting hours. What else *could* Israel expect of them? What better way to prove their fidelity? She never told her family of these suspicions; instead, she had tried to devise a fair solution. So while everyone else was stunned by Salmone's pronouncement, she stepped forward and proffered an alternative. It took every scrap of courage she possessed to speak before him. Inside, she was sick with dread. If her brothers' lives weren't at stake, she would never have opened her mouth in front of this man.

She dared not look him in the eye, but she couldn't resist peeking at him secretly to try and gauge his response. His face was as unreadable as the ancient Sphinx. His eyes burned into her as she finished, and she felt herself blushing. She bit her lip, wanting to kick herself for this ridiculous return to shy girlhood.

Salmone crossed his arms and took one step back. "And you thought of this argument just now, I suppose."

Rahab had promised herself that she would start right with these people if they accepted her. She knew the Lord would want her to speak truth, but telling the truth just then was like carving out her own tongue and handing it over as a goodwill present. She feared that this haughty Hebrew lord would think her a schemer for preparing a clever speech. She was sure that if she told the truth about her foresight and planning, he would think the worst of her. And she so desperately longed to give a favorable impression. To be accepted and well received. *O Lord, help me honor You.*

Rahab took a deep breath. "No. I have been thinking about it through the night."

She noticed his sharp inhale. A dark eyebrow arched after a moment. "Who told you that the men would have to go to war?"

"No one told me. I surmised it. You could expect no less of us than of your own people. More, if anything. Newcomers must prove their loyalty."

He uncrossed his arms. "Your suggestion has . . . merit." It seemed to her that he begrudged his own admission. "I'll think about it." He paused.

"In the meantime, none of you may enter the camp without learning the basics of the Law. Ezra, since you are here already, you might as well start with the fundamentals. Miriam, after Ezra is done with the Ten Commandments, why don't you instruct the women while Ezra teaches the men some of the more particular precepts of the Lord? You can return to the camp together later this evening."

Salmone added, "Make certain to speak to them in our dialect. Even though our languages share the same root, the differences in our dialects would make communication difficult for them once they arrive in Israel's camp. We cannot continue speaking to them in their speech, for few would extend that favor once they join Israel."

He turned to Rahab for a moment, and she thought he would speak more. He changed his mind, though, and turned to her older brother Karem, instead. "How many days' supplies do you have?"

"A week's worth of food—more if we are careful. We are short of water."

"I'll send water daily, and food when you need it. You have no tent, I see."

"We couldn't carry anything large during our escape. Anyhow, we're all right. The evenings are mild, and we have blankets."

"They're mild now. But come winter, you'll need appropriate shelter. Do you have gold or silver enough to buy a tent or two? Once you move into our camp, you'll find you shall need it."

Karem's brows knit in thought. "I'll see what we have between us if we pool our resources."

Salmone nodded. He turned to leave, hesitated, then turned back again. "Please understand. This step that you are taking is a life-and-death one. You are choosing to change your whole way of living. Completely. Count the cost before you commit yourselves." And then he left, not giving them a chance to bow or curtsy their respect.

Rahab sat down hard, realizing for the first time that her legs felt wobbly. She put her head on her knees and tried not to cry. Why did she feel this longing to be part of Israel? What was this desire that ate at her with a passion beyond any she had ever known? Her family still longed for Jericho. Still mourned the life they had lost. It was different for Rahab. Other than tearful thoughts of her friend Debir, Rahab never thought of her lost home. Her mind had become consumed with Israel.

Yet Salmone's warning was a fair one. What did she know about life with the Hebrews? And still for all of Salmone's warnings, she found herself more determined than ever to become a true worshiper of the Lord.

A soft hand touched her shoulder making her jump.

"Forgive me," Miriam said with a smile. "I didn't mean to startle you."

"My thoughts plagued me. An interruption is welcome."

"Don't let Salmone worry you. My brother doesn't know his own strength, sometimes. He has a good heart. He'll do right by you and your family. Anyway, Joshua himself has decreed that you can join us."

"Do you think I can really learn to fit in with your people?" Rahab asked, unable to keep the tremble out of her voice. She did not spell out her thought—she didn't say *a zonah like me*, but the implication was hard to miss.

"Of course you can. Anybody can see you already love the Lord. Judging by what Ezra told me, you are valiant and trustworthy. You care for your family. These are qualities that my people treasure. It may not be easy at first. Not everyone is kind to outsiders. But the worst of it will pass with time, if you persevere."

Rahab almost broke her reserve and hugged Miriam for her kindness. Concern that it might be deemed unacceptable behavior in Israel made her contain the impulse. Instead she smiled and nodded her thanks self-consciously.

Throughout that day, Ezra and Miriam taught them about the Lord and the laws that governed Israel. Rahab listened to every phrase, and tucked every new piece of knowledge into her memory to ponder over later.

"So who is your king?" Joa asked partway through a discourse on leadership.

"The Lord is our King," Ezra replied.

"Yes, yes. But who is your earthly king?"

"We have no earthly king."

"Then who is your prince? Is Joshua a prince? Or Salmone?"

Ezra shook his head. "We have no kings or princes. The Lord has anointed Joshua to lead Israel. There are twelve tribes, and each tribe has its own leader. The leader of the tribe of Judah is Caleb, who is Joshua's age and a man of stout heart. Under the heads of the tribes, we have leaders and officers of the people. We have commanders of thousands, which is what Salmone is, and under them we have commanders of hundreds. Then we have heads of families. We bring our disputes to judges. There is no need for kings and princes, who can grow vain and cruel."

Imri shook his head. "I've never heard of the like."

"It works well. Our respect for one another rises out of our trust in the Lord. Joshua has proven himself a mighty leader a hundred times over by now. But the real reason we trust and follow him into gravest danger is that we know the Lord has chosen and empowered him."

Izzie squirmed a little closer. "So if you have been traveling for almost forty years in the wilderness, you can have no houses. No shops. No temples. No roads. No walls. How do you manage?"

Miriam didn't quite grin, Rahab noted, but a dimple peeped at the side of her mouth. "We do have a sanctuary for the Lord—a tabernacle. You are right, though; it isn't a temple as you are accustomed to, though it is far grander than it sounds. There are curtains of twisted linen in blue and purple and scarlet, with cherubim worked into them, and many exquisite articles of gold and silver. Yet it is God Himself who makes the tabernacle awesome to behold, for the presence of the Lord when manifested is more wondrous than the greatest temple carved by human hands."

Rahab's heart trembled at these words. The thought of one day entering the tabernacle of the Lord, experiencing His glory and being touched by His presence rendered her both terrified and filled with delight.

"We live in tents instead of homes," Miriam continued. "Some are very large and comfortable. Everything has to be mobile, so we have few pieces of heavy furniture outside of what has been consecrated for the Lord's use. We have no shops. Men and women barter amongst themselves."

Izzie's eyes brightened. "I can weave well."

Miriam bent a little closer and touched Izzie's robe. "This is beautiful. Did you weave it yourself?"

She nodded. "It took half a year. I wove these patterns that you see at the edge right into the fabric."

"How delicate and soft you have managed to make it. What is it made of?"

Rahab noticed her sister's cheeks colored with pleasure. "I wove wool and linen together."

An odd look crossed Miriam's face. She bit the corner of her thumb and looked over to Ezra. He was busy talking to Imri. Rahab could tell that something was bothering Miriam, though she couldn't understand what it might be. Her sister seemed to miss the rising tension and discoursed happily on the virtues of mixing various yarns. Miriam seemed to grow more dismayed by the minute.

Finally, during a silent interlude Rahab asked, "Miriam, may I speak with you alone for a moment?"

"Of course." Miriam followed Rahab to the scanty shade of a palm.

"Will you tell me what is wrong? It's plain something is bothering you."

She groaned. "Your poor sister. I haven't the heart to tell her."

"Tell her what?"

"Her robe. She can't wear it when she joins us. We are forbidden from wearing clothing made of wool and linen woven together. And she'll have to leave behind everything else of mixed fabric. Such beautiful workmanship. Oh, Rahab, your poor sister."

Rahab opened her mouth and closed it again. Izzie was bound to take this hard. She had worked long hours on that robe. It wasn't as if she had dozens of garments. And she had salvaged the best from Jericho's ruin.

"I'm so sorry," Miriam said

Rahab bit her lip and thought for a moment. "It can't be helped."

Back with the others, Rahab tackled the problem right away. "Izzie, dear, I'm afraid I have some bad news," she began, preparing herself for a difficult scene. "In fact this applies to all of us. We won't be allowed to wear garments of wool and linen woven together. We can only bring those things that are made of one or the other."

"What?" Her sister's yelp drew every eye. "What are you talking about?"

Miriam stepped forward. "I'm so sorry. Your robe is beautiful. I'm sure every woman in Israel would admire it as much as I. Only, you see, we aren't allowed to wear clothes that are woven with a mix of wool and linen."

"Why in the name of all the gods not? That's ludicrous!"

Ezra lost a bit of color at that first exclamation. Rahab could read confusion and distress in his expression. She supposed he was trying to figure out why a woman who had lost home and hearth with a certain amount of aplomb would lose her composure over one measly garment.

Into the shocked silence, Ezra said, "Pardon me, I pray. I can see this is very difficult. But please understand if you wish to live amongst us, you must not resort to expletives about other gods, even in anger or carelessness. And if that were the name of the Lord you were taking in vain, it would be even worse, as I explained this morning."

Izzie looked at him as though he had grown a donkey's tail. "We are discussing my robe," she stated, her voice only a shade warmer than ice.

"Yes, but . . ." Miriam put a restraining hand on Ezra's arm and he fell silent. Rahab started taking deep breaths to try and calm herself. Would they tell Salmone? Would he come to the conclusion that they were beyond reform and ban them from joining Israel? This was proving to be so much more convoluted than she expected.

Miriam walked over to Izzie and took her hand. "It must seem unreasonable to you, Izzie. I would feel the same if I stood in your shoes. There is a principle behind this requirement, though. Let me explain it to you, because it's going to apply to almost every part of your life with us.

"The Lord has called His people to be set apart for Him. We are to belong to Him, and follow only His ways and plans. We are not to be like other people. He knows how quickly we can stray from His side. It would be easy for us to start chasing after Canaanite beliefs. So the Lord has given us these outward rules to help us remember every day that we belong to Him and no other. That our thoughts and actions must differ from the world around us."

Ezra raised a finger. "Some even say that by forbidding the mixing of different threads, God is symbolically reminding us that we cannot mix with people of other faiths."

Miriam pressed Izzie's hand. "I do not understand such mysteries. What I do know is that I would rather obey the Lord without understanding than follow my own limited knowledge.

"Perhaps a day might come when God's people will no longer need these outward reminders. Perhaps one day, He will write His Law on our hearts and we shall be able to give up living by these stringent rules. Until such a time, however, we must abide by His will.

"It is a sacrifice we choose to make for His sake. We know He isn't being cruel when He directs us in these minute details of life. He is being a protective Father who wishes to keep His children out of trouble. In these daily acts of obedience, we learn the larger principles of a righteous life.

"The Lord knows how much it will cost you to give up that robe, Izzie. But you will make His heart glad if you do."

Rahab drew closer to her sister and gave her an enveloping hug. "Do it for the Lord. Don't do it because of the rules, or because of Israel. If you do it for Him, you will have joy. If you do it for them, you will grow resentful."

Miriam looked at Rahab with widened eyes. "That is wisely spoken, Rahab." Izzie deliberated silently. The rigid slash of her mouth began to soften. She walked behind the blanket they were using as a screen. When she emerged a few moments later, she was wrapped in a simple linen shift and carried the disputed garment over her arm. She marched over to the fire, still burning from the noon meal, and after an infinitesimal hesitation, dropped the exquisite garment into the flames. They watched in stunned awe. Rahab saw her mother turn back and search through her own pile. She pulled out a couple of garments and threw them on the fire. One by one, they went through their meager belongings and burned every mixed garment.

Rahab supposed the more practical thing would have been to save these valuable articles and try to sell them in some Canaanite city. Their sacrifices, however, brought a subtle joy. It was almost as if Rahab could feel the pleasure of the Lord with their decision to honor Him above their own desires.

When it was time for Miriam and Ezra to take their leave, Rahab accompanied them a short way, a common gesture of courtesy amongst Canaanites. Miriam slowed her gait until the two of them fell behind Ezra. "How did you know about giving up the robe for the Lord and not for other people? That was admirable advice, Rahab. I've walked with the Lord my whole life and have only begun to understand that lesson myself."

"You credit me with too much, Miriam. I don't deserve your good opinion." Rahab came to a halt and reached out a hand, clutching at the younger woman's fingers. She hesitated, swallowing a few times before she could force herself to plow forward. "Living in Jericho—my family and I—we've done awful things. You know I was a *zonah*. My father, he asked it of me, when I was fifteen. And I chose not to stop when I could have.

I've had a dozen lovers, which is not many for such a profession, but a dozen too many for Israel and the Lord."

She paused and continued. "Izzie sacrificed her son to Molech. The string of our sins and failures goes on and on. You must become aware of these things, Miriam. Tell your brother. Tell Joshua. They should give their consent knowing everything. Nothing is hidden from God, so it would be useless for us to join you under false pretenses. It would break my heart if you reject us. But it would do my heart no good if you accept us not understanding who we are."

Rahab took a deep breath. There, she had said it. She had confessed. She kept her eyes lowered, desperate to avoid seeing the revulsion that was sure to be reflected in Miriam's face. Now she would recoil from Rahab and take back every generous compliment she had given her. The silence stretched, and then to her shock, Rahab found herself enveloped in an embrace that almost knocked her to the ground.

"I'm so sorry. I'm so sorry for all you've been through."

"What?"

"Your life sounds so hard. Such burdens you have borne. Did you think I would reject you when God has accepted you? If He buries your past, then so shall I."

"Your brother? Joshua?" Rahab asked in a faint voice.

"Joshua will do what the Lord tells him. And Salmone will do what Joshua tells him, although there might be grumbling involved. Stiffen your resolve, Rahab. Rely on God's approval. Salmone will catch up."

The problem, Rahab reflected as she trudged back home, was that she wasn't particularly sure of God's approval. Deceiving herself into believing that God accepted her seemed a far more likely event than winning His genuine acceptance. In the meantime, there was Salmone, who definitely did not approve of her.

CHAPTER TEN

Salmone's sister had prepared lentil stew for supper. The lentils crunched under Salmone's teeth, half-cooked. The bread, raw in the middle, stuck to the roof of his mouth. Miriam slopped another ladleful of soup into his still overflowing bowl, her mind so preoccupied she didn't even notice that half the soup sloshed over the side and onto Salmone's hand.

He winced. "Miriam, what's bothering you?"

"Hmm?" Miriam blinked and stood up from her cross-legged seat on the floor to clean up the supper dishes, unmindful that she had refilled his bowl only moments before. Salmone was relieved. At least that meant he wouldn't have to pretend to eat more.

"Speak your mind, girl. Tell me what's troubling you. And can you fetch me a rag? If you insist on scalding me with stew, the least you can do is clean it up."

"Oh, of course," she said and handed him a long piece of fabric. It was Salmone's best belt. Salmone set the belt aside with his dry hand and grabbed some water and walked outside to rinse his fingers and sleeve. Then he marched back inside.

"Now sister, tell me what has beset you."

"Can you tell? How observant you are."

"Miriam!"

"If you insist." She flopped on a cushion across from where he lounged. "I've been talking to Rahab."

"I might have guessed," Salmone shot back. He slapped the carpet next to him and jumped up. "First day and already with the problems."

"I like her, Salmone. I like her a lot. And if you stop being so mule-headed, you would too."

"Fine. What's the difficulty then?"

"She talked with me about her past. She told me about some of her sins, hers and her family's, because she desires to hide nothing from you and Joshua. She's desperate to join us, but she does not want to do so under false pretenses. She wants you to consent to their presence with the full knowledge of who they are and what they have done. I thought her confession was admirable. Not many would be so forthright under the circumstances. She is determined to do everything right. She prefers to lose her dream for the sake of her integrity if it comes to that."

Salmone expelled a long-suffering sigh and dropped back down on the cushions. "So. Tell me about this past."

In succinct sentences, Miriam explained to her brother what Rahab had revealed. Salmone shook his head, struggling between a grudging admiration and exasperation. "How am I supposed to make these people fit with us, Miriam? Child sacrifice? Selling your own daughter into prostitution? Adultery? Joshua has set me upon an impossibility. Let him be the one to solve it. Go ask him."

"I already have."

"Of course," Salmone muttered, leaning back. "How foolish of me not to remember you've lately become bosom friends with the leader of Israel. And what did he have to say, pray tell?"

"He said, 'What, and you think when I agreed to have Canaanites join us I expected them to be pure as the sons of Levi?'"

"How he can reconcile himself to this mountain of sin, I don't understand."

"He told me, 'Miriam, the past is God's domain. Our job is to rescue the present from its rotting carcass.' He also said he admires Rahab for being truthful."

"What an unparalleled paragon of virtue I serve." Salmone rubbed his aching temple. "There you have it, sister. Clearly, mine is the job of grave digging. I am to rid us of this hefty rotting carcass."

The next morning, a grudging Salmone went back to Rahab's camp, Miriam bouncing with jaunty steps at his side. He found the family gathered together and taking inventory of their finances. Crouching on one knee next to Karem, he asked, "Have you enough for tents?"

"Depends on what they cost." He told Salmone the sum of their net savings.

"You have sufficient for one large tent. It will be a tight fit for twelve people, but I think you will be able to manage. Then you'll have ample left to invest in several goats and perhaps a calf." He cast Izzie a sidelong glance. "And a few sheep. That way, you'll have milk and butter and cheese and yogurt, as well as wool. If you work hard in the land, by next year you'll be able to buy a second tent."

Rahab swiveled around toward him. "Work the land, my lord? Does that mean you've decided that my brothers and father can help cultivate farmland rather than go to war?"

"I thought that wouldn't slip by you," he drawled. "Yes, I have decided that we will benefit from their farming experience. Assuming that you will learn to abide by the Law, that is." Rahab dropped her head so that he could not read her expression. He perceived this to be a habitual tendency, one he found frustrating. He tightened his mouth and turned to Izzie. "Miriam told me what you did yesterday. That was courageous. Well done." Izzie flushed with pleasure.

Miriam stood up and moved to Izzie's side, carrying a folded piece of fabric. "This is for you," she said as she placed it in Izzie's hands. "I wove the fabric myself last year. It pales compared to your exquisite workmanship. I wish you would teach me how to weave like you. We have nothing so fine as your work in all of Israel."

"For me?" Izzie gulped.

Miriam laughed. "Well, it's not for your brothers. They would find it a tight fit." Salmone hid a smile.

Two weeks later, Salmone found himself at the Jericho camp. Again. He tried to concentrate on Joa's recitation on sacrifices, but his eyes wandered instead toward Rahab. She had one of her nieces on her lap, while trying to teach an older one how to spin yarn. He noticed that around the children she lost her guarded look, her full mouth softening with frequent smiles.

She was beautiful, he gave her that. At first, he found that very loveliness off-putting. It reminded him too well of her former profession. But he perceived nothing harlot-like about this woman. Her manner was reserved, bordering on shy. Her demeanor, though forthright, could match any Israelite maiden for modesty. Sometimes he almost forgot about her past and had to forcefully resurrect the memory. This wasn't exactly the kind of detail a man ought to waylay.

He dragged his attention back to the circle of men around him. Joa had lost his haunted air in the course of the past ten days. He seemed to take a genuine interest in the precepts of the Lord. They all did. "My lord, Salmone?"

"Hmm?"

"Why does the Lord demand an offering for unintentional sin? I mean, how can it be sin if you don't even know you are doing the wrong thing?"

"Whether you do the wrong thing intentionally or unintentionally, there are consequences. Let us say I break your leg on purpose because I have a grudge against you. My anger and lack of self-control causes you a lot of pain. Now supposing that I break your leg by accident. Will your bone ache any less because it was crushed by accident? Will you heal faster because I didn't intend to harm you? Sin is like that. Whether you know what you're doing or not, there is damage. There are consequences. The holiness of the Lord requires justice for these consequences.

It demands a covering for them. Yet, He is merciful with our mistakes. So He Himself gives us that covering by providing us with the sacrifice." Salmone shifted to make himself more comfortable, and as he turned, he noticed that Rahab had left her nieces to the care of their mother and scooted closer in order to hear their conversation. He had come to realize in the course of the past days that anything to do with God drew her like a butterfly to a colorful bloom.

She cleared her throat. "So the Lord forgives the one who errs by sinning unintentionally?"

Salmone turned toward her. "With the right sacrifice. Yes."

She kept her lashes lowered, hiding her expression from him. Salmone balled his hand at his side. He found that he was beginning to hate the way her eyes slid from him as if in dread. For all his objections to her, had he once mistreated her over the past two weeks? Had he insulted her? Demeaned her? Why did she smile for Ezra and Hanani and Miriam and every other human creature under the sun as far as he could tell, yet for him she only had reserve and distance? He itched to put his hand on her chin and turn her to face him. Instead, he tightened his fist.

"What about foreigners living among you?" she asked, her voice soft and without inflection.

"What about them?" he growled. He wasn't paying attention to her question. Instead, his mind was still grappling with her remoteness. Resentment rose up in him, unreasonable and sharp, coloring his voice with a harsher edge than he intended.

She sensed that edge and misunderstood it. Her pale skin turned a bright pink, and he realized too late that she was mortified. "Pardon, my lord. I didn't mean to interrupt your teaching," she said and moved to get up. Before he could think, Salmone reached out his hand and grabbed her wrist, pulling her back down.

"Stay. You weren't interrupting." For a moment she tried to pull her hand away, but he held fast, and pulled her down harder. Forcing his voice into gentleness, he said, "Ask your question again."

She grew very still. Salmone became aware that he was still holding her wrist and quickly released her. With a casual motion, he leaned back against his elbows, increasing the distance between them.

"I . . . I just wondered if the foreigner living with your people could also receive forgiveness by presenting an offering."

Not a question of ritual. Not a question that would help her fit in with Israel, or assist her to avoid costly mistakes. This wasn't a question of outward practicality. She was seeking to find forgiveness and redemption.

Would God give these things to one such as she? Did Salmone even know the answer? The echo of a distant teaching came to him. What had Moses taught about foreigners?

"Moses once said, speaking for the Lord, 'You and the foreigner shall be the same before the Lord: the same laws and regulations will apply both to you and to the foreigner residing among you.' He said this about offering sacrifices."

"He said that the foreigners shall be *the same* as you before the Lord?" In her eagerness, Rahab forgot to avoid Salmone's eyes. The veil lifted from her face, and she stared at him without her usual guardedness. Salmone took a sharp breath. He became aware, perhaps more than she herself, that her whole heart was in that question. She had ripped herself open, laid herself bare by asking it. For at the core of her words was the fragile offering of herself, her hunger to belong to the Lord and to Israel, knowing very well that she might be rejected, cast out and unacceptable.

He had wasted so much time worrying about her loyalty, worrying about the dangers of insidious Canaanite idolatry, worrying about her motives, when in fact, all Rahab wanted was to belong to the Lord. She thirsted for God. Hungered after Him. She couldn't seem to get enough of His precepts. And what she was searching for wasn't knowledge. It was belonging. She wanted the Lord Himself.

Could someone like her belong to God? Would He take her, accept her, receive her, cover her shame and sin? Was she the alien He had in mind when He spoke those words through Moses? Salmone didn't want to offer her empty promises. Silently, he asked the Lord for wisdom.

"Moses said those words, yes," he began. "He was speaking about sacrifices, and saying that the foreigners living with the community of Israel must live by the same rules. They must offer the same sacrifices." He stopped and sank into deep thought for some moments before continuing.

"We ought to remember that for Israel, sacrifices aren't a token ritual. They avail something real. Sacrifices are both the acknowledgment of our wrong and the price of our forgiveness. God wouldn't ask for a sacrifice if He weren't willing to pour out His forgiveness and acceptance in return."

He dipped his chin toward Rahab once in a gesture of reassurance. She looked like she was exploding with a hundred questions. Salmone watched the desire for answers tangle with something else, something more primal. *Fear*? Without a word, she slipped back behind her wall.

Frustration warred with relief. With a ferocity he barely understood, Salmone wanted to smash down that defense, to experience again her openness and trust. Yet he also knew that some of the questions she was desperate to ask would tie him up in tangles. *Will the Lord forgive me for my life of adultery? Will He forgive my father for asking me to become a harlot? Will He forgive my sister and her husband for offering their son to Molech? Will we have a new start, a clean slate?*

Salmone rubbed the back of his neck with a hand callused from the handle of a sword. What was the answer to these riddles? There were injunctions against every one of those sins, and serious consequences for each. Would God forgive? Would He give this family a second chance?

Miriam chose that thorny moment to come and join him. She had been speaking with Rahab's mother for the past hour. Salmone noticed the dark circles under his sister's eyes. She had risen from bed before him that morning, tending to the sick for several hours before coming with him to visit Rahab and her family. He should have noticed the exhaustion that etched her features sooner. Standing up in one fluid motion, he pulled her up with him.

"Time to return home." At the edge of the camp he hesitated. "Tomorrow, I'm going to speak to Joshua about getting you settled in our camp," he told them. "I think you are ready." Then maneuvering his sister ahead of him, he headed out of the meager oasis before the family's jubilant expressions of thanks could start to harp on his nerves.

"She loves the Lord, doesn't she?" Miriam said, breaking the silence. "Loves Him with a genuine desire that goes deep and wide. You don't find that kind of faith very often."

"Hmm?"

"Rahab. I overheard some of your conversation with her."

"Hmm."

"My brother the conversationalist. I'm serious, Salmone. Remember that day when they burned their clothes? I didn't tell you what Rahab told Izzie that day. When I had explained to Izzie that she couldn't bring her robe into our camp, Rahab said that Izzie should only give up her robe for the Lord. 'Don't do it because of the rules, or because of Israel,' she said. 'If you do it for Him, you will have joy. If you do it for them, you will grow resentful.' Her wisdom amazed me. She barely even understood the basic commandments then, yet she comprehended the difference between performance and worship. She understood that doing something as a willing offering to the Lord brings joy, whereas doing something to satisfy human expectations can only end in pain."

"She's . . . an unusual woman."

"Is that what brings you to their camp so often?"

"*What?*"

"Come, Salmone. You could send anyone to do this work. Any number of your men could have done the teaching. Yet as often as not, you have chosen to do it yourself. Two weeks ago, you were pulling out your hair in exasperation because Joshua had foisted them on you. Now you hardly stay away."

"I wanted to gauge their character for myself!"

Miriam sniffed, but she had enough discernment to hold her tongue.

Salmone ground his jaw. Her words struck too close to home. He had lost count of the arguments he had had with himself for the past two weeks. Every morning he lectured himself that he had better things to do with his life. And repeated the lecture even while of their own accord, his feet directed him back to Rahab's camp.

He tried to convince himself that the problems of grafting an enemy family into Israel merited his frequent visits. The potential pitfalls in this harebrained plan of Joshua's could give a young man white hair. The possibility of resentment, fomenting violence, immorality, division, and a host of other dangers hung over Jericho's survivors like a storm cloud. Salmone almost convinced himself that he visited them as often as he did in order to ensure that none of these dangers would become a reality.

The only thorn in this reasonable conviction had a name. Rahab. His thoughts strayed her way too often for comfort. His eyes rested on her without his volition. Although his physical attraction to the Canaanite woman plagued him, it paled in comparison to his increasing fascination with her as a whole. She had a brilliant mind, he had discovered. Quick-witted and savvy, she often seemed to be five steps ahead of everyone else in her family. She understood the ramifications of every decision with a precision that Salmone couldn't help but admire. Above all this, Rahab's faith drew Salmone. She awakened a longing that had old roots for him.

Salmone had been married at a young age. He had known his Anna from infancy. She had been his parents' choice, though a choice to which he had willingly submitted. In the short years of their marriage, he had known the kindness of a loyal wife. He had known the companionship of a patient and caring woman. But in his deepest heart, he had hungered for more. Anna believed in the Lord and followed His precepts. Yet she wasn't ardent for Him. She didn't speak to her husband about Him, growing excited with every new step of faith. When he tried to bring up the subject, she would avoid it. Salmone had longed to be able to bask in the mysteries of God with his wife, to share with her this most precious and sacred desire of his soul. His marriage, though pleasant and warm, lacked the fire of this greatest passion of Salmone's life.

In spite of the fact that Anna had been dead for many years now, Salmone had never remarried, because he remembered that barrenness and dreaded it. He wanted more than he had known with Anna. He felt disloyal just thinking about it, as if he accused Anna of a shortcoming. What fault had she, after all?

In Rahab, Salmone caught a glimpse of the passion, the intelligent searching mind, the hunger after the Lord that he longed for. In spite of her many gifts, however, she was utterly unsuitable. Her origins, not to mention her besmirched past, made her an unfitting companion for any Hebrew man, let alone one of Israel's leaders—*the son of Nahshon, once leader of the tribe of Judah, no less!* They would simply be incompatible.

And yet she drew him . . .

Salmone had allowed for every conceivable danger directed at Israel from Rahab and her family. This one contingency, however, had never occurred to him. That he would himself become the target of so inconvenient an attraction was an irony that he could do without. He would stay away from them starting tomorrow, he decided with finality. If Miriam was beginning to notice the leaning of his heart, then it was more than time to put a stop to it. He kicked at a stone as he walked beside Miriam, unintentionally causing a shower of sand to rise up. It flew into her mouth, which was open in a soft hum, and found its way up her nose.

"Yupphht! Hey!" she said, spitting out granules, sticky with her saliva. "Why are you declaring war on the sand?"

"Pardon." It wasn't the sand he was at war with. It was himself.

"Joshua, I think Rahab and her family are ready to move into the camp with us." Salmone sat alone with Joshua on a nubby hill. A few blades of tough grass grew around them in the rocky soil, waving now and again in the breeze.

Joshua gave a half-smile, quickly wiping it clean before turning to his protégé. Not quick enough for Salmone to miss, however. "I'm glad to hear it. So you have no more concerns?"

Salmone's lips twisted. "I wouldn't say that. I am simply satisfied that their desire to serve the Lord is genuine, and they bear no ill will toward Israel."

Joshua snorted. "That's mighty generous of you. The woman's faith is well known to half the camp already. In fact, I'd like to meet her. Why don't you bring her to me tomorrow?"

"I'll have Hanani fetch her for you."

"No, no. You bring her. I'd like to have you there too."

Salmone barely stopped himself from rolling his eyes. "Of course, Joshua," he said, his smile wooden.

CHAPTER ELEVEN

Yet again, Salmone found himself traipsing down the well-worn path to the oasis. At least this time it was Joshua's fault. Once there, he avoided meeting with Rahab for as long as possible by first finding her brothers and father.

"You can move to our camp this afternoon. I have located a tent that will suit your needs; I'll have it delivered to you when you arrive. After the noon meal is finished, a couple of men from my tribe will come to help you carry your things."

He nodded his head as the men thanked him, the effusion of their genuine excitement making him uncomfortable. A feeling too much like guilt clung to him. It occurred to him that given his attitude toward these people, he deserved their resentment more than their gratitude. Over time he had learned to treat them with respect; he had even relaxed his harsh reservations. He had not, however, behaved toward them with warmth and friendship.

He shrugged off the thought, and unable to avoid his real task any longer, turned to look for Rahab. She was on the other side of the camp, kneeling by the fire. He took his time ambling over to her, dreading her proximity. Anticipating her proximity. The opposing emotions made his stomach churn.

Too soon he arrived at her side, and for a moment stood towering over her. Her eyes widened with surprise before she lowered them. "Rahab," he said with a nod.

"My lord."

Without preamble he blurted, "Joshua wants to see you."

"Me?"

"Yes. You. Rahab." She didn't move. "Now, if you please."

"Now?"

"If you're going to repeat everything I say, this might become a lengthier conversation than I anticipated."

"But why does he want to see me? Have I done something wrong?"

Salmone hunkered down until his face became level with hers. He studied her for a moment. Her full lips trembled and she bit on them to keep them still. She knit her fingers together until they turned white. The honey eyes had grown dark with apprehension. He found himself wanting to wrap his arms around her in comfort until the fear drained out of her.

To stop himself from such rash foolishness, he shoved his hands behind his back. "Look, he wants to meet you, that is all. You saved his men; perhaps he might even thank you. There's nothing to grow anxious about. In fact, I've asked your family to move to our camp later this afternoon. Permanently. A couple of my men will come and fetch them."

"This afternoon?" She clapped a hand over her mouth for a moment. "I know, I know. I'm repeating your words. It's only that it feels like a dream. Shall we truly move in with Israel?"

"This very day."

She laughed, a tinkling sound full of relief and exultation. Salmone, who only two weeks before had fought tooth and nail to keep her out of his nation, found himself grinning right alongside her and wishing he could cause her joy more often.

"If I'm to meet Joshua, I'd better go and change. And I also need to pack if we are to move."

"Leave your packing to your family. Surely they can manage in your absence." He looked at her through veiled eyes. "You can change if you wish," he said, "but you look fine as you are."

Rahab drew a nervous hand down the side of her linen dress. "I better wear something more suitable. I won't be long." She lurched when she rose to her feet too abruptly. Salmone shot out his hand to steady her, his athletic reflexes working before wisdom held him back. For a tense moment they were connected, half leaning into each other, Salmone's hand on Rahab's arm. Her skin felt supple. Inviting. Unbidden, he felt an overwhelming kick of desire. His breath caught.

He pushed her away as he removed his hand and took a wide step back for good measure. Unreasonably, anger rose up in him. Anger against his own reactions to this woman, and irrationally, against her, for being the cause of so much unwanted emotional upheaval. She turned the color of pomegranate skin. "I . . . I won't be long," she repeated and raced away.

"You won't be long enough," Salmone muttered under his breath when Rahab was out of hearing range. Trying to erase the memory of the touch of her skin against his hand, he wiped his palm on his homespun tunic. This was Joshua's fault. He would dump Rahab at the doorstep of Israel's great leader and be done with the whole matter. Let Joshua deal with her. He would arrange for the family to purchase their tent and have it set up as far away from his own tent as the tribe of Judah could accommodate. If he was careful, he might not even run into her above once a month. Now that was a worthy plan.

Rahab reflected that in spite of Salmone's assurance, the robe she had on was wrinkled and far from fresh. The lack of water in their minuscule camp meant the precious supply they received from Israel was used only for food and drink and the most basic of necessary ablutions. Laundry was a luxury they hadn't been able to afford for many days now. She had had the prudence to set aside a fresh robe for the day they would move into Israel's camp, however.

During her last weeks in Jericho, before the army of Israel parked itself outside their walls, she had decided to sell most of her fine robes and veils. The night she promised God to change her life, they became useless to her. In their place, she had purchased several lengths of plain and sturdy fabric with which she made a few garments of modest design. Looking at the way Miriam dressed, she was glad of her foresight. If Miriam was typical of other Israelite women, then Rahab's new clothing would be considered luxurious but acceptable.

She washed briskly, using a rag and a basin of tepid water before changing into her fresh linen dress. Her hair hung unadorned in a braid down her back. Rummaging through a sack, she found a small jar of precious rose water and applied a little to her hair. Instantly, she regretted it. Would it remind Joshua of her past when he smelled it? Was perfume considered an immoral luxury among the women of Israel?

Frantically, she scrubbed the damp rag against her scalp until it hurt. Discarding the rag, she grabbed a long scarf and threw it over her head. Further delay would only put Salmone in a foul mood. A fouler mood, she conceded. He seemed short-tempered already. When she had stumbled, he had pushed her away as though she were an offense to him and to the heavens. She groaned, hating her desperation for winning his approval—hating the easy way he affected her with his smallest actions.

He barely gazed in her direction when she emerged from behind the makeshift curtain. Without a word, he began to walk, and she had to follow him as best she could. His legs were much longer than hers, and every few steps, she had to resort to a jog in order to catch up. If he noticed her predicament, he showed no sign.

"Is it far to Israel's camp?" she ventured to ask after a time.

"No."

Under the midmorning sun, she was puffing like a smoky fire, yet the turmoil in her mind was by far the greater discomfort. "Do you know Joshua well?" she asked. With every step, she grew more terrified at the prospect of meeting the commander of Israel. What if he detested her? What if after meeting her, he changed his mind about letting them remain?

Salmone slowed his steps. "I've known him my whole life."

"Is he . . . a good man?"

"He is the best of men." He gazed at Rahab for a moment and looked away. "Why are you fearful?"

She shrugged, too embarrassed to tell him of her self-doubt. In her own ears she sounded like a child in need of assurance.

"Why?" he asked again. "Tell me."

At times like this, it was easy to see why thousands followed Salmone's leadership. She could not dredge up the resources to resist the persuasive force of the man. "He might change his mind when he meets me," she said, her voice wavering.

"Why would he do that?"

She felt perilously close to tears. The nearer they drew to Israel, the more certain she grew that Joshua would dislike her. Her steps began to drag until she stopped. "Perhaps this is a mistake."

Salmone stopped a few cubits ahead of her. He hesitated, one step straining forward, another digging in the sand, as though he couldn't make up his mind whether to leave her there or come back. He gave a muffled groan and turned around. "Come. It's not a mistake."

She shook her head. "Joshua doesn't understand the defilement of our lives or he would never have allowed us to join you."

"He understands better than you know, Rahab. He still wants you."

She sat heavily in the sand and buried her head in her arms. To her shame, she couldn't control the tears. Before Salmone, of all people. She felt his breath on top of her head before she felt him kneel by her side.

"Shhh. It's all right," he whispered. For once, she detected no hint of criticism or exasperation in his voice. Perversely, his genuine sympathy made her cry harder. He lifted her hand with gentle fingers and held it between his own. His touch felt pure, safe. That alone shocked her. How long had it been since a man had touched her with purity?

In the security of his presence, the burdens of the past weeks came pouring out of her in a torrent of silent tears. Of all the people in Canaan, Salmone would have been the last person she would have chosen as her comforter. But she hadn't been able to let these tears out in front of her family because they were leaning on her strength. They relied on her resolve; she needed to be an anchor to them in this season of uncertainty.

"Forgive me," she gasped, after expelling what felt like the last drop of moisture from her body. "I don't know why I am so overcome."

He released her hand and sat back. "You've been courageous for a long time. Your strength has limits; that is all. But you needn't fear Joshua. Come now. Come and see for yourself."

Rahab nodded and stood up. Sand covered her new dress. Tears stained her face. Her nose ran.

"You're a mess," Salmone said with a gentle smile that had no sting to it.

"I know." She wiped her face with a kerchief and beat the sand out of her tunic. Salmone waited without comment. He didn't even tap his foot or drum his fingers to express his impatience. When they resumed their walk, he moved much more slowly, matching his footsteps to her smaller ones.

Joshua welcomed Rahab to his tent with a wide smile that could not ease her jangled nerves. Her heart pounded in her chest with such ridiculous force, she was sure everyone could hear it. She curtsied with care; displaying the deference she would have shown a king. She studied the leader of Israel, trying to gauge the man. He was striking, though in no measure handsome. The hawklike nose, the strong lips, the intense gaze bore witness to a resolute character that would not brook easy opposition. This was not a man to have for an enemy as she had good reason to know. But she suspected his friendship would be as sweet as his enmity harsh.

"I have looked forward to meeting you, Rahab," he said. But before he could speak more, a young man ran into his tent unannounced, covered in dirt, his clothes askew, his hair disheveled. Disconcerted, Rahab stepped to the side. Was this a normal occurrence, this rude access to the ruler of the nation of Israel? The newcomer panted hard, as if he had run a considerable distance, and his sentences came out in great bursts of breath.

"Joshua! O Joshua."

"Elam? What news of Ai?"

"We are defeated, Joshua! Routed by the men of Ai! They chased us from the city gate as far as the stone quarries and struck us down on the slopes. Thirty-six of our men were killed."

A heavy silence fell over Joshua's tent. Rahab knew of Ai. It was a piddling nation whose king ruled over twelve thousand people at best. Hardly worth the mention. How could the men who had defeated Og and Jericho be defeated by Ai? This news made no sense.

Salmone and Joshua both rounded on the man named Elam. The oppressive silence turned into a torrent of questions that only men of war could understand. Joshua must have forgotten about Rahab's presence, because his eyes widened when he saw her standing stiff and uncomfortable to the side. "Get her out of here, Salmone," he barked. "And get back quickly. Call the elders to me. We must come before the Lord and ask for His guidance."

Salmone was the color of ash. He grabbed Rahab's arm and half ran out of the tent. "I must find Miriam," he muttered.

She was stumbling beside him, infected with the urgency that drove him. This news was dire. Salmone came to a sudden stop while Rahab's momentum kept her going. She almost wrenched her arm in the process. Grimacing, she rubbed the bruised skin. Even with the overwhelming preoccupation of his mind, he noticed the gesture and released her instantly. "Did I hurt you?"

"It's nothing."

"Your pardon." He shoved both his hands through his dark hair, making it stand on end like wind-besieged waves. "Rahab. I need to ask you something. You must promise not to speak of what you've heard to anyone, not even to Miriam."

"Of course not. It would cause the people to lose confidence if they were to get wind of this news too soon or in the wrong way."

"Exactly. That's right." He sounded relieved. "I can trust you then, to keep the news about Ai to yourself?"

"Yes, Salmone."

"Good. That is good." He gazed into her eyes for a moment.

In spite of the tension and worry stamped over every feature, something like approval flashed across his face. "Now, I'm going to find Miriam and leave you with her. I don't know how long I'll be, but I won't have time to arrange for the purchase of your family's tent today."

"Don't concern yourself about us. Sleeping a few more nights under the stars won't harm us any. Can Miriam show us where to set up camp tonight?"

"Yes, she can. Tell her to ask Ezra for help."

He had started moving at a manic pace again. Running in the center of Israel's camp at breakneck speed was no easy task. The landscape was dotted with tents, people milling about, children playing, fires burning, and livestock hemmed in by makeshift pastures. City-bred and accustomed to streets and alleys, she could make no rhyme or reason of the setup, but Salmone negotiated the obstacle course with the ease of long familiarity. He had lived in camps like this his whole life, she remembered.

Without warning, he stopped before a roomy saffron-colored tent. The peremptory manner with which he lifted the tent flap suggested this was his residence.

"Miriam?"

Within the tent, several cleverly wrought linen hangings divided the area into private "rooms." From one of these Miriam emerged. "What are you two doing here?"

"Miriam, Joshua has some urgent business with me. Rahab will explain what she needs. I must go." He flew out before Miriam could form her first question.

"What set his cloak on fire?"

"Oh, you know. Joshua business."

Miriam laughed. "You haven't been here two hours and you're already speaking like him. Have you had anything to drink or eat? Of course not. Would that brother of mine think of anything so practical as a cup of water while the tribes need attention? Come over here and sit. You look done in."

Rahab sank down on a pile of feather-filled pillows, grateful for their softness. A blissful sigh escaped her lips. After two weeks of outdoor living, this simple tent seemed like a palace to her. "The joy of cushions," she murmured.

"You must be sore from sleeping on the ground with nothing but a blanket."

"I am blessed to be alive. I have no complaints."

"Nothing teaches gratitude like losing everything. I know a little about that too." Miriam gave a sad smile. "We were born into loss, my whole generation. It makes us thankful for every small thing."

Rahab thought, not for the first time, that Miriam was an extraordinary woman. "Is every woman in Israel as wise as you?" she asked on impulse.

"Heavens, no. I'm a jewel of great price."

They laughed together. "So what's this urgent Joshua business my brother is haring after now? He looked a bit pinched in the face."

Rahab was struck with guilt as she realized she had forgotten about Israel's great trial and her thirty-six dead men while she sat enjoying feather pillows and the wit of an innocent young woman. "It's a meeting of some sort, I think. Salmone will be busy most of today, I suspect. He asked that you and Ezra help my family set up camp here for tonight. He won't have a chance to arrange for the purchase of our tent yet."

"That's not like Salmone. I hope he has received no dire news."

"He'll tell us when we need to know. In the meantime, where's that water you promised me? If I'm going to traipse after another long-legged fellow today, I need something wet in my throat."

Miriam dimpled as she lifted the lid off a large clay jar and ladled some water into a cup for Rahab. "Ezra *is* long-legged. Then again, you know that quite well given that you had to bear the weight of him down the entire height of Jericho's wall. When Ezra first told us about it, some people made a few wisecracks about the size of Canaanite women. Wait till they see you for themselves. How did you manage that, Rahab? He must be twice your size."

"I suppose God gave me the strength. I had no choice, in any case. If I had let him go, he would have broken his neck."

"That would have been a pity. He has such a nice neck." Miriam grinned. "When will your family arrive?"

"Salmone said sometime this afternoon. He has arranged for a couple of his men to go and fetch them. It won't be for several hours though; when I left them, they hadn't started packing."

"That gives us time to prepare a few things. Let's go find Ezra and put him to work."

Miriam and Rahab fetched Ezra and they spent some hours choosing a suitable plot of land allocated to the tribe of Judah large enough to accommodate Rahab's family. Ezra said that when they purchased their tent, they could erect it on the same spot. In the meantime, he helped build a fire pit, fetched water, and strung rope between a few palm trees that, with the use of blankets, could be transformed into a private dwelling.

They were close to several other tents, and Miriam introduced Rahab to the women in charge of each household. Rahab noticed that the women she met responded with lukewarm reticence. She received no smiles or overtures of friendship. Though no one was rude, none of them displayed any warmth, either. Her insides curdled with apprehension.

"Don't worry, Rahab," Miriam whispered as they left the last tent. "They have heard your praises. Joshua called you a woman of faith when he spoke to the people after the fall of Jericho. In time, they'll welcome and accept you as Joshua has."

Rahab tried to ignore the queasy feeling in the pit of her belly. She hadn't managed to make any female friends while living among her own people these past ten years, so why should she expect to make them among the women of Israel? How could she hope to win their acceptance?

CHAPTER TWELVE

Rahab's family arrived before sundown. She explained Salmone's preoccupation with an emergency. "I was there when Joshua sent him off on his assignment. He won't have time to arrange the purchase of our tent for a few days. He worried about not keeping his promise to us, but I assured him we would manage."

"If an urgent situation prevented Salmone from procuring our tent, we needn't worry. Salmone merits our trust," Joa said with a dismissive shrug. Rahab studied her younger brother. Here was a reversal. In the past two weeks, Joa had often needed assurance. His reaction to the tent's absence testified to a profound change of heart.

Just then Hanani sauntered over, brimming with his usual joviality. Surrounded by Hanani and Ezra and Miriam's genuine care, Rahab could almost believe that other Israelites would come to accept them in time. Together, they spent a few hours getting settled with their belongings and becoming acquainted with their new home. The sound of laughter filled their modest campsite as they unpacked and discussed which way they would pitch their tent and where the livestock would go.

Ezra explained Israel's architectural setup to them, and Rahab realized that the camp was no jumbled maze, but carefully established according to precise codes.

"At the center of the camp stands the tabernacle and its courtyard," Ezra began. "The twelve tribes of Israel pitch up their tents around that central structure, each according to a predetermined order."

"I wonder if I passed by the tabernacle today," Rahab said. "What does it look like?"

"You would have noticed if you had seen it," Miriam cut in. "A white fence made of linen curtains hanging from pillars surrounds the whole structure. The fence is there to ensure that no one accidentally touches the tabernacle or the holy articles in the courtyard."

"How far is it from us?"

"About a fifteen-minute walk to the west," Ezra replied. "Judah is the largest tribe in Israel, with over seventy thousand men. So our campsite is enormous. Issachar is our neighbor to the north and Zebulun camps to our south."

Rahab's family began to ask questions about the other tribes, fascinated by their stories. Rahab listened with half an ear, her thoughts consumed with Ai. She tried to grapple with the possible outcomes of such a defeat. Why would the Lord allow His people to be overcome? They were now vulnerable to other attacks from Canaan. Having shown this first sign of weakness, they had proven themselves open to defeat. As ordinary as any other nation.

Later that night, as the noise of the enormous camp surrounding them faded into a lazy drone, the night was suddenly rent with the sound of a horn blowing. Rahab almost toppled over from the unexpectedness of it.

Hanani looked at Ezra with knotted brows. "That was the call to meeting. We must go to Joshua at once."

Joa stepped forward. "Us too?"

"Yes, everyone. All of Israel must attend, and you are now a part of us."

Joa's lips widened into a smile. "Is this a regular practice?" he asked. "Gathering late at night for meetings?"

Ezra frowned. "No, not at all. We'd better go and find out what it's about."

By the time they arrived, thousands had already gathered. Joshua stood on a hill so that his voice would carry. Even that wasn't sufficient to reach everyone, for God had blessed Israel and her numbers were great. To ensure that everyone heard Joshua, there were criers stationed at set points who repeated Joshua's words. No one would be left out of the proclamation.

The people were accustomed to such public summons, though seldom so late at night. No one shoved; no one pushed. Everyone took their spot in orderly fashion.

Rahab and her family were close enough to hear Joshua's own voice, and after giving the crowd time to settle, he began to speak. "I have grave news. You know that we only sent a small band of men to destroy Ai because it is a trifling nation. Earlier today news of the battle reached our camp. We have been defeated." A loud gasp rose from the crowd. Before terror could lodge in their hearts, Joshua lifted his hands.

"Listen to me, for I have more news. As soon as we received this report, the elders and I fell before the Lord, seeking His will on the matter. And He has spoken." The entire camp held its breath as Joshua paused and looked out across the gathering. "The Lord said to me, *Stand up! What are you doing on your face? Israel has sinned.* The reason we couldn't be victorious over our enemy is that there is one amongst us who has stolen what belongs to God and lied about it. We were told when we went into Jericho that everything must be destroyed except those items that were to be devoted to the Lord. Someone has broken that command. They have robbed what rightfully belongs to God. Tomorrow the Lord will show us who it is. I am sorrowful to death, for the consequences of this disobedience have been great. We have lost thirty-six of our best warriors, lives that would have been preserved if we had not betrayed the will of God. Tomorrow, no doubt more lives will be lost, for we have no sacrifice holy enough that would cover such a grave sin. More blood will be shed. I am filled with grief for this needless loss.

"Go tonight, and consecrate yourselves in preparation for tomorrow. In the morning you will present yourselves tribe by tribe until God points out the guilty person. Only then will the Lord give us the strength to stand against our enemies once more."

The heavy silence that met Joshua's pronouncement melted into the whisperings of thousands. People wondered who it could be, which tribe, which clan. They assured one another that it certainly was not them.

Joa said, "No wonder Salmone didn't have time to buy our

tent. He must have been dealing with this most of the day."

As Rahab and her family returned to their camp, they noticed that the gazes of their neighbors were even less friendly than before. She supposed it was natural that Israelites should jump to quick conclusions and suspect the citizens of Jericho. They had opportunity and motive. It was a bitter cup to swallow, all the same. Their wordless accusations stung. Her first night and she was already branded a thief.

Lord, You know we are innocent. We've done our best to honor You. And it's still not enough. Can we ever please these people? Can we ever vindicate ourselves in their eyes?

Like a whispering wind, a thought came into her churning mind. *You only need to please Me. And I am satisfied. Leave your vindication in My hands. I have called you and I am faithful.*

A sweet peace descended over her. God would be her vindicator. She didn't need to be defensive. She didn't need to point out her neighbors' unkindness to protect her own heart. She wouldn't have to put anyone down in order to raise herself up. God would take care of them. He was faithful. She smiled as she nestled deeper into the covering of peace He had bestowed upon her. Lifting her head, she looked up, her eyes shining with a joy that their precarious circumstances could not rob, and found herself staring straight into Salmone's eyes. The frown lines around his brows smoothed as his gaze locked with Rahab's. He crouched in front of her.

"I was worried about you." His voice was husky.

"About me?"

"About all of you, I mean. I assume the neighbors aren't being friendly?"

She grinned. "Not that I could tell. If looks could kill, you'd be digging fresh graves."

"It will be sorted out tomorrow. I know you are innocent of any wrongdoing in this matter. They will be ashamed of themselves by nightfall tomorrow."

Salmone believed them innocent. Without explanation, without a plea, he believed. Warmth filled Rahab. She knew that something frozen and old was starting to melt. Her mouth tasted dry. She swallowed convulsively. "It's all right," she said, though it came out a whisper. "God has given me His peace."

"I saw it in your eyes when you looked at me. More than peace; His joy rests on you."

Rahab nodded. "He gave me such reassurance! The load of my fears simply lifted. I only need to please Him, He said. Isn't that wonderful?"

"He spoke to you?"

"Not in an audible voice. More like a whisper within."

His eyes widened. "Perhaps His Spirit came upon you for a moment."

"Is that common?"

Salmone shook his head. "You've been more blessed than most."

She couldn't help grinning like a fool. "Right now I feel more blessed than most."

He rose up in a graceful motion. "I'd better get back. You don't seem to need my help."

"What will happen tomorrow?"

His face lost all expression. "Whatever is necessary."

Rahab didn't sleep that night. Wrapped in the security of

God's reassuring words, she held the memory of His presence close. Contentment enveloped her. Then Salmone's face flashed before her, his eyes dark as he whispered, "I was worried about you."

The next morning, the sun climbed over the horizon, sending bloodred rays through the sky portending the judgment to come. Hanani arrived at their makeshift camp not long after.

"Salmone sent me to fetch you. He thought you might find today's events confusing, being new to our ways." His manner lacked its usual cheer. The weight of last night's news clearly pressed on him like a millstone. Rahab's heart went out to him.

"That was thoughtful," Imri said. "I worried about what we were supposed to do."

"We are to gather by family. Each family stays within their clan. Clans gather in their tribes. You stay with the tribe of Judah, which is under Caleb. Joshua will call the leaders of the tribes forward first, so that he might determine to which tribe the guilty one belongs."

"Do we follow Salmone?"

"Yes. Stay near me and my family. We too belong to the same clan."

Again, Rahab was impressed with the extraordinary order with which Israel gathered about Joshua. After prayer and words of consecration, Joshua called the twelve heads of the tribes forward. They filed before Joshua solemnly, leader after leader. Each one came forward and waited until he was dismissed with a nod from Joshua's salt-and-pepper head. Then Caleb stepped forth, his back ramrod straight, his face grim. Joshua stared at his old friend and comrade for long moments. "Judah," he said, his voice sounding suddenly old. "God has shown me it is the tribe of Judah."

A loud murmur rose up in the crowd. Rahab became aware that those standing closest to her and her family were throwing them dagger looks. "Filthy dogs," a faceless voice shouted.

Out of nowhere, a small rock hurled through the air. Before Rahab had time to react, it struck her cheekbone and glanced off onto the ground nearby. Instinctively, she lifted a hand to the sting at the side of her face. Her fingers came away bloody. From the corner of her eye, she saw Hanani bolt toward her. He shoved her behind him with a protective gesture and shouted something that Rahab didn't catch. But the crowd's vindictive fury was not appeased. Rahab realized through a fog of disbelief that many near them were bending to pick up rocks.

"Stop!" Salmone's roar ripped through the buzzing of the people around them. "What do you think you are doing?" He stationed himself next to Rahab, his face a mask of rigid disbelief. These were Salmone's own people. He probably knew every one of them by name. "Have you lost your minds?" he bellowed again.

"Salmone, it's them," one man spat, still clutching a stone in his hand. "Joshua picked the tribe of Judah, you saw for yourself. And these Canaanites are the latest addition to our tribe. You know it's them!"

"I know only one thing, Jakim. It's God's job to choose the guilty party. Now unless He has given you information He hasn't yet revealed to Joshua, you'd better drop that stone. All of you!"

He faced them with a ferocity that would have daunted a less agitated crowd. Still, no one moved. Salmone took a step forward. One simple step, Rahab thought, and yet Salmone carried in his stance such authority that Jakim loosened his grip on the stone and it rolled to the ground. Others surrounding them did the same.

Salmone turned to Rahab's family. "Come with me. You must remain near me until the true culprit is found. You won't be safe until then." Even through the fog of shock and pain, Rahab noticed that his face looked ashen. As he walked, he maneuvered her so that she was sandwiched between her brother Joa and himself.

"Were you hurt?" he asked without looking at her.

"It's of no account." With some effort she managed to keep her voice steady.

An explosive breath escaped Salmone's lips, but he said nothing. When they arrived where his family were stationed, he turned toward her. "Let me see," he said.

"It's nothing. Just a minor cut," she said, desperate to avert attention from herself. Embarrassment at her public denouncement tangled her belly in knots.

"Let. Me. See." Salmone said, enunciating each word through gritted teeth. Rahab assumed he was angry with her for causing him trouble. He had objected to them joining Israel from the first, saying they would incite bad feelings by their presence and behavior. She supposed he was proven right enough, though it was through no fault of hers.

Feeling stiff with shame, with injured pride, and with the unfairness of Salmone's resentment, she considered walking away. That was childish as well as dangerous, she decided. Resigned, she turned her face toward him. Carefully, he examined the wound on her cheek. His touch was feather-soft. Still, she flinched with pain.

"I'm sorry," he said, his voice clipped as he removed his hand. "The bleeding has stopped, but you'll have a nasty bruise. When we go home, Miriam will give you some ointment, which will help with the swelling."

"Did you call my name?" Miriam crooned as she joined them. She gazed at Rahab's battered cheek and Salmone's barely checked rage. "What happened?" she exclaimed.

"Someone threw a rock at Rahab when Joshua announced that the thief was from the house of Judah," Salmone fumed. "They were ready to stone the lot of them, if you can believe it."

"It wasn't our fault," Rahab cried out, unable to hold her tongue any longer. The idea that Salmone blamed her became unbearable.

"What do you mean?" Salmone turned on her, his eyes wide with astonishment. "Who said it was your fault?"

"You! You're angry!"

"Of course I'm angry! My people have committed a terrible wrong. They could have hurt you badly if I hadn't stepped in. I'd like to knock a few of their heads together right now!" He paused, and then asked more quietly, "Why would you think I was angry with you?"

Rahab turned her head away. "You wouldn't have had this trouble if we weren't here."

Salmone rubbed the side of his face. "I'm not so unreasonable to hold that against you. You are the one harmed. Do you think I'm a madman that I should blame you for this?" he said, gesturing toward her discolored cheek.

Relief washed through Rahab. Her sister Izzie walked over and put a gentle arm around her shoulder, and Rahab clung to her for a long moment, avoiding Salmone's hawklike attention.

Different clans from the tribe of Judah were still walking before Joshua, being dismissed one at a time. Then the Zerahites came. With a lifted arm, Joshua detained them. Rahab knew that this choice, though not identifying the thief, instantly cleared her and her family from any wrongdoing. They had no connection with the Zerahites. After this, events moved at a rapid pace. The families belonging to the clan of the Zerahites began coming forward, and Zimri was detained. In the end, it was Zimri's grandson Achan who was taken.

Achan confessed his guilt within the first few moments of questioning, knowing perhaps that denial was futile. Bursting into tears, Achan said, "It's true. I've sinned against the Lord." Hidden in the ground inside his tent they found his forbidden treasures: gold, silver, and a beautiful Babylonian robe.

Joshua laid a hand on Achan's shoulder. "Son, was it worth soiling your heart for such useless treasures? What needless trouble you have brought on us and on everyone who loves you," he said and sank down, holding his head in his hands. After a few moments of silence, he raised his chin, saying, "And your own life too shall be forfeit because you disobeyed God and lied about it, and would have gone on lying about it if you hadn't been caught. Too cheaply have you sold your life."

Rahab, confused by Joshua's words, looked over at Salmone, knowing he comprehended Joshua's implicit judgment. Salmone bent his head back and stared unseeingly into the sky. "Miriam."

"Yes?"

"Miriam, you know what must happen?"

Miriam nodded, her expression grim.

"His sons and daughters must have known about it; the loot was right under the ground of their tent. And yet they said nothing. They too will partake of the punishment, no doubt."

"Oh, Salmone."

"You don't have to stay here. You should go home, Rahab. Leave with Miriam. Let her tend to your face. That swelling must be painful. Perhaps your family might wish to join you, as well."

Rahab bit her lip. "What will happen now?"

"The sentence is death. By stoning."

"Oh." Her hand crept up to her throbbing cheek. She had learned a little too personally what such a sentence would mean. "In Canaan thieves are put to death as well."

"The theft of property among us isn't usually punished by death. But Achan had the gall to steal from God's share. That shows not only exorbitant greed, but also a total disregard for the Lord. Did he think he could get away with it? That's why the punishment is so severe." He turned to look at the citizens of Jericho for a moment. "Quite a first day for you. Please feel free to leave; you can wait in my tent. It will be more comfortable than being outdoors in this sun."

Relief flooded through Rahab at the thought of going. She was beginning to tremble in the aftermath of the ugly attack on her life. Her cheek ached and her legs felt unsteady. Salmone's cool tent with its stuffed cushions and serene atmosphere beckoned like an oasis. With most of Israel absent from the camp, there would be unparalleled peace and quiet.

"Thank you. I would like to go." She looked at the members of her family to ascertain their preference. As if by prior consent, the women banded together and chose to go back, while the men elected to stay with Salmone and see Achan's fate through.

Miriam, who appeared relieved to miss this part of Achan's trial, led the way back through the confusing maze of Israel's camp. They walked in heavy silence, each stewing in her own thoughts. Inside the tent, Miriam tended the cut on Rahab's face, cleaning it with delicate care before treating it with a soothing ointment of her own making. "A little deeper," she said, "and I would have had to sew it up. As it is, the mark will fade in time. I will give you some of this ointment, which you must rub on the cut every day for the next week. Which one of those bovine wretches did this to you, did you see?"

"No. It happened too fast."

Everyone was soul-weary by this time, and Miriam suggested that they partake of a simple repast. Rahab's sisters-in-law and mother excused themselves to return to their own settlement, wanting to relieve Rahab's oldest niece who had been minding the younger children throughout the morning. But Rahab and Izzie remained with Miriam and, after eating barley cakes and vegetable soup, helped her clean up.

"Rahab, are you still in pain? You seem preoccupied," Miriam said as they put away the crockery into a covered basket.

"No. No more pain, thanks to your cure. I suppose I'm anxious. Do you think our neighbors will relent now that we've been proven innocent? Will they stop being suspicious of us?"

"I hope so. They'll certainly regret this morning's behavior. Would you like us to pray about it?"

Rahab had never prayed aloud with anyone. The prospect of starting with someone as experienced as Miriam seemed daunting. She feared she would appear foolish. Then again, to be able to pray alongside a friend was a joy she was loath to miss. "I don't know how to pray as I should. I'll sound ignorant," she admitted.

"I don't know how God measures ignorance, but I doubt He applies the same standards as we do. Salmone once told me that the Lord would speak to Moses face-to-face, as a man speaks with his friend. I have never forgotten that. I am no Moses, but I seek the friendship of God. I pray as I have been instructed: I speak the words of blessing that my father and mother taught me. But I pray also from my heart, as if I were speaking to a friend. As if I were speaking to a father. I have memorized some of the prayers of the great leaders of our people—the words Moses spoke to the Lord, or the song of Miriam. I can teach you these things. Most importantly, though, I believe God desires to hear us. It delights His heart when we turn to Him with open hearts, without artifice."

Rahab longed to experience the kind of intimacy that Miriam's words evoked. Izzie also wished to learn to pray. So the three women stood respectfully and Miriam began with the traditional blessings: *Blessed art Thou, O Lord our God, King of eternity.* She wove Moses's own words into her prayers:

Teach me Your ways so I may know You and continue to find favor with You. Rahab noticed that Miriam began to speak her own prayers, her words emerging humble and unembellished, sincere phrases flowing without self-consciousness. She felt emboldened to pray in the same way, remembering phrases from the Law and blessings that had been taught to her in her days outside Israel's camp. Izzie soon joined in. They stopped noticing the passage of time as they entered into a sweet realm that felt more real than the one they normally inhabited.

When they finished, Miriam fetched a battered harp and taught them the songs of Moses and Miriam. Rahab had never felt closer to God, or closer to experiencing true friendship.

CHAPTER THIRTEEN

Salmone entered his tent followed by a weary-looking Joshua. He heard the women's voices, lifted in a song of worship, before his eyes found them. Both men had left their shoes outside the tent, and their entrance made no sound. The women continued to sing, unaware of their new audience. Without thinking, Salmone's gaze sought Rahab. He searched the bent face, wanting to assure himself that she was well. Parallel to the narrow nose, an ugly gash ran down her white cheek, barely closed. He remembered the moment he had seen that rock fly, realizing it would find its target, maddeningly helpless to do anything about it. He had run, shoving people out of his way, knowing the while that he would be too late to protect her. He still shook when he thought of it. And it shook him still further that he was affected so deeply by the minor incident. He was a soldier who had seen the worst of war. One flying projectile against a relative stranger should barely perturb him.

But as he stood in the shadows, the quiet atmosphere of the tent began to settle his jangled nerves. The tension began to drain out of him, and Salmone became more aware of the women's familiar song than of the memory of the attack on Rahab, or even of Rahab herself. Before long, drawn irresistibly into the worshipful chant, Salmone and Joshua joined their baritone voices to that of the women:

> *In Your unfailing love You will lead*
> *The people You have redeemed.*

Feminine gasps mingled with masculine voices begging pardon.

"You must excuse us, my daughters, for intruding on you," Joshua said. "Walking in here was like walking out of a sandstorm and into a quiet garden. Salmone and I are grateful to you for your sweet song. It has revived my heart."

"My lord," his sister said, prostrating herself before Joshua, with Rahab and Izzie following suit.

"You honor Salmone and me by visiting our tent," Miriam said. "Let me bring you refreshments."

Joshua drew Miriam to her feet. "Rise daughters."

Rahab stood. "Izzie and I should return. Forgive our encroachment."

Joshua waved his hand. "Nonsense. It's you I've come to see."

"Me?"

"Watch out, Joshua," Salmone cut in. "She's likely to repeat everything you say when she is agitated."

"And why should she be agitated? Come, Rahab, and sit by me."

Rahab obeyed, her movements halting as she knelt by Joshua. It did not escape Salmone that she tucked her hands into a fold of her dress to hide their trembling. He frowned, not understanding her extreme apprehension around Joshua. Or himself. It was as if she always expected them to put her down. Or worse, to cast her out. Why couldn't the woman comprehend that she was safe now?

Rahab tried to quiet the rapid beating of her heart. It made little sense that a man of Joshua's stature would trouble himself on her account.

"Salmone told me what happened this morning." Joshua spoke as if on cue. "I wanted to see for myself that you had recovered."

"You shouldn't have concerned yourself, my lord. As you see, I'm well."

"What I see is the mark of my people's insolence on your lovely face." Joshua exhaled as though his breath weighed too much. "This has been the most abominable day. Achan is dead and buried in the valley beyond. Already the people call it the Valley of Achor for the trouble we have been through over this whole matter. It makes me furious that my people have added to our troubles by raising their hand against you. Please forgive us for our arrogance and prejudice, Rahab."

Rahab shook her head. "Their suspicion is understandable." *Wrenching, but understandable.* "I hope that in time, they'll come to trust us."

"I will do what I can for you. I can promise that none of our number shall lift a hand against you or your family again. They might remain cold and distant for a time, though. You must forbear until they come to know you better. Don't give way to discouragement."

"Thank you, my lord, for your help."

"No need to thank me." He gave a tired smile. "It's only your due. You're one of us now, no matter how the children of Israel treat you."

Rahab looked down. These were sweet words, by far some of the sweetest she had ever heard. Words of belonging. Words of vindication. Joshua was treating her as though he truly accepted her. Cared for her well-being, even. It seemed impossible that such a man—lofty in position as well as holiness—would stoop to provide for her needs. And yet here he was, exhausted from a sleepless night and burdened by a nightmare day, come expressly for the purpose of reassuring her.

Perhaps that was why she couldn't quite accept the validity of his words. She heard them. Her brain understood them. But in her deepest being, she could not receive them. In her secret heart she believed that it was a matter of time before Joshua would be disappointed with her. Like everyone else, he would turn his back on her when he came to know her. She bit her lip and frowned. Rahab knew that she would feel the bitterness of Joshua's rejection far more than the sweetness of his present support. The rejection would feel real. True. His praise felt hollow.

Joshua, misconstruing her expression, said to Salmone, "She's weary. Salmone, walk Rahab and her sister to their settlement and make sure their neighbors behave. Then come to my tent after supper, and I will tell the leaders about what we shall do regarding Ai."

They rose in respect as Joshua stood to leave, but he refused further escort outdoors. The tent seemed to shrink in his absence. Salmone turned to Rahab. "Would you like to rest here awhile before we go?"

"No, I'm well. And you don't need to see us home. Izzie and I can take care of ourselves."

"Can you?" Without warning, Salmone ran a finger down her cheek, just avoiding the livid wound that marked the tender flesh. Rahab shivered at his touch, and he drew his finger back, curling his hand into a fist. "I'll walk you home," he said through clenched teeth, and Rahab sensed that she had annoyed him again. What had she done wrong now?

Izzie, blissfully unmindful of this dense soup of emotions, gave a cheerful smile. "You're good to us. We'll be glad of your company."

Salmone's half smile was drenched in irony as it turned on Rahab. "A mutual feeling, I am sure."

Miriam packed some salve as well as a large ball of fresh cheese and half a dozen pan breads, which she insisted Izzie and Rahab take. "You've had a hard day. A little treat will cheer you." Rahab was too tired to argue and Izzie too cheerful a receiver to think of arguing.

Just as they were leaving, Miriam ran back into the tent and came out with a feather-filled cushion. "Rahab, take this. You'll need something softer than a blanket on sand for your cheek tonight."

"Oh no, I can't take your cushion. I've eaten your lunch. I've drunk your water. I've taken your cheese. I've received your bread. I've borrowed your salve. I can't take one more thing."

"Give me that cushion!" Salmone said. "You're not sleeping on sand tonight and that's final,"

"But—"

"Not another word. Not a sigh. Not a peep. Not one more objection out of you. Understand?"

"Salmone!" Miriam sounded shocked.

"That goes for you too, sister. We're going to have a quiet, peaceful, tranquil walk. Then I will knock some of our neighbors' heads together. And afterward I will have another quiet, peaceful, tranquil walk home."

The following day Rahab woke up clutching Miriam's cushion, groggy from disturbing dreams. Her nieces and nephews, already nauseatingly alert, shrieked about the camp, playing hide-and-seek. She sat up and winced. Her cheek hurt. Her head pounded. Her body revolted against sleeping so long without proper bedding. She wished she could be alone and quiet. Instead, a four-year-old boy and a five-year-old girl and their eight-year-old cousin piled on top of her, insisting Auntie Rahab hide them under her blankets. She held their cuddly bodies close to hers and dove under the covers. They giggled with abominable jubilation, moving about until they became a tangle of arms and legs.

"Don't wriggle so much or the others will find you," she warned her nephew. In his effort to quiet down, he raised an elbow and shoved it into Rahab's face, too close to her tender cheek.

"Oof!" Her head reverberated with jarring pain. Shoving the blanket down, she sat up. Salmone stood over her like a big oak tree, his face hidden by the blaze of the sun.

"I thought you would have risen by now," he commented.

Shading her eyes with a hand, she looked up and realized that the sun sat high in the sky. It was late morning already. "Oh."

"Not talkative in the mornings?"

"No." Her nieces and nephew started wriggling afresh, growing impatient. First one, then another, then the last sprang free from the blanket's grasp and ran off.

Salmone's eyes followed their progress with good-natured interest. Shifting his focus back to Rahab he said, "Do you always take so many people to bed with you?"

Shocked, she stared at him with widened eyes. He became very still, his face frozen, his skin turning a dark red. She realized he had simply blundered. He hadn't thought through what he was saying. Those same words, if uttered in deliberate sarcasm, would have reduced her to a defensive barb. Under the circumstances, however, they struck her as funny. She put her hand over her mouth, but the laughter leaked out. "Thank you," she said.

"What for?" He stared at her like she had misplaced her mind.

"For a moment you forgot my past. You'd never have said that if you remembered."

He frowned at her and took a step back. "I've brought your tent. I came to tell you. Your tent is here. A couple of my men helped me bring it. They'll stay and show you how to set it up. Your brothers and father aren't around. So I came to find you."

For Salmone this was babbling. The laughter dried up in her mouth. A wave of desolation settled over her as she sat there being the object Salmone tried to avoid looking at. He may have experienced a momentary lapse of memory, but clearly it was a mistake he preferred not to repeat. She was still Rahab, the Canaanite prostitute Joshua had foisted upon him, and he was still one of the high leaders of Israel, a man of honor and influence. The gap between them could never be bridged. Why she found these obvious realities so bleak, she could not explain. She became aware once more that her head was pounding and massaged her temple.

She had remained in bed too long. With an ungraceful motion she rose up. She had gone to sleep with her clothes on, too tired to change. Now she stood, decently covered from neck to calf, her clothes a rumpled mess. Salmone seemed to be finding his toes fascinating, so he wasn't likely to be offended by her appearance.

He had gone to considerable trouble to secure them this tent in the midst of a hectic, anxious time. Rather than focus on what he could not give her—respect, admiration, true belonging—she ought to focus on what he did offer. He was a generous man, helpful, fair, protective of his flock, even the flock of which he did not approve. "Thank you for the trouble you have taken on our behalf," she said.

Salmone nodded once, pivoted on his heel and left. She had never seen a man move so fast.

Sighing, she turned and noticed the two men who had helped him carry the tent, standing in the middle of their camp. They were busy conversing and took no notice of her. She glanced at the tent with curiosity. Behemoth-like, the thing spread on the ground giving no clue as to its beginning or ending. It was made of some kind of dung-colored hide, sturdy enough to hold off the rains and the heat of the sun. Enormous and thick, it must have required all three men to carry it. By no stretch of the imagination could it be construed as elegant. But it would be more comfortable than sleeping outdoors.

Rahab walked over to the men and introduced herself.

"You, we know," the skinny one said. They were both much younger than she had first thought, no older than seventeen.

The second one, more well-rounded and trying to grow his beard, asked, "Is it true that you let Ezra Ben Isaac down the wall of Jericho by yourself? This, I have to see. Show me how you managed that feat. Come. There is a tall rock near here. You can let me down just as you did Ezra."

Rahab held up her hands. "Some things are only meant to be experienced once."

"You won't show me your strength?"

"Not unless the Lord gives it to me again."

"Aaah," the skinny one said like he was the sage of Jerusalem.

"You fellows have more than enough strength to make up for my lack if you managed to carry that tent," she said.

"Well, Salmone helped. A little," he said with a distinct lisp.

"What are your names? You know mine."

"I'm Abel," the skinny one said. "And this is my cousin Adam."

"How do you do?"

"How do I do what?" asked Adam, puzzled. Abel elbowed him in the side.

"She means she's happy to meet you, genius."

Although their languages had sprung from the same root, and Rahab grew more accustomed to Israel's speech with each passing day, there remained differences in their accent and dialect that made communication interesting. Their etiquette too, though overlapping in some ways, offered challenging moments. In most ways, the citizens of Jericho conducted life with greater formality than the Israelites. Occasionally, however, they found that their Canaanite ways proved far more permissive than Israel's.

One afternoon when Hanani and Miriam were with them at the camp, Rahab's brother Joa casually passed wind. For the people of Jericho this was an acceptable means of relieving the tensions of the body. But Rahab noticed the Hebrews covering their mouths with their hands and turning puce.

"Is something funny?" Joa, always sensitive, growled.

In reply, Hanani shook his head, his face turning purple.

"Is it the lower cough?" Rahab guessed. "Do Hebrews not do that in public?"

"The *what?*" Hanani interjected, his expression arrested. "The lower cough, did you call it?" He threw a look at Miriam, and the two bent over double, their shoulders shaking.

Poor Joa stiffened with self-conscious indignation. "It's perfectly acceptable where I come from."

"Oh, I have no doubt," Miriam hurried to assure him. "We just . . . never heard—"

"What? You're going to tell me you never heard a lower cough before? Come! Even the children of Israel must do that sometimes," Joa exploded.

Miriam buried her face in her hands, her whole body quaking. Hanani interjected, "Yes, yes of course we do, though usually in more private circumstances. It's only that we never heard it referred to by that particular phrase."

Someone cleared his throat, drawing Rahab back to the present. She looked at her young helpers who had delivered her new home on their backs and bestowed a wide smile on them. "Salmone said you would help us set up this tent. Do you know how to do that?" She managed not to blurt out that they looked too young to tie their sandals.

"Sure. We've set them up and broken them down hundreds of times." Adam looked around. "You'd better set up your tent facing north this time of year. It will be cooler."

Abel shifted from foot to foot. "Where are your men? Setting up a tent requires muscle."

"I'm not sure. Let me find out." Rahab noticed Izzie stirring a pot of porridge. "Izzie, where are the men?"

Izzie rose and stretched her back. "They left at sunrise with Ezra. He wanted to show them some of the farms. Joshua is eager to start working the land."

"Well, our tent has arrived. We need them to set it up. Salmone has sent two young strapping fellows to help."

Izzie bit the inside of her cheek. "I don't know when they'll be back."

The sisters went over to the men and Rahab introduced Izzie. "How do you do?" Izzie asked.

Adam grinned at Abel. "I'm happy to meet you too."

"My brothers have gone with Ezra to examine farmlands. I'm not sure when we expect them back," Rahab explained.

Abel rubbed his clean-shaven chin. "We still have to fetch the rods, nails, and rings. It's near enough to noon. We'll stop and have lunch before returning. Perhaps they'll be back by then."

"Please have lunch with us. We would be honored if you would stay," Rahab offered.

Adam scratched his head. "Er, lunch? Umm, well, all right, I guess." Abel nodded with a sideway jerk of his head. She was so delighted to be able to give back a little in return for the favors they were receiving that she ignored their half-hearted responses.

Rahab seated them on a blanket they had spread under the shade of one of their neighboring tents. As they rested, the two sisters scrambled to put together a hearty lunch. To the porridge, Rahab added a few precious spices, which she had had the foresight to bring from Jericho. Izzie melted some of Miriam's cheese on the bread before serving it. The day before, Rahab had used a favorite family recipe to make raisin cakes. She knew this recipe broke none of Israel's stringent food laws, which Miriam had painstakingly taught them in the previous weeks. They set the food before their guests and joined them for the meal. After the first hesitant bites, Abel and Adam began to make impressive inroads into the food.

"This tastes marvelous!" Abel said around a mouthful of porridge and cheesy bread. For a skinny man, he certainly knew how to put away food. "I could eat a barrel full. What did you put in here?"

Izzie and Rahab grinned at each other. "Just spices. A little cinnamon and honey on the cakes, with the nuts ground very fine. That's the secret," Rahab replied.

"You women of Jericho can certainly cook," Adam said between mouthfuls. Rahab recalled that his generation had been raised on a mysterious substance called manna as their staple. In all likelihood, they had minimal familiarity with the use of spices or the art of cooking with different ingredients. She sat up straighter as she realized that there might be a few things she could do better than the women of Israel.

CHAPTER FOURTEEN

Rahab's brothers and father hadn't returned by the time Adam and Abel plodded back, panting with the effort of carrying several large wooden poles between them. They decided they could start the process by themselves and shooed Izzie and Rahab away. Rahab, suspecting that their work would last into the evening, fetched her sisters-in-law to plan an evening meal fit for their new companions.

Joa, Karem, and Imri sauntered into the camp within the hour, and if they felt weariness, they forgot about it once they saw the tent. By early evening, their tent was up in its full glory, looking similar to many of the other tents that dotted the camp's sprawling grounds. The whole family insisted that Adam and Abel stay for dinner, and they obliged far more readily than they had for the noonday meal.

They ate outside, enjoying the refreshing breeze as they admired their new domicile. Partway through the meal, Rahab noticed a couple of women lingering at the edge of their camp. A curly haired, snow-white lamb tottered on knobby legs between them. Rahab assumed they had been disturbed by their lively conversation and stood up with a quick apology on her lips.

One of them drew nearer. "You must be Rahab. Ezra has spoken so much about you. I'm his sister, Abigail. And this is Leah, Hanani's sister-in-law."

"Welcome. I am honored to meet you both." Rahab dipped a hasty curtsy before them. "Please come and join us. We are just sharing a meal."

"No, no. Thank you. We only came to bring you this." Abigail pulled on a short, tattered leash tied around the lamb's neck. "A gift from both our families for saving our brothers' lives. We ought to have been here sooner. Forgive our rudeness for the delay." She looked down.

"A gift? For me? But that's completely unnecessary. They saved our lives every bit as much as I saved theirs. It has been a joy to have your brothers as our friends. Indeed, they have helped us without cease. If there were a debt, which there is not, they have more than discharged it. With dividends."

Abigail shook her head and pulled the lamb forward. "These men mean the world to us. We wouldn't have stopped mourning them the length of our days should something have befallen them. We know the debt we owe you. 'Rahab saved our lives more than once,' they say. 'She has greater faith than our fathers and mothers,' they declare to anyone with ears. They praise you everywhere. You have been good to them, Rahab. You must let us thank you."

Rahab hesitated, reluctant to accept a gift for something she felt she didn't deserve. Yet she also loathed to offend anyone who belonged to Ezra and Hanani's families. She decided she had best humble herself rather than run the risk of insulting these women. "I thank you both. We will treasure our first lamb in our home amongst Israel."

Abigail and Leah both smiled at the same time. Without thinking, Rahab fumbled for Leah's hand and took it into her own. "Won't you join us for supper?"

"Come Abigail. It's the best meal you ever had," Adam pronounced from the fire.

Abigail knotted her brows for a moment. "Adam Ben Hosea, is that you with your mouth stuffed?"

"As yours would be if you had any sense, girl. Come and sit. You've never tasted food like this."

Abigail covered her mouth and looked at Rahab through widened eyes.

Rahab held up a palm in peace. "The food has been prepared according to Israel's laws. Salmone's sister, Miriam, taught us."

"Oh."

"Join us, please. Taste a little."

Leah came first, avoiding Abigail's accusing glare. She sat down next to Abel, who promptly dipped bread in one of the bowls and handed it to her. Abigail, who appeared a few years older than the others, squared her shoulders and joined the crowd. Rahab tied the lamb to one of the tent's posts, caressed its curly head, and returned to her guests. She sensed that Abigail had only joined the others with the intention of looking after them. With time, however, she noticed Abigail's guard slipping in increments until she was talking and laughing as freely as the rest, dipping her bread into the bowls without pause.

Rahab studied the scene about her and was struck by the

miraculous quality of it. In one day, God had provided them with a new home and new friends. Hope filled her chest, like a spring leaf, unfurling. She laughed at something Karem said, even though she hadn't heard what the words were. She realized that she was happy. When had she last tasted carefree joy, untainted with guilt or fear?

"You look much better than you did this morning," a voice said in her ear.

She twisted around, finding her face a breath away from Salmone's. She dragged in a gulp of air. "You startled me."

"Did I?"

"We're having a feast. We have guests and everything. Won't you join us? There's plenty of food."

"Thank you. No. I have little time. I came to say farewell. You should send the girls home too. Ezra and Hanani will be leaving with us tomorrow."

"Farewell? Where are you going?" But Rahab already knew the answer.

"To Ai. We must finish what we began. Other men are being sent ahead of us this evening. The rest of us leave before sunup."

In one moment, Rahab's fragile sense of happiness shattered. Salmone was going into battle. In a matter of hours, he would be facing arrows and swords and knives and violent men. The specter of Hamish's headless torso lying in front of her old inn rose up, making her want to wretch. She had had nightmares of that scene, could still smell the cloying odor of death, could still see the horsefly rising out of that gruesome, gaping mouth. What if that happened to Salmone? The thought throbbed like a gaping wound.

She turned, panicked that Salmone might see in her expression something of her churning horror. But as she began to move away, he took her hand and pulled her back.

His dark eyes bore into her. "What, no goodbye? And I came all this way."

Rahab tried to swallow past the stone that seemed lodged in her throat. She feared if she opened her mouth to speak, she would burst into tears. Or say words that revealed too much. She stared at him as dumb as her new sheep, unable to lower her gaze. "Goodbye," she grunted. It was the only thing she could manage before pulling her hand out of his and rushing headlong into the family's new tent.

As Salmone said his narrow-eyed goodbye, resentful of his own need to seek the Canaanite woman before going to battle, he was peripherally aware that thirty thousand of Israel's best fighting men were commencing a stealth ambush on Ai. Under the cover of deepest night, they made their way to the ridge of Jebel et-Tawil, out of sight of the watchmen at Ai or Bethel, but close enough to observe both cities. There, they would hide in silence, unobserved, biding the long hours until battle began.

At first light, Joshua led a second, much smaller army toward Ai. It was to this force that Salmone belonged. There was nothing secret about this march. The men approached the city with brazen intent and settled themselves just north of Ai in broad daylight. Unlike the men on the ambush mission who had covered their feet in tough canvas in order to mute the sound of their marching, Salmone and his fellow fighting men wore sandals with wooden soles. On the packed dirt of the rough countryside, their marching feet sounded like the beat of well-timed drums. Salmone's heart beat with that drum until he felt that he was one with it—a miniature cog in a seamless battering ram. He was ready. He was ready to show the men of Ai what the Lord could do. Like a mobile wall, the small force moved behind Joshua until they arrived at the narrow valley north of the city. They camped on the hilltop with the valley between them and Ai.

When the sun began to set, Joshua went into the valley in plain sight of the watchmen on the city walls. He paraded right under their noses and waved a friendly salute to the soldiers. They heard him laugh as their arrows fell short of his heart by cubits. Salmone gave a hard smile as Joshua scrambled back up the hill and joined his men. They would have to scramble faster than Joshua in the morning when the real fighting broke out.

A few silvery green trees dotted the hilltop, and Salmone found one of these to lean against. Somewhere out of sight of Israel and Ai, he knew many of his friends lay hidden for a second night, awaiting Joshua's signal. Like the night before most of the battles he had participated in, Salmone was too tense to sleep.

He thought of Miriam and her great hug as she had said her goodbyes to him. His heart softened at the thought of her. He wanted to provide a safe life for his sister. Sometimes, he felt a chafing frustration at having to pace his plans according to God's time. Sometimes, he wished God would hasten to establish them in security already. The thought made him turn red, and he was grateful for the dark that covered his face. Beneath the layers of godly obedience and faith, there still lay this unconquered chasm of self-will. He wanted to be his own master. He wanted to bend God to his own desires. Was it a wonder that Joshua had accused him of hypocrisy?

The thought brought Rahab to his mind. Or rather pulled her back to the forefront of his attention. He had hardly taken a step since their parting without a muted awareness of her filling his thoughts. When the call to battle had come from Joshua, Salmone had experienced a fierce need to seek her out. To etch her face into his memory. To say farewell, perhaps for the last time. He knew war could mean death. It was a reality he faced before every fight. Even those who vanquished sometimes fell in battle. You could win and still get injured. Still die. It wasn't the possibility of dying that tormented him, however. It was the thought of leaving without seeing Rahab.

He told himself he had no business seeking her out. She was nothing to him, and she could never become anything to him. Yet he felt that if he didn't go to her, see her, hear her voice, he would choke. And so he had trudged one unwilling step after another into her camp to find her laughing with his friends, looking like she had belonged to Israel all her born days.

He swallowed hard as he remembered her eyes when he had told her he was going to war. The beautiful golden eyes had filled with terror. Rahab was far from indifferent toward him. The realization offered an artesian well of satisfaction. The satisfaction merely vexed him more, and he growled under his breath. Ai was an easier enemy to manage than his own heart.

Before the sun had risen, the small force with Joshua was already falling into formation. With languid arrogance they made their way to a stretch of land overlooking Arabah. The location presented a poor choice from Israel's standpoint. They were exposed on every side, and Ai's warriors would have the advantage. Salmone knew they appeared like fools to a people who had already thrashed them once. Easy prey. Which was just as Joshua wanted it.

The king of Ai acted as expected. With the first faint rays of the sun he and his men charged out of the city, full of confidence and bluster as they shouted insults against the small army facing them.

Have you come back for more?

You want more corpses for your collection?

Our pigeons fight better than your warriors.

Would you like a few lessons from our little girls?

There was no shortage of insults that morning. Salmone did not allow his expression to change, but remained stony before every word. Pride held no place in this plan. In a few moments, he and his brothers would seem even greater fools than this. The men of Ai kept coming. But just before the first wave of Ai's army reached Israel's defensive line, Joshua screamed the shout to fall back. Israel's fighting men turned and ran toward the desert, away from the city. To the enemy, they looked like cowards, running away.

A great shout arose from the army of Ai. Some laughed, some whooped, twirling swords and clubs in the air. Salmone was aware that Israel's rapid retreat filled the hearts of her foe with new bravado. Everything in him itched to stop, to turn around, and engage this brash adversary with the courage that welled up in him. But instead he forced his feet to run faster, biding his time. Dust rose up from thousands of sandals pounding the wilderness terrain. Salmone tasted it with every breath, a dry earthy flavor that parched his throat and threatened to choke him. He swallowed, forcing himself to breathe rhythmically through his nostrils, keeping his lips locked shut. Throwing a quick look over his shoulder he saw with satisfaction that even the watchmen on the walls had left their posts and joined the chase. It was doubtful that any men remained in Ai or Bethel. Every man had joined in this pursuit, confident of victory.

Suddenly, Joshua stopped and turned around. He held a sword in one hand and a javelin in the other. Salmone saw Joshua raise the javelin toward Ai. As soon as he did this, the huge force waiting in ambush rose up from hiding and rushed into the city.

Unaware of the disaster entering their city, the men of Ai caught up with Joshua's smaller force and engaged them in battle. Swinging their swords enthusiastically they came against what they believed to be a vanquished and cowardly enemy. Salmone, ever in the front lines, found himself set upon by two men at once. The first was massive-shouldered and bulging with an impressive array of muscles. He wielded a broadsword, slashing it through the air with a manic flair Salmone couldn't help but admire. The other was armed with a knife that he handled with ease, flicking it from hand to hand with a steady, graceful grip. Salmone raised an eyebrow. These two were no mere farmers playing soldier during a national emergency. They were trained soldiers. And they seemed set on sampling Salmone's entrails for breakfast.

Salmone waved his fingers, beckoning. "How about we do this one-on-one?"

The man with the knife flicked it into the air and watched it twirl. "Too boring" he said, deftly catching it by the handle and pitching it straight toward Salmone's chest. Salmone pivoted with a lightning-quick movement, barely avoiding the knife and bringing his elbow crashing into his other opponent's broad back. The impact of bone on bone jarred the larger man, and he stumbled two awkward half steps—giving Salmone just enough time to run his sword into the man's massive right arm. The blade cut deep, tearing muscle and sinew and reaching bone.

Blood splattered across the warrior's chest, and he screamed with rage. To his credit, he did not lose his grip on his sword. Demonstrating considerable self-control, he shifted the sword to his left hand and brought it down against Salmone's midriff with uncanny precision. Salmone barely saw the arc of gleaming metal as it came toward him. He jumped back, bringing his own sword down to intercept the powerful strike. His quick reaction minimized the deadly force of the blow, but Salmone could not completely escape its sharp bite. It slashed across his abdomen, drawing a thin line of blood.

Salmone ignored the searing flash of pain, knowing the wound to be superficial. In his peripheral vision he saw the knife man pulling another weapon from his belt. "I'm as eager as you to finish this fight," Salmone shouted above the battle noise, "but I think it only fair to warn you that your city is on fire."

The man with the knife glanced over his shoulder, and then turned fully around to stare at the thick column of black smoke. But Salmone's other opponent refused to be sidetracked. "Shut up, Hebrew scum! You can try your trickery on the dead because I'm going to pulverize every one of your little chicken bones," he snarled.

Raising his sword, he came at Salmone with a lunge. Despite his injury, he executed a precise thrust. He was a more skillful swordsman than Salmone, wielding his weapon with lethal strength. But Salmone moved with greater agility. He dodged to the right to avoid a mortal thrust, then immediately feinted left. The broadsword followed left as he had hoped, and Salmone pivoted right instead, ramming straight into his opponent's body. It took the man only a flash to shift the sword back toward Salmone, but the move left his belly undefended. Salmone brought his sword straight down into the vulnerable flesh.

The man's eyes grew large with shock. A curious gurgle erupted from his throat, and he crumpled to the ground, motionless. Salmone grabbed the carved hilt of a dagger from the dead man's sash and tucked the weapon away in his own belt. "You won't be needing this where you're going." He wiped his bloody sword on the soldier's tunic, his eyes already scanning the area for further threat.

He spotted the knife-wielding soldier standing frozen some distance from the city walls, distracted by the attack on Ai. He was still in throwing range, Salmone realized. He hefted the carved hilt of his newly acquired knife, and was about to aim before spotting the larger force of Israel's army emerging from Ai. The men of Israel were running toward the battle. Soon, the knife-wielding warrior would be caught between Israel's two forces. He would have no hope of escape. Shrugging his shoulder, Salmone left him to his impending death and turned to the conflict closer at hand.

Within the hour, the battle thickened as both the armies of Israel drew close, surrounding the men of Bethel and Ai. Their enemies now fought with the desperation of fear rather than the bravado of victory. They fought with a reckless ferocity that required all of Israel's skill to repulse.

Salmone found himself fighting a wild bear of a man who wielded an ax, which he occasionally liked to use as a club. Salmone worked to keep his head attached to his neck, prancing around the colossal figure like a Canaanite dancing girl. Near him, Hanani was fighting a wiry man who wielded two swords, one whirling in each hand. Salmone noticed that Hanani was struggling, remaining on the defensive, trying to parry thrust after relentless thrust.

He realized he'd need to assist Hanani soon, but the bear he faced required his entire attention. He ducked low to escape a blow, and swung his sword at the man's legs, trying to cut him off from below. The man jumped a full cubit into the air, easily avoiding Salmone's sword. Salmone looked at him open-mouthed before rolling hastily out of the way of the club-like swing of the ax coming down toward his head as the man landed back on the ground.

Salmone took a few steps back, bringing him close to Hanani. "Hold fast. I'll be with you soon," he yelled. He noticed that Hanani hadn't the energy even to nod.

Salmone's opponent lunged with his ax, and Salmone spun to avoid being disemboweled. As he did so, he noticed the knife handler who had attacked him earlier, standing five cubits away, a knife held at the ready in his dexterous fingers. His gaze was fixed on Hanani.

CHAPTER FIFTEEN

"No!" Salmone roared. Frantically, he looked for aid. He found no one near enough to shield Hanani. This was his fault. He had ignored a dangerous foe, and now his friend would pay the price of his bad judgment. "No," he said again, this time making a promise.

He lifted his sword high, leaving himself completely open to the frontal attack of his opponent's ax. The man came at him without hesitation. Just before impact, Salmone twirled in a full circle so that the ax missed him by a hair. He brought his sword down under his arm and behind him at an impossible angle that the ax man had not anticipated. With a sickening thud, the sword's tip pierced through flesh and bone. The man folded with a strangled grunt.

Salmone wasted no time freeing his sword. Instead, he reached into his belt and pulled out the knife he had tucked there earlier. Almost in slow motion, he saw the man with the twirling knife lift the hilt, take aim and begin his throw. In the same moment, Salmone realized Hanani's opponent had managed to block

Hanani's sword with one of his own and was about to thrust his second sword into Hanani's stomach. It would be a deadly blow.

Salmone's breath caught. Two opponents—two lethal attacks, both trained on Hanani.

The two-handed sword man stood closer, his throat conveniently exposed. Salmone took quick aim and threw. The wiry soldier took the dagger in his jugular and crumpled to the ground with a great gush of blood. In the same fluid motion, Salmone pitched the full weight of his body into Hanani, knocking him to the ground. But the body-slam placed Salmone where Hanani had stood an instant before. Exactly where the dagger was flying. There was no time to evade it. With a force that brought Salmone to his knees, the knife penetrated his belt and robe and sunk into his stomach. The impact was excruciating. Then came a curious numbness.

Hanani sprung to his side looking as grey as the smoke rising out of Ai. "No, no, no! O Lord. O Lord, help us!" he cried.

Salmone began to shake violently. His body pitched backward. Hanani caught him just in time to prevent him from hitting his head on the rocky ground, bruising his skull and adding to his already considerable injuries. He set his friend down with careful hands. Salmone managed to reach up and grab a handful of Hanani's garment. "Pull this thing out of me," he gasped.

Hanani looked at him with eyes that were wide and tear-filled, and shook his head.

"Do it. Quickly."

Hanani stared into the sky for a moment, then wrapped his hand around the hilt of the dagger and pulled. The pain was beyond anything Salmone had ever experienced. He screamed in agony, unable to silence the animal sound that emerged from his throat. He was still conscious, taking labored breaths, aware of the flood of hot blood that gushed out of him. "Now get him," he whispered. "Before he hurts someone else." He shoved the dagger Hanani had just extracted back toward his friend.

Hanani nodded and stood, holding the knife that dripped with his friend's blood. Through a haze of pain Salmone raised his head, and noticed that Hanani had to wipe the tears from his eyes to be able to see. The knife man was trying to run out of their range, but the field was littered with fighting and fallen men, and it slowed his progress. Hanani took careful aim and let the dagger fly. Salmone managed to hold his head up long enough to see the dagger bury in the man's broad back. He dropped mid-stride and landed facedown.

For a moment Salmone lost his hold on consciousness, his head lolling back on the dirt. He came to in Hanani's arms. "Salmone!" Hanani's voice sounded hoarse. "Hold on!"

"It's all right."

"It should have been me! It should have been me!"

Salmone wanted to shake his head, but didn't have the strength. He looked down and saw the copious flow of blood staining his garments and soaking into the ground. He knew a mortal wound when he saw one. *Lord, have mercy on me.*

He forced his eyes open again and tried to focus on Hanani. "Not your fault. I had a chance to kill him earlier and didn't." He lifted his head to examine his bleeding belly. Beads of sweat covered his brow. "Looks bad. Take care of my sister for me, Hanani."

"Take care of your own sister! You stay alive, Salmone ben Nahshon, or I'll beat you to a pulp."

Salmone managed a trembling smile. "Go finish this battle, Hanani. I'll be fine here."

Hanani looked mutinous. Salmone managed to infuse his voice with a commander's authority. "Go!"

Hanani jerked down his chin. Untying his sash, he placed it under Salmone's head before running off. Salmone stared into the sky. It had turned into a beautiful day. White clouds dappled the horizon. A breeze rustled the trees, swaying them this way and that like royal fans. It had been so long since he had noticed the beauty of his surroundings. *Lord, is this the day I die? Into Your hands I give my life.* His breath caught as a stab of pain pierced through him, and for a few moments he was beyond coherent thought. As the pain diminished, he prayed again. *Please take care of my sister. Don't let any harm come to her in my absence.*

Another face, very different from Miriam's, haunted him. Large-eyed and full-lipped, filled with tenderness one moment and fear the next. A precious face. He took a laboring breath. *And Lord, take care of Rahab.* A sense of regret hit him with a force as sharp as the dagger that had pierced him. Regret for what never was. He groaned. It was the wound that was making him think crazy thoughts. How ironic that his last thoughts should be of a Canaanite . . . no. He could not say it. He could not think it of her. Whatever she had been, she was a different woman now. Her past was not the measure of her. If he had to think of her in these final hours of his life, he would not demean or dishonor her. *Lord, she is a woman of faith. Take care of her.*

"What have you gone and done to yourself?" A familiar voice interrupted his thoughts.

"Joshua?"

"And who were you expecting—the king of Ai? Let's have a look at you, young Salmone."

"It's not good. Please, will you promise to care for my sister?"

"Let me have a look before you pester me with unnecessary entreaties." Joshua attempted to be gentle as he examined the wound. Salmone feared he might be sick. A long groan escaped him. Joshua stopped. "I won't lie to you, son. This wound is grave. Fatal, perhaps."

"I told you so," Salmone said, grinning weakly, enjoying the sensation of putting Joshua in his place for once. Darkness pulled at him and he stopped resisting. Anything to stop the agony. The last image his eyes saw was that of Joshua praying.

Rahab sat on the floor of Miriam's tent making bandages. Since the deployment of Israel's army into Ai, she had fallen into the habit of visiting Miriam every day. The younger woman, already a veteran at the harrowing business of waiting out the outcome of wars, taught Rahab how to prepare for the care of the wounded. Just outside Israel's camp, a new tent had been set up to accommodate the warriors who would return injured from battle. Rahab never doubted Israel's victory. A conviction of their triumph undergirded her every thought. But she struggled with the knowledge that even triumphant battles could prove fatal for the victors. The thought paralyzed her with a fear she tried to hide from her friend. She was grateful for the time they spent in prayer, interceding for the protection of Israel's young men, for God to sustain them, for the safe return of Salmone. Their prayers saved her sanity.

Now as she rolled up newly laundered bandages, she wondered how many might be wounded in the battle of Ai, and what kind of care they would receive upon their return. "Do you have physicians in Israel, or is it the women who take care of the sick?" she asked Miriam.

"We have several talented physicians. Zuph ben Yudah is the most renowned. In fact, he left with Joshua's forces three days ago, so that he could treat wounded men as quickly as possible. Speed saves lives. He has trained a few of our women, I among them."

"How did he learn his skill? You have been roaming from nowhere to nowhere for forty years. Who taught him?"

Miriam grabbed an alabaster pot and began filling it with honey. "Our parents were slaves in Egypt where the world's greatest medical knowledge resides. Zuph's father worked under a skilled physician from boyhood. The man took a liking to Yudah, and shared some of his knowledge with him over the years. It must have been God's doing. Egyptian physicians are known to guard their trade secrets jealously. When we left Egypt, Yudah brought his knowledge with him, and taught his son Zuph everything he knew."

The tent flap flew open abruptly, and Hanani rushed in, forgetting to announce his presence to the women within.

Rahab and Miriam scrambled to their feet. "Salmone?" Miriam gasped.

"He's been injured. He asks for you."

"How bad?"

Hanani's eyes filled with tears, and he looked down. Miriam let out a wail and turned into Rahab's arms. Rahab felt the room begin to spin, but forced herself to hold Miriam, soothing her in this first panicked moment of discovery. She schooled her features into a bland mask, trying to hide her own churning emotions. Inside, she felt a crumbling more terrible than the falling walls of Jericho.

Miriam drew away and laid a trembling hand over her chest. "I'm sorry, I didn't mean to be such a coward. Rahab, will you come with me? You can help me care for him."

Rahab breathed in relief. She would be allowed to stay by his side. "Of course," she managed.

They seized several baskets, filling them with the supplies they had been preparing for the past three days. Just as they were about to emerge from the tent, a plump woman barged in, panting.

"Miriam, I just heard the news! Thank God we have won the battle and his sacrifice is not wasted. I will go with you and help nurse him. He must be in agony. War wounds hurt worse than anything, I'm told."

"Dinah!" Miriam stood stock still.

"Come, come. What are you waiting for? Time is short. He's probably dying as we speak," the woman named Dinah urged, pumping her arms up and down like an irate goose.

"Er, Dinah, thank you for your offer of help. Actually, I've asked Rahab to accompany me," Miriam said, already heading out of the tent.

"Who?"

"Rahab. Excuse me if I don't introduce you. As you mentioned, our time is short."

"You can't be serious! You can't take that woman to nurse Salmone at such an hour. It's . . . it's indecent! Besides, I'm his cousin. I should be by his side."

"And I am his sister and I will decide who should be by his side. And I choose Rahab. Good day to you, Dinah." Taking Rahab's hand in a firm hold, Miriam pulled her forward and followed Hanani at a run.

Zuph straightened from his examination of Salmone. "Hepatic wound. The knife penetrated the liver, cutting it almost in two." Absently, he rubbed his shoulder, his face grey with exhaustion. "Massive blood loss. He's very weak. Been unconscious for hours."

"But he lives," Miriam said, her lips white.

"I don't know if it's because he's so stubborn or because of Joshua's prayers. But yes, he lives."

Rahab could not take her eyes off Salmone. He lay still on his fresh pallet, orange as a gourd, his breaths so shallow she could not see his naked chest move with them. Bandages covered his middle. They must have been fresh, for on the sides the fabric remained pristine. But around the wound, they were covered in the scarlet of fresh blood.

O Lord, don't take him. Don't take him. Don't take him. The litany wouldn't stop in her head. She heard the conversations that went on around her, heard the moans of other wounded men in the tent, the low relieved laughter of those whose injuries were not grave, the comforting expressions of family members, heard all this and understood, and yet the litany went on. *Don't take him. Don't.*

"Can he be healed, Zuph?" Miriam's question brought Rahab's thoughts into sharp focus.

Zuph wrinkled his hooked nose in thought. "It's not likely, but it isn't impossible. The liver does have the ability to regenerate itself. If you can nurse some strength back into him, and if you can prevent putrefaction, perhaps he will survive."

"How?"

"He needs careful nursing day and night. His bandages need to be changed four times a day and twice at night. Use honey, and plenty of it. I've sutured the cut, taking care that the knots face upward and out of the wound, so they shouldn't pull the cut open when you change the dressing, but have a care. Rub olive oil into the thread to keep it soft. I wish I had date wine and frankincense. That would do him a world of good."

Rahab blinked. "I have both," she whispered.

Zuph glanced at her. "And you are?"

"This is Rahab," Miriam provided.

"From Jericho. I've heard of you. You have date wine you say?"

"And frankincense. I would be happy to give all I have."

Zuph nodded. "Good. That will serve well. Later, I'll show you both how to use the wine to cleanse the wound before you apply the honey bandages.

"For now, an immediate threat to his life is the massive blood loss. We need to get a lot of liquid down his throat. Because his liver has been damaged, he cannot have fatty foods. Not even a morsel. Give him barley water sweetened with honey or strong ox broth, well salted. Mind you, take the fat out before feeding it to him. While he is unconscious, you'll have to dribble it into him by force. Can you manage that?"

Both women nodded, their tongues too heavy for speech. Rahab ran back to her tent to fetch the wine and spices. Hastily, she shared the news of Salmone's injury with her family while heaving items out of her sack. By the time she found what she needed, clothes and bottles and amphorae were strewn every which way.

"Go, go," Izzie urged. "I'll tidy this."

Rahab nodded and flew out. She arrived back at the tent of the wounded out of breath and sick with worry. Handing her bundle to Zuph, she sank down next to Miriam.

Zuph took a modest sip of the wine and held it in his mouth for a moment before swallowing. "Good. And I see the frankincense is pure. This will serve us well. Now, I will show you how to change the bandage."

He untied the binding around Salmone's middle and pulled the linen away from the swollen flesh with deliberate care. In a couple of places, dried blood had adhered the suture to the fabric. These he detached delicately, using a miniature pair of iron tongs. The wound was covered with a thick layer of honey. Zuph looked up, making sure he had the women's attention. "The honey draws the poison out of the wound and helps to alleviate putrefaction. That's why it's so important to change the bandages often."

In a wooden bowl, he mixed a modest amount of frankincense in the wine and, soaking a fresh cloth in the mixture, he began to wipe the honey from the wound. As he removed most of the gooey paste, Rahab saw that a yellowish pus was oozing out of the inflamed cut. This, Zuph wiped with great care, dipping his cloth again and again into the wine mixture. The combined smell of old and fresh blood, decaying pus, expensive date wine, and exquisite spice was enough to make Rahab want to gag, and she barely held back the impulse. She could not believe this was Salmone, could not believe that the vital man whose mere look silenced an outraged crowd now lay here smelling of suppuration and decay.

Miriam sneaked out a hand and held Rahab's fingers in a bone-shattering hold. Finding the pressure reassuring in spite of the pain, Rahab held tight to that tiny soft hand. Together they watched the physician prepare a fresh bandage, covered with a thin coat of wild honey, before wrapping it around Salmone. The ministrations of the physician did not rouse Salmone from his deep sleep. Rahab thought it a blessing that he was absent from his own agony.

Zuph wiped his hands clean with the last of the wine mixture. "Be sure to cleanse your hands before and after touching the wound as you see me doing. Procure as much honey as you can. Given who he is, I don't doubt every family under his command will show up with their year's supply of it. If he survives this, it will be a long and arduous road for him. And for you, Miriam, as you care for him. It will not be a matter of days, you understand, but of weeks."

Miriam nodded. "I'll manage."

"You'll need help. Isn't your best friend Elizabeth expecting a baby? She's near her time, as I recall. She and her mother won't be able to come to you."

"I'll help," Rahab volunteered. "I mean, if . . . if you wish it, Miriam," she stammered. "Since I've already learned how to change the bandage."

"Thank you, Rahab. Of course I want your help."

CHAPTER SIXTEEN

Salmone felt himself choking. Hands held him down, and he thrashed against their hold. Sputtering, he opened his eyes. His vision was queer and bleary. A woman's face wavered over him. *Rahab?* He shifted and realized that his head was on her lap.

"What?" he croaked. His throat felt scratchy. He forced himself to go on with sheer tenacity. "What are you trying to do, kill me?" Another coughing fit shook him.

"Thank God! You're awake! Do you know who I am?"

Her voice sounded higher and thinner than he remembered. He brought a weak hand to his temple as memory flooded back. "You're in worse shape than me if you can't remember your name."

She gave a bark of laughter and with exquisitely gentle fingers laid his head back on the pallet. He felt a sense of loss as she moved away from him. "I'll wake Miriam. She'll be so relieved."

He saw his sister stretched out near him on another pallet. Her face, smooth in repose, appeared exhausted. "Let her sleep. Has she been nursing me long?"

"Eight days and nights. I convinced her to take a nap a short while ago. She hardly leaves your side and only sleeps in short snatches. This is the first time you've been awake long enough to speak in sentences. Everyone has been so worried about you."

Salmone frowned. He had no memory of being awake at all. A more urgent memory filled his mind. "The battle?"

"A complete victory for Israel."

Salmone closed his eyes with relief. He had been wounded just before the final outcome of the war had been determined. He opened his eyes again and trained them on Rahab, wondering at her presence. He must be in the tent of the wounded. What had brought the newest member of his tribe to his side in this place?

"You had better finish your broth before I change your dressing. That's why you were choking. I was trying to feed you."

"*You're* going to change my dressing?"

"Unless you prefer I wake Miriam to do it?"

"Of course not. I mean, where's Zuph? Why can't he do it?"

Rahab knelt near his head so he could see her without straining his neck. She seemed pale. "Because your dressing has to be changed many times, day and night, and Zuph has other patients beside you. He has taught Miriam and me, and we take great care to do it right."

"Miriam and you? You've been caring for me?"

Rahab shrugged and turned away to pick up a bowl. "You must drink this. You lost a lot of blood, and we need to build up your strength to battle the putrefaction. You have been feverish for many days."

Miriam must have asked for Rahab's help, he realized. He

knew his sister had a fondness for the woman, but of the plethora of women they knew, did she have to choose this one? The thought of being helpless in front of Rahab made Salmone squirm. Perversely, he also had to admit that he was reluctant to part with her company. He did not wish to send her away. He swallowed his pride as best he could. "It's not foul, is it?"

She smiled. "It's fresh broth. The women of Judah fight over the privilege of making it for you each day. This batch was made by Michael's wife, the mother of the pretty and unattached Judith, who delivered this portion by her own jasmine-scented hands this very morning."

"Just give me the bowl."

"I don't think—"

"Give it to me!"

"I'm sorry, but no. You can't hold it yet. You're too weak from the wound."

Salmone almost yelled at her to get out. Did he need a woman to tell him that he was as weak as a newborn? He swallowed his temper as he remembered his exhausted sister. Waking her up with his bellows might be unwise. He gave Rahab a dagger look. She seemed to pale under his displeasure, but scooted closer nonetheless and gently lifted his head onto her lap. His mouth went dry and he forgot the rest of his protests. She held the bowl against his lips and he drank, small sips that occasionally dribbled down the side of his mouth. He tasted nothing. Incensed by his helplessness, confused by Rahab's unusual closeness against his naked back, he swallowed each mouthful, resenting his ridiculous position with every gulp. She wiped his mouth and chin as she would a child's and laid him back down again.

"Now your bandage. Are you in pain?" Her voice sounded husky. Their closeness affected her also, it seemed. He smirked, forgetting to answer her.

He could tell Rahab was trying to be gentle, but by the time the old bandage had been removed, sweat soaked his hair. He lifted a weak hand to wipe his brow, and stopped midway, arrested. "By all that's holy, the light is strange in this tent. Do I not look an odd color to you?"

"It's your liver. That's where the knife pierced you. Zuph says the liver can regenerate itself. It will take some time though, and until then, you will have this yellow tinge. Right now, we must battle the putrefaction of the wound. That's why we change your bandage so often and wash the wound. The honey draws out the poison."

"Where did you find so much honey?"

"I believe every honeybee from here to Egypt faints at the very sight of a woman from the tribe of Judah. Your popularity astonishes even Joshua, who has stopped by twice each day to pray for you. He says he should be praying for the women of Israel instead." Rahab's tone was light, but the line of her lips thinned as she spoke.

She's jealous, he thought, trying not to smile. But he suspected he looked like a fox—orange and pleased.

Rahab awoke to the sound of Miriam and Salmone conversing in low tones. After staying up half the night, she had fallen into an exhausted stupor. She still felt tired and could not summon the energy to move, nor did she have the heart to interrupt the private moment between brother and sister. Well, not strictly private, as she could hear every word.

"Is it only the two of you, looking after me? Couldn't you find anyone else to help?" Salmone asked.

"Please. There are lines stretching out the tent. And you know who was at the head? Dinah."

"Heavens forefend me! I hope you turned her away?"

"I told her when you wake up you're likely going to marry her. She comes by on the hour to see if your eyes are open."

"You didn't!" Salmone's voice had the ring of real terror in it.

"Of course I didn't." When Miriam spoke again, her voice seemed clogged with tears. "I thought I might lose you. Rahab was with me when Hanani brought the news. I realize I haven't known her long, but she has been such a comfort to me since you left. So I asked her to come and help. Zuph showed us how to care for you, and she picked up every detail with the facility of a born healer. I don't know how I would have managed without her, Salmone. She's been as faithful as a sister. When my mind was a fog of worry, she remembered what had to be done and arranged for it. I could have asked others to join us, but I longed for quiet while we waited out the worst. Do you mind? I can ask her to leave if her presence bothers you."

Rahab held her breath. Oh, why had she not made them aware she was awake? She would have spared herself this mortifying rejection.

Salmone's response came agonizingly slow. "I mind being mewling and sick no matter who takes care of me. You don't have to ask her to leave. I'm glad she's been a good friend to you. And like you, I prefer fewer people fussing about me at a time like this."

"Good. Now drink some of this barley water. Zuph told us we must pour as much nourishment into you as possible."

"I can feed myself. You two women are going to drive me to distraction if you insist on the feeding and the wiping and who-knows-what else you are doing. I won't have it. And please get some men in here to visit me before I go mad. While we're at it, they can help me with my personal needs from now on. I don't want women around for that."

Rahab decided she had waited enough and shifted on the pallet, making exaggerated noises to warn Miriam and Salmone she could hear them. She felt a fraud. "Peace to you," she whispered and slithered out the tent as fast as her sleepy senses allowed. The stars were still out; she had not slept long. As she strode rapidly out of the tent, she tripped over a sleeping form. Hanani.

The unintended sandal in the middle of his back brought Hanani awake in an instant. He sat bolt upright. "Has something happened?"

She crouched by his side. "No, Hanani. He is awake and asking for his friends. He would appreciate a visit from you. A short one, though. He may not want to admit it, but he needs rest."

Hanani scrambled up so fast his feet grew tangled in his trailing belt. Rahab placed a steadying hand on his shoulder. "And then go home and get some rest. You haven't left this place since you brought us the news. You haven't even returned to your tent to change since the war, Hanani."

He shook his head. "It's my fault he's in there," he mumbled, his voice wobbly as he shoved the tent flap aside and stumbled in. Rahab's eyes followed him for a moment and then, sighing, she turned. She had heard the story of Salmone's injury from Joshua. Several people had tried to persuade Hanani that he was guiltless, Ezra and Joshua among them. The young man would have none of it. He kept vigil outside the tent of the wounded, barely taking time to eat.

Rahab shook her head and walked a little farther until she reached a trickling stream. Kneeling down, she began to wash as thoroughly as modesty allowed in such a public place. In the dark warm night, the chill water refreshed and soothed. She hadn't had time to think since she had begun to nurse Salmone. Now that the danger of death seemed to have passed, a sudden rush of tears overtook her. She sobbed out the tension in great silent heaves. He would not die. He would not die. She shied away from thinking through why this man's life and well-being had come to mean so much to her. Relief flooded her senses and that sufficed.

When Rahab returned to the tent, Salmone and Hanani had both fallen asleep, snoring in soft tandem breaths. Miriam smiled. "I feel certain he is past the worst," she whispered.

"Yes, I thought so too. His fever has lowered. Zuph should be here soon to confirm our hopes; it's near dawn."

"The challenge now is to force my brother to rest. He's mulish to the extreme. I didn't dare tell him how long his process of recuperation is likely to last. He's bound to go unhinged once he learns he'll be the only one left in this tent by next week." Miriam laughed, thinking of it. "You realize he'll make our lives a misery with his grumbling, don't you?" And then she burst into tears.

Rahab, who had broken down not one hour before, enfolded her friend in a tight embrace. "He's like an overgrown child!" Miriam snorted when her crying had subsided. Rahab released her and stepped back. It wouldn't do to agree too wholeheartedly.

She gathered used bandages and dirty crockery to take out and wash. Zuph walked in as she left, and she gave him a small curtsy. Ingrained habits, she found, had a way of asserting themselves. In spite of growing more at ease among the Israelites, she retained some of the formality of her manners. Zuph gave her a lopsided smile and nodded acknowledgment before walking in to visit his patients.

Rahab lingered at her chore, wanting to give Miriam time alone with the physician. In truth, she needed time alone, herself. For nine years, she had lived a predominantly solitary life. She had enjoyed long stretches of privacy. In the past seven weeks, she had nearly forgotten the meaning of the word. People everywhere. She rarely managed to be alone with her thoughts. A great exhaustion swept over her. When was the last time she had slept through the night?

She hung the clean bandages on a few branches to dry and walked back into the tent. Zuph must have already examined Salmone and left. Miriam knelt near him, her face more at peace than Rahab had seen in days. "Good news?" she asked as she settled herself next to her friend.

Miriam nodded. "The cut is healing well. We still need to nurse him vigilantly, until the wound is completely closed. But the immediate danger is past. He needs rest and proper nourishment. He can have visitors now, thank God. That ought to keep him entertained. He's still not allowed to rise out of bed. Not for another week, at least. Zuph says it's a miracle he has recovered this much, but there is now a good chance that he will recover completely."

Rahab closed her eyes for a moment. They had agonized, without daring to speak of it even to each other, over the possibility that Salmone might never regain the fullness of his health. That would be a great loss to such a man, perhaps an unbearable one. Opening her eyes, she smiled at Miriam. "So much good news. I think we should celebrate. You shall eat a proper breakfast, which I'll make you, and then sleep before you collapse. I do not want to nurse two of you."

"What about you? You're as weary as I am."

"I will sleep when you wake up. Now, what have the good women of Judah brought us to eat?" Rahab found flour and olive oil and made fresh flat breads, which she served with cheese and walnuts and a few dates. She and Miriam ate their fill, their appetites returning with Zuph's encouraging news.

Hanani was still asleep on the pallet next to Salmone, and they hadn't the heart to wake him. Rahab set up new bedding in the back of the tent for Miriam. She found a pillow and light sheet from amongst the multitude of things visitors kept dropping off for them. From one sack, brought by Izzie the day before, she pulled out a flask of rose water. With a smile, she sprinkled a couple of drops on the pillow. Let Miriam be surrounded by beauty for a few hours instead of the smell of sickness. It was a measure of Miriam's physical and emotional weariness that she did not even argue about being put to bed while Rahab kept vigil. She fell asleep before her head sank into the pillow.

Rahab came back to sit next to Salmone. She wrinkled her nose as a ripe smell filled her nostrils. Really, she would insist that Hanani go and wash and consecrate himself once he woke up. As if on cue, he opened his eyes and stretched. "How is he?" he whispered.

"Very well. Zuph was here and told Miriam that he would likely be beating your heads together as hard as he ever did. But we must try to keep him from rising out of bed too soon."

A slow smile appeared on Hanani's face. "Don't worry. I'll tie him down myself."

"Before you come anywhere near him, you might consider a wash, if you please. Donning fresh clothing might improve your presentation, as well."

Hanani scratched his chest. "I forgot. I didn't want to leave his side. I will return soon, smelling like spring flowers."

"Good. Bring Ezra and some of Salmone's less boisterous friends. He's allowed visitors now. Tell them to mind their manners. He's still sick, though he may not acknowledge it."

Hanani looked like his old self, or at least a dirtier version of his old self, as he strode out of the tent, the spring back in his step. Bending over her patient, Rahab shifted the sheet. It was time to change his dressing. When she undid the bandages, she discovered that the bleeding had stopped. Though the wound still suppurated, the infection had decreased considerably. Rahab no longer felt bothered by the sight or smell of it; she had grown accustomed to the routine of cleansing, wiping, washing, oiling, balming, and binding the weeping wound as though it were the most natural part of her day. Sometimes, she would visit the other men who were in the confines of the tent and, alongside Miriam, helped their families with nursing chores. She grew to like the sensation of usefulness that came with caring for the sick.

Salmone slept through her ministrations as she made a new honey poultice, and with expert movements, wrapped it about him. In an effort to draw out the last of the fever, she dipped a fresh cloth in a mix of cool water and date wine, and began to wipe his torso with featherlight motions so as not to wake him. She washed his feet and hands and forehead last, which Zuph had taught her drew out heat more rapidly than other body parts.

When she had finished, she rinsed her hands in wine and water and leaned back against a sturdy tent pole. She surveyed the mound of dirty rags, but could not summon the energy to wash them. Her head drooped as she thought of her next chore—heating broth for Salmone and trying to feed him without choking him—an impossible task.

A soft touch on her hand made her look up. Salmone's eyes bore into her. "You look spent," he said, his voice gravelly with sleep.

She shook her head and smiled. "It's good you're awake. I was worrying how to feed you."

"Thank you for all you've done."

"I'm glad to help." She tried to straighten her rumpled tunic. It had been days since she had had a chance to change. She probably didn't look much better than Hanani.

"It was a good day when you joined Israel," he said into the silence.

"What?" she asked, her mouth falling open. She forgot her

concern about her appearance and stared at him. She could not have heard aright. Not those words from Salmone. "What?" she said again.

His mouth softened into a lazy smile. "I see you've given up repeating me. Now you're repeating yourself."

CHAPTER SEVENTEEN

After eighteen days of wretched inactivity, Salmone rose from his sick bed long enough to take a few faltering steps around the tent. His legs wobbled as he moved, but they carried him, for which he thanked God.

A steady stream of friends had been trying to cheer him since Zuph allowed visitors. Because his strength had contracted to a fraction of its usual vigor, he often fell asleep in the middle of conversations, like an old grandmother. Zuph warned him that it would take weeks before he felt himself again. Joshua scoffed at his impatience and told him he ought to be grateful he lived. He knew this to be true, yet it did not help the chafing impatience when he had to be helped every time he ate or sat or emptied his bowels.

Aside from the awful infirmity, pain dogged his every conscious hour. Deep inside his gut, the lacerations in the layers of muscle and organ ached with a tenderness that made him catch his breath as he moved.

Rahab and Miriam smiled when he barked at them, not taking any offense. He felt as grateful for this grace as he was for their incessant care. Their casual acceptance of his foul moods made it easier to bear himself. They spared him the debt of guilt he owed for snapping at them when he should be considerate. With Miriam, whom he had known since infancy, he already felt a level of comfort that long familiarity had established. Now his enforced intimacy with Rahab birthed a similar comfort. He found her easy company, never intrusive or demanding. She soothed him without trying. He liked her conversation. She often surprised him by her insights. Only the night before she had told him how the Passover had come alive for her during the siege of Jericho. He had asked what she meant.

"Hanani and Ezra told me how, in Egypt, the Pharaoh would not let your people go," she said. "So the Lord brought down plague after plague upon the people of Egypt, and in the end, death came against all the firstborn of the land. They told me, on that day, the people of Israel were instructed to remain inside their homes, with their doors closed, and the blood of lambs marking their doorframes. When the Lord sent the destroyer to go through the land and strike down the Egyptians, the destroyer passed over the homes of Israel by this sign.

"My family and I were in Jericho when God sent destruction and death against our nation. We too were told to stay inside our home. We were given no sacrifice, not belonging to Israel then. But God chose a scarlet cord the color of blood to hang outside my door as a sign that would preserve us from death. Shut up in my house, surrounded by death and yet being spared from it, I felt a little of what your fathers and mothers must have known—that it was God alone who held our lives in the palm of His hand."

Salmone had been amazed at Rahab's profound insights. Her conversation often enlivened his otherwise monotonous day. But she was also at ease with quiet. She didn't need to converse every moment of the day.

Though he knew it to be a selfish decision, he chose not to insist that the women conscript others into helping with his care. He sensed few women would understand his needs as well as the two who had tended him since the beginning. Reluctant to expose himself to the unbearable clucking of some overbearing matron or doe-eyed young girl, he hunkered down on his pallet and allowed his weary nurses to have their way.

His world, usually so large and encompassing, had shrunk to the size of a tent. When on the twentieth day of his confinement he took his first steps outside and saw the sun, he almost wept with relief. His friends set up a chair of sorts for him, and piled it with feather pillows. Nestled in its depths, Salmone held court for his horde of visitors.

In spite of the thick knot of people that surrounded him and vied for his attention, Salmone became aware that he had not seen Rahab for hours that day. He stopped Miriam on her way to fetch water and said in her ear, "Where's Rahab?"

She straightened and crossed her arms over her chest. "With this army of admirers, you can't bear to lose one?"

Salmone drew his eyebrows into a frown. "Where is she?" he insisted, feeling a knot in his stomach. Her absence grated on him more than he cared to admit.

"In the women's tent."

"Oh. How long will that be?"

Miriam rolled her eyes. "As long as it takes." She played with the tip of her fingernail. "Don't worry. Abigail is coming to help me instead. She can manage now that your nursing needs are so much lighter."

Salmone turned his head away, vexed. What did he care for Abigail and nursing? He wanted Rahab. He swallowed hard as the thought sank in. He missed her. He wanted her back. Scowling, he huddled down in his chair and ignored a question directed at him. The one benefit of sickness was that people pretended not to notice when he was rude.

In the evening, Joshua came to visit him as he had often done in the course of Salmone's convalescence—a high honor given the man's list of unending responsibilities. He always managed to come at the time when other visitors had disappeared, and the tent of the wounded, now empty of every patient save Salmone, had grown deserted.

Salmone had been ensconced back in his pallet by the time Joshua arrived that night. The day outside had tired him, and he lay on his thick bedding feeling sluggish and useless.

"I hear half of Israel came to visit you on your first outing today," Joshua commented as he made himself comfortable on the floor next to Salmone.

"At least. Tomorrow, I expect even more visitors. I am such an entertaining fellow."

Joshua ignored him and looked around. "Let's pray. Shall we invite the women? I don't see Rahab."

"In the women's tent." Salmone could not wipe the resentment from his voice.

"She didn't do it to inconvenience you," Joshua said, amusement coloring his voice. "It's God's design."

"Did I say anything? I'm not *that* simpleminded."

"Are you sure?" Joshua guffawed.

"It's a relief someone in this tent is amused."

Joshua leaned forward. "What are you going to do about Rahab?" he asked, all trace of laughter gone.

Salmone pretended not to understand. "What's to do? As you said, it's God's design."

Joshua threw him a stern look. "Your feelings for Rahab. Are those God's design too?"

The simple question hit him like a punch in his injured gut. A lungful of air leaked out of him. Had he been so transparent? He could refuse to discuss the matter, he supposed. Or he could unburden himself with the one man he respected above every other. He shoved his fingers into his hair. "I don't know what to do."

"Do you love her?"

Salmone had run from that question the way sheep run from a mountain lion. Yet, it always caught up with him. Could he love a woman from Canaan? Could he pollute his lineage and his father's honored memory with a harlot from Jericho? Yet, the woman he had come to know, the loyal friend who placed others before herself, who spoke truth and showed kindness even under ugly provocation, the woman whose tenderness had perhaps saved his life, bore no resemblance to the *zonah* he had envisioned. His thinking became muddled when he placed these considerations next to each other—*who Rahab was* and *what Rahab had done.*

He shook his head. "I don't know, Joshua. I'm confused."

"Confusion is not of God. You must look to your heart and find the source of it. Let me tell you one thing. If you do love her, I will stand behind you. I will accept your marriage. I admire her, Salmone, and as I have said from the beginning, God Himself brought her to us. You would have my blessing. But only if you love her. Both of you deserve nothing less."

Salmone stared at Joshua in disbelief. Had the leader of Israel just given him permission to marry a Canaanite woman who had once made a living entertaining men in her bed?

A week later Rahab returned to the tent of the wounded wearing a pale blue linen dress and a shuttered expression. She avoided Salmone's eye as she circumvented his cluster of friends who had gathered outside the tent of the wounded, and went straight inside to seek Miriam. Salmone had to battle the urge to get up and follow. Why had she not greeted him? Why had she seemed so distant? After what seemed an interminable time, Salmone made an excuse and pulled himself out of his chair to enter the tent. Rahab was already helping Miriam, listening to his sister's update from the previous week. Salmone shuffled over, his gait that of an aging man suffering from a double hernia. He stood over Rahab as she knelt on the floor, binding clean bandages. His heart did a flip at the sight of her. "Welcome," he said.

"Thank you." She glanced up at him and down again. "You look improved. Less orange."

"You look paler. Didn't you like the women's tent? I'd heard it was a pleasant place to spend a week."

She flushed scarlet. At first he thought he had embarrassed her. Did Canaanites not speak of such things openly? Then a new suspicion made him lower his brows in a fierce frown. "Did they mistreat you? Did someone offend you?"

Rahab waved a hand in the air. "It's nothing."

Salmone's back stiffened. "It isn't *nothing*. What happened? Tell me."

"Please, Salmone. Let it go. I don't wish to speak of it." Her voice sounded small. Salmone wanted to explode with frustration. He could not force her to talk. He could not force the women of Israel to show respect to one who had given their nation nothing but loyalty. He could not even force his injured body to bend down so he could comfort her. With a muffled growl, he turned his back and walked to the other side of the tent.

Miriam came to him and put a calming hand on his arm. "This is ridiculous," he hissed.

"I'm afraid it's partly my fault. Abigail told me that some of the women felt snubbed because I chose Rahab alone to help me nurse you. They won't hold it against me, or you, of course. But they blame her for worming her way into our affections. They doubt her sincerity."

"Is she to suffer because of her kindness to us? I won't have it."

"Salmone, you can't do anything about it. It will merely make matters worse. You must trust God to vindicate her."

Salmone crossed his arms and raised his chin. "You want me to sit around and do nothing while the women of Israel torment Rahab because of her goodness to me?"

"I want you to trust God. Leave it in His hands."

Salmone made an irritated sound in his throat and stormed out.

Rahab walked aimlessly, wandering much farther from the tent of the wounded than she had planned. She had only meant to step out for a few moments of fresh air and calm. Miriam and Salmone and even Abigail had assiduously avoided the topic of her seven days in the women's tent, avoided it so well, in fact, that they were driving her distracted. They treated her as though she might fall apart with one wrong word. She wanted to get past the seven hellish days in that tent. She wanted to pretend no one had derided her. Forget that seven days out of each month, while her menstrual period made her unclean, she would have to return to that place. She wanted to move on. She had no need of anyone's pity.

The thought made her fume, and her feet picked up speed. The sound of a childish whimper brought her to a sudden halt. She looked about her. She had managed to walk away from the camp, well into the wilderness. Could she have heard aright? What would a child be doing out here, in the middle of nowhere? It must have been an animal. She tensed, her skin prickling. She whipped around, intending to flee whatever danger lurked near.

The whimper came again. She had not been mistaken; this was a child's voice. A frightened child. Rahab followed the direction of the sound. "Is anyone here?"

A wail ripped into the sky, sending a shiver down Rahab's back. It was the sound of pure terror. Rahab began to run, dread spurring her to speed. "I'm coming. Hold on. I'm coming." Where was the child?

She almost ran past an outcropping of rock when a bit of color at the top caught her eye. Backtracking, she began to climb. Near the top, she saw the child's head—a little girl with big curls, sitting scrunched up into a crevice on the other side of the rock face. Her clothes identified her as an Israelite. From Rahab's vantage, she could only see the child's back, but she looked to be no older than three or four.

"Don't be scared, sweetheart. I'm here now." The girl didn't move, didn't swivel her head to acknowledge the call. Rahab found this strange. A terrified child would surely respond to the reassurance of an adult. What kept her glued to that spot, unmoving, her back rigid? *One more step, and then I can reach her.* Rahab placed her foot on a secure ledge, reaching forward. And froze.

The length of a man's arm from the little girl sat a snake, a deadly desert viper whose poison would surely kill the child.

Rahab swallowed, bile rising in her throat. She had no suitable weapon. Even armed, she would have been half paralyzed with fear. Snakes petrified her. *Blight!* She closed her eyes, knowing time would be short.

"Almighty God. You made that snake. Make it go away." The viper sat unmoving, its tongue slithering in and out. Its scales were the same color as the sand, patterned with darker markings, and though not long in length, Rahab knew it contained enough poison to bring down a grown man. *Oh, why won't You make it go away?*

The snake moved.

Closer.

Rahab gasped. "You want me to kill that thing, Lord?" she whispered. "Show me the way!" From the corner of her eye, she saw a stone, flat, oval, and heavy, lying next to her hand. Warily, she picked it up, the whole while keeping her eye on the serpent. It ignored her, remaining rigid and alert at its post in front of the child.

"You're going to be fine, little one," Rahab crooned to the girl. "I'm going to get rid of that snake. Then we'll go and find your mama. All right?" The child moved her head with a cautious motion and looked at Rahab. Her dark brown eyes were dilated with terror. Rahab nodded at her, trying to smile with encouragement. Her hands were slick with sweat. Her brow dripped with perspiration. She knew she had one chance. Only one.

Lord, You know I have terrible aim. Please improve it. Move my hand. Move this stone. Save Your little girl from harm. She wiped the sweat from her eyes, bit her lip, and took aim. The stone flew. It twirled. It landed with a heavy thud, on the snake's head. For a fraction of a moment, the snake lay still. Then it moved. It lived! Injured, bleeding, and furious, it lived.

Rahab screamed at the same time as she put her arms around the little girl and yanked. The snake turned toward where the girl was and struck, its mouth open, scarlet, and venomous. Its fangs found the little girl's shoe and closed with a mighty force. But the shoe was empty. It had fallen off as Rahab lifted the child into the air. The snake, confused by its injury, wasted time striking at the empty leather until its senses picked out the dangling form of the girl above. It rose up to strike again, this time

at the girl's bare foot. Rahab scrambled down the other side of
the rock one-handed, clinging to the child with the other. The
snake's fangs missed her flesh by a hairbreadth. Rahab clam-
bered with more haste than care, scraping her side and fingers
in her desperation to get down.

She kept running as she hit the ground, her little passenger
clinging to her with frantic strength. Rahab's legs pumped furi-
ously until her lungs felt like they would burst. Logic told her
they had left the serpent far behind, yet an irrational fear that
snakes were slithering everywhere, chasing her, ready to bite
her at every step, made her keep going. Finally, she stopped,
out of breath, bent over with the effort of pulling air into her
burning chest. She settled the child on the ground, first making
certain that nothing crawled or coiled nearby.

"Are you well?" she asked, trying to inject calm into her voice.

The little girl nodded her head and burst into wailing tears.
Rahab hugged her close. "I know. I know. It was very scary. You
were so brave. What's your name? I'm Rahab. How about you?"

"Ha . . . Ha . . . Hannah."

"Hannah. I'm going to tell everyone how brave you've been.
But first, I'm going to take you to my friends Miriam and Salmone. They'll help me find your parents. What were you doing
up on that rock in the middle of nowhere, Hannah? Did you
get lost?"

The little girl pursed her exquisite lips and nodded. "I went
off by myself. That was naughty, wasn't it?"

Rahab smiled. "A little."

The sand would be too hot on Hannah's bare foot, so she
would have to be carried the rest of the way. Picking the child

up again, Rahab hefted her against her side. "Your parents must be very worried. Let's go find them."

Rahab brought Hannah to the tent of the wounded, hoping Salmone or Miriam might be able to help locate her family. As usual, Salmone had several visitors. The buzz of conversation ground to a halt as Rahab approached, holding Hannah. She realized that she presented quite a sight, her clothes disheveled, her hands scraped bloody, holding a Hebrew child who sported only one shoe.

Salmone rose from his chair with a slow, deliberate motion. "What happened?"

"I found her when I went for a walk. She was lost."

"Rahab saved me from the bad snake," Hannah said, squirming to come out of her rescuer's arms.

"*The what?*"

"The snake! It sat in front of me for ever so long until Rahab came. She threw a rock at it. Then we ran and ran. Rahab runs fast."

Salmone turned to Rahab. "*What?*"

Every pair of eyes there turned to Rahab. She flushed. "Her parents must be worried. Perhaps we should send for them?"

A young man jumped up. "I know Hannah's family. I'll go fetch them right away."

Miriam brought water for Hannah and Rahab and gave the little girl a sweet cake. After making sure that Hannah was unharmed, she turned her attention to her friend's scraped palms. Rahab, exhausted from her ordeal, would have preferred to disappear inside the tent, but everyone insisted on hearing the full tale of their adventure. In order to placate the oceans of curiosity, she gave a brief account of the events, punctuated by Hannah's lengthier and more colorful explanations.

Salmone interrupted her clipped account. "A viper?" At her nod, he turned pale. He was not the only one.

A weeping woman accompanied by a more subdued man ran into their midst. "My Hannah!" the woman wailed. "Where's my girl?"

Hannah dropped her sweet and ran into her mother's arms. Father, mother, and child melded into one solid heaving form, their laughter and tears mingling. Rahab stepped back, stiffening as she recognized the woman.

This was Hannah's mother? *Elizabeth!* She had been one of Rahab's chief tormentors in the women's tent.

Rahab began to back away as inconspicuously as she could. Just before she managed to disappear inside the tent, someone told the child's parents, "Rahab saved your Hannah from a poisonous serpent. She's right here. Without her, your daughter would be dead."

Elizabeth stumbled as she spun to find Rahab. A myriad of expressions flickered across her face. Astonishment. Disbelief. Denial. "You saved Hannah's life?" Her lip curled, as if she suspected Rahab of making up a tale.

Not understanding Elizabeth's accusing tone, Hannah pulled on her hand insistently. "She did, *Eym*," she said, using the formal Hebrew word for mother. "The snake wouldn't leave me alone. Then Rahab came and threw a stone at its ugly head. I was so scared. But Rahab said I was very brave. Wasn't I, Rahab?"

Elizabeth stared at her daughter, her mouth sagging. While she might doubt Rahab's story, she could not deny the testimony of her own child. After an awkward silence, the child's father stepped forward. "Our thanks, Rahab. We owe you more than we can say."

Elizabeth's face turned rigid.

Miriam stepped forward. "Wait. Elizabeth, how do you know Rahab?"

"Who said I do?"

"Come now. It's clear you are acquainted. Were you in the women's tent together?"

Rahab's chin dropped. How had Miriam surmised the reason behind the stiffness in Elizabeth's manner?

"What of it?" Elizabeth asked, her tone sharp.

"It occurred to me, you see, that the timing is astonishing. God must have put Rahab in your path, knowing that she would shortly save your daughter's life. I'm sure you befriended her there. Perhaps God is returning your kindness to Rahab by using her to save Hannah."

Elizabeth pursed her lips.

Miriam smiled sweetly. "After all, the Lord commanded that the foreigner living with us must be treated as one of our native-born. We are to love such a one as ourselves, are we not? For we were ourselves aliens in Egypt. I know you would have obeyed the Lord."

Rahab bit her lip to stop from laughing. Without another word, Elizabeth cuddled Hannah to her bosom and strode away, leaving her husband to catch up.

"Bye, Rahab!" Hannah called over her mother's shoulder. "Come and play with me."

In the morning, Rahab awoke bruised and aching from her scramble down the rock. A procession of women was already lining up outside the tent of the wounded, gift in hand. This was not in itself an unusual sight. Since Miriam could not leave Salmone to attend to daily chores, and their servant was often busy with the family's business at the campsite, many of their friends and acquaintances brought them food and necessities each morning. But these gifts were not for Salmone or Miriam. They were for Rahab. Rahab sat stunned as woman after woman welcomed her formally to Israel. By early afternoon, piles of gifts surrounded her. Almonds, honey cakes, wool, dyes, olive oil, a carved comb. And still the women came.

Salmone perched near her when her visitors dwindled. "You had more guests than I, today."

She shook her head. "I don't understand. What happened? Last week these women couldn't stand the sight of me. Now they shower me with presents."

He reached out for her hand and turned it over in his. Her palm looked raw and scabbed in places. He drew his thumb softly over the surface. A shiver ran down Rahab's spine, and she snatched her hand away. Salmone leaned back, his face unreadable. "You saved Hannah's life. They realize you had nothing to gain by it. I suppose they are finally acknowledging that they misjudged you."

Rahab thought of the strange events that had led to this change in her circumstances. "I can hardly believe the words I am about to say, but I'm grateful for that snake. God didn't answer my prayers, but He certainly brought good to me through that serpent."

"What do you mean?"

"You want to know the truth? I was angry with God yesterday. I wanted Him to make the snake go away. That's what I prayed for, and I know God could have done it. Easily. He could have made that creature turn around and go visit its cousins in Egypt. He could have struck it with lightning. He could have made it fall asleep. Instead, it coiled on that rock, refusing to budge in spite of my pleading and prayer. Why wouldn't the Lord answer my cry? He knew my limitations. What was the point of forcing me to fight a poisonous serpent?

"But that snake softened the hearts of the women of Israel. Because I fought for that child's life, mothers in Judah now think better of me. God spared Hannah's life, and mine, but *His* plan benefited me more than my way could have done. At the time, I only wanted Hannah's safety. And God did answer that prayer. But in a way that purchased the good opinion of Israel's women toward me. His inscrutable plans exceed our best schemes."

Salmone leaned forward until his face drew even with Rahab's. The deep brown of his eyes were speckled with black flecks. She felt as though her heart could be captured by those eyes, tethered like a wild horse in the hands of an expert trainer. He smiled faintly, as though sensing her thoughts. She dropped her chin. Salmone stretched his fingers to her cheek and gently drew her face back up toward him. "Don't turn away. I want to tell you something."

"My lord?" she croaked.

"I like the way you see God in everything. It's a rare quality. I really admire . . . that."

CHAPTER EIGHTEEN

Sleepless, Salmone stretched against the mountain of cushions at his back. It was the middle of the night and he lay in his own bed, a luxury he still savored after two weeks of being home. Joshua refused to allow him to return to his heaviest duties yet, goaded by Zuph's conservative precautions. So Salmone avoided military training. In every other aspect, his life had returned to normal. To his dismay, he chafed under a routine that had seemed perfectly satisfactory in the past. A nagging longing gnawed at his bones, until the shadow of discontentment dogged his every step. Nothing satisfied.

He punched a pillow behind him, trying to make himself more comfortable. The luxury of painlessness, of health, of freedom from the tent of the wounded ought to have been enough to give him peaceful nights of sleep and days filled with gratification. Instead he grew more restless by the hour. His garrulous thoughts led him in circles without resolution.

All this brooding, this mental rambling that robbed him of rest, centered on the same vortex: his feelings for Rahab. He had spent more than a month in her company. He had grown accustomed to her presence, her uncomplaining care, her quick-witted deductions, her charitable humor, her soft tenderness, her iron-hard faith.

Salmone covered his eyes with his hand. Since he had returned home, he had avoided her. He had sent his manservant over with a small fortune in sheep as an appreciation gift for her help. Politely, she had kept one and returned the rest. The one, she had said, she would give to God as a thanks offering for his safety. Salmone had been too embarrassed to insist she keep his gift. He knew there was an offense at the root of his offering, as though he wanted to buy himself out of her debt. As though he wanted to pay her off and owe her nothing in emotion and friendship.

He kept his sheep and his company to himself. He hadn't seen the sight of her, heard that softly accented voice, felt the cool touch of her long fingers in fourteen days. And it made him sleepless not because he was in her debt, but because . . . he loved her.

There. He had said it. He had admitted it to himself. He had confessed it in the caverns of his own squirming mind. He loved her and he wanted her and he missed her. And this separation was driving him to distraction. *Oh God, what am I supposed to do?*

Had she been another woman, a daughter of Israel, pure, unsullied, uncontaminated, he would have rejoiced in his feelings. He had begun to fear that he would never feel this way for a woman—that he was not made for it. He had desperately wanted to experience that soul-consuming passion. To fall in love was once his dearest personal desire. Now his wish had come true and he could not be more miserable. How was he to reconcile himself to having a Canaanite harlot for a wife? How were his children to get along in Israel with such a heritage? What could become of his line? Would God not reduce it? Condemn it? Destroy it down through the coils of time?

Another punch to another unfortunate pillow made the feathers cringe in one lumpy corner.

And yet Joshua said that he would approve of his marriage to Rahab. Would Joshua ever sanction what God would not? Was this really God's problem or Salmone's? His jealousy, his prodigious pride, his vanity, were these the true monsters that lay at the root of his struggles? Was it just that Salmone wanted a wife of whom everyone could approve—an admirable wife who would be the envy of his friends and the desire of his enemies? Was he afraid that somehow *he* would be reduced by her past?

A hard kick shifted the sheet off his naked torso and Salmone shoved the rest away and rose up. In the unrelieved darkness of a moonless night he found his way to the entrance of the tent and tried to calm his bursting head by breathing in fresh air.

His pride and Rahab's past made impossible bedfellows. Her past could not be magically undone, and his pride seemed as unmovable an obstacle as her past. He was the son of Nahshon, the leader of the people of Judah who had ruled over seventy thousand people! His father's sister had married Aaron, Moses's own brother. He was cousin to some of the most prominent people in Israel. How could he bind himself to a Canaanite harlot?

What were his choices, then? To tear her from his heart and move on. Could he do that? The memory of her beloved face filled his mind. She was so beautiful to him; the way she moved, the way she smiled, the way her eyelashes swept down when she wanted to hold her secrets. He loved being with her. Her companionship was at once comfortable and exciting to him. He loved her keenness for the Lord. Joshua had once said that she followed hard after God. Her passion for the Lord matched his own, and was perhaps even more faithful than his in some ways. Could he give up so much for the sake of his pride?

In turmoil, he took a few steps out, unmindful that he was covered only in a loincloth. The goats in a nearby paddock looked balefully at the naked form disturbing their sleep and turned away with disinterest. Their disdain made Salmone smile. He wished he could be as disdainful of his own struggles.

Could he give Rahab up? See her marry another man, hold him, be tender to him, care for him, smile for him, give him children? The thought filled him with a rage so sharp he gasped. This was a new consideration to him. Merely because he rejected Rahab, it did not follow that other men would. She was a prize. He knew that. Could he give her up? *No. No. No.* His heart and mind shouted in unison. In this, at least they were united.

His inscrutable plans exceed our best schemes, she had said. Could this love, like Rahab's snake, represent a deeper plan of God's? Even before Salmone had acknowledged that his feelings for Rahab were love, he had prayed that God would remove them from his deepest soul; he had prayed it with the same fervor that Rahab must have prayed for God to remove that snake. God seemed as uncooperative regarding Salmone's prayer as He had Rahab's. Perhaps He had a reason.

Lord, tell me what to do! Give me peace. I cannot bear this turmoil. He shuffled back inside and crawled into bed. *I will do what You tell me. Just tell me. Please.*

Sharing a tent with eleven people was proving complicated. After years of independence, Rahab found the lack of privacy hard to bear. Upon occasion, the total absence of quiet punctuated by irritating expectations threatened to suffocate her.

There was one good side effect to the demands of her new life. They distracted her from the pain that was gnawing at the marrow of her soul. Somewhere between learning Israel's laws from Salmone in that cramped oasis and taking care of his wounded body, she had managed to fall desperately in love with the man. She could not point to a moment or an hour. She could not fathom how she had made such an egregious error in judgment. She only knew that when she returned home from the tent of the wounded, she felt as though she had torn off a fragment of herself and left it behind in his keeping.

For his part, Salmone made his feelings clear. He had not even stopped by once since the priests had pronounced him clean and sent him home. With his herd of fat sheep sent courtesy of a servant boy, he expressed his gratitude to Rahab. But he avoided her company now that he was mobile and able to choose whom he pleased for his friends. His rejection hurt more than the knowledge that he could never love her. In the tent of the wounded they had at least been friends. He seemed to enjoy her presence there. To like her companionship. Now, with the breadth of his world opened up to him once more, he had jettisoned her the way he had discarded his stained bandages.

Rahab sneaked out of her pallet and made her way through the winding maze of tents toward the wilderness. It was early hours yet, and her family remained asleep, which meant that she was able to leave without annoying explanations. She picked her way with care, making little noise as she moved through Judah's enormous campsite, walking south through Zebulun. Apart from a few early risers and goats, no one stirred. Finally Rahab came to the edge of Israel's camp and found the winding path she sought. She had discovered that this path led to an oasis, which to her astonishment was often invitingly empty. In the bustle of her people-filled life, the seclusion of the spot offered a haven that Rahab sought with increasing frequency.

Here, she could think of Salmone and the tangle of her emotions. How had she allowed herself to become so vulnerable to the man? How had he managed to get past the high walls around her heart and settle himself inside as though he owned everything that was within? Rahab had spent her adult life keeping men at bay. She might have flirted with an outrageous and almost scientific precision. She might have bestowed her selective company on a chosen few and on occasion even offered friendship. She might have entertained men with her body. But she had always guarded her heart. She had never given away her deepest self. Until Salmone.

The thief! The pilfering thief! Without effort, without design, he had taken what he hadn't wanted, and it wasn't even in his power to give it back.

What was she to do? How was she to survive such an impossible love? Of all the men on this earth, why had she fallen in love with the one most likely to spurn her? *O God! Cure me of this love, I beg. Spare me this added hurt.*

Rahab turned the last bend on the path and walked with sluggish steps toward a skinny palm. Her steps faltered. A man rested against its trunk, his back to her, his dark head bent in an attitude of prayer. He must have heard her, for he rose abruptly and turned.

"Salmone!" Rahab almost choked on the name. The object of her fretting thoughts stood before her, looking impossibly handsome in his crisp white tunic.

"Rahab?"

"I beg your pardon. I didn't realize anyone else was here. Excuse me." She turned on her heels, wanting to run in the other direction. She hoped he did not think she had followed him.

A hand wrapped around her waist. Salmone pulled her back against him. "Wait," he whispered into her veil-covered hair. "Wait."

Rahab froze. What was he doing holding her like this? Her heart pounded so hard she felt certain he must feel it. She remained rigid under his touch, unable to turn around. Salmone moved his hands to her shoulders and forced her to face him. "I was just praying about you when you came," he said cryptically.

Her eyes widened. "About me?"

He gave a twisted smile and stepped away from her. "Yes, about you. Did you know I was here?"

She shook her head with such vehemence, her veil slipped back. "No, I swear. I didn't mean to bother you." He had been praying about *her*? He was probably chafing under the debt of gratitude he owed her for taking care of him. If he brought it up, she would wallop his pretty nose. What she had given, she had given as a gift of friendship. A free gift. His insistence on repayment insulted her.

"Come and sit with me. I want to talk to you." He pulled on her hand and she stumbled after him, desperate to be near him, and wishing herself on the other side of the world at the same time. Being with Salmone was as painful as being without him.

What could he have to say to her? Nothing she would like to hear, probably. She sat near him, drawing her knees to her chest and wrapping her arms around herself until she looked like a knot, drawn in and clinched tight.

Salmone leaned back against the tree, cloaked in silence. Several times, he opened his mouth to speak and then closed it again, as if he could not find the right words. Rahab studied him nervously, not able to understand his mood.

"I was making a decision when you came," he said finally. "About you." His voice faltered. "Rahab, I would like it if you looked at me while I spoke to you."

Rahab's eyes darted up. A sudden cringing fear made her mouth dry. What could he have to decide regarding her? Was he speaking as a leader of Judah? Had she crossed an unknown line? Had she broken a law, offended a neighbor, made a dreadful mistake, failed to please God? What had she done wrong?

Salmone frowned. "And it would help if you didn't look at me with such dread."

"I . . ." Rahab faltered, at a loss.

He grimaced. "This is a wretched beginning. I'm still trying to wrap my head around the fact that you walked in here when you did."

"Truly, I didn't know you were here. I wouldn't have dreamed of interrupting you if—"

He leaned forward and put a hand on her mouth, effectively cutting off her words. He let his fingers rest against her lips for a moment, and then shifted, removing his hand with somnolent reluctance. "Why do you so often assume that I'm angry with you? Or that I think you've done something wrong? I don't. I was glad to see you today. Incredulous, but glad."

"*You were?*"

"I've thought of you often since I came home."

Rahab narrowed her gaze. "Indeed?" In spite of her best effort, a hard edge of sarcasm tainted the single word. She closed her hand into a fist.

His responding smile was lazy. "I missed you."

"Then why did you never come to me? You could have come with Miriam if you had wanted. Instead, you avoided me and sent me sheep."

"I did avoid you. I needed time to sort through my feelings. Seeing you would only have confused matters."

Rahab grew very still. "You have feelings for me?"

"Surely you must have noticed. Just as I noticed you are not indifferent to me."

Rahab jerked back. "Pardon?"

"Look me in the eye and tell me you don't love me." Rahab did not miss the smug satisfaction that colored the dark eyes.

271

She shot up in a whirl of motion, intent on leaving. Shame covered her with icy fingers. It was one thing to strive with unrequited feelings of love for the man, quite another to have those feelings discovered, named, and thrown in her face. Salmone stood up at the same time, blocking her path.

"Will you listen to me?" He grabbed her arm and pulled her close.

"I've heard enough. Let me go! I'm sure you wouldn't handle a Hebrew maiden in such a manner."

"No, I wouldn't. But then I'm not about to ask any Hebrew maiden to marry me."

"*What?*"

"I'm trying to tell you. I came here to think this morning. To decide what to do about you. Perhaps I am being presumptuous, but as I prayed, I felt God's approval. And for the first time in days, the turmoil that has plagued me turned into unwavering peace. I had just made up my mind to go speak with your father when you arrived. I almost fell over when I saw you. I often come to this oasis early in the mornings, and I have never before seen you here. And just at the very moment when I had made up my mind to join my life to yours, you came to me. It felt like a confirmation, seeing you in that moment."

Rahab's world began to tilt on its axis. Salmone's declaration started to sink in—the meaning, the implications, the outcome. He was changing her whole future with his words. The impossible had happened. Salmone had fallen in love with her. He had gazed into her past and wanted her anyway. Like a person frozen near to death, the thawing came slow. Her heart was hard to convince.

"You really want to marry *me*?"

The sound of his laughter, rich and low filled her ears. Instead of answering, he bent his head and kissed her. To Rahab, whose mouth was stamped with the memory of a dozen men's kisses, his caresses came as an utter shock. This simple kiss, this sweet, uncomplicated possessive touching of Salmone's flesh against hers was a first for her. It was the first time that she kissed a man she loved. It was the first time that a touch rose out of mutual affection, mutual wanting, mutual commitment. She felt as if this was her first kiss. Nothing in all her experience compared to this. A sense of belonging enveloped her, melted her.

Salmone lifted his head and she gasped. She felt dazed and disoriented. He studied her wordlessly, his perceptive eyes half-hooded. "You're always a surprise," he said and stepped away.

So many questions swirled about in Rahab's mind, she couldn't decide which to express first. *Do you really love me? Do you believe God approves of such a marriage? What will Israel say to our union? Can you forget my past—let it go—live with it?* "Joshua," she remembered abruptly. "What will he think?"

"Joshua gave me his approval before I knew for certain how I felt about you."

Rahab felt stunned. She had expected sober objections if not outright hostility. In spite of his goodness to her, having one of his great leaders united in marriage with a former *zonah* must represent a disastrous precedent, not to mention an unsavory example. How had she managed to win Joshua's approval? "I don't know what to say."

Salmone wrapped his arm around her waist and pulled her to him. "Say you'll marry me."

Flushed and overwhelmed, she repeated, "I will marry you."

Salmone gave a grunt of satisfaction and kissed her again, a hard and brief kiss that sealed his delight over her trembling flesh. When he drew back, she leaned against him for support, and he laughed softly.

"Rahab, I have one request of you."

"Yes?"

"I don't want to wait long. We are a nation at war. Battles are a certainty. I learned at Ai that I am not invincible. I don't want to waste the life I have left in the waiting."

Rahab lifted her head. "I don't know about this whole proposal. I think you should take time and practice some more." She felt the rumble of a chuckle against her cheek. The thought that this man had chosen to bind his life to hers still felt like a dream.

"You are not impressed by my proposal?" he asked. "I suppose I should have gone to your father first, as is proper. But the sight of you loosened my resolve and I blurted my feelings."

"You did not. You blurted *my* feelings."

He gave a shout of laughter and pulled her closer to him. "Pardon. What else did I do wrong?"

"Just now you hinted at an uncertain future. You should know that I do not cherish the thought of being a widow before I'm a bride. So take this as warning, Salmone ben Nahshon. Don't you even consider death and dying."

"I will do my best to comply."

"See that you do, my lord."

"You're not going to turn into a bossy wife, are you?"

"I said *my lord*, didn't I?"

Rahab spent the rest of the day in a haze of shock. She would wonder in sudden bursts of disbelief if she had dreamed Salmone's proposal. Then she would remember his kisses. She could never have imagined those feelings.

Salmone had promised to come to her father that very night. He intended to arrange for the bride price and the betrothal contract right away. And then it would become official and known to everyone that Rahab the Canaanite was going to marry a leader of the tribe of Judah.

No one knew her secret yet, and her family gave her strange looks as she walked around in a daze, not hearing their comments or responding to their requests.

"Are you sick, Rahab?" Izzie inquired in the early afternoon.

"How nice," Rahab responded. From Izzie's frown, Rahab registered that her words were an ill match for her sister's question.

As the astonishment at Salmone's proposal began to settle like fine dust after a herd has run past, Rahab began to wonder how she could have been so mistaken in his feelings. How had she missed his affection? It had never occurred to her that the man felt deeply for her. Once or twice, she had wondered if he desired her. The thought gave her no satisfaction. Given his strict sense of honor, he could only begrudge such feelings, and resent her for inspiring a most unwelcome passion. But love? Where had that been hiding?

She had little confidence in herself where Salmone was concerned. In the presence of his clean, blameless past, she felt the sins of her own more keenly. The interiors of her imagination could not stretch enough to allow such a man to love such a woman. She didn't feel good enough for him.

Surely, she would learn to be secure in him once they married. Surely his love expressed in so public and binding a commitment would sink in and she would accept that she was, indeed, lovable in his eyes? Surely they would make each other happy in marriage, bringing reassurance into the uncertainties of past and present?

Moonlight brightened Salmone's path when he came to visit his future father-in-law. With him came his sister Miriam, grinning from one ear to the next, and his mother's oldest niece, Esther, who appeared pale and jarred. Everyone from his father's line had produced polite excuses for not joining him. Joshua strode near Salmone, discussing the details of the coming betrothal. He had not only reiterated his blessing on Salmone's choice of wife, but had offered to stand in for the father of the groom. His presence soothed Salmone's hurt at the absence of other kin.

Imri saw them first as they stepped into his campsite. From his blank face, Salmone deduced that Rahab had said nothing to prepare her family for the coming proposal. A wave of amusement washed over him. This ought to prove interesting. The family, drawn by the loftiness of their unexpected guests, gathered round and made their respectful bows. Salmone stretched his neck for a glimpse of Rahab and experienced a stab of disappointment when he found her absent.

With his customary air of authority, Joshua asked to see Imri and his wife alone. In the modest family tent, the Jewish delegation was treated with gratifying hospitality. Joshua, sipping from a cup of barley water said, "Imri, we are here for a purpose. I stand in the place of Salmone's father this night, and I am here to ask for your daughter's hand."

Imri looked like he was about to topple over. "Hand, my lord? As in marriage? That kind of hand?"

"Precisely."

"But your servant only has one unmarried daughter—Rahab."

"That would be the one."

Imri's jowls shook as he turned his head with bewilderment, looking from Joshua to Salmone to his wife. "My lord Salmone wishes to marry Rahab?"

"That's what I said. So if you are willing, we would like to draw the betrothal contract."

At first, Salmone found Imri's dazed acquiescence diverting. But the alacrity with which he agreed to every one of Joshua's stipulations, and the ridiculous eagerness he displayed to satisfy Salmone's requests, soon began to grate on him. The man practically gave his daughter away for free. The bride price he almost waived, unmindful of the affront it showed to his daughter. Not once did he address Salmone and take him to account as a protective father would have done. Not once did he insist that Salmone should treat his daughter with proper consideration. It was as if he could not believe his good fortune in finding anyone to want Rahab at all. Did Imri not see the value of his own flesh and blood? Why did he not stand up for her? Salmone began mentally to withdraw from the proceedings, trying to calm his mounting anger. By the time Joshua finished the details of the contract, the prospective bridegroom barely knew what he was agreeing upon.

It was time to call for Rahab, and Miriam volunteered to fetch her. Salmone began to unclench his jaw. The prospect of seeing Rahab washed away his bristling affront. His breath hitched when she walked in. She had dressed in a simple tunic the color of cream, a woven sash tied around the narrow waist, emphasizing the deep curves of her figure. He stood up, and as was customary, took her hand in his and led her to sit next to him. Though her face appeared calm, her fingers trembled in his.

"Rahab." He waited until she lifted her head. "Your father has given his consent that we wed. Do you also give your consent?" This was, of course, a formality. She had already given her agreement in the dawn hours, and he intended to hold her to it.

"I do." Her voice came soft and unwavering. Salmone's heart contracted.

"Your father and Joshua have agreed on a betrothal settlement. Here is your bride price." He poured a handful of gold coins into her palms. With an instinctive gesture she caught them before they spilled on the floor. The gold, in fact, belonged to her father as long as he lived. But Salmone wanted her to know by this tangible means that her value in his eyes was great.

"I have another gift. This belonged to my mother." He placed the delicate gold, lapis lazuli, and pearl earrings on top of the mound of coins. "When we left Egypt, the Egyptians gave us articles of silver and gold on our way out. We gave most of it for use in the tabernacle. But many of us still have token pieces left from that season of our history. I remember my mother wearing these. It would please me to see them on you."

With an almost careless flick of her wrist, Rahab dropped the gold coins Salmone had poured into her hands in order to examine the earrings with minute care. "You're giving me your mother's jewels?"

"They will look beautiful on you."

Rahab caressed the fragile gold and lapis beads that dangled from the frame. Her fingers lingered on the single teardrop pearl in the center of each earring. He could tell she was pleased. In comparison to the value of the coins, the earrings were a trifle. Yet, somehow, they meant more to her. *You're giving me your mother's jewels?* she had asked. She was moved by the emotional weight of the gift. Because it meant something to him, she treasured it.

Salmone found himself staring at her with open delight. His overt interest was observed, and there were several suppressed grins and meaningful looks directed his way.

He cleared his throat and rose. "It's growing late." He was glad that he had insisted on a short betrothal. This was going to be a tortured three months. Turning to Rahab, he gave the traditional promise. "I go to prepare a place for you. I will return again unto you."

CHAPTER NINETEEN

Miriam, Izzie, and Abigail accompanied Rahab as she went for her ritual *mikvah* on the morning of her wedding. The Jordan had calmed its swells, and though cold, presented several safe bathing spots. The women picked a secluded location and spread their things on the banks of the river.

No sooner did Rahab wade in than her teeth began to chatter. She took a deep breath before dipping her head under water. She was certain her lips were blue by the time she emerged.

Izzie sat down on the bank and dipped her toes in the water. "Don't worry. Your bridegroom will warm you tonight." Everyone giggled except for Rahab who threw her sister a quelling glance.

There was no one with whom she could share her increasing sense of tension. Who would comprehend a Canaanite *zonah* being nervous on her wedding night? She barely understood it herself. She only knew that Izzie's silly jokes fingered a fear that went too deep to examine.

The women did not linger at the ritual immersion of *mikvah* since the water was too frigid. As soon as they had washed and spoken the words of blessing, they scrambled out of the waters and put on clean clothes. Then they accompanied Rahab to her parents' tent in order to prepare her for the wedding feast.

For her wedding, Rahab had decided to borrow an exquisite robe belonging to Izzie, woven from pale blue linen. Back in their tent, Izzie drew out the dress, and Rahab gasped. Sometime in the past few weeks, Izzie had managed secretly to embroider the hem and neckline with tiny white blossoms.

"This is yours to keep," Izzie said with a warm smile.

Miriam, who had apparently been party to the conspiracy, presented Rahab with a belt made of a long row of silver blossoms.

"I set this belt aside for your wedding present the day Salmone told me he had decided to marry you. When Izzie saw it, she conspired to decorate your wedding dress to match."

In spite of years of wearing rich garments and gilded baubles, Rahab had never felt so beautifully attired. Hugging Miriam and Izzie, she whispered, "I could not imagine lovelier wedding garments. I shall never forget your generosity."

"We did it because we love you," Miriam said. "You know, it is a pity to hide such a beautiful bride under this *badecken*. But in Israel, brides must be covered by a veil."

"I welcome it. The thought of hundreds of people staring at me for hours makes me want to run away. But before you put it on, I need one last thing." She fetched the earrings Salmone had given her and put them on. Shaking her head to make the pearls dangle she said, "Now I'm ready."

Imri, Joa, Karem, and Gerazim supported the poles of Rahab's bridal canopy as she made her way toward Salmone's tent. Hanani and Ezra, who had come to fetch her with a shout of "Behold, the bridegroom comes," led the way. Halfway, Salmone met with the company, and stepped inside the canopy beside Rahab.

He squeezed her hand. Rahab, whose nerves were growing closer to the shattering point with every step, let her hand lie in his, but did not squeeze back.

"I would say you look beautiful. But I can't see anything. I'm surprised you haven't tripped and fallen on your face. How can you see your way from under there?"

Rahab realized that Salmone was doing his best to soothe her. He wasn't succeeding. His very closeness made her more anxious. She did not want him to notice her tension, however. More than anyone on earth, she loved this man. And she wanted to make him happy. She forced herself to sound casual as she responded. "I'm following the smell of Hanani's washing oil. I think he used every last drop in his coffers in honor of our wedding."

Salmone pressed her hand again. "Do you see those lights twinkling ahead?"

"Yes."

"That's an aisle lined with torches on either side. At the end of that aisle, Joshua and Caleb are waiting to pronounce the marriage blessing over us."

"Good."

"I shall remove your veil then."

"Perfect."

283

"You're not speaking very much tonight. I'm starting to wonder if your father is pulling a switch on me the way Laban did to Jacob. You're not Izzie under there, are you?"

"No. Gerazim had a few objections to that plan. You're definitely stuck with Rahab."

"She's the one I want."

Perspiration dampened the back of Rahab's neck under the *badecken*. *What am I doing? This union can never work.* Was it too late to start running the other way? She thought of what it would do to Salmone if she refused to marry him at this late hour. How could she humiliate the man she cherished beyond her own life? It would destroy him. And yet, what if she married him and let him down? What if she fell short of his every expectation?

Her thoughts were such a jumble that she barely noticed they had arrived in front of Caleb and Joshua. Wedding guests filled every nook and cranny of available space. Joshua began the seven blessings, and Caleb followed. Rahab only heard snatches. *To honor, support, and maintain her in truth ... I bless their union ... That they may be fruitful ...*

Rahab felt faint. The *badecken* over her face had grown cloying. Hands led her in a circle around Salmone three times. She moved, feeling disconnected from the proceedings, from Salmone, from herself. Fingers pressed her to a stop. Salmone lifted the opaque *badecken* from her head and dropped it to the ground. She blinked at him, and he bent to take her mouth in a kiss, at once chaste and full of promise. A small quiver of reassurance passed through her and, leaning into him, she told herself everything would be well.

People cheered and pressed in for noisy congratulations. Salmone pulled her into his arms for a reassuring moment. "Let's inaugurate the feast. Then we can slip away and be alone for a few minutes. I have something to tell you."

Rahab forced herself to follow Salmone. She put her foot where he put his, smiled when he smiled, lifted her cup when he lifted his. She tasted a morsel of food and feared she might be sick. Then Salmone pulled her behind him out of the conclave of activity and somehow managed to lead them to a secluded spot. Without preamble he turned to her. "What is it? You are shaking. What's wrong?"

Rahab didn't know how to respond since she herself did not comprehend the root of her crumbling composure. "I think I'm afraid that I will disappoint you and you will regret marrying me," she confessed.

He drew her into a tight embrace. "That won't happen." He stepped back from her, keeping his hands on her waist, his arms a bridge linking them. "Rahab, I should have said this to you earlier. But we were hardly left alone for the past three months. I want you to know something. Your past is dead to me. It's dead between us. Never speak of it. Never allude to it. It is gone and over with. I never want to be reminded of it. I know you for who you are now. That other Rahab doesn't exist. We will build our lives on today and we'll bury the past."

Rahab's mouth turned dry. She understood that this speech was intended to make her feel better. More accepted. Her new husband was trying to reassure her. Only his words were having the opposite effect. How was she supposed to kill her past? How was she supposed to shield him from any reminders of it? What if she did or said something that would unintentionally awaken a memory of that time? Instead of making her feel steady and safe, Salmone's reassurance catapulted her into even more paralyzing dread.

Unaware that his speech had caused his bride greater misery, he enfolded her in a lighthearted embrace. "We need to go back to the feast or our guests will start wondering if we have absconded. We'll have seven uninterrupted days in the bridal bower to talk about everything. Right now, though, if we don't return, we'll be the target of every bawdy joke in Judah for a month."

Rahab nodded, unable to speak.

To the bride, the wedding feast seemed a nightmare. More than anything she wished to retire somewhere quiet and think through the ramifications of Salmone's declaration. But there was no solitude to be had on this night of all nights. Her every smile was a lie, her every word a misdirection. She only felt capable of fear this night—fear of failing her husband's wishes. Fear of being, in the end, discarded by the very person whose acceptance had given her a new hope.

As bad as the feast was, going into the bridal bower proved worse. Here, her marriage would be consummated. Here, she would be a virtual prisoner for seven days and nights with her bridegroom. Here, she would have to keep the past from entering her marriage bed and defiling it. How was she supposed to contrive that miracle?

Salmone's own tent had been set up as the bridal chamber. Miriam had decorated it with care for the occasion before leaving to spend two months at her friend Elizabeth's tent. How desperately Rahab wished for her sister-in-law's presence. But only the bride and groom were allowed in the bower.

Finally alone, Salmone cupped her face and lowered his mouth to hers, kissing her with a passion he had banked in the previous months. "My beautiful Rahab," he murmured, his voice low. Always, she had felt a melting kind of belonging in his arms. His kisses had been the most exquisite physical experience she had ever known. But on this night his words rang in her head, too well remembered. *I never want to be reminded of it,* he had said of her past. Well, if she kissed him back passionately, wouldn't that remind him? If she were responsive, wouldn't he wonder where she had learned to do this or that? From the early days of their engagement, she had harbored a belief that she did not deserve this man. Eventually, he would wake up to the fact of her inadequacies. He would grow disappointed, disenchanted. His proclamation tonight confirmed every one of these suspicions. In the intimacy of their bed, he would see reflected the faces of her past sins, and he would hate her for them.

With every new thought, Rahab grew more paralyzed with fear. She turned to stone in Salmone's arms. He seemed puzzled by her coldness. At first, he construed it as leftover wedding jitters. He spoke comforting words. His caresses were tender and soothing. He laid her on a mattress scented with myrrh and kissed her over and over. Rahab grew more frozen with every touch. The more he tried to call a response out of her, the more she shut down.

Finally Salmone withdrew. "Is something wrong?" His voice had no edge of vexation, only a puzzled concern.

His kindness seeped under her skin. She may not be able to let herself feel passion for him, but if she lay there like a corpse, surely that would not please him either. What was she supposed to do? She couldn't explain her feelings, not without wrenching the past right into bed with them. "A little apprehensive. Don't stop."

He didn't move. She reached out to him and drew him back down to her. Forcing her body to grow as pliant as the creeping tension allowed, she did her best to give him the message that she wanted this. In a way she did. She wanted to give him everything he asked. But she was too bound up in wounds and fears to be able to receive anything from him. The chains of her bondage and his incomprehension were wrapped too tightly around them for the consummation of their marriage to be anything but disappointing to both. When it was long over, Rahab wept herself silently to sleep next to her dry-eyed and wakeful bridegroom.

The seven worst days of his life were almost at an end. The woman he loved had morphed into a clam, shut up tight, and withdrawn. Following several disastrous tries, he had stopped touching her altogether. She became a block of marble in his arms. He could not understand it. The first time he had kissed her mouth, she had melted into him like she wanted nothing better than to become a part of him. Afterward, she had gazed at him with a wonder that had shaken him to his core. She had looked like she had never been kissed before. Like he was the only man on earth.

Now, when he kissed her, she turned to stone. He had wondered at first, with a nauseating uncertainty, if perhaps he wasn't as competent as the Canaanite men she had known. Was he somehow deficient? He knew from his years with Anna that this was an unlikely conclusion, but had felt pressed to ask her. Her shocked look, full of horrified dismay, had at least put to rest that crippling self-doubt.

He had tried to make her open up to him; to explain her inscrutable behavior. That was when she had turned mute. Her answers became monosyllabic and unenlightening. His witty, intelligent Rahab diminished into a wisp of herself.

This silence grated worse than her physical unresponsiveness. It stank of mistrust. She was keeping him at bay in her heart. He felt his frustration mount into anger; his anger festered into resentment, and the resentment spilled over. One out of every two words he said to her was tinged with sarcasm. He felt ashamed of himself for treating her this way. The shame just made him more resentful. He was the one wronged, wasn't he? Why should he feel bad about it?

He prayed, and was aware that she did also. But they prayed separately, never sharing the experience with each other. His prayers brought him no relief. He knew that his marriage was not a mistake, even though it was a disaster. Every time he prayed, he felt a reassurance that marrying her had been God's will. He was glad that God, at least, was happy about it. It was not a happiness Salmone could share.

His wife walked into the living area of the tent where he was lounging. In the past few days, she had contrived to avoid him as much as possible, leaving any place he entered with a predictability that would have been comical if it weren't so disillusioning.

She had left her hair loose down her back, a mass of curls twinkling red in the firelight. How often he had imagined sinking his fingers into that hair. Why shouldn't he? She was his wife. He didn't comprehend what nonsense kept her away from him, but he wasn't going to capitulate to it anymore.

He stalked over to her. She became rigid at his nearness. He saw the flicker of panic on her face and something in his heart softened. Capturing her chin in his hand he lifted her face to him. "You love me. Why are you running from me?"

She shook her head. He pulled her close. "You love me. Say it."

"I love you," she said obediently, her body shaking.

"Not like that. Say it like it means something to you. Say it like this," he said and covered her lips with his, kissing her with the force of a passion too long pent up. The kiss lengthened, became wild and deep, and to his delight, he felt her grow gradually pliant in his embrace.

"Rahab," he whispered, digging his hands into her perfumed hair. "Rahab, my bride."

It took him a few moments to realize that she had gone cold and unresponsive again. He groaned with frustration and pulled away. "Tell me! Tell me what ails you. Stop fighting me!"

She shook her head again, her face white. He flung her away from him and strode off in disgust. He had married a woman in a wall. Wooing her was like running at full speed into brick and mortar. After seven days he had enough bruises to last him a lifetime.

CHAPTER TWENTY

Salmone's face hid his inner turmoil. Now that the marriage week was over, at least he could immerse himself in the activities of daily work. For the past ten days, he had left his tent before dawn and come home long after dusk. Rahab seemed to grow worse every day, more distant, more of a shell. In her own way, she also tried to find solace in work. She cooked meticulous, elaborate meals that he rarely bothered to taste. She washed his clothes and mended them. She wove wool. She even took care of the livestock, a job that his servant and the shepherd boy he hired were perfectly capable of performing. But unlike him, she wasn't merely trying to get lost in activity. He realized with a bitterness he couldn't conceal that she was trying to appease him. As if working hard made up for what she withheld from him. Did she think she could perform her way into his approval?

He had managed to evade Joshua during this time, half worried that he might notice something was amiss. But his good fortune ran out as he made his way back to his tent one evening.

Joshua, seeming to appear out of nowhere, attached himself to Salmone's side.

"And how is my young bridegroom?"

"Well, thank you," Salmone lied, keeping his voice pleasant.

"Then why is it I am told you hardly visit your tent? Out and about before sunup and home after nightfall? Is this any way for a newly married man to conduct himself?"

Salmone frowned darkly. "When I come and when I go is my business if you please."

"I don't please, as it happens. A man who takes a new wife shall not go out with the army, according to the law—"

"And I have not!"

"And he is not to engage in heavy public duty."

Salmone had nothing to say to that. Joshua wrapped a brown hand around his rigid arm. "Do you know, I've found a convenient little oasis not far from our camp. I feel the need for a refreshing stroll. Would you accompany me, my friend?"

Salmone wasn't fooled by Joshua's pleasant words. He had his iron-will face on, and would not be refused. Clenching his jaw, Salmone fell into step with the leader of Israel. As if by mutual consent, at first they avoided the sensitive topic of Salmone's marriage. They spoke of the twelve tribes, issues of settlement, farming, and the certainty of upcoming wars, until they arrived at Joshua's oasis. Ironically, it was the very spot where Salmone had proposed to Rahab. He swallowed his bitterness and sat against the trunk where he had prayed about his future.

Joshua crossed his legs comfortably in front of him. "I wished you would speak to me. I can see you are suffering."

"There are some things a man can't share. Not even with you, Joshua."

"Doubtless you are right. But are you sure this is one of them? Or is it your pride that keeps you from speaking to me?" Salmone laid his head back against the peeling palm. "I don't know. I don't know anything anymore."

Joshua reached out a hand and placed it on Salmone's shoulder. "Son, talk to me."

Unbidden, Salmone's eyes filled with tears—tears of frustration and anger, tears of disillusionment, tears of hurt. He couldn't resist the proffered comfort and wisdom. He had scant hope that even Joshua would be able to change things. Yet the thought of unburdening himself to someone he trusted proved too tempting, and he began, in halting and sometimes embarrassed sentences, to tell Joshua of his married life.

When he was finished, Joshua scratched his beard. "Let me see if I comprehend this. On your wedding day, you told Rahab that she was never to speak of the past. Never allude to it. That you never wanted to be reminded of it, yes?"

"Exactly. You can bear witness yourself that I've done everything I can to woo this woman. Make her feel cherished."

Joshua covered his mouth with his hand.

"What?" Salmone barked, annoyed. "Don't you lay the blame of this on me."

"It's not a question of blame. It's a question of understanding. Your wife needs to know that you accept her past, not that you're pretending it doesn't exist."

"I don't see any difference."

"There's a world of difference. Son, a woman needs to feel

safe in love. She needs to know her husband accepts everything about her and still loves her. To be known through and through, including the failures of her past, the shortcomings of her character, and still be loved, that's the Promised Land of a woman's heart. That's where she finds rest."

"So?"

"When you say to your wife that you want to avoid every mention of her past, aren't you in fact telling her that this one thing about her you cannot bear? That there is a piece of her that is unacceptable to you? You cannot tolerate this part of her? You cannot contend with it? You cannot look into the depth of her mistakes and still desire her? Aren't you saying that the only way you can want her is to pretend that part of her life never existed?

"It seems to me that what you're offering her is a conditional love, at best. What she needs from you is to take her as she is and love her as she is. I'm not saying approve of her wrongdoing. But, Salmone, she already knows full well what she did wrong. What she needs is for you to offer her *your* acceptance. For you to show her that what she did is not who she is. She needs to receive this message from you, receive it over and over until her heart believes it. Instead, you have shown Rahab that she is not safe in your love. It's plain that she already doesn't feel good enough for you. Add to that the judgments of your heart, and is it a wonder the woman has turned into stone?

"Another thing, more practical. When you say to a woman that you never want to be reminded of her past, it places her in a wretched dilemma. I dare say she freezes in your arms because she is afraid if she does something that reminds you she had lovers before you, you will discard her. You will stop loving her. You have put limits on your love, and she is trying to stay within them."

Something rebellious and hard rose up in Salmone. He wanted to refute Joshua's charges. He wanted to defend himself. He kept his mouth shut by sheer force of discipline. Several times, he swallowed the bile that rose up in his fierce desire to vindicate himself. Joshua was too wise to interrupt and waited out as Salmone calmed down enough to think through Joshua's words. Was there justice in them? This question became more paramount than his bitter need to vindicate himself. Could Joshua be right?

The more Salmone thought, the more he felt like someone had punched him in the gut. Joshua's recriminations started to bore through his hard defenses. He sagged against the tree as he finally acknowledged the truth behind Joshua's words: he had never let go of his wife's past. Not honestly.

"I fooled myself into believing that I had accepted Rahab's life in Jericho," he muttered. "Now I realize that I buried it, but I never accepted it. Joshua, what am I to do? How am I to change my heart? How am I to offer her the kind of security you say she needs when I don't have it in me? If it is the limits of my love she fears, she has a right. They are there. I hate what she did. It cools my ardor to remember it. And I cannot fathom how to change myself."

"That's because it cannot be done. Not by you, in any case. But with God, all things are possible. Now that you have seen into your true heart and accepted the responsibility of your own failures, He can have His way. He can transform you."

"I've been so angry, so full of resentment toward her, and it's been me. I am the culprit. I haven't cherished Rahab the way she deserves because my devotion has many limitations."

Joshua held up a hand. "Wait, now. This is not all you. Rahab comes with her own burdens. You can't tell me that a girl sold into adultery at fifteen by her own father doesn't have a few gashes in her soul. I have told you one, which is that she feels beneath you. Not good enough for you. For a marriage to work well, husband and wife need to know their own value before God. But that old hurt in Rahab can be healed. Though it may appear improbable now, God can use you, Salmone, as a means of restoration in her life. If you are willing."

Oh, he was willing! The thought made Salmone's heart beat like a drum. More than anything, he wanted to bring healing to Rahab. An image of her changing his bandages, cleansing the oozing pus with patient fingers, gently washing away the putrefaction of his broken body, flashed across his mind. Could he do this for her soul? Could he help bring healing into the wreck of her heart? God would have to deal with his own hard heart first, teach him real love, set him free of his own bondage before he could be of use to Rahab.

"I fear I may fail her," he choked out.

"You may."

"Joshua!"

"Don't expect perfection from yourself, son. Or from her. You shall both make mistakes on this journey. You won't have a good marriage because you won't fail your wife, or she you. It is what you do in response to those failures that will determine the course of your marriage. Now, shall we pray and ask for God's help?"

After praying for Salmone, Joshua left him to think. It was pitch-black now, and Salmone could barely make out the shape of the bent palms and skinny terebinth. He felt spent, unprepared to face Rahab, yet. He understood that God alone could help him win this battle. Without frequent prayer, he would fall to discouragement and wrong thinking. A picture of Jericho rose up in his mind. The walls of Jericho—enormous, daunting, ancient—filled his mind with unusual clarity. *This is Rahab*, he thought. *She is bound up in so many walls—walls of fear, of rejection, of loneliness, of unworthiness.*

But God brought Jericho's walls down because Israel clung to the Lord and not to their own understanding: *he would cling to God.* God brought Jericho's walls down because Israel persisted: *he would persist with his wife.* God brought Jericho's walls down because He wanted to give Israel that territory: *God wanted to give Rahab to Salmone.* He believed this with single-minded conviction.

Rahab's freedom was God's will. And it was that will that would win them the victory. As he had been a warrior for God against the walls of Jericho, so he would be a warrior for God against the walls that trapped his precious wife. He would demonstrate the same obedience, the same patience and persistence, the same unyielding resolve to win over his wife that he had shown in battle against Canaan's cities. The soldier in him smiled.

Long into the night Salmone then wrestled with his own judgment of Rahab. Once, he had been disgusted with Imri for not knowing his daughter's worth. He saw, now, that in his own way, he had failed to value his bride. He had made of her two women, the one lovable and precious, the other tainted, unde-sirable. She had grown paralyzed with that division, not know-ing how to keep the two halves apart for him. Because within her own soul she was shamed and belittled by her past, she did not have the resources to stand against his unspoken recrimi-nations. She took them in and felt them just. She believed them the true measure of herself.

Salmone wanted to love her right. He wanted to cherish her and make her feel secure in him. He wanted the limitations of his love removed until his bride felt that she belonged to him. Was safe in him. For hours he prayed that God would teach him to love Rahab like that. He repented. He confessed. He strove in prayer until he was spent. For a few hours he fell asleep be-neath the shade of the tree where God had first told him that he could marry Rahab. When the sun shone high in the pale sky, Salmone made his way home. For the first time in days, joy accompanied his steps. He walked like a warrior intent on conquering a priceless territory.

Rahab jumped as Salmone entered their tent. It was late morning. He had not come home for the night, and she had fretted through the wakeful hours that he had left her. Secretly, she studied the handsome face. He seemed inscrutable to her. Was he angry?

He drew close without touching her. Something in her wanted desperately to step back and put more distance between them. She resisted the impulse, knowing it would annoy him.

His silence goaded her to speak. "Have you . . . have you eaten? Would you like some food? I just finished baking some bread. There is trout and goat cheese too."

"Sounds delicious."

With relief she turned away to fetch the food. He grabbed her wrist and pulled her back to him. "Would you pack it for us? I thought we could go outside the camp and be alone for the afternoon."

"Alone?"

His smile deepened the grooves in his cheeks. It was the first smile he had given her in days. Rahab's heart quickened at the sight of it. "That was the idea, yes. You. Me. Food. We could go past the tent of the wounded. You used to walk near there. Remember?"

"Y-y-yes." Was this a peace offering? Encouraged, Rahab dared a slight smile back. But the burgeoning hope proved short-lived. How long would his benevolence last? How long before she ruined it with a wrong word or action?

"Would you like help with the food?"

"I can manage. Thank you." Rahab found a clean sack and put the still-warm barley bread inside. She took her time wrapping a slice of soft cheese in cloth. Her movements were slow as she added the fish to her bundle. She grabbed a wooden cup for water, and tried to think of something else that might delay their departure. She didn't want to go. It would only end in disappointment. She knew her reluctance did not escape Salmone's notice. He was frighteningly perceptive. And yet he did not seem perturbed by it. He sat on a rug, whistling a jaunty tune under his breath as he changed into sturdier sandals. When she couldn't delay anymore, she came to him and dangled her bundle.

"Lunch is ready." She tried to make her voice sound carefree.

"Oh, but this won't do."

"What?" she asked, alarmed.

"Your shoes. Much too delicate for a trek outside the camp. You'll get blisters in those flimsy things. Come here."

Rahab went to him, heart pounding. He made a motion for her to sit near and she obeyed. He fetched her walking shoes, and she extended her hand to take them from him.

"I'll take care of it." He knelt before her and lifted her foot. Gently, he undid her sandal.

Rahab's throat went dry. She tried to pull her foot free. "My feet aren't clean."

He held tight to her ankle, not letting go when she struggled. Seeing the determination in his eyes, she grew still. He gave her a small smile full of approbation. Pulling off her sandals, he wiped her feet with a damp cloth, and strapped on her sturdy shoes.

"That wasn't so hard, was it?" He took a moment to rinse his hand in a pitcher before rising. "Well, wife, are you coming or are you going to keep clinging to the rug all day?"

Rahab had forgotten she was sitting. An openmouthed confusion had dulled her thinking. Had he truly done the work of slaves—washed her feet and tenderly strapped on her sandals for her? What was he up to, this husband of hers who was an utter mystery to her? What was he doing here at home in the middle of the day, acting like nothing was wrong between them? Where had he spent the previous night? From the stubborn angle of his jaw she suspected that she wouldn't discover any answers until he was good and ready to tell her.

She scrambled to her feet and was startled when he took her hand, lacing his fingers through hers. Bending to pick up the bundle of food she had made, he flashed a smile. "Be a shame if we forgot this. I feel hungry for the first time in days."

Salmone set the pace, ambling with his long-legged gait until he realized that Rahab was scrambling to keep up. He slowed his steps immediately. "I'm sorry. I often do that to you. Force of habit, I suppose. Miriam complains that I walk like a mountain goat."

As they walked, he began to regale her with stories from his work, discussing the challenges of settlement and farming that faced their community in the immediate future. With flattering frequency, he asked her opinion, considering her responses with serious interest. By the time they had made their way out of the perimeter of Israel's boundaries, Rahab found herself calmer.

Salmone chose a path that led to a narrow brook. "Let's cross to the other side. There are some pretty acacia trees over there, as I recall."

Rahab stepped forward, intending to submerge her foot into the water. Without warning, Salmone grabbed her around the waist and swung her high into his arms. "No need for us both to get wet," he said, grinning.

Without her volition Rahab felt herself tense. Being this close to him was torture. Salmone's handsome face softened. "Be at your ease. I won't harm you, Rahab." His voice, low and quiet, held no edge, no irony. Relief flooded her. Relief that her uncontrollable reactions were not turning him away from her as they often did. She let herself go limp, but could not bring herself to raise her arms and clasp him about the neck.

On the other side of the brook, Salmone lowered her to the ground, letting her body slide down against his in slow motion. Heat rushed to Rahab's cheeks, but if Salmone noticed it, he made no comment. "What do you think of this spot? We can sit on that low rock under the shade of the acacia tree."

Rahab nodded. She would have agreed to sit down on a dunghill if he had suggested it, she was so utterly befuddled by his actions. He handed her bread and fish, which she could only play with. Her stomach churned at the thought of food.

"You need to put that in your mouth and start chewing. You've lost too much weight."

Rahab was deaf to the concern in his words and could only focus on the implied criticism. Did he think she was losing her looks? Did he find her unattractive? She shoved a piece of bread in her mouth and swallowed with determination. It stuck in her throat, choking her, and she hunched over, coughing.

"Drink this," he commanded, holding a cup filled with water from the brook to her lips. She managed a sip. Then another, until the coughing began to subside. "It would help if you chewed before swallowing. You know of chewing? It's when you move your teeth up and down."

Rahab smiled in spite of herself. "You've lost weight yourself. It's good to see you eat."

He grew earnest and thoughtful at her words. "It hasn't been an easy time for either of us."

"No."

"Rahab, I brought you here because I wanted us to come to a quiet place where we could talk openly."

She felt a wave of nausea at the thought of one more conversation with Salmone. He would now press her for answers, answers she could not give. "Must we, Salmone? We are having a pleasant day. Let's not ruin it." She rose up and turned her back to him. Everything in her strained to run—from this place and from this man with his probing questions.

Salmone's voice sounded calm. "We can't hide from this trouble. We must face it together. I don't fault you for feeling as you do. I've made many mistakes, Rahab. I ask your pardon."

Rahab's heart contracted. A painful certainty began to creep over her. He wanted to set her aside—divorce her. That was why he was apologizing. That was the mistake to which he referred. No wonder he had stayed away all night and arrived home in good humor. He was resolved already. And who could blame him? The entirety of Israel would sigh with relief. *Oh God, I cannot bear it. I cannot.*

"Please don't, Salmone," she cried, her heart in her throat.

In a flash he was beside her. "Don't what, Rahab? What is it?"

She almost begged, begged for him not to leave her, not to abandon her. But she had gulped down a lifetime of entreaties, knowing them useless. Why belittle herself further by starting now? One thing she could try to salvage was the vestiges of her bruised pride. She hung her head in defeat, beseeching God in the silence of her agonized thoughts. *Give me courage to let him go.* "You're right," she said, her voice cracking like dry tinder. "Divorce would be best."

CHAPTER TWENTY-ONE

The silence that greeted her outburst held an ominous thunder. Rahab was surprised to see an expression of despair flicker across Salmone's face. "Why do you bring up divorce? I said nothing about us parting."

"But you were thinking it. It's all right. I don't blame you. I suppose I see no other solution myself."

"I never thought it. Never even considered it. Never will."

He had *never* thought about it? It occurred to her, with a kind of astonished wonder, that she had wounded him by her suggestion. He was hurt. Hurt that she would wish to end their marriage. And why had she proposed divorce? Only to spare her pride. She had reacted as she always did to the horrors of life. She had hidden her real feelings behind a pretense of strength, and in the process, wounded the man she was supposed to protect. In order to save face, she had hurt him.

"I . . . I didn't mean it," she gasped. "I thought you wanted it; that's why I said it."

She saw some of the tension leaving his features. "Come with me. Come and sit by my side."

As she followed him, it began to sink into her benumbed brain that he didn't mean to set her aside. Relief flooded her until she grew weak with it. She loved this man beyond any limits she had set for her heart. She loved him so much that the thought of losing him hurt worse than death.

"Rahab," Salmone began when they sat face-to-face. "What made you think I wanted to divorce you?"

"Things have been so difficult between us."

"Yes, and part of that is my fault. But merely because our marriage is difficult at present doesn't mean that I want to end it. What I want is to work it out, make it into the marriage God intends for us to have.

"Some of our trouble is due to me. I've done wrong by you, Rahab. I didn't mean to, but that doesn't change the outcome. I placed an unreasonable prohibition on you, and I am deeply sorry for it. I should never have said that I didn't want to be reminded of your past. It was foolish of me. I now realize that I placed you in an impossible position.

"What I want, is to start over."

Rahab lowered her eyes. What he had said on their wedding day had been a glimpse of his true feelings. He had shown her by those words that he could not bear her sins, or the sins done against her. Those words captured Salmone's real sentiments. "I wish that were possible," she said with slow deliberation. "But I see no way. You can't change your heart. You can't alter your feelings even if you want to. My past won't disappear. How I wish it would! But it will always remain between us."

Saying the words aloud made her feel more hopeless than ever.

Salmone leaned toward her. "Who says my heart can't be changed? Didn't God change yours? I can't alter myself; it's true. But God can transform me as much as He did you."

"I'm the same as I always was. How am I altered?"

"A life lived differently shows a change in the soul. Can't you see that your very desire for God shows how He has transformed you from the inside out? Trust God if you don't trust yourself. You certainly don't trust my love—I know this. You expect it to fail. To come to an end and let you down eventually, like your father's did."

It had never occurred to Rahab that her father's failure to love her would reflect in her relationship with her husband. Was she, as he hinted, incapable of trusting Salmone because her father had taught her that all loves fail in the end? Was she punishing him for her father's sins? She put her head in her hands and sighed.

He reached out and cupped her cheek. "This is going to take more than words. My little Jericho, I'll have to be very persistent to win you to me."

"What did you call me?" She pulled away from his hand.

"It's my own special name for you."

"I don't want to be called that," she objected in frigid tones, offended at the comparison, remembering a city decrepit in its character.

"Don't you want to know why I call you that before you forbid me?"

"No! Yes."

"It's a picture God gave me. You don't know this perhaps,

but for Israel, conquering Jericho represented an impossibility. Those high walls." He shook his head. "How were we to climb them? Smash them? In the end, God did the work. Our job was to show up, day after day, ignoring every discouragement, persisting in what He had asked us to do. Those walls came down not because of our strength, but because of God's.

"You are that walled city, Rahab. In my flesh, I didn't have the resources to win you. But God is dealing with us both. He is transforming me as much as He seeks to transform you."

"You see yourself as the one God will use to pull down my defenses. Is that what you mean?"

"If I let Him. And if you let me."

"It sounds painful. You forget, I was there the day Jericho's walls came down. You want me to go through that?"

"Yes, if it means you'll be restored."

Rahab leaned back, her heart beating fast. She drew her knees to her chest and held them tightly in the circle of her arms. "What do you mean to do?"

Salmone gazed at her, his eyes unflinching, boring into her with the precision of one of Zuph's knives. "Whatever I must."

Dread grabbed hold of her and she felt herself pale. "I don't know if I can do this, Salmone."

"There is nothing for you to do but learn to trust me. The One who parted the Jordan has more than enough power to heal our marriage. I don't intend to give up. You'll learn to believe that in time."

His face was set with an unrelenting resolve. The force of it struck Rahab dumb. She had a feeling that her life was about to turn on its head.

Salmone stood and stretched his hand toward her. She grasped it without thinking. He pulled her up in one swift movement, dislodging her equilibrium so that she was thrown against his chest. His arms wrapped about her for a precious moment, steadying her, and then as soon as she found her footing, he released her. The distance came as a relief to her. She needed the safety of some room between them. As though cognizant of her emotions, he did not insist on carrying her across the shallow stream this time, and forbearing comment, he let her splash in, wetting her feet.

Rahab thought with relief that he was finished for now. That he had sheathed his sword in its scabbard for now. She discovered she was wrong.

"Months ago, when you were first seeking to join us, Miriam told me about your father. He is the one who asked you to become a *zonah*, as I recall. When you were fifteen. Am I right?"

Rahab stiffened. Why did he have to bring that up? "Yes."

"Will you tell me about it?"

As her husband, he had every right to ask her. What would be the harm in telling him? He knew the worst, anyway. Hadn't she been the one to insist on disclosing the facts of her life before joining Israel? Hadn't she risked her future for the sake of honesty? So what held her back at this moment?

With Miriam, she had divulged only what she wanted. She had spoken the truth, but painted by a broad brush. The barebones facts that she had disclosed didn't reveal her inner struggles. Her shame. And that had been hard enough. She had felt like she had cut herself just by telling that much. But Salmone asked for more. He wanted to glimpse her soul.

She thought of her father's decision that fateful day, the decision that had turned the tide of her future. It still made her tremble to remember it. Her own father had thought her expendable. With unexpected clarity, Rahab saw that she had learned to agree with him. Her mind held him accountable for his sin against her, held him responsible for a violation she would never have committed against a child of her own. But in her deepest heart, she realized that she believed her father's conclusion. She *was* expendable. She was worthy of being discarded. And she feared that Salmone would realize it once he heard her story. If her own father thought her of no consequence, wouldn't Salmone, in hearing it, come to realize this was his wife's true worth?

As they walked through the wilderness toward Israel's camp, she could feel the heat of his body as his arm brushed against hers, feel the solid dependability of his strength. He waited for her answer with uncharacteristic patience.

He wanted her to trust him. Even though he had confessed that his love was limited and perhaps unable to withstand the ravages of her former life, he wanted her to trust him. *No, not him. God.* He wanted her to trust God at work in him and in her.

Was this a matter of faith, then? Once, she had risked her whole life for the sake of her faith. She had been utterly convinced that the Lord would bring down Jericho's walls and wrest victory from Israel's enemies. Could she not have faith that this God was big enough to conquer her heart and Salmone's too?

Here were her choices then: to trust God or to trust the monstrous fears of her heart. And Salmone had the same choice before him. It would take both of them for this marriage to have a chance at fulfillment. She could not control Salmone's choices, but she *could* control her own.

She stopped in the middle of the path. "I will tell you, Salmone. I'll tell you whatever you want to know about my father."

Salmone's eyes turned liquid soft. He drew her to a rock and they sat next to each other, exposed to the hot afternoon sun. With slow, broken sentences, Rahab told her story. She avoided her husband's eyes, petrified that she might find coldness or detachment in them. She spoke of her father, and of the circumstances that had forced his betrayal. She didn't mention much about Zedek, the man who had purchased her untutored favors when she was merely fifteen, knowing that he would have his own day of reckoning. Salmone would not leave that stone unturned, she guessed. For now, however, she only had enough strength to speak of her father's choice and her own role in the ensuing events.

Salmone listened without interrupting, except for a few exclamations. When she revealed that she had refused to join the temples though it would have made life so much easier, he burst out, "Even then you resisted idolatry. No wonder God set you apart for Himself."

This was the first time she had verbalized her story to anyone. It was cathartic to tell, but other emotions besmirched the relief. Weariness. Shame. Guilt. She felt exposed and vulnerable. Holding herself stiff, she separated herself from Salmone. If she chose to withhold herself from him, it wouldn't hurt so much as having him rebuff her.

"Stop it," he rasped. "Stop drawing away from me." He pulled her into his arms. "Stay with me."

Rahab lay against his chest, her heart pounding. He hadn't reviled her. Though he knew that she had capitulated to her father's demands, he hadn't judged her. She had helped her parents plan so that they could reap the greatest financial benefit. He knew this and still held her, tenderness etched on his soft lips.

With a shy movement Rahab did the boldest thing she had yet done in her life. She reached for Salmone's hand and held it. It cost her more courage than it had to hide Israel's spies from the king's men. It cost her every drop of her inner strength to make this move toward him, instead of waiting on him to reach for her.

Salmone grasped her fingers with a force that almost crushed her hand. "My brave girl," he whispered, and kissed her. He kissed her and kissed her, not letting go of her trembling hand until she melted against him.

It was the Sabbath and Israel rested. No one cooked. No one mended. No one worked. Rahab loved the Sabbath now, though in her first days after escaping Jericho, having a full day of inactivity while so many chores remained undone felt more frustrating than restful. With time, she had come to see the Sabbath as an expression of God's concern for her. Now she kept it gladly no matter how many seemingly important things she had to ignore.

She sat in the weak autumn sun, her legs stretched before her, quietly reciting the *Shema*, while covering her eyes with her right hand: *Hear O Israel, the Lord our God, the Lord is one.*

The earth moved gently. Beneath her hand Rahab raised her eyebrows. That was odd; she had never experienced that before when she had recited the *Shema*. Distracted, she began once more. *Hear O Israel . . .*

The earth moved again, harder this time. She realized the movement wasn't a figment of her imagination. Salmone's cry as he ran from the tent made Rahab sit bolt upright. "Earthquake!"

Again, the earth trembled, this time unmistakably. Rahab gasped. Absently, she noticed that sheep and goats were running loose, freed from their pens by the force of the tremors. The sound of shouts grew loud around them.

Salmone dropped beside her and pulled her into his arms. "It's all right. It's all right."

Held in the circle of his arms, she began to feel the fear drain out of her. She knew Salmone did not have power over the earth; he couldn't make it stop trembling. Yet irrationally, his simple presence made her feel safe. She clung to him tightly for long moments.

"I think it's over," Salmone said, pulling back a little. He surveyed the landscape around them. "There doesn't seem to be much damage. It was a minor quake."

One of the neighbors' loosed goats nuzzled Rahab's shoulder. She laughed, patting the coarse wool on the beast's neck. "I've found a new friend."

Salmone smiled, scanning the area. "It will be a chore sorting the animals out. But for now, it's still Sabbath. Let them roam. We'll take care of them after sundown."

"You'd think the earth would know better than to make such

a fuss on the Lord's Day," Rahab said, indignant at the rude interruption of her restful prayers.

"I will lodge a letter of complaint, shall I?"

"A very long one."

Salmone's eyes crinkled in the corners. He took Rahab back into his arms. A sense of peace washed over her. Salmone was himself not unlike an earthquake, dislodging her world with the force of his will. Yet, astonishingly, no one made her feel so protected as this man.

Too soon, the peace in Salmone ben Nahshon's household came to a painful end. He had spent several challenging days dealing with a quarrel between two headstrong men. Although Caleb, the leader of the tribe of Judah, had curtailed many of his duties due to his recent marriage, he was allowed the work of arbitration, a duty he usually enjoyed. But when two hot-tempered blockheads refused to concede on any point, arbitration took a slippery slide into hair-raising exasperation.

He brought some of his frustrations home. They stuck under his skin, interfering with his prayers, and Salmone found himself at the wrong end of a clash with his wife when he was least prepared for it.

A scream tore through the night, jolting Salmone out of sleep. His soldier's instincts kicked in with instant alertness. Rahab moaned, and he realized that she was caught in the grip of a nightmare.

He shook her gently, concerned when she would not wake.

"Rahab! Rahab!" he cried.

She snapped awake with a gasp. Salmone ran a comforting hand across her shoulder, surprised to find her skin cold and damp. Her glazed eyes stared into space.

"It was a nightmare," he said, drawing her gently into his arms. Pulling a corner of the blanket over her, he cradled her through its thick folds, trying to impart a sense of safety into her shivering body.

She nodded. He tightened his arms around her and held her as if she were a child. "What was it about, can you tell me?"

She stiffened and pulled away. "Nothing really. I get them often."

"Tell me about this one."

"I want to forget it."

Salmone let out a sigh of annoyance. They had lived in a happy truce since their conversation in the wilderness some weeks before. He had not pressured her to divulge any more details of her former life. Yet given their recent camaraderie, he expected more trust from her. What did he have to do to win her over?

"Who was in it?" he insisted.

She licked her lips. The skin was dry and cracking. "Zedek."

Salmone recognized the name instantly and pounced on it. "The goldsmith. The one to whom your father sold you."

"For a season."

"Did he abuse you?" Try as he might, he could not make his voice temperate. There was an edge to every word. "Is that why you have nightmares about him?"

"No. He . . . he was gentle enough."

"I see. And this is why you wake up screaming in the night."

"I wake up screaming because I didn't want him! I didn't want him, but I did what he asked. Every single thing he asked, do you hear me? Every single thing he paid for. I refused him nothing." She rose from the mattress, shaking now with agitation rather than fear.

Salmone felt himself go cold. Too late, he realized that he wasn't ready for this confrontation. He wasn't prepared to extend love to his wife in exchange for her brutal choices. This picture of her unresisting compliance made him sick. She had been a willing participant. He tried to dredge up some compassion for her, but the best he could do was to silence the words of judgment that trembled on his lips.

"And then, when the three months were over, he dismissed me without once looking back." She covered her face with her hands and began to sob. "He didn't want me anymore."

Salmone's heart began to pound so that he could barely hear his own voice. "Did you love him? Is that what you're saying?"

She raised her head, her tearstained face bleak. "Love him? He made my skin crawl."

"I should think," he said, his voice like ice, "I should think having such a man release you would be a relief rather than a cause for tears. I don't understand you, Rahab."

She sank down onto their bed as if her legs couldn't support her anymore. "I may not have loved him, but I would have preferred to stay with one man than be passed around from one to another. In the end, I suppose I wasn't good enough for him. He had enough of me within three months."

Salmone's mind became a whirl of confusion. The thought of another man pawing at his wife while she willingly let him made his stomach turn. The thought of her writhing in agony over his rejection annoyed him. She should have been conceiving of ways to escape the man rather than be so downcast about the end of the liaison. He knew that he was supposed to comfort her now, but he could not. Without a word, he grabbed his cloak and went outside. The sound of his wife's weeping tore at him as he walked out, but he kept right on going.

By the goat pen he sank to the ground, leaning his back against the fence. The pungent odor of goat dung barely penetrated his senses. His guts cramped with the turmoil that whirled in him like a windstorm. Fisting a calloused hand, he punched the ground, twice, three times, until the sting of the hard dirt cutting into his skin brought him to his senses and he stopped.

He drew his knees against his belly and laid his head on top of them. For a few minutes, he continued to stew in his anger, anger against Zedek, against Imri, against Rahab, against life. Against God. *Why did You do it? Why did You let her live like that? Why did You bring her into my life?*

A great silence met his raving. Salmone gulped in big lungfuls of air, trying to keep the tears from coming. In slow increments, the seething anger passed over him. He gave up ranting and began talking. Then listening. As he began to pray, his heart grew soft, changing within him.

He realized that every time he fought this battle, he gained a bit of ground. He didn't land back where he had been before. It seemed to flow out of him the same at first—the same judgment, the same conditional love. But when he worked through it as he had now—God with him, guiding him—Salmone knew that his feelings had undergone a shift that was real. A change that was permanent. Before much time had passed he went back into the tent, back to his wife, who lay still weeping on the ground near their rumpled mattress.

His stomach tightened at the sight of her. There had been so many occasions that should have led her to tears—endless tears. War. The destruction of her world. The meanness of her new neighbors. Her unspoken love for him. Yet she had been frugal with those tears. Tonight, she was crying as if she would not stop.

He went on his knees before her. "Forgive me, Rahab."

She shook her head and cried harder. He felt like she was shredding his insides with her sobs. "You won't forgive me?"

"No. I mean yes. I mean there's nothing to forgive."

"Of course there is. I didn't stand by you as I should have. But I'm here now. Not like Zedek, see? I'm back for you."

She shook her head again, saying nothing.

"Rahab, it's hard for me to hear about you with other men. I won't deny it. And tonight, it was especially hard, because I am exhausted and because I had not prayed. That's no excuse—more an explanation. I grew angry and I shouldn't have. What's worse is that I'll probably do it again. But beloved, I have returned. I am here, and I want you. I want you for always. I am no Zedek."

"Please, Salmone. Can we just let it go? Let's go to sleep."

The haunted expression on her face told Salmone that he had to give up for the night. She was too fragile to take in his pleas, to grasp the truth of them. He leaned away from her, his jaw set. He had lost some ground. Tomorrow, he would gain it back. And more. Joshua had warned him that he would fail Rahab, and that she would also fail him. Victory, he remembered, was not so much in being perfect toward each other. Rather, victory would flow out of how they dealt with their failures.

"All right. We'll talk another time. Come to bed now." He wanted, with an itching desire, to pick her up and carry her to their now cold bed. But he sensed that in her present state of mind any form of intimacy with him would cause her to be more distraught.

With jerky movements she crawled back to the pallet. Setting his jaw, he stopped himself from lifting her, helping her, holding her. He lay next to her, careful to avoid physical contact. He had not been intimate with her since those painfully awkward attempts in the early days of their marriage. The story she had shared with him about her father had convinced him that he needed to earn her trust before their marriage bed could become a place of joy to them. So he had restrained his desire. Yet at the same time he had made some inroads in teaching her to enjoy his touch. His casual caresses no longer turned her to stone. Now he felt her body respond to him when he kissed her lips. Tonight, he had forfeited some of that ground. The loss grated on him, inasmuch as he felt it was his own fault. He vowed with a single-minded resolve that he would take back what he had lost.

It took him considerable time to fall asleep. When he woke up, it was late. His breakfast was laid out, and his wife was gone.

CHAPTER TWENTY-TWO

It took every bit of Rahab's self-control to keep still as she lay next to her husband. She could not rest. She felt mortified by the previous night's events. It was humiliating enough to wake up screaming like a madwoman. Her husband must have thought he was being attacked by savage Canaanites before he realized that it was his own wife having a wrestling match with her nightmares. As though that weren't enough, she had spoken about her disgrace.

Poor Salmone. How much could an honorable man take? He hadn't raved, but she had sensed his seething anger riding hard beneath the surface of his stretched resources. She knew that he had returned to her out of guilt. His well-intentioned determination to abide by her had driven him back to her side. But he had seen a glimpse of her real heart, and no amount of good intention could make excuses for that.

In a moment of weakness, she had revealed her true nature to him. He had been confronted with the awful truth that his wife was a harlot in her soul as much as in her body. She was no good. And now he realized it, and it was only compunction that kept him by her side, sleeping so still in the predawn darkness.

Rahab began praying with silent desperation, slipping first into words she knew well. *Blessed art Thou, O Lord, our God.* But she could not focus on the familiar blessing; the wail deep inside her needed the expression of her own words. *Lord, my hope is gone—gone. I am heavyhearted, cut off from my husband, from my future, from Your love. But You are able to restore life to me. Raise me up from this grave of despair: give me a new life and a new hope, I ask.*

Sighing, she rose up, hardly making a sound as she prepared her husband's breakfast, and then left the tent in her bare feet, carrying her sandals in her hand to ensure she did not disturb him.

Thankfully, she had prearranged to meet with Miriam today, which gave her the perfect excuse to delay speaking to her husband again. Before leaving, she gave a message to the sleepy servant who was feeding the goats, informing Salmone of her plans. Like a coward, Rahab snuck out before Salmone had a chance to force another discussion upon them. She had no wish to face him. For the length of this day, at least, she would have a hiding place.

Twice a week, without fail, Miriam packed up food, medicine, and bandages and took herself outside Israel's camp to the tent of the sick. She nursed anyone who happened to be there, often without having met them before. Family members, weary from endless cycles of care, accepted her intervention with relief. Zuph and other physicians had come to respect the young woman's ability and entrusted some of their complicated cases to her.

During her long days of nursing Salmone, Rahab had also

found herself drawn to the hard work of attending the sick. The awareness that she could be of indispensable use thrilled her. Overcoming her shyness, she asked to join Miriam on her weekly visits to the sick. Today was to be her first trial.

Miriam bounded to her side, enveloping her in a fierce embrace that warmed Rahab's cold bones. "I missed you so much."

Rahab smiled, tucking away sad thoughts. "I saw you the day before yesterday."

"Too long. Do you know how desperately I've been wanting a sister of my own?"

Rahab loved it when Miriam referred to her as her sister and demonstrated her preference for Rahab's company over most others. She weaved her arm through the younger woman's. "Well, sister, are you ready to go cure some sick people?"

"Cure, is it? You have set your standards high for your first day."

"I rely on you to do the curing."

Miriam rolled her eyes. "You, I will cure ... of that high opinion. Before the end of the day, I reckon."

The layout of the tent of the sick intrigued Rahab from the moment she entered it. Made from animal hide and stained a light shade of grey, the tent was one of the largest she had ever seen. By means of openings in the walls of the tent, fresh air circulated throughout the space. Each opening had a flap that could be shut in inclement weather. Rows of well-maintained pallets lined the ground in orderly fashion, separated into sections by hanging curtains made from spun goat hair. Patients were assigned to specific sections, depending on their conditions. This tent boasted a sophistication that made the tent of the wounded seem minuscule in comparison.

Surprisingly few pallets were occupied, given the breadth of Israel's population. Some of the invalids moaned with pain, their cries weak from repetition. Others felt well enough to bear their burden in silence. Still others slept, finding solace in the gift of unconsciousness.

A peculiar odor filled the tent—a mix of the sweet scent of incense, which they burned constantly, combined with the sour stench of sweat and urine and old food. That odor alone could sap hope dry. At the side of most patients, family members squatted, hollow-eyed with worry and lack of sleep.

Miriam, accustomed to the tent's sights and sounds, seemed immune to its atmosphere.

Rahab found the rhythm of nursing had not deserted her. With quick, intuitive steps, she picked up new skills from one hour to the next. She found Miriam was welcomed wherever she went, even when she served in the midst of strangers. Among the sick, she had developed a reputation. Patients who had dwelled in the tent longer recommended her to the newcomers. "Miriam of Judah has the kindest touch. You'll be blessed if she tends you."

Rahab's respect for the young woman she called sister grew as she observed her tenderhearted ministrations. Miriam didn't have to be here. She chose to help the most needy in her society. There was no compulsion behind her goodness. Rahab wished she could be half as good, as lovable, as giving as her new sister.

On their way back to the camp that afternoon Rahab disclosed some of her admiration, trying to convey her high regard for the woman Miriam was.

"I believe you labor under a misapprehension," she responded, laughing off Rahab's compliments. "You make it sound as though I have somehow managed to escape Adam and Eve's fate and have arrived into this world in a state of near perfection. A greater falsity you couldn't find in the teachings of a Canaanite priest. My flaws would fill the temple."

"Please! What flaws?"

Miriam's steps ground to a halt. "You're serious?"

"Of course. You are pure and good, but never proud. You haven't once judged me in spite of what you know about me. Add to this funny, pretty, kind, easy to please, and what more can you want? Everyone is fond of you. You have hordes of admirers."

"And I enjoy their good opinion a great deal. In fact, inwardly, I often worry about what others think of me. This, dear sister, is a form of pride, of which God heartily disapproves. I should strive to please God, and spend far less time and effort trying to earn the good opinions of those around me. The Lord has an objection or two to being second best.

"You say I don't judge you. How could I, when I am convicted by my own idolatry? Rahab, don't you know that when God requires the blood of sacrifices to cover the uncleanness of the people of Israel, He is thinking of me as much as of you?

"God's standards measure my heart, not any illusion of righteousness I might contrive to achieve with my actions. And before those standards I fail every day."

Rahab drew her eyebrows together until they met in a deep frown. "You exaggerate. What have you done that's so wrong? My life on the other hand . . . You can't compare yourself to me."

"I don't. I compare myself to the holy standard God sets for us. Your problem is that you compare yourself to *me*, and conclude yourself a great failure. But your standards are skewed. In a way, each one of us is a ruin before God. The wonder is the lengths He goes to in order to save us both from our ruination."

The women walked the rest of the way in silence, each wrapped in her private reflections. To Rahab, her sister-in-law's confession of her sense of shortcoming and sin came as a revelation. She would never have guessed it about Miriam, who seemed the picture of confidence. More curious still was Miriam's understanding of God. A God who was as dissatisfied with a woman like Miriam as one like Rahab. A God who held all of Israel to account. And judging each one guilty, provided a way to cover that guilt. The idea that before such a God she stood on equal ground with the likes of Miriam dazzled her mind.

Partway through the camp of Judah, Rahab bid her sister-in-law good day. On a whim, she decided to visit her family whom she had not seen for several days. As the intended call offered the perfect excuse for delaying time alone with her husband, her steps took her to her family's tent with more eagerness than usual. When she had finished greeting everyone, Izzie pulled her away.

"Come with me. I have some news for you." Izzie's eyes sparkled as she grasped Rahab's hand and began to pull her in haphazard fashion through the maze of the tents around them. Rahab threw a longing look back at her parents' tent. She had spent her morning in back-numbing labor, and the past forty minutes traipsing through the wilderness. The prospect of yet another energetic trek through the busy byways of Judah's camp made her stomach heave.

"Izzie, I'm tired."

"And grumpy," Izzie added with dreadful cheer.

"Where are you taking me?"

"Nowhere particular. I just want to have some privacy."

"In Israel?"

"You have a point. Fine. I'll tell you here." She hopped to a stop and grabbed both Rahab's hands. "I'm going to have a baby!"

Rahab's mouth fell open. After these many years of barrenness, they had all concluded that Izzie would never conceive again. She squeaked with delight. "Truly?"

Izzie bounced on her feet. "I'm so happy! It's the Lord's doing. He has blessed Gerazim and me. Rahab, I could burst out of my skin with joy!"

Rahab embraced her sister and did a small twirling dance. Her head spun with astonishment. Izzie started to walk again, holding on to one of Rahab's hands. Rahab forgot her tiredness and thirst. As they trotted forward, haphazardly navigating narrow lanes, Izzie began unfolding the story of events leading to her pregnancy, a story that astounded Rahab.

"Before your wedding, Gerazim and I decided to take a new lamb to the tabernacle to offer to the Lord. As a sin offering for giving our son to . . . for our great sin. I was desperate to ask for His forgiveness, though I didn't really believe that God would ever be willing to pardon me."

She put her hand on her chest as though it throbbed inside. "My son. My sweet son. When I think of what I did, I can hardly bear it. I wish I had listened to you. I will always bear the ache of that loss."

Her hand dropped to her side, and her face took on a dreamy expression. "Gerazim and I went to the tabernacle with an unblemished lamb, the best we owned, and we stood before the priest. My knees were knocking together. I thought the priest would spit into my face and show me the way out when I began my confession. He didn't, though his eyes grew as wide as plates. When he had finished the rites, he said a blessing over me, and it was as if every word was a burning coal that I swallowed. I cried out; I felt that I was on fire. But the strange sensation passed and in its place, I experienced a restful quiet that I have never known before. My mind, my heart, my will, my body were all at peace. I floated in this state of tranquility for . . ." she shrugged. "I cannot say how long. Deep down, in my marrow, I felt a conviction that God had forgiven Gerazim and me. I cannot explain it. I know I don't deserve it. But so it was.

"I thought this was the end, and for me, it would have been enough. The gift of forgiveness for the first time since the day I offered my son as a sacrifice. Yet the Lord had more to give me.

"I conceived that very night. I have waited this long to be sure before telling anyone. Gerazim has known from the beginning, of course, but next to him you're the first to find out."

Rahab and Izzie spent the next hour rejoicing over the baby, planning and plotting for his birth, and thinking of names. Every once in a while, one of them would give a shriek of delight and envelop the other in a mighty embrace.

The sun had long retired from the sky when Rahab took her leave from Izzie. She had lived through a full and topsy-turvy day. Her bones were desperate for rest, but her mind clamored. She wasn't ready to face Salmone. She did not wish to look into his long, sleepy eyes and read the condemnation in them. She did not want to see the full shapely lips pressed hard with the effort to hold back words. So instead of going home, she sat behind a tent and ruminated.

In a way, the events of this day had turned many of her assumptions on their head. She had found that God held someone as seemingly perfect as Miriam to account for sins that were graver to Him than they appeared to Rahab, while at the same time forgiving and blessing someone as ruined by the worst of acts as Izzie. He wiped out Jericho, and He saved a harlot. What kind of God was this? He seemed at once impossibly holy and ridiculously merciful. How could you tie those two incongruities together?

Rahab sighed, no closer to understanding than when she first began. She became aware as she caught sight of the moon high and bright in the sky that she could not linger away from home anymore. As it was, she had neglected to prepare her husband's supper by her lateness. With weighted steps, she made her way back.

She found Salmone marching back and forth in front of their tent. He came to a halt when he spotted her. "Where have you been?" he cried.

"I told the servant to tell you—"

He clenched his jaw until the bones jutted out. "That was hours ago. Miriam's been back since before supper. I checked."

Rahab took a cautious step back. "I went to visit my family."

"You could have sent someone to let me know." He stepped closer until he was towering over her. She tilted her head back to study him and realized with a jolt that he was shaking.

"I . . . I'm sorry," she said without much conviction, not understanding why he was livid. Was it because she had not prepared his food? Could a missed supper rile the man so?

"Sorry?" he shouted. Then closing his mouth abruptly, he grabbed her hand and pulled her into the tent, dropping the flap behind him. Two or three oil lamps lit up the interior with enough light to illuminate his expression. Nostrils flaring, eyes narrowed, lips flat, he stood with his feet apart, and the veins on his neck bulging. Rahab's mouth turned dry. Instead of releasing her, he pulled her against his chest. "Do you know what I've been through since before sundown not knowing where you had disappeared to?"

"You were *worried*?" All this fuming was rising out of worry? This was a new revelation. Her years of independent living had taught her to be master of her own time. Even the months of living with her family in Israel's camp hadn't prepared her for this. There, if she could manage to get away from the various demands that dogged her steps, her time was her own. She gave no one explanations of where and when she came or went. No one, so far as she knew, grew anxious about her being gone for two or three hours longer than usual.

"What do you expect? You disappeared without a word. What was I to conclude? After last night I thought . . ." He stopped mid-sentence and took a small step back, enough to put some breathing space between them.

His reference to the previous night caused Rahab to grind her teeth. Then she realized he meant he felt concerned for her well-being after a difficult night. "You worried about me?" she repeated with wonder. Something about that knowledge, about the fact that he had been anxious over her began to loosen the knot in her belly. "I ask your pardon," she said, her voice soft, this time meaning the words.

He shoved her away from him and turned away. "Let it be. It's over."

"But—"

"Let it be, I said. I'm going to bed." To Rahab's astonishment, he grabbed a blanket and a folded mattress and strode to the far side of the tent. Flipping the curtain, he walked through to the space they set apart for guests. Openmouthed, Rahab followed him. He made up his makeshift bed with a few jerky moves and crawled under the covers. Except for the night that he hadn't come home, he had never slept apart from her since their marriage. Not even in the midst of their worst struggles.

"Salmone!"

"Rahab, you need your own space. This I understand. Now you have it. Run along and enjoy."

"But let me explain."

He waved his hand. "Woman, this whole day long I have sat adjudicating as people explained. I'm done with explanations."

Rahab turned on her heel and left him. She fumed her way to bed. What ailed the man? Had he lost all sense? Why this uncharacteristic careening from fury to worry to childlike huffiness? Because she had been a few hours late?

You disappeared without a word. Her unexplained absence had fretted his mind. And through the hours of waiting, he must have grown increasingly resentful of her thoughtlessness, swerving between fear of the worst and anger over her cavalier disappearance. But his insistence on sleeping alone verged on a childish tantrum. How could a man who had withstood the worst she had thrown at him be provoked to such a degree by a minor incident?

Rahab twisted in bed. *You need your own space,* he had said, his voice too calm. Did he think that she was avoiding him? In truth she was. However, she was not avoiding the man, his company, his presence, or his society. These things she loved. She was avoiding his disappointment. Avoiding his regret at having married a woman not good enough. Did he not know that? Had he, perhaps, for once, misread her? Had he left in a huff because he felt hurt and unwanted? By *her*?

CHAPTER TWENTY-THREE

Tossing in bed did not help, and turning was no improve-
ment either. Rahab's anger had long since evaporated.
Instead she wrestled with the odd idea that her self-assured
husband might be laboring under the false notion that *she* had
spurned *him*.

He had once accused that she expected his love to fail. Well,
perhaps it had, a little, the night before. He had left her behind,
alone with her tears, his mien cold as he walked out.

And when she had stayed away from home all these hours,
had he thought she was making an indictment against him as
a husband? Had he thought she had stayed away from home
because he had failed her? That she avoided him because she
was disappointed with him?

Salmone, her lion of a husband who fought the enemy with
legendary courage, who led thousands every day through times
of peace and war, whose confidence seemed to her unshakable,
was at this moment lying in another bed not because he didn't
want her, but because he thought she didn't want *him*. She sat

up straight. If she was right, she was sleeping in the wrong bed. And if she was mistaken, she was about to suffer another mortification.

Rising, Rahab took the time to straighten her shift and push her tumbled hair off her shoulders. Making little noise on her bare feet, she padded to the back of the tent and swished the curtain aside. In the darkness she could make out Salmone's shape, his back turned to her. Before doubts could sap her courage, she marched forward, lifted the blankets and slid under. Salmone remained inert, his quiet breaths rising and falling as before.

"What are you doing?" he barked just as Rahab relaxed.

"S-s-s-sleeping in my bed."

"This is not your bed," he said, his back still turned to her.

"My bed is with my husband." Biting her lip, Rahab forced herself to lift her hand. It felt like it belonged to someone else. She willed it to move and placed it on Salmone's shoulder. "My place is with you, Salmone. I don't want to leave."

He sighed. A few moments passed. Then he turned around, his face so near, she could feel his breath stirring against her hair. "Stay, if you want. But not out of duty."

"I want to be with you," she confessed, trying to infuse her voice with the love and longing that had become her constant companions. In the thick darkness, she felt his hand move about her waist. With a strong push and pull of fingers, he drew her into his arms and held her. For the first time since waking many hours before, Rahab felt her muscles unclench.

The unspoken things that remained unresolved lay between them, still, but ignored for the moment. Rahab was content to be near him, embraced by him. She sensed that he was as wakeful as she. "My sister is with child," she blurted, wanting to share the precious news with him.

He propped his head on his palm. "I am happy for her. She's been barren for many years, hasn't she?"

Rahab told him the story Izzie had shared. "Salmone, why do you think God blessed her? He seems to act out of His holy justice when I would expect mercy, and pour out mercy when I would have doled out judgment."

He drew a finger down her cheek. The simple touch made her shiver, and noticing, he gave the ghost of a smile before withdrawing his hand. "I suppose our sins warp our expectations."

"I don't understand."

"I mean that the reason God seems to act in ways that make no sense to us is that our perceptions are wrong. Our expectations are subtly twisted. We long for things that harm us and run from the things that grow and heal us. We think good is bad and bad is good. God acts rightly, but to us, it seems confusing. Or sometimes plain wrong."

Rahab digested Salmone's response. "Do you . . . do you think my perceptions about my past are wrong too?"

Salmone was quiet for a moment, gathering his words. "I think they are a mixture of truth and lie, which make them very convincing, and therefore very dangerous. But it seems likely that where you would believe yourself deserving of condemnation, the Lord would desire to give you mercy."

Rahab sank into silence. How would her life change if she could, in the secret interior places of her heart, begin to believe the promise that lay at the root of Salmone's words? As a woman, as a wife, as a lover, as a daughter, as a friend—would she arise a different creature from the one she was now if she put her faith in the merciful goodness of God? If she truly believed that God forgave her, accepted her, counted her as one who belonged to Him—would that change her life?

Fatigue began to have its way with her body, and sleep clouded her thoughts. In the periphery of her drowsy mind, Rahab was aware that Salmone held her, and that God held her too, no less tightly and securely at that moment. Then she sank into a dreamless sleep, deep and uninterrupted.

Rahab had begun making a wool tunic for Salmone the day after their engagement because she had wanted to present him with a special gift. She had limited material resources of her own. Most of what she had when she escaped Jericho she had given to her family toward the purchase of their tent and flock. What could she give a man who seemed content with simple things?

Then she noticed that Salmone owned few garments, and those he had were old and well worn. She thought of lesser men she had known, men without her husband's goodness, who had possessed so much, inhabiting a world overflowing with lavish riches. She was determined to make her husband something opulent. Something that demonstrated how highly she thought of him. She wanted to surprise him before the start of winter. But she wasn't that clever a weaver.

Fortunately, her sister was. With a satisfied smile, she watched Izzie's fingers fly over a particularly difficult section.

She had asked Izzie to come to her tent to help with the weaving while Salmone was occupied with the business of Judah.

"Oh." Izzie gasped suddenly and stopped working.

"Are you unwell?" Rahab asked, concerned.

"It will pass. Or perhaps not. Excuse me." She ran toward a bowl at the mouth of the tent and bent her retching head into it. After a few unpleasant moments she sat back. Silently, Rahab handed her a cup of fresh water and a cloth.

"It passes as quickly as it comes. I feel perfectly well now."

"How often do you feel ill?"

Izzie waved a careless hand. "Once or twice a day. I would spend the whole day with my head in a bowl for this child. He is worth every discomfort."

Just then a young boy knocked at the outer post of their tent, asking permission to enter.

"Come," Rahab called.

The boy took time to politely remove his sandals before entering the interior of the tent. "Master Salmone sent me. He fears he will be very late this evening, and asks that you sup without him."

After giving the boy a raisin cake for his trouble, Rahab settled back near her sister. "That man works harder than a poor farmer's ox. This is the third evening in a row he has missed dinner."

"Perhaps he doesn't like your cooking. I could teach you a few things, if you want."

"Go on with you. A child in your belly and suddenly you know everything. My husband likes my cooking well enough, I thank you. He has too much on his shoulders, that's the problem."

Izzie became instantly serious. "Are you worried for him?"

Rahab shrugged. "He works too hard. But then there is so much to do. I hear Gerazim and our brothers are gone from sunup to sundown as well."

"That, they are. Well, at least you will have extra hours to work on this tunic. Another week like this and you might even finish it."

Late into the night and with only a modest fire and small lamp for light, Rahab concentrated on Salmone's gift, finally setting it aside when she heard his footsteps outside the tent. She could not wait to see his face when she gave it to him.

Tired from too many late nights, Rahab woke up later than usual the next morning. Through bleary eyes she saw Salmone settled on feather-filled cushions, absently munching on raisin cakes. He noticed she was awake and sauntered over.

"Sleep well?"

She raised herself up on an elbow. "Yes, thank you." It occurred to her that his presence in the tent at this hour was unusual. He left long before this on most days. "Aren't you going to work?"

"Not right away." He was standing over her, and she tipped her head up to accommodate the great difference in height. Noticing her discomfort, he lowered himself on the mattress near her, his hip close to her thigh. The unexpected closeness distracted her.

"Rahab?"

"Yes, Salmone?" She gave him a sweet smile, thinking of the tunic she had hidden in her chest.

"We need to talk."

She frowned. "Why?"

He wriggled closer. "Rahab, I have allowed a whole week to go by without resolving our differences. It's enough time. If we don't work through this tangle, it might fester."

Rahab suppressed a groan. Couldn't he see that she had barely opened her eyes? He wasn't a man; he was a wolf who lunged at every opportunity. "Can I wash first?" she snapped.

He ignored the edge in her voice. "Of course."

She took her time rising out of bed. She knew he would have to leave for work soon enough. The slower she moved, the less time they would have for this unpalatable discussion. He watched her as she sauntered to the curtain, his eyes cool. "If you aren't ready by the time I eat this raisin cake, I'm coming to fetch you," he drawled.

Rahab spun around. The implacable set of his jaw told her he meant it. With deliberate movements, he broke off a large chunk of the raisin cake and put it in his mouth. She whipped around and ran off in haste. Could the maddening man not let anything go? What use was there in rehashing through her painful past?

She rushed through her wash and pulled on a shapeless wool dress. Combing through her hair would take time and patience, neither of which she possessed. She lifted the red-brown curls away from her shoulders intending to tie them with a string when Salmone prowled over. He took the string from her nerveless fingers. "My raisin cake is finished."

She turned to face him. "What are we discussing?"

"Zedek."

She slashed at the air with a dismissive hand. "We already did that."

"We started, but we didn't finish. I want to tell you what I've been thinking, but I'm not going to do it standing here like a caravan camel." Without waiting to see if she followed, he went back into the main area of the tent, which was strewn with comfortable pillows and colorful rugs. Rahab followed behind, resenting every step. When he sat on a cushion, she chose a rug. When he stretched his legs, she gathered hers into her chest. When he leaned forward, she leaned back.

Salmone ignored her wordless acts of rebellion with the same unruffled immovability he might have shown a child. "We're going to talk about your nightmare."

Rahab, who had not expected him to reach for the jugular with such rapidity, sprung to her feet.

"*Sit down.*" He planted himself before her, a wall of muscle and bone that refused to be budged. She wilted, feeling helpless, and sank back down.

"That's better."

"For you, perhaps."

"True. Now. The nightmare. People have nightmares because they're afraid of something. What is it you think you're afraid of?"

"Nosy people?"

He ignored her again. Physical resistance didn't work. Sarcasm didn't work. What was going to penetrate his thick skin with the reality that he was wasting his effort and causing her a thousand pains in the process?

"You said that night that you have nightmares because you gave in to Zedek's every demand. You capitulated to his desires. What you were saying, though I was too dense to see it at the time, was that you were filled with shame about your willing participation. Guilt and shame have eaten at you year after year, increasing with every willing act of adultery."

Nausea rose up in waves. Large beads of sweat broke out on her forehead. "I don't want to talk about this," she said brokenly.

Salmone bent forward. "But you are going to." A cup of water rested near his hand. He raised it to Rahab's lips. "Drink this." She shook her head. "Don't say no to me. It will settle your stomach. Drink."

She drank, too weak to deny him.

"Better?" he asked, as she drank the last drop of water.

"No," she replied, though the water helped quiet her roiling belly.

"I regret that," he murmured. His eyes were at once soft and intractable. "I've found a strange thing about guilt. Sometimes it's real—the expression of something wrong that must be appeased. Forgiven. Sometimes, though, it's guilt for something not really our fault, not really a sin. The right kind of guilt, the kind planted inside us by God's Spirit, leads us to repentance. Leads us to change. Leads us to the forgiveness of God. It leads to peace, Rahab. But when you become more and more tangled in shame without a way out, without real access to repentance and forgiveness, then you are closing the door to God and to His restoration. There are few things more destructive than unrelenting shame. Your problem is that your insides are tangled between shame and honest guilt, and you can't tell the difference."

Rahab snorted. "There's nothing false about my shame."

"Isn't there? Let's talk about Zedek. He took advantage of your poverty. Of your need. If he had been a man of honor, he would have helped you without exacting a selfish price. Instead, he used you. You were fifteen years old! Stuck between a father whose weakness outweighed his love and a man whose lust outweighed his integrity."

Rahab doubled over. "I should have resisted him. You said so yourself, that night."

Salmone let out his breath like a giant had stepped on his chest. "Oh, Rahab. The words of a hurting husband don't always make for truth. Set aside my sinful anger for a minute. Let's sort through this from God's point of view. Ideally, if you were a woman grown, if you had the resources to stand against this wrong, yes, you are right. You should not have capitulated. But you were young and helpless. You had been taught to obey your father and mother. You had been impressed with the direness of your family's need. So you used your considerable intelligence to work within the parameters that were given you. What sin you committed pales in comparison to the sins committed against you."

Rahab wanted to believe Salmone's words, and she wanted to believe that he believed them. Her mind even began to soften a little to the logic of his argument. Her heart, however, would not bend. It insisted on being mired in shame. She could not step out of that shame through the door of well-expressed argument.

"You forget that I went on with that life even after I was freed from Zedek. Even after I grew into womanhood and established my independence." Each word, as it left her mouth, held a bitter taste. Why was she telling him these things? Was she trying to goad him into hating her? Leaving her?

"I told you that what you need to sort through is where your guilt is real and where it is imagined. Miriam told me your story. It always puzzled me that a *zonah* would only have a dozen lovers. Could you have had more if you wanted?"

Rahab avoided looking at him. "Of course," she said, half hysterical at the thought of discussing such things with her husband.

"I have always wondered about that, Rahab. You're so beautiful; surely men vied to be with you?"

Something too close to pride nipped at her heel. Her popularity had been one of the few things in her life that had given her a sense of well-being, albeit fleeting. Here with her husband, that popularity could not count for much, not with her sins hanging out like so much dirty laundry for him to sort through. "Men did want me," she murmured.

"And you denied them. Why? Wouldn't you have been wealthier if you had—" Salmone broke off, looking lost for the right words, then pressed forward. "If you had kept company with greater numbers?"

"Please! Can't we stop this?"

"Not yet. Tell me what I asked."

She stared at him with unconscious appeal. He narrowed his eyes. "Tell me," he insisted, refusing to relent.

She threw her hands in the air. "Oh, why won't you just let me be?"

"Answer my question. The sooner you do, the sooner it will be over."

She groaned. "I wanted to be with as few men as I could."

"Why?"

"I felt helpless—caught in this life that I believed I could not change. So I tried to limit the horror of it. Limit my own transgression."

Salmone leaned forward and stroked her shoulder, his fingers trailing down her arm with a fleeting motion before withdrawing. "I think the Lord takes note of such choices. Takes note of a heart that tries so hard to avoid sin. You had deceived yourself into believing you were helpless—that you could not stop. Of this deception you must repent. Of the acts of adultery that it led you to, you must also repent. But you must let go of the guilt that stands over you like a corrupt judge, always accusing and condemning. When you accept these false accusations, you are willingly participating in them. That is like me helping the men of Ai attack me instead of fighting against them. You have to begin fighting against this condemnation instead of agreeing with it."

"I don't know how. Besides, I've already repented to the Lord, and nothing has changed."

"That's because you don't understand the mercy of God. You can't believe, and therefore can't receive His forgiveness. Do you believe He would extend the same goodness to you that He has offered Izzie?"

No. She gazed at his calm face with mute helplessness.

Salmone sighed. "Promise you will think about what I've said."

Rahab gave a bitter smile. "Now you want my thoughts too."

He twined his fingers in her hair and pulled her to him. His mouth pressed against hers, a demanding, searching touch that gave no quarter. Into her lips he murmured, "I want everything."

CHAPTER TWENTY-FOUR

She had married an annoying hound of a man. Always poking into places she would rather ignore. Yet, Salmone proved his steadfastness in a dozen ways each day. Even his prodding questions demonstrated his commitment. Annoyance aside, Rahab's love for him grew by the hour. She wanted to shower him with some tangible show of affection but could think of few things that might please him.

It occurred to her that he had not spent much time with old friends since their wedding. Before his marriage, he had been able to entertain close companions with more casual ease. Rahab wondered if a modest supper with dear friends might please him. As soon as the thought came to her, she decided to act on it that very night.

She set out to find him, knowing he would prefer a forewarning of her plans. He was still entangled in a difficult case involving two influential families. The families in question lived near each other, which aggravated their problems, but helped Rahab locate Salmone quickly. She found him sitting cross-legged outside a luxurious brown tent, the leaders of the two families on either side of him. One of the men was speaking, his thin lips moving fast so that small droplets of spittle flew out of his mouth, landing on his beard and mustache and Salmone's tunic. Every once in a while, he gesticulated with a wild motion of his ruddy hands, pointing this way and that. Salmone sat stone still, his countenance blank. Rahab had come to know that expression well. It meant he was not pleased. She felt sorry for the spitting fellow. Perhaps this was the wrong time to disturb her husband with something as inane as a feast. She could wait for another night. Swallowing her disappointment, she turned away.

"Rahab!"

Too late. He had seen her. She felt ridiculous now, interrupting an important discussion for a frivolous request. He ran up to her, his eyebrows locked in a frown. "Is something wrong?"

"No. Nothing. I'm sorry to intrude on you. I only have a silly question."

"An intrusion would be welcome, believe me. Ask your question."

"I thought, if you are agreeable, to invite a few friends for dinner. Your sister and Ezra, Hanani and Abigail, and my sister and her husband."

"That's a fine idea. I would enjoy that."

"May I use an extra portion of the grain for supper?"

His brows shifted back to a frown. "You don't need to ask. It's your grain. Do as you like, Rahab." His brusque tone hinted at exasperation.

"Most husbands get annoyed if their wives *don't* ask permission before spending their riches."

Salmone bent forward, his lips close to her ear. "I'm not most husbands. Haven't you noticed yet?" And he left before she could tell him that oh, she had noticed. How she had noticed.

The guests arrived before the host, who came late to his own feast. When eventually he showed up, his steps hurried and march-like, his face looked frozen with tension. But within moments of being with trusted friends, he began to smile, his body relaxing. Pleasure washed through Rahab as she noticed the change.

Dinner, according to unanimous opinion, would satisfy a king. Israelite men were easy to please, having for most of their lives feasted on simple and uniform fare. And Israelite women were eager to learn and admire.

It had grown late by the time everyone left. Rahab and Salmone walked outside with their guests, accompanying them partway. Cleaning up lasted longer than usual since Rahab had sent the servant to bed. The boy had already fetched fresh water, and Rahab rinsed the dishes in the dark, using sand to scour the rough clay.

When she finally undressed and went to bed, she found her husband fast asleep. Quietly, so as not to disturb him, she slid next to him. The last thing she saw as she closed her eyes was an image of Salmone's face wreathed in laughter during supper. She had managed to do something that made her husband happy.

Rahab searched again through the bedroll, the sheets, the floor of the tent, the folds of her cream dress. Nothing. She shook her striped veil with a vigor born of impatience. Still nothing. She could find no sign of it. She had gone to bed forgetting to remove her earrings. And she had risen from bed with one of them missing. Where could it be? Pillows tumbled, curtains swished, floor mats shook under her searching fingers. No earring turned up. Rahab sank to the floor, her face in her hands. She could not believe she had lost the earring that had belonged to Salmone's mother. Out of all she possessed, those earrings meant the most to her. She could not bear to lose one.

Salmone returned to a disheveled home. His wife sat staring into space. Her dress was askew and a dark smudge that looked suspiciously like soot marred her cheek. She wore no veil and her hair hung in tangled curls down her back. One earring hung from her ear, a single tear-shaped pearl dancing amongst dark blue lapis lazuli. He advanced into the tent. She did not heed him. He approached her. She continued staring.

"Is something the matter?"

Her head whipped around. "I didn't hear you."

"I noticed. What's happened?"

"Oh, Salmone, I've lost my earring," she wailed. "I forgot to take them off before coming to bed last night, and in the morning, I found only one in my ear. I've looked everywhere to no avail. It's gone!"

"I'm sorry."

She made a funny, kitten sound in her throat and flung her hands to either side in despair. He could tell her distress went deep. "They weren't all that valuable, Rahab."

"They were to me!"

"I can help you look for it."

"I've looked for hours. Nothing. It's disappeared into the air."

"Where have you looked?"

"I've turned this tent inside out. I even went through the ashes of the fire."

That explained the mess. And the soot. He crouched down in front of her. "How about outside? We walked the guests out. And then you washed the dishes in the dark. You might have dropped it before you ever came to bed."

"Oh." *Embers of hope sparked in her eyes.* "I didn't think of that."

"Let's go look."

"No, no. I'll search for it later. You've been working hard all day; you must be tired. Come and have your supper. I'll look after you are finished."

The earrings had some sentimental value for him, it was true. They had belonged to his mother, and he could still picture her with them dangling against her cheek. But the sentiment was superficial. In truth he would prefer nothing more than to sit down, drink a glass of barley water, and eat his wife's cooking. The distress on her face, however, made that plan null. He'd choke on his food if he made her wait in the throes of her anxiety. "We'll look now," he said and pulled her up. Her unresisting

351

acquiescence and the expression of relief on her face confirmed he had made the right decision.

The best strategy would be to make a systematic sweep of the area, he decided. First, they took a snail's walk along the lanes that they had covered the previous night. It had been a rainless day with enough wind to cover something as minuscule as an earring with plenty of sand. Their search had to be methodical, and to Salmone's grumbling belly, agonizingly slow.

Their careful exploration produced no fruit. Salmone was cognizant that, after a windy night, even the most minute search might miss a prize as small as a piece of jewelry. Still, he kept his doubts to himself, seeing no reason to cause discouragement until it became necessary.

They returned to the area outside the tent, focusing on the side where Rahab's nocturnal cleaning had taken place. Kneeling with their heads close to the ground, they swept the sand. Salmone tried to remember the direction of the winds that morning, and began to widen his search. He noticed Rahab sitting back, abandoning hope, her features spelling dejection. He kept up the search, refusing to give up, a gnawing feeling goading him on.

His index finger touched something solid and cold. He seized upon the spot and quickly wiped away the sand. There it was! Rahab's treasure—forgotten, abandoned, lost on the ground. From the mark of footsteps, more than one pair of sandals had trod on the delicate gold and pearl. The sight made him narrow his eyes with dawning comprehension.

Rahab, who had been watching his movements with desultory interest, became aware that his search had in fact borne fruit. She gasped and sprang to her feet, rushing over with a haste that overturned a pot.

"You found it!" she cried.

"Mmmm."

She threw herself down by his side and reached out for her earring. He pushed her hand away. "Leave it," he commanded.

"What do you mean *leave it*?"

"I mean it's no good anymore. It's been lying in the sand a whole night and day. See the mark of the footsteps? It's been trampled on again and again. It's ruined."

"No, it's not! I can see it is fine. It needs a careful washing perhaps, but it will be good as new as soon as I give it some proper care."

"People have stepped on it, I tell you. It's worthless now."

"Of course it isn't. Jewels don't lose their value just because they're dirty. It's still a pearl even if it's been stepped on. What's wrong with you? Why are you acting this way? Give me my earring!"

"Not until you understand."

"*What?*" Rahab's irritation colored her voice as she reached for the earring.

He held it away from her. "You are this earring."

"You've been in the sun too long. Let's get you some fig wine."

"I don't need fig wine. I need you to see something. Rahab, you seem to value this earring above your other possessions. You appreciate its inherent value as gold and pearl, but even beyond gold and pearl it means something more to you. It represents great worth in your sight.

"Don't you see, beloved, God looks upon you the way you

look upon this delicate jewel? Only with so much more tenderness. So much more delight."

He waited, giving her time to hear his words before continuing. "Do you remember the story of creation? God fashioned you in His own image. He called you *very good*. Don't you see? That means that He considers you to have profound worth. You are like this precious jewel to Him.

"You tell me that in spite of the fact that this earring has been lost, abandoned in the dirt, and trampled underfoot, it is still of great worth to you. It remains a valuable piece of jewelry. You tell me that even though people have stepped on it, it is no less precious.

"Can't you see that the same holds true for you, Rahab? You may have been discarded by your father, or by Zedek, but that has not robbed you of your true worth. You may have been stepped on by many others, but that has not changed who and what you are: a child of God, made in His image."

"I just wanted my earring," Rahab mumbled, turning pale. "Why do you bring Zedek into it?"

Salmone could taste her distress, but he went on, ruthless in his need to restore her life. "Because I want you to be free of him. His actions turned you into this earring. Instead of being cherished and treasured, you were tossed into the dust. And when he was done, he left you there. But he didn't grow tired because you are tiresome, Rahab. He didn't leave you because you are not good enough. He left you because of his own sin. It wasn't any lack in you that caused him to abandon you; it was a lack in him. The same is true for your father. They lost a treasure in you when they didn't appreciate you. Like throwing gold in the dirt and walking away from it, the loss is theirs.

"Rahab, look at this earring. Is it ruined and worthless now because it's been in the dust? Tell me it's spoiled beyond repair. Tell me you don't want it anymore."

He watched her, and then continued. "God can't say those things about *you* either. You are His precious gold. You are His irreplaceable pearl. And you have never lost the value you were born with."

Tears filled her honey eyes. She reached for the jewel, not grabbing this time, not seizing, but touching with a reverence that made Salmone hold his breath. "I'm this earring?" She gasped, her voice breaking.

He nodded. With an aching wonder she stared at it twinkling in the palm of her hand. There was little damage to the gold or the gems. As she had predicted, they needed a good washing and a few adjustments to the soft wires that had become bent under the weight of careless feet. But the earring was as valuable as ever. Its gold was still gold, the pearl solid and lustrous. Rahab closed her fist around the ornament and brought her hand to rest on her heart.

Something in her broke—Salmone could see the shattering of it. A keening noise escaped her lips, like the sorrowful wail of a confused and hurting child. His heart almost cracked at the sound, at the ancient pain it contained. He pulled her into his strong, protective arms. Her whole body shook against him.

"Hush, sweet. Hush," he murmured. He knew the mountain of pain erupting needed release and didn't intend to end it before its time. Yet he wanted her to experience his comfort as she went through the releasing of this monumental sorrow.

It occurred to him that he could never judge her again after this, after witnessing the suffering child who had finally seen a glimpse of her true image in God's eyes. He could never think of her past as a pollution of his pure bloodlines. He could never condemn her again for having been with a dozen men before him. Far from loving her less, he loved her more fiercely than ever. God had shown him that earring as much for his sake as for hers. He needed this lesson every bit as much as she. She was a jewel beyond price to him, and nothing could ever again diminish her value in his sight.

Her convulsive trembling began to subside and the keening wail turned into ordinary tears. He held her tight through all of it, kissing her temple, caressing her hair. Every instinct to protect, to cherish, rose up in him. An overpowering tenderness welled up so he could barely form the words. "I love you," he whispered. The declaration came out of him in a natural rush of emotion he could not suppress.

She clung to him, arms wrapped about his neck and back, pressing her whole self into him in an abandonment of trust and need that melted him from the inside. He had never felt so wholly close to another human in his life. Into the crook of his neck, she whispered something, which he missed at first, and then he realized that she was telling him that she loved him, she loved him, over and over. Salmone thought he would burst with the joy that flooded inside him.

It took him a long time to realize that someone else stood near them, clearing his throat awkwardly. His movements sluggish, Salmone lifted his head, still clinging to his wife. Only when he saw how bleary his vision was as he tried to focus on

Ezra's face did he come to realize that his lashes were stuck together with tears.

"Ezra?" he croaked, annoyed at being interrupted, wanting the whole world to disappear and leave him alone with his wife.

"I am sorry to intrude," Ezra said, avoiding eye contact. "Joshua sent me to fetch the leaders of Judah. I was here once earlier and left. But you're the last one I need to round up."

"Joshua wants me now? What is it?"

"A delegation of men arrived on donkeys several hours ago. They want to make a treaty with us. Joshua has asked the leaders to gather and advise him."

"A delegation! Well, Joshua can do without me on this one decision. I can't leave my wife just now."

Against his neck, Rahab's words tickled with gentle exhalations of air. "Go, my love. You can't keep Joshua waiting. I'm all right."

Salmone shook his head. "I won't leave you, not unless it's absolutely necessary. Ezra, will you tell Joshua my wife needs me, please? If it's urgent, I will come. But if he can do without me, I'd rather stay with Rahab. Find out more details in either case and come back and tell me."

"You need not have lingered with me," Rahab said, when Ezra left. "Israel needs you. I understand." Her face was blotchy from crying, and her alluring eyes had turned red and puffy. She had never seemed so beautiful to him. He still held her, unable to bring himself to release her. The thought of putting the smallest distance between them seemed unbearable.

"I will leave if I must. Right now, I don't want to be anywhere but here."

357

"Perhaps we should go inside."

Salmone realized suddenly that he had been clutching his wife outside their tent in plain view of any neighbor who might happen to wander outdoors. Night had fallen, providing a cover of sorts. But he would rather have some dregs of privacy. Shifting his weight, he hefted Rahab into his arms and walked into the tent. She clasped him about the neck, her head against his heart. In her long-fingered fist, she clutched the earring. He smiled at the sight of it—at the sight of her.

Once inside, he sat down on a rug, leaning against a post, Rahab still in his arms.

"Let me fetch you some food and drink," she whispered.

It dawned on him that she must be utterly worn out from weeping. Food and drink would do her good. "I'll fetch us some," he said.

She gave him a dismayed look. "That's my job. You've worked endless hours, and Joshua might still call you back. I can at least do this for you."

"Any day—every day—for the rest of our lives, if you want. But tonight, let me take care of you." To his delight, she nodded, though he could tell that it came hard to her, this giving over to his care. He wanted her to understand that she was not a burden to him, that caring for her did not make her less precious in his sight. *Years. I'll need years to teach her that.* He managed to find leftover sweet cakes from the night before and cheese and stale flat bread. She made the best barley water he had ever tasted, and long ago, he had learned where she stored it. Bringing over the whole earthen vessel, he set it next to them along with the deepest cups he could find.

Before eating, he blessed God as was his habit. But he took time to pray longer, to praise God for His provision and guidance and mercy. He praised God for his wife, for their marriage, for their future, for the plans God had for them whatever they be. And he praised God for opening his eyes and Rahab's to truth. Only God could take a lost earring and turn it into an instrument of healing.

CHAPTER TWENTY-FIVE

Salmone was relieved when Ezra returned bearing the message that Joshua had excused his absence and did not require him to come. Rahab offered their guest a plump cushion and barley water. Salmone frowned; he wanted her to rest and not rush about, burdened with duties. He scowled at Ezra when Rahab offered him some food. Ezra hastily refused.

"Where is this delegation of men from?" Salmone asked, his curiosity roused.

"They have come from a distant country," Ezra said after taking a sip of his drink. "When Joshua asked them why they had come to us, they replied that the fame of the Lord has spread. They know we've defeated Og and Sihon, and they have heard of the miracle of our escape from Egypt. Which is why the leaders of their nation have dispatched them here to make a treaty of peace with us."

"How do we know they are what they say?" Salmone asked. "How do we know they don't live nearby?"

"Joshua said the same. But they had the leaders of Israel examine their provisions. Their bread was moldy, their wineskins cracked, and their clothes and sandals worn out as by a long journey."

"I see. I take it we will be praying and seeking God's will before responding?"

"Well . . . no, actually. As it happens, the leaders thought the evidence good enough to make a decision. They gave their word to make a treaty with these people."

"Without inquiring of the Lord!"

Ezra held up a hand in a gesture of surrender. "I'm only the messenger. All I know is that the other leaders were convinced of the delegation's claims."

Salmone took a deep breath. "Pardon. If I wanted to voice my opinion I should have gone to meet the delegation." He turned to Rahab. "And I don't regret not going."

"Speaking of going," Ezra said as he rose to his feet, "it's time I found my own tent."

Salmone and Rahab rose up with him. "Thank you for bringing me the news, Ezra."

When Ezra's shadow had melted into the night, Salmone said, "It's late. Let's go to bed." Try as he might, he could not keep his voice light. The thought of Rahab and bed in one sentence tugged so many strings to his mind and body, he could not breathe.

He had to set his longings aside. She was not ready. Just because she had taken a significant step did not mean he should pounce on her. He felt a sense of loss—of anger even—for what had been stolen from them. He made the decision not to give in to such discouragement. His job was to take back the territory that had been stolen, to reclaim every particle of Rahab's mind, heart, and body from the ravages of the past.

One day, like Joseph, he would say of those who had harmed his wife, and thereby him, "You intended it for evil, but God meant it for good." Like Rahab's snake, like his own near-fatal wound, like the lost earring, God could take the very worst and use it for good. In the meantime, though . . . in the meantime, he had to grit his teeth and abide.

The night had turned unseasonably warm, and Rahab joined him in bed wrapped in a light shift. Half of him longed to hold her close, to experience that incomparable sense of connectedness. The other half groaned with the frustration of holding her, but only so far. She took the decision out of his hands by snuggling against his body with a shy wriggle of arms and legs. He knew how much such an overt demonstration of affection cost her, knew that she usually feared rejection too much to reach out to him first. Not for the world would he withdraw from her now. Twisting his body, he reached for her and pulled her close. The scent of her hair, infused with roses and some indefinable element that was pure Rahab, filled his senses. Without his volition, his fingers bunched in her hair and pulled her head back for his kiss. It wasn't a kiss of comfort, of gentle contact, of belonging. It was a searing kiss of passion and wanting and need. He tingled with the desire to have her, and his kiss told her so as it hungrily drank in everything she had to give. More than anything, he wanted her to feel this way about him, to long for him as he did for her.

She was soft in his arms. Yielding. Everything about her fit him so right. It required a prayer, a silent desperate cry to the

Lord, to stop him. *O God, give me the strength to wait,* he cried in mute anguish before withdrawing.

It took a while to calm his harsh breathing. "A foretaste of things to come," he murmured with a lopsided smile.

She gazed at him large-eyed. "You . . . you really know how to do that well," she said, her voice breathless.

It dawned on him that she was deeply affected by his touch, that she had felt a portion of his own churning need. His impatience quieted at the knowledge. Unable to stop himself from grinning, he whispered, "You can count on it." He kissed her again, this time taming his need and basking in the joy of her awakening wonder. His body's satisfaction might have to wait, but his soul was well pleased. He gave a contented sigh and lay back on his pillow.

"I forgot to tell you!" Rahab burst out, sitting up straight.

"What? What did you forget?"

"My father is giving a feast in honor of Izzie and Gerazim tomorrow evening. We are to go to their tent after sunset."

"Ah. I'm afraid I'll be late. No doubt you'll want to go early and help them prepare?"

"If it's all right with you."

"Of course. I'll meet you there as soon as I can."

Salmone found visiting his in-laws a chore. He had a hard time letting go of his anger against Rahab's parents. Because he knew better than anybody the price their choices had exacted from their daughter, he found it torturous to sit and pretend everything was well. Sometimes, he felt like screaming at the man and woman who had sold their daughter for a handful of silver. He wanted to ask if they had any idea what their full bellies had cost her. Years of leadership had taught him to control his temper. The frustration, however, would only be ruled and not banished. He chafed at the necessity of holding his tongue, knowing that a confrontation would serve only to hurt Rahab more.

Clamping down a sigh, he drew his wife closer and settled for sleep. One evening of suppressed resentment would not kill him.

Rahab spent half the night going over the inconceivable discovery that God truly valued her. She would never be able to wipe the memory of that moment of comprehension from her mind. It was as if a shaft of love pierced her walled-in soul, and she felt, for the first time, that she was loved beyond reason. Esteemed far beyond what she deserved. Seeing this glimpse of God's heart made her see, made her believe, that even a man like Salmone might love a woman like her. She was worthy of such a man. It had been years since she'd nurtured that tattered hope. *The hope that she would be chosen, claimed, cherished.*

In those moments of dizzy revelation, of feeling immersed in love and acceptance, she had heard the unmistakable whisper of the Spirit of God in her soul. "You are My gift to Salmone. You are the treasure I wanted him to have." Though he was doubtless a gift to her, she realized God had blessed Salmone by giving *her* to him. Because, inconceivably, in God's sight, she—Rahab— was a treasure.

And that was why when Salmone held her with exquisite tenderness and whispered that he loved her . . . she believed him. For the first time, she believed him in the depths of her heart. She felt secure in his love.

Rahab realized that she would have to take more steps in this journey to wholeness. She knew that other circumstances might shake her assurance. Diminish her confidence. But having come through the darkest valley, she now understood that God would see her through other battles. He would shatter other lies that lingered in her soul and, bit by bit, set her free.

In Jericho, when she had first placed her faith in the Lord, she had known Him to be mighty. Great. But last night, she had learned to place her faith in His mercy. He bestowed His love to those who did not deserve it. He ascribed worth upon His children who could not earn it.

Izzie had learned this lesson with her pregnancy. She would appreciate Rahab's sense of wonder and gratitude in a way that no one else could. The thought of spending a whole day in her sister's company made Rahab hurry through her morning chores with a smile. Even the grueling task of preparing for a large feast under her mother's direction could not diminish Rahab's joy. This was a day of celebration—for Izzie and Gerazim and, in the secret places of her mind, for her and Salmone.

The sun seemed to move with perverse sluggishness that day. Even Izzie's precious company could not distract Rahab from her sense of impatience to be with her husband. She missed him. Following the overwhelming closeness of the previous evening, his absence left a hole. She told herself that she was behaving like a young virgin, mooning after a man she had seen just that morning. Her best cynical lecture fell on deaf ears. She didn't care if she was acting with the impetuous longing of the young. She wanted her husband, and he would be late on this night of all nights.

The grounds surrounding the family tent overflowed with guests by early evening, testimony to the new acquaintances the men had formed as they helped the tribes of Israel with the challenges of farming. An herb-stuffed lamb roasted on a pit, sending mouth-watering aromas into the air. Rahab milled about, offering fresh pan bread. The bread would be used in place of plates when the lamb was served. Rahab felt her stomach rumble and remembered that she had not eaten since morning when she had broken her fast with Salmone. She stretched her neck this way and that, hoping to catch sight of him as he arrived.

Joa carved the lamb, and Rahab began circulating a heavy platter loaded with pieces of choice meat. A man who seemed vaguely familiar cut her off as she walked by him.

"How about giving me some attention," he said in a nasal voice, his lips glistening wet through a stringy mustache.

She turned in a half circle, a spontaneous smile on her lips, the platter stretched forward. To her surprise, she found the man staring at her with unbecoming boldness, his gaze lingering openly on the curves of her figure. Her blue wool dress was modest, appropriate for a matron of Israel. Nothing in her behavior or apparel signaled an invitation for such unpleasant scrutiny. Nothing except that she was Rahab of Jericho. She blushed, feeling the old shame claw at her insides. Then Salmone's words rose up in her memory: *you are this earring . . . you are His precious gold.*

He wasn't ogling her because of *her* wrongdoing. *His* sin was the culprit, not hers. With calculated coldness she withdrew the platter and turned away from the man, not bothering with an answer. To her dismay, he grabbed her wrist, almost spilling the lamb. "I said, how about some attention," he drawled.

"If you're so desperate for attention, I'll be happy to give you some," a dagger-sharp voice growled from behind Rahab. *Salmone.* "Care to let go of my wife? Or can I help you with that as well?" His thin smile was no disguise for the meaning of his words.

The man released Rahab's wrist as if it were on fire.

"Just looking for some lamb," he managed, failing to look convincing.

"I think you've had enough. Wouldn't you agree?"

"Ah, sure," he said, even though he hadn't tasted the tantalizing roast yet.

"No reason to hang about anymore then, is there?"

"No, I don't suppose so." He took a long, yearning look at the platter, and trudged off.

"Ill-mannered man." Rahab sniffed. "I would have put him in his place if you hadn't."

"I know you would have, but it gave me pleasure to do it. You don't mind?"

"No. I quite enjoyed it."

Salmone smiled into her eyes. "I'll need to get used to beating off your admirers. Serves me right for marrying such a beautiful woman."

Rahab's heart skipped a beat. He had managed to coax a compliment from a stranger's ogling. To Salmone, the man had been drawn to her because of her worth, not her uncleanness. She rewarded him with a dazzling smile.

Imri came over to where they were standing, wiping perspiration from his high forehead. "Good evening, Salmone. Rahab, will you come and dance?"

Rahab choked. "Dance? I think not, Father."

Imri ignored her emphatic response and turned to his son-in-law. "Salmone, have you ever seen your wife dance?"

"No."

"Well, you should. She was famed for her dancing in Jericho. There were few to compare with her grace."

"Father!" Rahab filled the single word with volumes of censure.

"Bah," Imri said. "Come and show them what real dancing is."

Her father's claim was true enough; Rahab's skillful dancing had once been admired by many. She had never performed the provocative dances customary among other *zonah* in Jericho, though. Her performances exhibited more emotion than sensuality, a surprisingly decorous dance that drew admirers from both sexes. But Rahab had no desire to become the center of attention. She longed for a discreet, quiet existence. She wanted to blend in, not to stand out. "I am not dancing," she insisted

"I would like to see you," Salmone interjected, his voice soft.

Her jaw dropped. Her father and Salmone joining forces! Rahab had enough feminine vanity to want to satisfy her husband's curiosity. Being the object of his admiration offered a temptation she could not resist. "I will dance . . . but only for you," she said. He drew in his breath and his skin took on a ruddy shade.

"Bah!" Imri exclaimed again, and walked off.

Rahab giggled. "I better serve this lamb before it grows cold."

"*Lamb?* What about my dance?"

"In good time."

"My beard is turning white as I wait."

"You'll look more distinguished," Rahab exclaimed without sympathy.

The guests clamored for the delicious meat, and the platter emptied rapidly. Salmone claimed her before her family could give her a new chore.

"Come and bide with me for a while," he insisted, drawing her to a less crowded corner. He managed to find an unoccupied stump for Rahab to sit on and settled on the ground next to her. "Did you notice the pride on your father's face when he bragged about your dancing?"

Rahab threw her husband a doubtful look. "No."

"He lit up as he talked about you. He *is* fond of you."

She mulled over his words in silence. "In some ways, that makes it worse."

"How do you mean?"

"Because he loved me, I trusted him with my whole heart. And I believed his words about me, the good and the bad, the right and the wrong. I believed the underlying message of his actions too. To this day I fight with the notion that he was right about me. His conclusions ring truer than my own. If he had been an evil man, I might have been able to ignore his pronouncements. I might have learned to discredit his opinions. As it was, I have believed him my whole life. Except for the Lord, and your love, I would not have been able to escape the false convictions he unwittingly forced upon me."

"I hadn't thought of that. I admit, I find it hard not to feel angry with him. So much of our lives has been impacted by Imri's actions. It's hard to let go of my resentment."

Rahab nodded, understanding. "That's the problem with bad choices. They spill into other people's lives. Here you are, a man of Israel, impacted by a decision my father made eleven years ago in Jericho. My consolation is that the Lord can overcome our failures."

"It makes me happy to hear you say that, Rahab." He came to his feet. "Can we leave? I have news I must share with you."

Rahab felt a stab of worry. "Is it bad news?"

His face became inscrutable. "Not necessarily. Just private."

A knot squeezed her stomach. Whatever he wished to share with her must be serious. Marriage to a leader in Israel presented its own painful challenges. "I'll tell Izzie."

Salmone held her hand as they walked back. She sensed that he wished to wait for the confines of their tent before speaking, and though anxiety harangued her insides, she respected his wish. Pressing her lips shut, she just held on to his hand. She couldn't wait another moment when they arrived at the tent. Before Salmone had the chance to light a lamp, she turned to him.

"Tell me."

He finished lighting the lamp and set it down. "I'm uneasy about the visitors who made a treaty of peace with us yesterday. I want to follow them and discover if they told us the truth."

"The ones with the moldy bread and worn shoes?"

"The same. Something about their story troubles me. It's a precaution, nothing more. I aim to follow them for a couple of days to verify their claim."

Rahab thought through the implications of his errand. Spying missions were not safe for any Israelite on Canaan's highways. Every step deeper into unconquered Canaanite territory represented a multitude of threats. If the visitors were what they claimed, travel would be his gravest source of danger. If not, the delegation might not take kindly to a nosy Jewish man bent on discovering their secrets.

"Aren't newly married men supposed to be exempt from war?"

"I am not going to war."

"Heavy duties, then."

"I am merely . . ." He searched for the right word.

"Snooping?"

"Precisely. I don't believe I would violate the intention of the Law by going."

She had married a soldier. Soldiers walked into danger. As his wife, her responsibility was to make his job as easy as possible. Adding her worries to his burdens would be of no help to him. She forced herself to sound calm. "Will you go alone?"

"Ezra and Hanani have volunteered to accompany me."

Rahab's smile was haunted. "They do have experience as spies."

Salmone's laugh seemed forced. "Three is a good number. We can move fast and hide easily if need be. We are behind by a whole day, so we'll ride."

"What do you plan to do when you find them?"

"Return and inform Joshua. We can't attack them because we've made a treaty with them, and that remains binding. But we need to know the truth."

"Shall I pack food for the three of you? How many days' worth, do you reckon?"

"Hanani and Ezra will bring their own food. Four days ought to suffice. I'll show you how to put together a light pack. Speed is our greatest concern, so we can't be weighed down by supplies."

Rahab nodded and on impulse, clasped him hard against her. "I'll miss you."

He cupped her face in his hand. "You're wonderful, you know. I dreaded telling you. I didn't want a fuss. It happens to some of my friends every time they go away. Tears and wailing." He shuddered. "I should have known better than to expect that reaction from you. Then again, no man wants to leave a cold wife who doesn't seem to care. Somehow, you expressed the perfect measure of tenderness and composure. Thank you for that. It makes going away easier."

CHAPTER TWENTY-SIX

Rahab prepared for bed, wrapped in a fog. Salmone would leave in the morning on a dangerous mission. She might never see him again, never hold him, never hear his beautiful voice speaking to her. She could not bear to linger long over that possibility. Even being apart for a few hours that day had felt wrenching. The idea of being apart for days seemed unbearable.

She crawled into bed next to him. Though motionless, the rigidity of his body belied sleep. He had once shared with her that he often could not sleep well the night before a mission.

They lay next to each other for some moments, neither speaking, neither touching. With a sudden motion, Salmone twisted on his side and gathered her in his arms. "Rahab," he whispered, and pressed his lips against hers. He lingered over that kiss, lingered with excruciating patience and tenderness until she clung to him. With a deliberate movement he shifted her body until she lay half under him. His hands touched her and his breathing grew ragged as he kissed the curve of her neck.

Rahab was caught between an overwhelming desire, utterly new in her experience, and a terror that was all too familiar. Old fears crowded her mind. Fear that here in his arms, in his bed, she came closest to the Rahab of Jericho. Half of her felt that she would shrivel up if he stopped his exquisite caresses and the other half dreaded that she would shatter if he went on.

Sensing her hesitation, he drew in a ragged breath and lifted himself on an elbow. "I'm sorry. You aren't ready."

She took his dear face in her hands. "It's not that. You give me more pleasure than I ever thought possible to find."

He bent down and kissed her on the mouth. His voice was hoarse when he lifted his head. "Tell me why you're struggling. Help me understand."

She felt close to tears. "It's so hard to talk about this."

"I realize. But I'm asking you to plow through that pain. Trust me."

"Will you hold me?" Her voice sounded brittle and young.

With a swift motion, he enclosed her in his arms. "You're safe with me. Just talk to me." He studied her face in the dim light of the lamp, his eyes intent. She recognized that look, the one that dissected your insides and read your mind in the hiding places you thought no one could find. She gave herself up to that scrutiny, wanting to hide nothing from him.

Her breath, as she drew it into her burning lungs, was agitated. Tomorrow her husband would leave on a mission that threatened his life. She wanted to send him on his way with no walls between them. For that, she would risk anything, even his rejection. "Salmone, you're the only man I have ever loved." She made a sweeping gesture with her hand that took in their bed. "Before you, all this was about pretense for me. Pretense, performance, work. If there was any pleasure, it was rare and mixed with such shame. I am terrified every time you touch me that the old me is going to leak out, and that you'll know. I don't know how to be, how to act with you, here in your bed. I don't know how to be a wife."

"Then let me be a husband to you," he soothed. "Let me take the lead. You don't need to perform for me. You don't need to act, or do anything unless something wells up in you out of love, or out of your own desire. I want nothing from you except what is freely given.

"When I touch you, it is an outward expression of a love that fills every part of my being. I long to be connected to you. My body demonstrates the longing of my soul. I have no interest in using you to slake my lust. I have no interest in using you at all. What I want is an intimacy that encompasses every aspect of our being. Together. Let me touch you like that. And you touch me the same way. I have no expectations of you, beloved. There's no need to perform. Just love me, and I will feel it and be satisfied."

Rahab was silent as she digested his words. With more courage than confidence, she lifted her hand and placed it over his chest. "I want to try your way," she declared, her voice raw.

Salmone's flinty gaze as he studied her was unflinching. "There is one condition over which I will not compromise. The moment you slip back into old memories, the moment your mind turns my touch into work, or shame, I want you to stop me. As hard as that might be for me, it would be a thousand times worse to find out afterward that I caused you to feel

377

besmirched. The thought of harming you in any way turns my stomach. Can you understand? Will you promise to do as I ask?"

"I promise," she whispered. She knew it would not be an easy promise to keep. Stopping him partway because *she* didn't feel right seemed to her the most selfish behavior imaginable. Would he not resent and revile her for being such a bundle of needs? Such a burden of requirements? And yet she had to trust him when he said that he would feel worse if she did not express her needs. She had to believe he could bear the weight of her brokenness and not give up on her.

Almost as though reading her thoughts, he whispered again, "Trust me," and then kissed her, his hands twining in her hair and lifting up her face to deepen the kiss.

"Do you like this?" he asked later, and forced her to answer when she would rather stay mute. "And this?" he insisted, not giving quarter until she learned to be honest with what she felt. "I want to know what you like. Tell me," he said. "Do you want this? Shall I stop?"

"No!" she cried out, and he laughed, a triumphant, wholly masculine sound that sent shivers down her spine.

That night Rahab learned purity in the bed of her husband. She learned that there was nothing dirty or sinful or corrupt about being touched, being possessed by one to whom God had joined her. And she began to comprehend that Salmone could willingly bear being delayed for her sake. He enjoyed only what she could mutually enjoy with him, and he held no grudges for the differences between them. The more freedom he gave her, the greater her ability grew to find pleasure in his arms. That night, Rahab left Jericho and its massive walls behind her.

Morning came much too soon. Salmone's goodbye was wrenching. Rahab could tell by his distracted air that half his mind was already on his mission. She gave him a swift embrace, trying to memorize the contours of his lips against hers, the shape of his hands branding her back, the tickle of his clean beard, the expanse of chest that seemed to envelop her. Then she let him go, sensing his impatience to be on the road. She walked with him to Caleb's tent where Ezra and Hanani and Miriam already awaited. Joshua had arranged for three swift donkeys to be given to the men, and these stood at the ready, peacefully chewing fodder. Here in public, her goodbye was formal and constrained. But Salmone, obviously not suffering from shyness, pulled her into his arms and held her with passionate possessiveness. "I'll be back for more," he whispered in her ear, and was gone.

To Rahab's delight, Miriam moved back home that evening. She helped Miriam put her folded garments back into her carved chest. By the standards of Jericho, Miriam's belongings appeared meager, though they met the needs of a maiden of Israel. Rahab promised herself to weave fabric for a new tunic for her sister-in-law as soon as she finished the one she was making for Salmone.

It would have been unbearable, Rahab reflected, to go through the agonizing hours of her husband's absence by herself. She found a respite in Miriam's company. They had already learned to live together from their days in the tent of the wounded. Neither grated on the other; neither intruded upon the other. They made a good match, Miriam easygoing and eager to help, Rahab well-organized, without being overbearing. Together, they often prayed. Rahab felt closest to God in those times, buoyed by hope in the face of near constant anxiety for Salmone's well-being.

On the second day of Miriam's return, the two women rose with the sun and set out for the tent of the sick, bundles of supplies under their arms. To Rahab's amazement, the greatest diversion of the day came from an entirely unforeseen source: Miriam. Her usually placid sister-in-law entered into a heated argument with the wife of one of her patients. Rahab thought Miriam's anger understandable since the wife of the patient, a man by the name of Benjamin, was an unpleasant complainer who would have tested the patience of an angel.

Zuph had assigned Benjamin, who suffered from a wasting disease, to Miriam's care, hoping that her meticulous ministrations might help improve his condition. Rahab had begun laying an extra blanket on a sleeping boy, when Benjamin's wife came into the tent.

Discovering Miriam tending her husband, she shrieked, "What are you doing?"

With characteristic calm, Miriam responded, "I am Miriam of Judah; I help with the sick. Zuph sent me to look after your husband."

The woman curled her lip. "That incompetent jackal, Zuph? As if I would depend on anything he said."

Miriam stiffened. "Would you like me to stop caring for your husband?"

"Caring? You call what you people do caring? You've caused

him more damage than good, I shouldn't wonder. Get your hands off him."

Miriam tightened her lips and rose up. "As you wish." Her patience, worn thin already, ran out completely when she observed the woman feeding Benjamin the kind of solid food Zuph had expressly forbidden.

"Stop giving him that! You'll make him sicker."

"And who do you think you are, telling me what to feed my husband?"

"You're doing him no service by giving him that food. He needs light liquids."

"Can't you see how skinny he is? And should I starve him more when he's wasting away already? Mind your own business, meddlesome Judean wench. I know what's best for my own husband."

Miriam stormed forward to stand very close to the woman. "If he dies, his death will be on your head. I've never seen such an ill-mannered, selfish, ignorant woman in all Israel."

Rahab stood up, certain that if someone did not interfere, matters would turn ugly. Fortunately, Zuph must have arrived at the same conclusion. He walked up to the two women and, taking Miriam by the arm, pulled her away. "She cannot be reasoned with, child. Let it go," he murmured.

On the way home Miriam kept silent. They were in the territory of Judah by the time she opened her mouth. "Well, at least now I have disabused you of the notion that I am without fault."

"What did you say that she didn't deserve?" Rahab responded. "Most people would have exploded long before you did."

"I am not saying she wasn't wrong. It's my response to her behavior that's the problem. She was in anguish, Rahab. Filled with worry for her husband. I could have been more understanding."

Rahab frowned. "Miriam, I was there, and believe me when I tell you, you were the one wronged."

"I am aware of that. But she's answerable to God for her wrongdoing, not to me. I should have reacted out of mercy. That's why God provides me with a sacrifice when I make wrong choices, isn't it? So He can extend mercy to me. Should I not treat others the same? Yet, I'm struggling to forgive her, Rahab. I don't want to. I like holding on to my grievances. It helps me focus on her wrong rather than mine."

Rahab was quiet. Miriam's words prodded an old agony for her. She had her own struggles with forgiveness and mercy, struggles more profound than Miriam's current situation. She had never forgiven her father. Not truly. She had helped him financially and preserved his life during Jericho's downfall, but these many years she had also held his failure against him, not letting go of the wrong he had committed against her. The last time she had called him *Abba*, she was fifteen.

Her sister-in-law was battling with herself because she wanted to extend to others the pardon she received from God. Although she hadn't achieved that desire toward Benjamin's wife yet, at least she was striving to. Ought not Rahab do the same for her father? Ought she not ask God for a change of heart? Now it was Rahab's turn to stew in silence. It seemed almost too much to ask, such forgiveness.

That evening, after they had finished supper, Rahab disclosed some of these thoughts to Miriam. The kind of openness required for such a conversation represented a new territory for Rahab. The openness vulnerability she had learned in her relationship with Salmone had begun to influence her other relationships as well. Rather than holding her secrets close to her chest for fear of being rebuffed, she shared them candidly with Miriam. Feeling secure in the young woman's love, she was able to be honest about her shortcomings.

Strangely, instead of feeling shame for her painful disclosures as she once would have done, she now experienced an intimate belonging. She felt truly connected to Miriam. Befriended by her. Known by her. And the more she shared, the less lonely she felt.

Miriam was thoughtful when Rahab had finished speaking. "I think you are right in believing that you need to forgive him. But it may not come so easily. Has he ever asked your pardon?"

"No."

"Perhaps he isn't even aware that he needs to. It's possible that he has excused his decision in his own mind. Which means you must learn to forgive an impenitent man. Not the easiest thing to do, Rahab, but the right one."

Rahab pressed her hands to her stomach. "The thought of it gives me indigestion."

"Let's ask God for His help. If this is what He wants, He must impart the strength to you. Here I am struggling with forgiving Benjamin's blighted wife. I can't begin to imagine how hard it is for you."

After prayer, Rahab went outside to wash a few dishes. From the corner of her eye, she noticed a man walking toward their tent. Even in the distance, she sensed something familiar about him. The long-legged, graceful gait, the broad shoulders. She gasped. "Salmone!" She dropped the dishes with a clatter, picked up her skirts, and ran to him. He laughed out loud when she pitched herself into his waiting arms.

"Such a welcome for two days' absence. What will you do if I'm gone for two weeks?"

"Don't make me find out, you wretch."

He kissed her soundly. "I thought I must have embellished this in my imagination," he murmured. "I haven't."

Rahab clung to him, not willing to loosen her hold just yet. "Come and greet Miriam. She's come back home and will be so happy to see you."

He smiled. "I can't really walk with you hanging on me like this."

She slapped his arm. "Of course you can."

"You're right," he declared and swung her way up into his arms, making her squeal with delight. Miriam squealed with equal delight to see the hearty form of her brother returned safe from his mission.

Over a supper of smoked fish and raisin cakes, Salmone shared his news. "As I suspected, the men with whom Israel made a peace treaty live very close to here. They came from Gibeon and several other connected towns."

"Gibeon? But that's a major city!" Rahab said.

"One of the royal cities, and quite a bit larger than Ai." Salmone sighed. "There's more alarming news. I found evidence that Adoni-Zedek, the king of Jerusalem, is attempting to gather the kings of Hebron, Jarmuth, Lachish, and Eglon into one enormous army."

"What will you do?"

"To begin with, Joshua has sent a few leaders back to the Gibeonites to understand the motive behind their charade. In any case, since we gave our word, we can't turn against them. But Joshua has his own scheme. He intends to make them woodcutters and water carriers for Israel. From now on, they will be reduced to menial labor. That's their curse for deceiving us."

"What about the army Adoni-Zedek is gathering?" Miriam asked

Salmone looked down. "Big armies only mean one thing."

No one said the word, but all three knew. *War.*

As it turned out, the five Amorite kings devised a trick of their own. Rather than attacking Israel directly, they attacked Gibeon and the other provinces that had entered into peace with Israel. Rahab knew as soon as she heard the news that Israel would go into battle. They would not sit back and allow an ally to be destroyed by its neighbors.

Joshua chose to lead out the army late in the evening, marching all night from Gilgal in order to take Adoni-Zedek by surprise. The Law forbade Salmone from joining the army only weeks after his wedding. He found it hard to remain home in safety while his comrades bore the brunt of the fight. That night, Rahab and Salmone sat sleepless, praying for their friends and for the future of their nation.

Just before dawn, Salmone fell into a restless asleep. In the silence, left alone with her thoughts, Rahab realized that one day soon, her husband too would be gone, and she would be the one sitting on her lonely pallet, praying while Salmone waged war. On this austere night, as they waited the outcome of Israel's new battle, Salmone's departure did not feel like a distant event. It felt real and inevitable.

Rahab felt the vein pounding in her temple. Nausea clawed up her throat. Her heart could not bear the thought of losing her husband. Her mind became a wailing storm. She felt like her skin could not contain her. She wanted to run out of her body and leave it behind, leave behind the intensity of fear that clawed at her. She tried, but there was no reasoning with the terror that consumed her. It did not comprehend comfort. It raged with an illogical fervor that would not end.

Suddenly, in the midst of this near-unbearable squall, she heard a whisper, one short phrase: *My daughter.* She recognized that voice, that combination of immense power and inordinate love. *My daughter.* The terror left abruptly.

She was not alone. One by one, she rehearsed what was true. Israel did not battle as other nations. The Lord was her Warrior. He went ahead of His people. He opened miraculous doors to victory. Most importantly, she recalled that Salmone belonged more to God than to her. The Lord would see to Salmone. And He would see to her. Her fate, her well-being, her future were not in Salmone's hands. They were in God's. Whatever became of Salmone during the conflicts to come—Rahab could trust her destiny to the One who had brought her through so much already. She needed to remember that Salmone was not her Lord, only her husband.

She could not entirely shake the feelings of anxiety for the man she loved. But the fear no longer consumed her. In her inmost being, God had grown greater than fear.

Later that morning, Rahab went to visit her family, taking with her fig cakes, which she had prepared the previous day.

Her father loved this particular recipe. She found him in the family tent, working on a malfunctioning lamp. A memory flashed in her mind as she saw him rise up from the lamp and stretch his arms to loosen his knotted muscles. It was the memory of her father picking her up when she was three years old, twirling her around, shouting, *My daughter.* The very words God had spoken to her in her hours of panic. It occurred to Rahab that the Lord wanted her to understand something. God had covered the gap of her father. He had loved and protected her where her father could not. And He wanted her to remember that, regardless of his grave failure, her father also loved her.

In that moment the thought of forgiving him, of letting go of the bitterness of his betrayal became not only possible, but also irresistible. She might have other days when she would need to renew the struggle internally, let it go again, and give up the resentment afresh. For now, she could take this step with peace.

She considered how to convey this tremendous change of heart to her father. If she told him she forgave him, he might take offense rather than be comforted. If, as Miriam suggested, he had justified his actions, Rahab's forgiveness would only make him defensive. It would smack of an indictment. Every act of forgiveness by its inherent nature hinted at a wrongdoing. Her father might feel judged instead of relieved by her words. And yet Rahab could not leave him without communicating that some impediment between them had been shattered that day.

With soft steps, she went over to him, proffering the fig cakes in one upturned palm. "For you, *Abba.*" It had been eleven years since she had called him that.

His eyes widened, and for an uncertain moment he stood and stared at her. Tears filled his eyes. He ignored the cakes.

"What did you call me?" he asked, his voice shaking.

"*Abba.*"

He reached a trembling hand to the top of Rahab's head and patted it once. "My daughter," he whispered, his voice breaking. Then he strode outside. Rahab laid the cakes down on a platter and wiped away tears as she straightened.

That day, an astounding event shook the nation of Israel. The sun stopped right in the middle of the sky. It hung there, at high noon, for hours. *For an entire day.* The people marveled, walking out of their tents again and again as if to verify that they weren't dreaming. No one had ever heard of such a thing. Ever.

Finally, when they had all lost track of time, a runner brought news from the army. Joshua had prayed that the sun would stand still over Gibeon so that he could finish the battle and vanquish their enemies. To everyone's astonishment, the sun obeyed, for God had honored Joshua's improbable request. Rahab doubted the world would see such a day ever again.

And, yet, which was the greater miracle? That the sun should delay going down for a day, or that a woman would forgive her father's gravest sin against her?

Salmone welcomed his friends as they returned home from battle, exhausted but unharmed. He lingered with each one, listening to their stories, his eyes full of pride. Rahab watched her husband as he moved from man to man, always with an encouraging word, an understanding response, and felt no small pride of her own.

The next day, when he had finished his rounds of visitation, and ate a small supper, she gave him the robe she had finally managed to finish.

"What is this?"

"A gift."

"But why?"

"Because I am proud to be the wife of such a good man."

His cheeks darkened and he lowered his eyes. For a long time, he said nothing. When he raised his head, she saw the gleam of tears in his eyes. She caressed his cheek. He grabbed her hand and pressed a hot kiss against her palm.

When he lifted his lips, he had schooled his features back into calm. With a shake, he undid the careful folds in the wool and held it against his torso. "It's the finest garment in all Israel!" He rubbed the soft wool. "I shall become spoilt beyond repair."

"I can live with that."

That night, Rahab danced for Salmone for the first time. Her dance lasted only moments. Before she had a chance to show him one of her more elaborate moves, she found herself pulled roughly into his arms.

"I'm not finished," she mocked.

"Neither am I," he assured.

Later, as they lay cozily in each other's arms, Rahab mused innocently, "I think Ezra is a fine man. Don't you, my lord?"

Salmone's lids, already half shut, snapped open. "Excuse me?"

"Ezra, I said. Such an admirable man."

"Is there a point to this discussion about the fine qualities of another man while we lie in our marriage bed?"

"Miriam would likely do a better job of answering that."

Salmone pushed the sheet off his chest and sat up. "Miriam? What does Miriam have to do with it?"

"Well, I think she would agree about Ezra's having many admirable qualities."

"Miriam is just a child," Salmone retorted.

Rahab giggled. "That may be, but most young women her age are already bearing their firstborn."

Salmone frowned. "I grant you, she's grown up a little in the past month or two."

Rahab covered her mouth with her hand and looked down. Salmone crossed his arms. "What of it, anyway?"

"Ezra seems quite fond of her."

"That boy has been following her with his eyes for nigh on a year. Don't you think I've noticed?"

"Hardly a boy, husband. Why, half the women in Judah would court him as a bridegroom. And Miriam is fond of him."

"Has she said so?"

"She might have."

Salmone punched a pillow and gave Rahab a fierce look. "Why hasn't the boy . . . all right, the man . . . come forward then? Why should my wife be telling me about this in the peace of my bed?"

"The way you scowl at him every time he approaches Miriam? He can hardly expect a warm reception what with your frowns dogging his every step. And his only sin is to love your sister."

Salmone held up his hands. "Peace, woman. Have it your way, then. Ezra is an admirable man, and I will stop scowling at him. Anything more?"

"You are the very soul of generosity, my lord."

Salmone bent over and kissed his wife. "I am only grateful you are on the side of Israel," he murmured. Then he kissed her again before she could respond.

EPILOGUE

The baby screamed with single-minded insistence. Salmone picked him up and bounced him. "Calm yourself, my son, or your mother will accuse you of being greedy."

"He is greedy," Rahab mumbled, cracking one eye open. "He just *finished* feeding." She lifted her arms, and Salmone put their son into her hands.

"Shush, sweet. Mama's here. She'll take care of you."

The baby began to suckle with noisy abandon.

Salmone laughed. "He definitely doesn't have your manners." As if on cue, the child passed gas, a gurgling sound that made them both laugh. "Well, perhaps he has your brother's manners."

"Oh, it's just a lower cough. Leave him be."

"I have no problem with it. But the woman he marries might have a few objections."

"I wonder who that will be?" Rahab reflected.

Salmone bent over and kissed his cheek. "Son, whatever you do, wait for the right woman. Even if you are old and grey by the time she shows up, don't settle. Wait patiently."

"And treat your wife well from the *first* moment you lay eyes on her. Unlike some people who may be related to you."

"I don't know who your mother has in mind."

"Oh, Salmone, I pray he will be as happy as we are. I pray God will bless him with a good wife who will bring him joy—and a son to continue your line."

"And yours," he whispered, bending down to kiss her. Straightening, he moved to the open tent flap, where the sun's rays were shining through. "I wonder what will become of our lineage, Rahab. I wonder what manner of men and women will be born through us, and what lives they will live."

"I wonder how God will use them."

"Yes, that most of all."

As if by silent consent, their hands reached toward each other, and entwined over the head of their beautiful boy. Their eyes locked. Without words, they shared a thousand joys, the joys of a man and woman who truly knew each other, and accepted every foible and scar along the delights they brought each other. Neither one spoke. Yet in the silence, love flowed and settled over them. Beyond their tent, wars were waging, kings were rising, cities were falling. But in their small chamber, all was peace.

ACKNOWLEDGMENTS

Profound thanks to Wendy Lawton from *Books and Such* Literary Agency, who took me under her professional wings, and proceeded to change my life. Words cannot express my gratitude to Paul Santhouse from Moody Publishers who believed in this book and championed it so faithfully. I also wish to thank Duane Sherman and the other dedicated staff at Moody whose incredible encouragement and hard work made every part of the publication process pure joy.

Writing is a solitary process, but even the most self-contained writers need the companionship of a few special friends. To those who supported me along this journey, read my first drafts, and loved me and prayed for me through every step: Karen Connors, Janice Johnson, Cheryl Mallon, Tegan Willard, Kathi Smith, Linda Stricland, and Emi Trowbridge, my dearest thanks. I would have given up many times without your encouragement. And Millie Tolley, for your prayers and eyes that saw, I am so grateful. Thanks also to Leslie Goetler who in the midst of crazy residency hours took the time to give me medical information, and Persh Parker who showed me how a raging river can be crossed.

A special thanks to my closest friend, Rebecca Rhee, who brought me a Christmas tree when I had no time and made me soup on cold long nights. Rebecca and Beth, your friendship through the years has been one of the most profound blessings of my life. What would I do without you?

Many thanks to my father and mother for the generous freedoms they bestowed on me all my life, including letting me read at the dinner table when I was a child and allowing me to love Jesus freely when I grew up.

And to the many women who inspired this story with their valiant battle against the sorrows of life—sorrows that led to self-condemnation and shame: you are women of worth (Ruth 3:11).

ACKNOWLEDGMENTS FOR
THE ANNIVERSARY EDITION

I have left the original acknowledgment section for this book intact, because I will always be grateful for the people I have named there. I would also like to name a few additional individuals without whose help I would not have been able to complete this updated edition.

First and foremost, my thanks to Judy Dunagan, Acquisitions Editor at Moody Publishers, without whose support this new project would never have happened. With grace, gentleness, and wisdom, Judy has been there for me through every step. Pam Pugh has worked on this manuscript with me one word at a time, believed in it, loved it, nurtured it, and made it better. What do you say to an editor like that? Thank you seems so little. I can't tell you how much I appreciate Connor Sterchi's detailed eye, saving me from making many embarrassing mistakes. I am deeply grateful to Erik Peterson and his team for creating a stunning cover and interior design. They've made this Anniversary Edition something truly memorable. I owe an inestimable debt to Moody Publishers for believing in this project from the start, and for allowing me to release this revised edition.

A special thank you to my hubby, whose very presence is strength to me. Besides, he reads my books and underlines them! I landed a gem, right?

Finally, my deepest gratitude to my readers around the world whose encouragement and trust humbles me beyond words. I love you people. Thanks for sharing my world.

If you read this book, you will discover that God is the greatest love of my life. I hope He is yours too. I know He is smiling over you.

The title of this novel and the use of pearls in the story are the result of literary license. While Egyptians used mother-of-pearl in their jewelry during this era, no archaeological evidence for the use of pearls exists until centuries later. However, *Mother-of-Pearl in the Sand* wouldn't have quite the same ring.

The Bible tells us that Rahab was a harlot (*innkeeper* was a euphemism for prostitution). Biblical Hebrew has two distinct words for describing prostitution. The first, *kedeshah*, refers to temple prostitutes. The second, *zonah*, refers to the garden-variety kind. Wherever Rahab's profession is mentioned, the word *zonah* is used. Our story deals with this distinction.

Many of the references made to Rahab both in the Old and New Testaments include the term *zonah* (Rahab the *zonah*), which is to say that the people of Israel never quite forgot her background. Though most of the descriptions of her have a distinctly positive slant, this juxtaposition indicates that Rahab may have experienced a mixed reception in her new home. Welcomed and admired, yet never quite outliving her past.

Salmone's name appears with several different spellings in the original Hebrew, including *Salmon, Shalmon,* and *Salmone.* While most English translations of the Bible use the first version of the name, this novel uses the final version. Naming my hero after a fish seemed unappealing both to me and to my readers.

Wherever possible, this book has been based on biblical and archaeological sources. The scene in chapter 17 comparing Rahab's experience in Jericho with Israel's experience in Egypt during the first Passover was inspired by a chapter in Tivka Frymer-Kensky's book *Reading the Women of the Bible* (New York: Schocken Books, 2002, pages 297–300). Ultimately, however, this is a novel—a fictional account of a historical woman who holds great importance for both Jews and Christians. The Hebrew Bible discloses that after the destruction of Jericho Rahab settles in Israel permanently, but we are not given further details about her life (Joshua 6:25). For Christians, Rahab's destiny is revealed in one third of a verse in Matthew's genealogy of Jesus. These simple words reveal Rahab's amazing destiny: *Salmon the father of Boaz, whose mother was Rahab* (Matthew 1:5). In other words, Salmone and Rahab were married and had a son.

The Bible gives us a glimpse into Salmone's background through several genealogies (1 Chronicles 2:11; Ruth 4:20–21). Clearly, he comes from a highly distinguished family in the house of Judah; his father Nahshon is the leader of the people of Judah, and his father's sister is wife to Aaron (Numbers 2:3–4). Of Salmone's own specific accomplishments and activities nothing is known. But the verse in Matthew is still shocking. How could a man who is practically a Jewish aristocrat, significant enough to get his name recorded in the Scriptures, marry a Canaanite woman who has earned her living entertaining gentlemen? Much of this novel deals with that question. Needless to say, this aspect of the story is purely fictional. We only know that Salmone married Rahab and had a son by her, and that Jesus Himself counts this Canaanite harlot as one of His ancestors. On how such a marriage came about or what obstacles it faced, the Bible is silent.

The best way to study the Bible is not through a novel, but simply to read the original. This story can in no way replace the transformative power that the reader will encounter in the Scriptures. For the biblical account of Rahab, refer to Joshua 1–10, the book of Ruth, and Matthew 1:1–17.

DISCUSSION QUESTIONS

1. In chapter 1, we see overt and subtle ways that Rahab's family fails to love and protect her. Describe some of these situations.

2. What emotional wounds does Rahab sustain as a result?

3. In your own life, were there ways in which your family failed to love and protect you?

4. How do you feel these circumstances have affected you?

5. In chapter 2, Rahab befriends Debir. What are some of the qualities in Debir that draw Rahab to him? What defects do you detect in him as a friend?

6. Describe the qualities you would like to see in an ideal friend. How many of these qualities do *you* possess?

7. In chapter 3, we see Rahab being drawn to the Lord. What qualities does she perceive in God that draw her to Him?

8. Use three words to describe God as you understand Him.

9. What made Rahab willing to risk her life in order to save the Jewish spies?

10. In chapter 6, what principles can we learn from Joshua's encounter with the commander of the army of the Lord?

11. In chapter 8, Joshua accuses Salmone of growing judgmental in his attempt to become righteous. What do you think that means?

12. Do you see any judgmental attitudes in yourself?

13. In chapter 17, Rahab says that she is grateful for the snake. What do you think she means?

14. Are there snakes in your life for which you have learned to be grateful? Share why.

15. In chapter 21, Salmone calls Rahab his Jericho. What does he mean?

16. Ancient cities were often surrounded by defensive walls meant to keep harmful elements out and allow good to come in. Rahab's heart has walls that act in the opposite direction: they allow harm in (for example pride, the belief that she isn't lovable or worthy, fear), and keep love and intimacy out. In what ways are the defensive walls of your heart reversed like Rahab's?

17. In chapter 23, Salmone tries to explain the difference between shame and true guilt. Explain this in your own words.

18. In chapter 24, Rahab and Salmone both comprehend the true source of Rahab's worth through the lesson of the pearl earring. What gives you your sense of worth? In what ways does your life show this?

19. How do you think God feels about you?

20. In chapter 26, Rahab learns purity in the bed of her husband. What does that mean to you?

21. Rahab finally forgives her father. What do you think helps her do that?

22. Are there still unforgiving places in your heart? What will help you overcome these feelings?

23. In what ways do you feel you are like Rahab?

24. What are some of God's qualities discussed in this story that touched your heart? Why?

Two women. All alone. With no provision...
Can they find hope in a foreign land?

More from Tessa Afshar

The prophet Nehemiah's cousin Sarah can speak several languages, keep complex accounts, write on parchment and tablets of clay, and solve great mysteries. She becomes a scribe who rubs elbows with royalty and solves intrigues for the Queen. There is only one problem: She's a woman in a man's court.

978-0-8024-0558-6

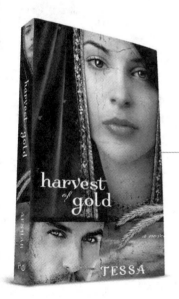

Darius remains skeptical that his Jewish wife is the right choice for him, particularly when Sarah conspires with her cousin Nehemiah to rebuild the walls of Jerusalem. Will the journey there help Darius to see the hand of God at work in his life and even in his marriage to Sarah?

978-0-8024-0559-3

also available as ebook and audiobook

MOODY
Publishers®

From the Word to Life®

Enter the story of Ruth like never before
through this 6-week Bible study

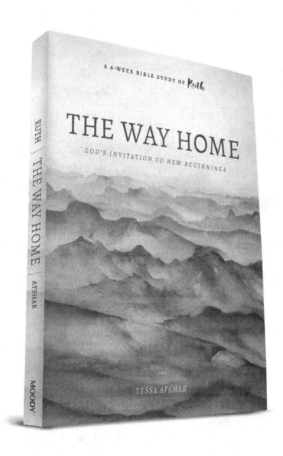

Bible Studies for Women

IN-DEPTH. CHRIST-CENTERED. REAL IMPACT.

7 FEASTS
978-0-8024-1955-2

KEEPING THE FAITH
978-0-8024-1931-6

AN UNEXPLAINABLE LIFE
978-0-8024-1473-1

THE UNEXPLAINABLE CHURCH
978-0-8024-1742-8

UNEXPLAINABLE JESUS
978-0-8024-1909-5

AN UNEXPECTED REVIVAL
978-0-8024-2500-3

WHO DO YOU SAY THAT I AM?
978-0-8024-1550-9

HE IS ENOUGH
978-0-8024-1686-5

IF GOD IS FOR US
978-0-8024-1713-8

ON BENDED KNEE
978-0-8024-1919-4

HIS LAST WORDS
978-0-8024-1467-0

I AM FOUND
978-0-8024-1468-7

INCLUDED IN CHRIST
978-0-8024-1591-2

HABAKKUK
978-0-8024-1980-4

THE WAY HOME
978-0-8024-1983-5

Explore our Bible studies at
moodypublisherswomen.com

Also available as eBooks

MOODY PUBLISHERS
WOMEN
BIBLE STUDIES